I0700308

KANO'S GRASP

RELEASE DAY SAGA
BY RYAN MATTHEWS

RELEASE DAY

KANO'S GRASP

ARJUN'S PATH

ZEPHYR'S HOPE

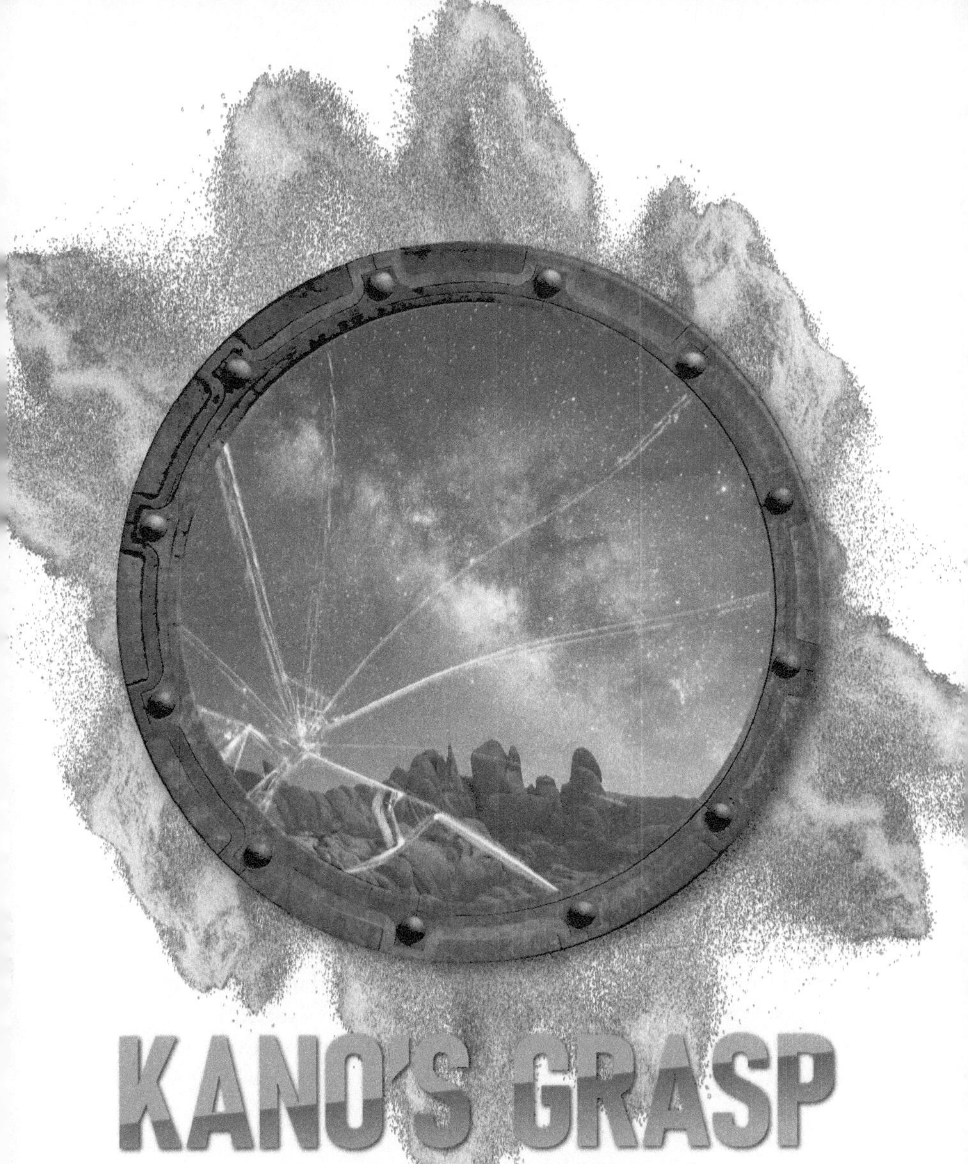

KANO'S GRASP

RYAN MATTHEWS

Copyright © 2022 by Ryan Matthews.

All rights reserved. Published by Battlehill Press.
Friendship, Tennessee.

www.battlehillpress.com

No part of this book may be reproduced in any form on by an electronic
or mechanical means, including information storage and retrieval systems,
without permission in writing from the publisher, except by a reviewer who
may quote brief passages in a review.

This is a work of fiction. Names, characters, places, and incidents either
are the product of the author's imagination or are used fictitiously. Any
resemblance to actual persons, living or dead, events, or locales is entirely
coincidental.

Layout and cover design by Ryan Matthews
Images used under license from Shutterstock.com.

Library of Congress Control Number: 2022916470

ISBN 979-8-9865388-2-2 (paperback)
ISBN 979-8-9865388-3-9 (hardcover)
ISBN 979-8-9865388-4-6 (ebook)

First Edition: October 2022

*For Travis and Fae, my grandparents, who
always kept their home, fried potatoes, and
card deck warm.*

CHAPTER 1: LOLADE

I never should've changed the name of the boat.

The sea voyage began innocently enough. In addition to the typical manifest, we were taking on several passengers at Mueller's request, something I wouldn't have done otherwise. You'd think if anything, my years of experience would've taught me to trust my gut. I've worked in the arduous and unforgiving transportation trade since I left Kano, the pod of my birth. After spending years proving myself as a capable leader, fighting the stigma associated with my gender, I finally climbed to the rank of captain on UTES-110H, the underwater boat that operated the southern Atlantic route of the global transportation system.

Growing up in such a harsh underground environment helped to prepare me for what I would be forced to deal with on the surface. As a young candidate, I was coerced to do things that I'm not proud of, but they were things that dispelled my weaknesses—increasing the likelihood of my survival. I distinctly remember the first time our trainers released live inverts within the confines of the pod, tasking the candidates to take them down. We had awoken to alarms blaring throughout the city, our instructions following shortly on the communication system. The administration was led by Ndulue Zabu, our barbaric prime minister who thought nothing of the loss of innocent human life. Over the decades, candidates had made the perilous journey to our pod on their own Paths to Citizenship only to find the living conditions just as brutal as what they had endured on their way there. The idea of releasing the invading alien species in our populated pod for our training was nothing short of insanity.

That was the morning I watched my brother, Tayo, die. He was always courageous, doing everything he could to protect others and demonstrate his bravery. He was a few years ahead of me, but we had always known we were brother and sister. We had a bond that two strangers don't just have. It was him that I found myself fighting alongside as the bone arachnids clawed their way into each inhabited district, making short work of their populace. Eights don't eat much on their own, but they slaughter everything that moves, intending to return to it later. The state of decomposition doesn't faze their unceasing appetites. Back when our pod was renowned for its research, they used to tell us that leaving their dead victims was a way the Arthropods provided for each other. Despite their aptitude for cannibalism, everything they did was ultimately for the advancement of their kind.

That day, as I stepped over the corpses scattered to and fro in the market a few levels up from my dorm, all I saw was red. The entire district was bathed in human blood. No sign of the distinct, dark hemolymph of the inverts. It was a massacre. The innocent and unprepared residents hadn't even put up a fight. The vibrant colors of the market stalls, normally a pleasing contrast to the dingy surroundings, were now uniform in their stained appearance. Despite the sweltering heat and humidity of the pod, added to by the moisture from the fallen, my skin prickled as though I was freezing. It appeared that the eight we were tracking had already moved on from this area. I could hear screams coming from levels below, but the distance led me to the conclusion that it was one of the others. I advanced slowly, having lost sight of Tayo. I knew the creature could be lurking anywhere, but I had been trained for tracking, though I never thought I'd be using my skills in our pod. I stepped through a collapsed blue market stall, noticing the owner and her produce were scattered all over. I held the back of my hand to my mouth as I stifled a gag.

Food inequality has always been a problem in our pod. It was the haves versus the have-nots. One day, Tayo was desperate for food. As an advanced candidate and a male, he was allotted more food than me. Due to his concern for my well-being, he shared his food with me. What I didn't realize was that he was, in fact, giving me all of it. One day I woke up to find him so hungry he was hallucinating. At first, he thought I was an invert, but he was so weak that keeping him from grabbing his knife—a normally impossible task—was effortless. I had ration points, but they were virtually worthless in the lower levels, where people preferred something more functional. Barter was the way of things, but we had nothing to trade. Desperate to help him, I went to the market a few levels up and attempted to steal a handful of overripe carrots. Even in my desperation, I rationalized the theft as something the owner would discard anyway. No sooner had I turned to leave, than I felt a deceivingly strong hand on my shoulder.

"Where do you think you're going with my carrots, *kadan*?" she asked.

"I'm sorry," I said, pleading. "It's for my brother, he's starving."

"We're all starving, *kadan*," she said. "It's no excuse for thievery."

"Where are we going?"

"To the guards. If you're lucky, they'll just take your hand."

"What? No! They were old carrots. He's dying!" I pleaded.

The small woman shoved me against the wall. I could feel the slime growing on the corroded surface, slick on the nape of my neck.

"Carrots are carrots and they are how I survive!"

I began to sob.

"Oh, *kadan*," she said, muttering and drooping her head. "Take the carrots. May the gods reward me in my next life. They sure as hell haven't in this one."

I thanked her profusely and sprinted back to my brother, who I had to force-fed the semi-rotten produce. I eventually fell asleep on him, waking the next morning to find him caressing my head. He knew what I had done to keep him alive. That's how it was. We watched out for each other.

As I stepped through the old woman's tattered stall, I couldn't help but shed a tear for her. It was she that had kept my brother alive and me, whole.

"May the gods reward you," I said before continuing on.

Trapped within my memories, I had forgotten one of the first rules of tracking: Never let your prey know you are tracking them. My little eulogy had alerted the eight, who had been hiding in wait, to my presence. With mind-boggling speed, it flew from its refuge, lunging towards me with its dripping fangs out. My trepidation escalated as terror seized my bones. Giving in to my instinct to flee and find a more defensive spot, I turned and ran up the nearest stairway where I could have the high ground. I ran as fast as my body could go. I rounded the corner and felt my feet slip out from under me, the blood having lubricated the already slick concrete floor. Everything happened slowly. I slid down onto my side as I watched the creature leap up over me, preparing to administer its death blow. Just as it reared back, I closed my eyes, coming to peace with my inability to do anything to defend myself. I waited for the chest-crushing blow, but it never happened. I slowly opened my eyes to see why time had stopped. There the eight stood. Motionless, but seemingly alive. My eyes followed the length of its arachnid body to find that it had my brother's blade buried to the hilt in the weak patch of its abdomen. My brother stood behind the creature, smiling, as blood dripped from the corner of his mouth. I realized then that the creature's venomous stinger had sunken deep in his chest. Tayo had given his life to save me—his final act of bravery.

"I love you, sister," he whispered before his head lolled to the side.

●●●●●●●●

I've spent the last four years as captain of the *Tayo*, which I rechristened in my brother's honor, infuriating the crew who still adhered to the ancient maritime superstitions. It was possibly this action that the universe was punishing me for. I thought I had encountered almost everything the Arthropods had to offer, but I was wrong. On what felt like another routine leg, Mueller had surprised me with some extra live cargo. He explained the importance of the candidates' earth-shattering mission, but to me they were just more cargo. Once on board, I supplied them with our extra berths, which were normally folded away. It was going to be a long trip for the eight of them, sharing a space that would be cramped for half their number. Not to mention, the crew would be irritated that some of their recreational space would be unavailable for the ten-day duration of the crossing.

After Kofi, the pump house attendant, refueled us, Mueller, Otto, and the others helped us load the boat. I had taken the news of the substantial loss of the Misfits with difficulty. Lately, I had been hearing far more bad news than good. I began my career with optimism, but every day, a little more pessimism seeped in. I wondered how long it would be before there was no hope left. I didn't put any faith into this mission, but there was an almost imperceptible spark in me that hoped for its success.

We got underway as soon as possible, not wishing to waste any more time within reach of the enemy. Water meant safety. Land meant death. Initially, everything was going pretty smoothly. The passengers tried to help around the boat but did nothing more than get in the experienced crew's way. Before the end of the first day, the men were becoming irritated. Even navigating the boat with the extra bodies was making tempers flare. The next morning, while eating our highly anticipated breakfast of fresh fruit, a luxury we only enjoyed once per passing, I addressed those on board.

"Attention crew and guests," I said, after rapping my aluminum coffee cup with my spoon.

"Aye," the crew responded in unison as our passengers looked on, unsure.

"While I appreciate your efforts to help," I said, addressing our guests, "It will be best if you confine yourselves to the section of your berths for the duration of the trip, barring trips to the head. We'll stop once a day to have an hour of surface time at which time you may join us. Master-at-Arms Kebe will see to your needs."

I could see the looks of dismay and irritation on their faces, but they were too polite to say anything to the effect. I admired the fact they could follow orders. They apparently trained them well in Pod Horizonte. The one called Huck, who appeared to be their leader, stared down at the table, his black hair obscuring his face. Ever since he had come aboard, something had seemed off about him. I had asked Kebe to keep an eye on all of them but particularly that one. He also had special instructions to keep the exclusively male crew away from the three female passengers, all of which would be just as highly sought after as the sweet fruit after a long period of abstinence. My boat would never be as lawless as it was when I had joined the crew.

The third day of the trip started out as normal as any other day. The men would bring me lists of all the new damages found, and I would authorize their repairs based on materials available and priority. Our eighth-generation u-boat was getting perilously close to the end of its serviceable life, and I could tell. There wasn't a surface without corrosion or a pipe without a patch. It wasn't a matter of if the hull was leaking but rather how much it was. The boat was fully submersible but rarely did we ever need to. Far out on the open ocean, the inverts never bothered us. I wasn't sure how deep the boat could even go given its present condition.

It was during that moment of going through the morning's lists when the commotion began to stir. I was in the bow when I began to hear yelling emanating from the stern where Huck and his companions were housed. I sprinted back as fast as the narrow hatches in the bulkhead would allow.

"Kill the invert!" I heard yelled as I made my way closer to the fray.

Still ducking through the last hatch into the supremely overcrowded room, I screamed "Hold positions! Make way for your captain!"

The crowd parted, and I saw something I was wholly unprepared for. Writhing on the floor was Huck, surrounded by my men armed with pipes. The crew was in a standoff with Huck's friends as Ariadne attempted to administer aid to her agonizing victim. Huck was writhing on his stomach and drooling on the floor, his back dotted with multiple large red blood stains. From the center of several of the stains, yellow larvae were emerging.

"Throw him overboard immediately," I said.

CHAPTER 2: HUCK

It was a common occurrence for candidates to get injured during training. They would frequently talk about changes in time perception, feelings of weightlessness, and an absence of pain. The morning the chomper larvae decided to hatch from their little homes throughout my back, I felt pain. Every. Single. Bit. Time changed alright. Time crept along agonizingly as I was carried topside to be thrown overboard. The only floating sensation I would feel was in the ocean as I watched any hope of survival drift away under its twin natural gas-powered props.

My back had itched incessantly ever since the day we were attacked by the split wings on the barge. The infectious parasites carried with them the ability to numb their host, the only pain I recall from the day was what felt like a few impacts on my back. By the end of that dismal rainy day, I was soaked in a mix of precipitation and blood, unable to determine the blood's source. With adrenaline still flowing through my veins, I changed my jumpsuit as quickly as I could and wasn't any wiser about what had happened. By the time the itching started, it didn't occur to me what it might be. As a matter of fact, it was as if my mind didn't want to figure out what it was. Every time I thought about going to Ariadne for help, I would feel a pressing desire to do something else.

Itching aside, we were repeatedly pounded by discouragement. We were losing people at an unsustainable rate to the inverts as they slowed our progress to Tank Town. When they ambushed us, I would've sworn it would've been our demise. Among those we lost that day was my best friend and roommate, Zeke. I would never get over my doubt about the decision to spare Arjun's life over his. He made the decision, but I was the one who administered the serum, saving Arjun. *Had I made the right choice?* Krista certainly didn't think so. She had become closed off to all of us, even her best friend Ariadne. Her mood grew increasingly darker through the sinister emotions toward us that seemed to pervade her thoughts, her beautiful smile had vanished as quickly as people after the Arthropod Landing.

After our surprising defeat of the spine back, the gargantuan Arthropod that the inverts had deployed as a secret weapon, we finally arrived at the much sought-after coast. The battle with the spine back, which our friend Otto had dubbed the Nightmare, gave me confidence that we were on the right track. The bloody inverts felt threatened by us, though the optimism was overshadowed by the large number of casualties we'd experienced. Mueller and Otto's Misfits would never be the same. Once what was left of the transporter cargo was loaded aboard Captain Lolade's u-boat and Hemant was begrudgingly convinced to travel on open water, I stood with the others on the deck and waved to Mueller, Otto, and Kofi as we departed.

We were out of sight of land within minutes, surrounded by a sea of white-capped blue ocean. The experience was a disconcerting one after having spent the majority of my life surrounded by land underground. In one of what would be many lecturing moments, Master-at-Arms Kebe informed me that at some points of our crossing, the ocean floor would be as far as five kilometers below us. When he had said that, Hemant, normally a wheat complexion, turned as pale as Ciro. I leaned out over the dorsal railing as I watched the waves crash against the hull. I was startled when an alarm wailed, looking at Kebe in a panic.

"Relax, my friend," said the master. "There's no need for anxiety here. That's just the sound of the dive alarm warning us to go below. Let us go down the hatch."

I nodded and followed the stout man down the narrow passage. The sub looked as though it was pieced together from a junkyard. Everywhere my eyes fell were haphazard repairs and patches of tan goo. It was reminiscent of the interior of Pod Horizonte and felt like an appropriate metaphor for humanity—falling apart at the seams. The smell of lubricants was overpowering at first, giving me a horrendous headache, but after the first day, I had adapted to this new undersea existence. It was only coming back into the boat after our daily surface time when the smells would burn my nostrils again. Every interior surface of the vessel was covered in controls of some sort—knobs, valves, gauges, dials, lights. I was always afraid to set my hand down on any surface, lest I send us careening to the bottom of the ocean. I was amazed at what humanity was still capable of engineering, even with the Arthropod-generated electromagnetic fields restricting our use of microcircuitry.

I spent the first few days doing what I could to help out, but I was mostly yelled at. "Noob" seemed to be the chosen word for everyone in our party. Part of me was thankful when Captain Lolade confined us all to our berths, though the looks of disdain from the crew were still unnerving. I thought the lack of privacy on the barge was bad. At least there we had vehicles to hide behind. Here, all eight of us were in a very small space situated between two frequently accessed sections of the boat. While we had been ordered to remain in place, crew traffic through our space was frustratingly regular and inconvenient.

I had awoken on the third morning of our crossing with the itching incessant and painful. My back burned as though I'd spent the night leaning against a nuclear reactor. I couldn't stop scratching. As I pulled my hand back to look at my fingers, I saw that my fingers were covered in a dark, warm liquid. Even in the red nighttime lights, I knew what it was.

"Ariadne!" I screamed, waking Hemant next to me with a start.

"Oh god!" Hemant said, jumping out of the bunk.

Ariadne slung herself over Krista's groggy form and came to my aid, rolling me onto my side.

"Oh my god!" she said. "Krista, get Lolade! See if anyone on this boat has medical training!"

Before she could act, a crew member came to see what the early-morning ruckus was about.

"Inverts!" he screamed, waking the crew. "Inverts on board!"

Laying on my stomach, I saw the boots of the entire boat's crew thunder into the small space, ready to bludgeon me into smithereens. At that moment, all I could focus on was the searing pain in my back. If the chompers used a numbing agent when they deposited their eggs, it was the reverse now. It felt as though my intestines were trying to worm their way out of my back as I convulsed on the frigid floor. I felt a metallic taste on my tongue as a viscous liquid filled my mouth before I spewed it onto the deck.

"Don't waste any time, boys!" yelled someone above me. "Paste them all!"

"Like hell, you will," said Omar, challenging their leader.

I heard the others answering in agreement.

"Kill the invert!" another said.

"Hold positions! Make way for your captain!" yelled Lolade,

barely audible above the fray. Then after a pause, "Throw him overboard immediately."

•••••••••

Next thing I knew, I was face-down again. I must have passed out. This time, I was on the surface of the boat's hull, my face pushed into the metal grating that provided the grip when walking on the slick surface. I could feel from the bite of the studs that I was no longer wearing a jumpsuit. Behind me, I heard ripping sounds and winced as a bandage was callously applied to my back.

"You'll survive," said Ariadne. "You're going to be sore as hell for a few days, maybe longer if the split wing larvae left any excretions in your body."

"Are they all gone?" I asked.

"Yeah. They were in the process of hatching. They hadn't really started devouring you yet. I pulled them all out and squished them. That's that pile of green goop next to your head."

I turned my head to see a sickening green, black, and red pile of mucous, then promptly vomited into the grating.

"Thanks, Ariadne," I said, wiping my mouth and feeling the stabbing pain in my shoulder.

"Don't thank me yet," she said. "We're out here because I pleaded with Lolade to let me treat you. At the moment, we're locked out of the boat and they have no intention of letting any of us back in."

"Any of us?" I raised my head as much as possible with the pain and noticed the other six of us from Horizonte sitting in the shadow of the conning tower. *Damn. Some sort of leader I am.*

"Are any of you guys hurt?" I asked.

"We're fine," replied Omar.

"You could've told us you were infected, Huck," said Mei.

"I'm sorry. I don't know what came over me," I said.

"If you weren't in so much pain already, I'd kick your ass."

I looked at her and managed a weak smile. She didn't smile back.

"It's going to be a long seven days under this sun," I mumbled.

I heard the distinct squeal of the hatch opening and saw Kebe emerging, struggling to balance his ascent on the ladder with several trays of food.

"Here's dinner," he said. "No surprise, it's fish."

Kebe closed the hatch behind him and leaned against the tower, pulling out a cigarette from the pack retained by his suspenders before igniting it.

"It shouldn't be any surprise, but the captain is pissed you brought a threat onto her boat."

"I had no—" I began.

"Shut up and listen," said Kebe. "She knows you had no idea. She's just pissed. Now she has to keep the men from mutinying and drowning the lot of you."

"How can they do that?" asked Ariadne. "She couldn't have known!"

"Mariners are a damned superstitious lot. A woman controlling a boat, bad. Naming a boat after a male, bad. Renaming a boat, very bad," he said, taking a long drag. "You, Huck, are the embodiment of all the bad luck Lolade represents."

"You could let us back in," said Hemant. "We could help defend her until our arrival."

"I won't go against my captain's orders. You'd be a fool to think otherwise. Lolade will be fine. She's the toughest captain I've ever met, and the third I served under. Like this boat, my time is coming to an end. I remember when this boat was so new it still smelled like the satay the engineers ate while they assembled it at Pod Bandung."

"What can we do?" asked Omar.

"It's clear. We camp out here for the next eight days," said Arjun. "Master Kebe, could you bring us our gear?"

"Kebe is fine. You guys aren't exactly crew," he said. "Probably. I'll run it by Lolade first, but I doubt she'll have a problem with it. I'll bring you some ropes as well. You'll want something to tie down with should a squall come up."

"A squall?" asked Krista.

"It's a storm that arises quickly, catching you off guard," said Ciro. "Many sailors from history have been lost overboard to squalls."

"Very good, young man," said Kebe.

Krista turned her smoldering focus back on her knees. That was the most I'd heard her say since we came aboard.

"If there's nothing else, I'll bring your gear up when I come back to collect your trays," said Kebe as he opened the hatch and vanished inside the vessel.

"This certainly isn't how I expected to travel to the Saharan Territory," I said.

"We're certainly not being treated like heroes," said Mei.

"We're not exactly heroes yet," said Ariadne.

"This couldn't get any worse," said Krista, pouting, just as a light rain began to fall.

CHAPTER 3: HEMANT

My companions never grasped just how much I don't like open water. I didn't like traveling up the Strider River. I didn't like floating in the middle of Mountain Lake, despite its spectacular views. And yet I find myself traveling across the Atlantic Ocean on the *outside* of a boat. I'll just add it to my growing list of unpleasantries.

I hadn't missed Huck's excessive scratching throughout the last leg of our journey. It was stupid of me not to say anything, but everything's always more obvious in hindsight. I was still alive, which is more than I can say for most of the company we traveled with. My heart nearly exploded when I thought I was watching Arjun die in front of me. Everything I had done to protect my brother failed in an instant. For that brief moment, I was powerless. I had become too complacent after our battle with the Nightmare, but the inverts wasted no time in teaching me to never let my guard down again—and I never will. They knew we were coming for them, and it was only a matter of time until the next confrontation. I resisted the urge to walk across the boat's slippery deck and wrap him in a tight hug. Instead, I watched him and Ciro palling around under the shade of the conning tower's deck, no doubt comparing the merits of seaweed in the diet or something equally mundane. I was thrilled he was still alive, but the sting of Zeke's death was still fresh on my mind. The inverts would pay. They would pay for Zeke, Leni, Kurt, and everyone else they'd taken.

Thankfully yesterday's rain had subsided. So far, the crossing has been smooth. Aside from the constant surveillance of the aerial network, we hadn't seen any sign of the inverts since before we had set sail. I practiced drilling and sparring with Omar every day, wanting to stay in perfect shape for whatever the inverts might throw at us when we made landfall. I was happy to have regained all of my previous strength. The others jogged back and forth on the deck or sparred if their weapons allowed. Kebe had stayed true to his word. He climbed the narrow ladder every day to bring us a decent meal. In addition to supplying us with the promised ropes to tie ourselves down, he taught us myriad marine knots. As the monotonous days drifted past like the sea buffeting the hull, Kebe passed more and more of his time with us. I realized that he was a wealth of maritime knowledge. Arjun and Ciro were intent on soaking up as much of it as they could before we would depart from his company. The three of them would sit on the bow for hours, talking about the plethora of ocean life and the mysteries of the deep. Judging by his deep grin, Kebe enjoyed the conversations as much as the boys did, smoking and talking incessantly until a crew member would call him down for one of his numerous duties.

Thankfully, there was enough room under the tower's deck for all of us to escape the baking sun. Otherwise, I would've peeled like a desiccated onion from Horizonte's market district. None of us would escape this crossing without some skin damage. Some mornings, the wind and salty water felt so abrasive, that it was as though the air itself was shaving off my skin layer by layer. I was in no hurry to return to the claustrophobic pod living, but being out of the elements even for a few hours would be a marvelous reprieve. Despite my extreme distaste for the open water, I had begun to appreciate the calming nature of the waves' sounds as they lapped against the smooth metal. The ocean smells were equally satisfying as I grew more accustomed to the rocking motion of the vessel. The fishing skills we'd learned from Kurt came in handy during the crew's deck time. Though they limited their contact for fear of contagions, they had no qualms about sharing rods with us or letting us help catch the fish that the boat's chef would prepare for our dinner. I would be glad when we could eat something other than fish. Even a boney snake was beginning to sound appetizing again.

With little else to do, I constantly dwelt on Arjun's place in the future of our mission. The temptation was to leave him at Baghdad where he would be safe, but I knew his knowledge had proved critical for our survival. Additionally, I knew he wanted to remain with me. If we were going to carry this bomb from Kano to the near-unreachable Hive, it would likely mean our deaths. Two lives for all of humanity seemed like an easy decision on paper, but was I willing to pay if the cost was Arjun's life? Maybe he could go all the way with us to the Hive. If I could intensely train at Pod Bhopal, maybe I could be all the more prepared to protect him. I still had time to think about that. Kano was thousands of kilometers away and Baghdad even further.

Our seventh day on the ocean began like any other, but not long after sunrise it took a turn for the worst. I had woken up that morning to a heated discussion between Ariadne and Huck, watching them gesture towards a gray skyline.

"That's a freaking squall, Huck! We need to strap down!" said Ariadne.

"How do we know it's not just rain, like the other day?" asked Huck.

"The other day there were scattered gray clouds. The entire bloody skyline is gray! Look, see that curtain? That's rain, Huck, and a hell of a lot of it!"

"How can you be sure?"

"Fine," she said. "We'll tie ourselves down and you can wander about the deck, but don't expect me to jump in after your stubborn ass!"

"Huck, Ariadne's correct. We should prepare for a rough ride," added Arjun.

"Fine," said Huck. "Everyone tie yourselves down!"

"As if we needed your permission, *Captain*," said Ariadne.

Nothing like a morning quarrel. We were all a little short-tempered after spending so many miserable days limited to the hot metal grating of the boat. I grabbed the ropes which were fastened down next to me and began to pass them out. Though it was breakfast time, the crew must have seen the same thing on the periscope, because, as punctual as Kebe was, there was no sign of him coming out of the hatch with our breakfast. *Great, riding out a storm and I don't even get coffee. At least I won't have anything to puke.* Once we were tied down, there was nothing to do but watch the squall's advance, which it did with surprising speed. What had been a relatively smooth ride on a calm ocean rapidly became anything but. The waves picked up and the boat bobbed up and down unlike anything I had ever experienced before. *God, I never want to be on a boat again.* Motion sickness overcame Mei. She started heaving in time with the boat's rise and fall. Thankfully, she was on the far side of the group, the wind directing her expulsion aft. Otherwise, we would've all been covered in her vomit. I felt sorry for her as she continued to dry heave, nothing remaining in her stomach but bile.

The bouncing was bad enough, but then we hit the storm's face. It raged around us. The whipping wind and sheeting water tore at our faces, drenching us instantly. Despite the warmth of the climate, the water wicked the heat directly from my body as if it was feeding the ocean's wrath. I closed my eyes, desperately trying to keep my calm. Meditation proved impossible, and any semblance of calm eluded me. Squeezing my eyelids closed was only making things worse. Opting to focus on the horizon, I opened my eyes to see the largest wave of my life about to swallow our boat. *Maybe I was better off with my eyes closed!* The massive wave slammed down over the boat, bow first, completely submerging us as the sea bubbled overhead. *They're never going to get me back on the freaking water!* When the water finally receded, I saw that Arjun was no longer in place at my side.

"Arjun! Arjun!" I screamed, hearing Ciro echoing me.

"I'm here!" I heard a voice crack from over the side amid fits of coughing.

The sub was rocking to and fro, but there didn't appear to be any more imminent super waves. I untied myself, ignoring the pleas from the others. I followed Arjun's rope to the edge, using it to balance myself and guide me as the salty spray blinded me. One side of his rope had come untied, but amazingly, he had managed to hang on to the knotted end as the wave had pummeled us. If not for his adrenaline-fueled grip, I never would have located him. I looked down the side, there was Arjun, the rope twisted around his forearm, which bled profusely and drained down his body before diffusing into the ocean. With a burst of superhuman strength, I pulled him up and helped him back to the shelter of the tower before lashing him back in place.

"Are you alright?" I screamed at Arjun over the crashing waves.

Arjun nodded, frozen in place by the onslaught of water. "It's just a bad abrasion. I'm not losing enough blood to be of consequence."

After taking care of his rope, I twisted one arm into my rope and my other in his. I could feel the course strands biting into my skin, but I wasn't letting go of Arjun again. It didn't matter how tight our tethers were, they would never be tight enough. The idea of Arjun staying on at Baghdad sounded better and better, even though I'd miss him fiercely, the idea of him tucked away safely was enough to offset that.

I have no idea how long the storm lasted, but it felt like days. We finally saw the first hints of sunlight through the squall, signaling the end. As we passed through the storm's final veil, I realized it was a setting sun. We had spent the entire day riding through a storm.

"We did it!" I screamed, exhausted.

I was joined by most of the others in my celebration. I looked at everyone. Even though it had been one of the most miserable days of our lives, we all had smiles on our faces simply because we had survived unscathed, even Mei. Everyone but Krista, who just sat there, stone-faced as always. Whatever she was going through didn't seem like the Shock. It seemed like something else—like fury. What concerned me the most was that I wasn't sure who that fury was aimed at.

•••••••••

On the morning of the tenth day, we finally pulled into what the crew referred to as Freeport, having crossed an entire ocean. The journey from the Latin Territory to the Saharan Territory felt like quite an accomplishment even though it was a regular occurrence by the crew of the *Tayo*. Captain Lolade had the ocean crossing down to an art. She let us back inside the boat once we neared the shore, figuring our quarantine was no longer necessary with Huck fully recovered, aside from the occasional whine about his injuries. I awkwardly squeezed past the crew in the narrow walkways, suffering their suspicious glares and frigid treatment. Navigating the claustrophobia-inducing spaces was difficult, to begin with, but made even more so by my cumbersome war hammer. It certainly wasn't a weapon designed for close-quarters combat, which is exactly why we all carried a dagger as our secondary weapon. Omar didn't have it any easier with his naginata. After an embarrassing moment when I blocked the main ladder up, we were on the surface of the boat prepared to disembark with all of our gear.

I watched as the boat pulled gently into the derelict port and recognized the ubiquitous pump house from which the u-boat's natural gas tanks would be refilled for its return crossing. I was the first to descend the gangplank and forced myself to resist the urge to collapse onto the ground, immensely grateful for the cessation of constant motion. As the men cleared the quay of some scavenging inverts, we helped unload the cargo for the Saharan transporters, Captain Lolade and Master-at-Arms Kebe stepped down to see us off.

"I hope you all fare well in your mission," she said, her unrevealing eyes as deep as the ocean we had just crossed. "If you are successful, you could change the tides of this never-ending war. My place will always be the sea, but I look forward to a day when I can set foot on land and let down my guard." Turning to Huck, "I see that you are well from your *encounter*. First and foremost comes the safety of my crew, even if they are all bastards. I was able to keep their anarchy tamped down this time, but you will understand if I never allow you on my boat again."

"I do," said Huck. "Thank you for carrying us across."

"Yes, thanks," I added as the others did the same.

"Arjun. Ciro. You would be wise to remember the lessons of the deep. They will serve you well in your understanding of all the animals. A word to the wise," Kebe said, coming closer to where Huck, Ariadne, and I were standing, "Watch yourselves in Kano. You'll find it isn't the most welcoming to outsiders. I understand a critical component of your mission lies with the scientists there. My advice is that you do whatever it is you need to do and move on. Should you run into any trouble, I have an old friend, Ekon, who frequents the place. He's a strange one, but he has the kindest of hearts and will help you should the need arise."

Clapping Huck on the shoulders, he smiled as he and Lolade returned to directing the unloaded men.

"How long will it take to get to Kano?" asked Ariadne.

"At least as long as it took us to cross the ocean. Maybe longer," said Ciro. "There are too many variables to know for sure."

"What was all that about Kano?" asked Omar.

"I don't know. I was looking forward to a hot shower and some real food, nutrition be damned, but now I've got something else to worry about."

"What Master Kebe said was concerning," said Arjun. "I would be interested in what our contact, Dieter, has to say."

I scanned the horizon for any sign of the next group of transporters, wondering how we were going to convince this particular group to carry us around. I felt like a parasite in my own right. At least there were no signs of inverts. The landscape was dry, desolate, and filled with the disintegrating remnants of shipping containers from ages past. I could see some greenery in the landscape, but considering the deceiving nature of the region, there was no telling how far away it actually was. I caught myself wishing Mueller and the Misfits would come pulling around the corner, but all I saw was a cloud of dust in the distance, signaling that the group was en route.

"Now what?" I said, turning to Huck.

"We wait for whoever that is," he said, gesturing towards the plume.

CHAPTER 4: ARIADNE

I stood with Krista and watched the cloud of dust grow closer and closer. The swirls in the wind put me on edge. We had been told the Saharan transporters would be arriving shortly, but my experiences made me wary of anything rapidly approaching our position. After the ambush that killed Leni and gave us a glimpse into the intelligence of the inverts, it's no wonder I was anxious. I hoped that this experience with the transporters would be as pleasant as the last one turned out to be. After their initial gruffness had worn off, we had grown close, even being adopted into their culture. Mueller and Otto would forever be close friends. Kurt, who had been killed in a polie bombing, would live on through the knowledge he shared with me. I was feeling the losses particularly hard this morning and seeking comfort, I reached my arm around Krista who forcefully shrugged it off.

"Leave me alone, Ariadne," she said, before distancing herself.

"I…" I stammered but stopped when I realized she was no longer listening.

I had nothing to do with Zeke's death, but Krista held it against me just like she did everyone else. The only person she had spoken to since leaving the Latin Territory was Omar. Somehow, they had found a commonality in their anger—Krista with her loss of Zeke and Omar with his hatred of his father, the Prime Minister Carvalho of Pod Horizonte. Krista had always been a bubbly personality, always managing to brighten a dark room, which was always appreciated in the dank confines of our former home, Pod Horizonte. What I thought to be her strongest attribute was vanishing before my eyes. I hoped she could come to terms with what happened before losing herself. None of us would ever be the same people we were before Release Day, that much was clear, but I desperately wanted to see some semblance of the Krista I grew up with.

Through the dilapidated shipping containers sprawled over the cracked concrete of the port, I could begin to make out the first vehicle in the transporter's caravan. It looked akin to the Misfit's personnel carrier. I took a deep breath and tried to suppress the anxiety I felt about these new people. If they chose not to take us to Kano, I was uncertain how we would make it on our own—especially being hunted like we were.

"Maybe we should leave out the fact we are being targeted by the inverts," I said to Huck.

"No kidding," he said with a wry smile. "Anyone else wishing it was Mueller and Otto?"

"Yeah," came the nearly unanimous reply, followed by nervous chuckling.

"Let Lolade do the talking," said Huck. "She's got something in mind."

As the caravan arrived, I could make out the rest of the vehicles. Attached to the first of two personnel carriers was a large all-terrain buggy. It was a strange sight. All the transporter vehicles we'd seen to date appeared very utilitarian. The first carrier and buggy were brightly decorated in an almost garish scheme. *Who are these people?* After the first carrier, the rest of the vehicles had the typical nondescript appearance equivalent to the Misfit's loadout. Once all the vehicles had come to a stop near the pump house, from which the attendant had already emerged, the men began to jump from the vehicles, shouting at each other in a language other than United English.

United was based on the English spoken on a worldwide basis at the time of the United Territories of Earth. Upon the initiative to build the pods, it was chosen to be the *lingua franca* for the inhabitants of the world's pods. All instruction to future generations was mandated to be in United. Of course, there were pockets of languages that filtered down, incorporating various slang into each pod's vernacular, but on the whole, people groups weren't supposed to be using anything aside from United. As a general rule, the further down you went in Horizonte, the less United you heard. I wondered if it was the same in the other pod cities.

The lack of use of United wasn't the only thing that set these transporters apart from the Misfits. Instead of thick rugged apparel made of canvas, these transporters wore flowing, loose-fitting fabric that prized ventilation over durability. On their heads, they wore wraps to protect them from the glaring sun's heat that poured down even more mercilessly than in the Latin Territory. Unlike most of the residents of Horizonte, the Saharans' skin was generally a darker complexion than my own, offering them further protection from the sun's rays. Already noting the difference in culture and appearance, a horrifying thought crossed my mind. *If the people are different, are the Arthropods too?* Sadly, I knew it wouldn't be long before we found out. I wasn't excited to see new enemies. At least the hooks and eights were known foes. We had been taught everything our trainers knew about, but since we had left the pod, there had been no shortage of surprises.

Eventually, a large man emerged from the first gaudy vehicle. The man was the fattest person I had ever laid eyes on. After being raised in the food desert of the pod, being overweight was an anomaly usually only seen in the high-level residents. It usually, but not always, was an indicator of corruption and greed and put me on my guard. The man wore the same billowy material and wrap as the others, but his garments appeared far more ornate than theirs. A smaller man emerged immediately after him carrying a sun shade, frantically trying to keep it elevated over the large man's head.

"Who the hell…?" Omar muttered.

The rotund man walked over to Captain Lolade without even a cursory glance in our direction.

"Captain Lolade," he said in a patronizing tone as he kissed her cheeks. "How good it is to see you once again. What gifts from the lesser jungle have you brought me this time?"

"Much the same, Yanus," she said.

After being put on the hull of the boat, I hadn't spent a ton of time with Lolade, but even as limited as my interactions with her were, I knew when she was concealing her annoyance.

"A pity," he said. "Keep an eye out for anything of interest. You know how I appreciate anything from *before*."

"You never let me forget," she said. "The supplies are less than normal. The Misfits encountered heavy losses on their last trip, both human and material. The remaining cargo is mostly communications, supplies, and those passengers over there. They are part of your load."

"Passengers? I've never taken candidates in my supply runs," he said, disdainfully. "Why should I waste my precious resources on them?"

"Because those are your orders, Yanus. They come from Prime Minister Carvalho himself," lied Lolade.

"Carvalho? That bastard has no power here."

"Fine. See what Prime Minister Zabu says when he learns that you've left his most anticipated cargo on the side of the road."

At the mention of Zabu's name, Yanus stood up straighter and tensed.

"I'll carry them, but they can expect no coddling from me!" he said, turning in a huff and taking out his anger on his men in their foreign language.

"Well he seems like a bowl of sunshine," said Hemant.

"Ten days, Arjun?" I asked.

"Yes. I fear it will feel longer if this is the attitude we can expect," Arjun replied.

●●●●●●●●●

Yanus was correct. We received no coddling. After bidding farewell to Lolade and Kebe, we were unceremoniously escorted to the cargo hauler, which would remain mostly empty due to the destruction of the Misfit's cargo. For their small size and innocuous appearance, those stupid pill bugs had proven to be a menace. It was because of them that humanity was down to nine pods. Once the bugs realized or demonstrated, not sure which, their ability to drop them like bombs, we began to realize the inverts were far more intelligent than we had given them credit for.

The hauler was sweltering in the heat of the region. Any benefit the shade of its bed offered was negated by the limited ventilation. The only sign of airflow was the ever-increasing amount of road dust at our feet. The hauler, not made for comfort, rattled us to our bones with every bump as we repeatedly slammed down into the metal plating covering its bed. The diamond-textured plate, instead of providing us with rough friction to keep us from sliding around, only scratched mercilessly at our backsides. Under the best of circumstances, this trip was going to be miserable. Eventually, we all got the hang of riding. Mei and I stretched across the bed, using our legs to hold each other into place. It was still miserable, but with the rest following suit, at least we weren't being banged around like rag dolls.

By the time we came to a stop at the end of the agonizing first day of Saharan travel, I looked and felt as though I had been through a battle. We sought a place of privacy away from our newfound friends to relieve ourselves. When I unzipped my jumpsuit, I saw that my legs were covered in the purple hue of bruises, my muscles screaming from the exertion needed to keep Mei and me in place. When I finally looked at my surroundings, I could barely breathe. I forgot all about my discomfort. It was beautiful! We were surrounded by tall trees with long snaking vines hanging down from the canopy arching above. The smells of green foliage and wet earthy decay filled the air accompanied by the sounds of the local insects. I glanced at Huck and smiled, noticing that he was in awe of the surroundings much like I was. What had started out looking like a dry and barren landscape had changed into a luscious jungle reminiscent but different from the Latin jungles. Though he meant to be condescending, now I understood why Yanus had referred to it as the lesser jungle.

I was snapped from my sense of awe by a heavy blanket smacking me in the chest, hurled by one of the men. He was attempting to explain something to me in his native language, but I couldn't understand.

"Do you speak United?" I asked. "I don't understand you."

"No," he said and began to walk away, then turning, he walked back to me. *"Mashi,"* he said, patting the blanket. I looked at the others questioningly, noticing we had all been given one.

"Mashi?" I asked, gesturing to the thick olive-drab blanket.

He nodded.

"Thank you," I said as he walked away.

"I guess their word for blanket is *mashi,*" I said, shrugging to the others.

"If we're going to be with them for ten days, it would serve us to learn some of their language," said Ciro. "I'll start keeping a list of terms. Maybe we can establish some basic communication. I think we're on our own."

"Yanus doesn't seem interested in helping us," said Mei. "He's treating us more like animals than people."

"Speaking of animals," said Ciro, "Can you imagine what this place would've looked like before the Arthropods decimated the local fauna? Do any of you remember from your classes what a monkey was? Or a hippopotamus?"

"A hippa what?" asked Hemant, laughing.

"I know what a monkey is," said Omar, "That would be Hemant."

I started laughing, the pressure in my chest reminding me of the day's bruising.

"I'm glad that you all are enjoying yourselves while my men take care of the work," said Yanus, who had approached us in stealth despite his girth. "Those who don't work, don't eat. I'll forgive you this time since you are new to our ways, but tomorrow, failure to contribute will result in your hunger."

"I'm sorry, Yanus," said Huck. "What can we help with?"

"You will never directly address me as Yanus, young one!" said Yanus, perturbed. "You will refer to me only as Protector Yanus! Get to work setting up your bivvies. The general camp work seems to be finished. Any hunters among you would do well to join the hunting party if you wish to prove your value here."

"Yes, Protector Yanus," Huck said, doing his best to reign in his sarcasm.

Once Yanus had disappeared back into his dedicated carrier, I let out a sigh of relief.

"Dear God," Hemant said. "Who the hell does he think he is? The only thing he looks like he's ever protected was his lunch."

I stifled a snicker.

"Either way, I've got to go prove my dignity and find us something to eat. Maybe *Protector* Yanus will let me borrow a spear," I said, thinking back to our discouraging battle with the Nightmare that killed Leni and left me without a bow. "Ciro, Mei, you guys coming?"

They both nodded and we set off into the unknown woods, with unknown threats, with the unknown hunting party.

CHAPTER 5: DIETER

I listened to the air hiss between my lips as I methodically took a deep, calming breath and opened the hatch of my apartment. With each passing day, the harassment increased in our department, driving my anxiety up and up and up. There was a day when Pod Kano was world-renowned for its scientific research. Some of the smartest candidates from the furthest pods risked their lives to journey here where they could participate in cutting-edge weapon research and development that could turn the tide of war in our favor. As I walked down the gunk-caked, trash-strewn corridor to the elevator, I tried to focus my mind on my personal mission: put the finishing touches on the bomb and find a way to smuggle it out. How I was going to do that, I had no idea. The last few missions sent to the Hive to gather information had never returned. If the teams arrived, they never made it back to tell.

I stepped into the elevator and selected the floor of the science lab using enough pressure to move the plastic button through its gummed-up track. Since Zabu's hostile takeover of the pod nearing two decades ago, everything from infrastructure to society had gone completely to hell. Scientists were still held in decent regard and though the pod was struggling, having long since exceeded its operational life, things were tolerable for the academics, provided they regularly demonstrated their worth to the minister and his cronies. In a military coup, Zabu, at the time a grand general, saw the way things were going and decided he could run the pod more effectively. Without going through the normal democratic channels, he assassinated the former prime minister and claimed the title for himself. Anyone who questioned him had a similar fate. It was difficult to stand up to a guy who walked everywhere armed with a blood-crusted machete.

With a ding, the elevator doors parted, scraping against a wad of paper caught in its tracks. I trudged along the path through the overripe garden district. The conditions in the pod were bad enough before, but in an effort to quell dissent, he had executed many of the most knowledgeable people in the pod. Now those tending the city's crumbling infrastructure lacked the wisdom to operate them under the best of circumstances. Furthering the issue, when someone couldn't perform effectively, Zabu's militia would execute them as well. The pod's inhabitants had three viable life choices: join the corrupt militia for a guarantee of decent treatment, silently fulfill their duties while still risking unjustified execution, or abandon their post to live on the fringes of society doing illicit work to make ends meet. Zabu's reign had brought the worst out in everyone.

As I approached our lab, I looked up at the looming Nucleus and further suppressed my anger at the way things had declined over the years. The wind coming from the central shaft was cooler than usual, giving me a slight shiver. I came across one of Zabu's men, fornicating with a young woman against the dingy wall of the poorly-illuminated corridor. *Probably how she's providing for her family,* I thought, with sadness. I mistakenly made eye contact with her as I bustled past. She looked at me with an offering smile. The man stopped his motion long enough to look at me.

"He wouldn't know what to do with you anyway. The only anatomy he knows is invert," he said laughing, before resuming his motion.

I diverted my eyes and picked up my pace. This is what life had come to in the city. The only reason the scientists were kept alive was that Zabu had a devious aspiration to take over Pod Baghdad. He was exhausting the resources in our pod and wanted to raid and subjugate Baghdad as well. Just like the Arthropods, he would come in like a biblical plague of locusts and unsustainably consume everything in sight. Of all the research we'd done into the invading species, I still wasn't completely sure how the Arthropods continued to thrive, having depleted most of the natural fauna on the surface. It sickened me to think that our practice of releasing candidates could be a significant source of their sustained momentum. That and cannibalism. A second shiver passed at the thought.

I arrived at the lab, punching in my code under the stuttering fluorescent bulb above. Upon entering, I was greeted with the welcome scent of cleaners. The lab was one of the few places left in the pod that was immaculate. Since Zabu had retasked me and the other scientists to build a Baghdad-busting bomb, we were some of the few teams allowed to function autonomously. Under the previous minister's reign, we had very limited access to dangerous and explosive materials. This change was one of the few that benefited us in our search for a way to defeat the Arthropods. Every time the minister or his minions pressed us for the completed weapon, we always pleaded for more time. I would die before I gave our maniacal leader a method to carry his ilk to another of humanity's savior cities. What he wasn't aware of was that we had nearly completed the weapon, though it wasn't exactly the weapon of his desires.

I rearranged my station, moving beakers, burners, and scopes to look as though I was doing a different project every day. Emile,

Rupert, and I would execute the silly charade so we could get to our real work: our chemo-nuclear bomb. It was a labor of love built straight from the pages of history. The nuclear design was based on a Cold-War era device built by a socialist group called the Soviets and combined with a chemical disbursement system based on an early American invention from their involvement in the Vietnam War. Pre-landing humanity seemed to have a penchant for killing each other. It was crazy to think that we were hanging our hopes of humanity's survival on four-hundred-year-old wartime technology.

Emile and Rupert had arrived at the lab before me, having already begun their work. They had traveled together from Pod Munich, the pod city of my origin as well. They obtained their citizenship on arrival and came to serve under me as the lead scientist. We had become fast friends and with our similar upbringing, could anticipate each other's needs in the lab. Sadly, we represented most of the remaining core of the scientific minds in the pod. We had been working in tandem with Pod Baghdad to develop weapons based on their Arthropod research. As a result, we found favor in Zabu's eyes, something that the other scientists didn't have. They had become just as scarce as the experienced greenskeepers and professors.

"Emile, check the viewport," I said.

Emile walked to the port and after a cursory glance back and forth said, "All clear."

We took turns manning the watch and today was Emile's. Rupert and I walked back to the corner of the lab where the large water lines to the labs were located. Since Zabu's takeover, one particular water main was one of the numerous systems that had fallen into disrepair. We had sent multiple requests to the labor department down in the lower levels, but they had all gone unanswered. Zabu had rounded up many of the labor class, the ones with the largest chips on their shoulders, and had used them as the backbone of his militia when he staged his coup. The lack of maintenance, like the access to explosives, had benefited us. The unused pipe now served as a shroud for our bomb. We had dissected the large white pipe for easy access, hinged out of sight on the rear and opening under a large tin plate of warnings.

Rupert opened the pipe, and we looked down onto the canvas-wrapped package. Neither of us was particularly strong, so it took the two of us to lift it from the recess and lower it onto our cart. I unfurled the wrap and admired the years of work. The bomb was slightly less than a meter in length and the diameter of a dessert plate, looking no more threatening than a giant battery.

"I know we've discussed this, but are you sure we're ready to fill the chemical tanks?" Rupert asked, still carrying hints of his Eurasian accent all these years later.

"It's time. The device needs to be ready to go at a moment's notice. Once the tanks are full, I want to attach the carrying straps," I said.

"But you still haven't heard anything from your friend, Memo."

"I know. I also know him. He'll do everything in his power to help. We're running out of time. I'm betting on the transporters bringing something—anything—to help us."

"I must admit, I am struggling to hold onto hope, Dieter, but I hope you are correct."

"They're coming!" Emile shouted, as loud as he dared.

Rupert and I haphazardly stashed the weapon back into the vacant pipe and the three of us hastily proceeded to look busy at our stations. Within seconds, three armed militia members entered to provide us with our regular harassment.

"All clear," one shouted into the corridor outside the lab.

My heart skipped a beat as I watched Prime Minister Ndulue Zabu swagger into our lab. I swallowed dryly.

"Good morning, gentlemen," he said, his calm demeanor adding even more to my disconcerted feeling. "Where is my weapon? I would very much like to lay my eyes on it."

I could hear Rupert gulp from where he stood. "It's… It's still not ready, Prime Minister. There are still many theories we are working through. It has to work in theory before—"

"Theory. Theory?" he said, approaching Rupert to within centimeters of his quivering face. "Theory should've been over a year ago when I assigned you this task. I have waited long enough. Let me see what you have."

"We… uh… you wouldn't understand our technical drawings and specifications. It's very complex."

Eying him closely, Zabu stepped back and took his signature machete from one of his men, fresh blood glinting under the lab's bright lights. He took the flat of the blade and ever so slowly rubbed it across Rupert's chest, uncomfortably close to his neck and changing the color of his white lab coat collar to crimson.

"Do you understand my work?" he asked, his words soft and slow.

"Yes. Yes, sir. I do," stammered Rupert.

"Then why wouldn't I understand your work?" he asked, then with a flick of his head, one of his men kicked Rupert in the back of his knees, knocking him to the ground while the other grabbed his arm and held it down extended across the black slab of the tabletop. In a swift rehearsed motion, he cleaved off Rupert's right hand. Rupert screamed as his face contorted in pain, cradling his spurting arm. I winced but held fast.

"Show me your work," Zabu said again, his voice unchanged.

Emile looked at me pleading, his eyes darting to the pipe. The tension in my chest was unbearable, but I knew that giving him the bomb we had created would not only kill everyone in Baghdad but also bathe its contents in radiation. Our creation was meant to turn the tide of the war against Arthropods, not to squabble over resources with humanity's remnants.

"We've been working on technical drawings and scale models," I volunteered, as I picked up a submersible pump out of its housing that I had been repairing, praying he wouldn't know the difference.

Zabu chuckled. "Scale models."

In the blink of an eye, his relaxed facade vanished and in a burst of wrath, he turned to Rupert and began to mercilessly hack him apart with the short blade, spattering my friend's blood, fat, and bone all over the once sterile lab as my heart exploded within my chest. When the violent act concluded, Zabu turned, covered from head to toe in the crimson fluid. He removed a pure white handkerchief from the pocket of one of his men and dabbed at his face and hands, barely reducing the glossy coating.

"You dare to presume I don't know a pump from a bomb when I see one," he said to me. "Your friend bore *your* punishment. You have thirty days to have a fully-functional complete model delivered to me. Thirty days. If it is not in my possession by then, you'll plead for a death like your friend's."

Zabu and his men cleared out of the lab, leaving Emile and me to deal with pieces of Rupert's corpse. On the way out I heard Zabu laughingly say to one of his men, "Ruling is such messy work." I watched as Emile collapsed next to what was left of Rupert and put my hand on his shoulder. If he hadn't been in such a daze, I'm sure he would've shrugged it off.

"We could've saved him," Emile whispered.

"At the cost of every soul in Baghdad," I responded.

I hoped Zabu would come to an end appropriate to how he introduced others to theirs. He had forced the final leg of our plan into motion. We had a timeline. We had to get our bomb out of Pod Kano and we had thirty days to do it.

God, I hope Memo comes through.

CHAPTER 6: HUCK

Once Ariadne and the hunting party departed, the five of us remaining behind sat up our team's bivvies and tried to make ourselves look busy until Yanus was out of sight. Krista wasn't much help, her behavior mimicked Leni's experience with the Shock before she improved. I thought about asking if she needed anything, but every time I looked at her, she could sense what I was about to say and answered with a glare. I collapsed onto a downed tree, feeling the give of rot eating away at its interior. Exhausted, I began to painfully slip off my boots. It wasn't the safest thing in the world, but my feet needed the fresh air.

"Huck, come take a look at this," said Arjun.

"You've got to be kidding me," I muttered. "Do I have to?" I asked. "I just took off my boots."

"I think you are safe to walk barefoot, but you need to see this."

I grunted as I stood and stretched, feeling my spine crack, relieving some of the day's tension. I really hoped what he had to show me was worth breaking my rest. Then I felt a pang of guilt when I realized that the others were still out hunting while my lazy ass chilled on a log. I stepped carefully over to where Arjun had been wandering around the clearing examining the local flora.

"What's up, Arjun?"

"Take a look at this kola tree," he replied, pointing at a nearby tree dwarfed by the others in the canopy.

"It's a tree," I said, shrugging.

"One, it's not just any tree. Here, chew on this," he said, handing me what looked like a nut.

"Sure," I said and popped the large nut into my mouth. Instantly, a bitter taste coated my tongue. Before I could spit it out, Arjun said, "Don't spit, keep chewing." I kept chewing and sure enough, the taste got better and I felt a little better too. I looked at Arjun, surprised.

"What is this?"

"It's a kola tree. The nuts have caffeine. You looked like you needed a pick-me-up."

"Thanks, man. How do you remember all of this stuff?"

"Remember, I was planning on going to Pod Baghdad after my Release. This was the route I was going to take, so I familiarized myself with all the edible plants and animals I might encounter."

"I'm thankful for that then." I turned, heeding the call of the log.

"Wait. That's not actually why I called you over her. Look at the tree it came from."

I looked back at the tree, this time with a little more patience. Sure enough, there was something weird there. Up and down the trunk were centimeter-sized holes that extended completely through its trunk, so neat, they almost looked drilled.

"I'm surprised the tree is still alive. What do you think caused that?" I asked.

"This tree isn't very soft wood. I don't know of anything that would have enough power to pierce this so cleanly."

"We barely knew what we were doing on the other continent. Now we're in a whole new place with all new dangers. Just keep your eyes open, okay? Let's stay together too. I don't trust these guys. I hope the others come back soon."

"I feel the same. They seem safe enough, but they have not earned my trust."

With Yanus gone and nothing pressing to do, I sat down with my journal and sketched the weird pattern in the tree. It seemed prudent to document our strange findings during our journey. Everything was alien here. Only a handful of humans had been eking out an existence on the surface over the centuries. If we were ever able to retake our planet, humanity would have to relearn, well, everything. Maybe one day my sketchbook would be part of history. The thought brought a smile to my face.

After an hour had passed, Ariadne, Mei, and Ciro returned exhausted and irritated from their hunt with the others.

"That sucked," Ariadne said, throwing down a strange spear onto the leaf-strewn jungle floor with a thud. "If I had wanted a babysitter, I would've stayed with the matriarchs back in the pod."

"Why? What happened?" Hemant asked.

"At first they just gestured and fussed at us in whatever they're speaking, then—" Ariadne began.

"She's mad they wouldn't let her use a bow," interrupted Mei. "They gave us each these short, pronged spears."

"Yeah. They're actually pretty good," said Ciro. "I killed three lizards, though I missed a lot more than that. It's pretty similar to the spears we were trained on. Same basic principles. I don't think they'd do anything against inverts though."

"I have no idea what they are saying, but they kept saying *mashi* today. It's either the word for spear and blanket or their favorite word," said Mei.

"Maybe it's their equivalent of thingy," Ciro added, laughing.

"Excuse me, My name is Taha," said Yanus' attendant, walking from between twin trees. "I'm sorry to interrupt. The men are preparing the caught game. It's best to be on your guard as this is when we're at the highest risk of discovery."

"You speak United. What a relief to have someone other than…" I said, before catching myself. *Why the hell did I say that? We're walking the rest of the way for sure.*

"Than Yanus?" Taha said with the slightest hint of a smile. "He is a good leader. He raised me, teaching me United English as well as mathematics. He can also be… difficult."

"It's a pleasure to meet you, Taha," said Ariadne, invigorated by the new face. "I'm Ariadne. Would you like to eat with us tonight?"

"I know all of your names, and the pleasure is mine," said Taha. "You'll find I am quiet, but a good listener. Alas, I'm afraid I cannot. I have to serve Yanus dinner and sing for the occasion. He would surely miss my absence."

"Sing?" asked Omar.

"Yes, Master Omar. In Pod Baghdad, where most of us are from, the human voice is the most regarded instrument in our musical history. I'm grateful. It was my voice that saved me. He heard me singing one day in the market and insisted I accompany him. As a result, I had very little training in the arts of warcraft."

"Just Omar, please," Omar said, surprising me. I thought he would have reveled in the master thing. "Why don't the men speak United? I understood that was obligatory when the pods were developed."

"It was," said Taha. "The people of the Mideast Region are strong-willed and cultural-centric. They've held on to many more traditions than the other pods. The working class mostly speaks an evolved version of pre-landing Arabic, whereas the educated are bilingual. You'll find that—"

"Taha!" Yanus bellowed, then said something in Arabic to which Taha lowered his head and followed him sheepishly back to the ornate rig.

"He might have raised him, but he treats him like a dog," said Hemant.

"I hope he finds a better life than this," I said. "Maybe one day he'll be the leader of these guys."

"Food's ready," whispered Krista as she pushed her way between us to the fire pit.

With that, we followed to the pit where another unappetizing lizard was being dug up. It smelled worse than snake and even after spending most of the last month on the water, fish seemed more desirable. In the end, it wasn't too bad. Being ravenously hungry helped.

•••••••••

The following morning, we grudgingly loaded our things into the uncomfortable cargo truck and departed camp. I had slept restlessly all night. Between the Saharan Territory's different sounds, bruising from the rough ride the day before, healing injuries from the parasites, and anticipation of invert retaliation, it was no wonder sleep eluded me. The trip this far had been remarkably calm—unnervingly calm, really. Aside from the aerials, we'd seen no sign of the Arthropods, but I knew they were aware of our presence. I felt it every time my back had a phantom itch.

My sore muscles felt every bump in the undulating road. I had thrown my sleeping pad in the back hoping for some relief, but even doubled over, it wasn't enough. Judging by the grimaces on the other's faces, we'd all be walking stiffly for the next few days if our bodies didn't get used to the pummeling. It's too bad Yanus didn't have any real seats to spare. I bet there was ample space in his carrier, not that he would share it with anyone other than his servant.

I tried to make conversation with Hemant across from me, but over the noise of the half-tracks trundling below us, I quickly gave up. Making matters worse, I couldn't even nod off. The second exhaustion would overwhelm me; there would be a back-breaking drop that would jar me awake. Arjun estimated this to be a ten-day ride. I had no idea how I could endure nine more days of this nonsense. I made up my mind to talk to Yanus the second we got out for a break.

Whether it was hours or minutes later, I don't know, but we felt a noticeable deceleration. My ears rang with the newfound silence. The motion calmed enough for us to break out of our supportive positions and scan the horizon from peep slits of the hauler's armor.

"That terrain looks rough," said Mei. "It's no wonder we slowed down."

"Rough?" asked Hemant. "As in, that wasn't rough back there?"

"Fine. Rougher," she replied.

"Well at least they slowed down," said Hemant.

"Wait, where are my knives?" Mei said, panicking.

I panned the truck, the bed's vibrations making it too difficult to crouch. After a second, I saw where Mei's pouch rested on Krista's leg.

"There, by Krista."

"Krista, would you throw me my knives?" Mei asked.

Krista turned her head in the other direction toward the rear viewport of the hauler.

"Are you freaking kidding me?" said Mei.

Omar, who was also seated at the back acting as Krista's supporting partner, reached over and grabbed the pouch before tossing it to Mei.

"Thanks, Omar," said Mei, then addressing Krista. "It's not like I haven't been saving your ass on a daily basis. The least you could do is help your teammate out."

Krista turned in a fury. "Like you helped Zeke?! Don't talk to me about help! There might have been enough in that bottle for both of them, but did you give it a chance? No! Huck may have held the bottle, but his death is on your hands."

"You're right. We didn't know, but Zeke chose! He—"

With a lurch, I rolled forward, smacking into the firewall separating the cab from the bed, and narrowly missed the bottom of the gun turret with my forehead. Immediately, there was a secondary impact as another body collided with me. *Great, more bruises.* The hauler had come to a dead stop and judging from the dead quiet, so had the other vehicles. I untangled myself from the pile of limbs, dusting myself off as I stood as much as the space would allow.

Wham! I was flung into the shrouded metal sides of the hauler as it tipped onto its side and fell over. I saw nothing but lightning after the impact on my head. Then the rush of pain hit. My head, my chest, and my shoulder were all screaming in agony. I didn't know as much about medicine as Ariadne, but I was betting I had a concussion. I wanted to jump up fighting, feeling the imminent attack, but when I stood, a spell of dizziness sent me right back to the ground.

I regained my balance and took a cursory glance around. The others were in a similar state to my own. I could hear a commotion outside, but couldn't parse out what was happening over the thunderous ringing in my ears. I helped Omar stand before turning to Hemant. He had blood pouring in rivulets down his face, but thankfully, it was superficial. Arjun and Ciro were already standing and helping Mei tend to an unconscious Ariadne. I rushed over to her to see if there was anything I could do.

"I don't see anything wrong with her, but I think we're under attack," said Mei. "You guys go see if you can help. I'll stay with her."

"Good idea," I said. "Everyone out. Be ready for anything. We can't let them take the hauler!"

Omar had already manned the door.

"I've got the handle budged, when I open it, rush out," he said. "I'll slam it closed behind us."

I nodded and stepped out into the overwhelmingly bright light.

CHAPTER 7: HEMANT

I smeared the trail of blood away from my eye as Omar flung the door to the cargo hauler open. *Here goes nothing.* I stepped out after Huck and was temporarily stupefied by the ensuing chaos. Scores of inverts were overrunning our caravan from all sides. Fewer than the battle with the spine back, but still legions of them. I was mesmerized by the fluidity of the Saharan transporters who were out in force battling the aggressors. I had mistakenly judged they weren't warriors from their appearance, but I couldn't have been more wrong. All around, the transporters spun, flipped, and slashed in a beautiful flowing style that was more reminiscent of a dance than a battle. Their tan garments floated on the breeze as they wielded their heavy curved blades like artists, painting the ground with jet black pigment.

Omar prodded me in the back, reminding me that I was gawking in the middle of a life and death scenario. I had only been on the surface of the planet for a month, and I was already desensitized to battle. I focused my mind on the present and launched myself into the fray, protecting our flank. With no trouble, I ascertained the source of our overturned vehicle. Next to the road were two thrashing multipedes with partially crushed frontal carapaces.

"They're a damn battering ram!" I yelled to no one.

I began delivering crushing blows to each segment of the pedes within the reach of my long-handled war hammer. Even with their self-inflicted injuries, they proved to be a challenging foe, always writhing to keep their heads out of my hammer's blows. With each segment I destroyed, the more the creatures' back ends became liabilities dragging them down. Between the dervish-like transporters and myself, it was only a matter of time before the pedes met their demise. The men and I grinned at each other through the fray, our camaraderie speaking in a universal language. I turned to see where else I was needed in the battle just in time to hear cheers erupt. We had sustained a few losses among the transporters but had successfully quelled our first direct attack in the new land. Even Taha, the youngest of the group, was spattered with hemolymph. I walked over to Huck, embracing him. It was good to get moving again, even if it was under the threat of battle. I had spent too long sedentary, and it wouldn't serve to lose my edge, especially if I had any desire to join forces with the elite fighters in Pod Bhopal.

"How'd you fare?" I asked him.

"I took down a few eights and hooks," said Huck.

"If we're keeping count, I think I killed four," said Ciro.

"Five," said Omar.

"The men we're traveling with are quite impressive," said Arjun.

"Agreed," I said. "I've never seen anything like it.

"It's a traditional style practiced by my people and adapted to the Arthropods," said Taha, joining us. "We were semi-prepared. This place is perfectly shaped for an ambush, so we always ready ourselves. We're attacked frequently, but we've never seen an attack of this magnitude."

"I need to go check on Ariadne," said Huck.

"You!" yelled Yanus, approaching me from behind.

"Me?" I asked, pointing to my chest.

"All of you!" Yanus said. "What are you playing at? You haven't been honest with me!"

"What are you talking about?" said Huck, stepping in. "The caravan was under attack. We helped defend everyone."

"Don't play coy with me!" Yanus yelled, the veins in his neck full to bursting. "This was a targeted attack! How many vehicles do you see overturned, *hmm?*"

I looked up and down the convoy. Yanus was right. Only the cargo hauler was flipped on its side.

"I'm sure it was a target of opportunity," I said.

"Target of opportunity, you say? Come. Come."

We followed Yanus to the head of the convoy where his carrier had been immobilized by flat front tires. As we walked, I noticed how unblemished his clothes were—not a dark blot nor torn hem. I looked around at all of those who had participated in the onslaught, no one had spotless or intact garments. I lost that train of thought when I followed Yanus' finger to the ground and felt the air leave my lungs. Buried in the earth, low enough to remain unseen, but high enough that its spikes protruded above ground was a dead multipede.

"Tell me, Henam, what about this says *target of opportunity?*" asked Yanus.

"My name's Hemant. And I agree, this is unnerving."

"I don't care what your name is. You're cargo! And just like cargo, you don't think," Yanus said, infuriating me by poking my forehead with his chubby finger. "Once we're to safety, you'll have five minutes to explain to me what you are doing and why I should carry you *any further,* or I'll bring you right back here and leave you as an invert buffet!"

•••••••••

After the attack, the damaged tires on the lead vehicle were replaced with spares and we made a beeline out of the area before the inverts could cannibalize their fallen. That evening, after cleaning up, we were permitted to enter Yanus' carrier. We checked on Ariadne after Yanus' blow up. She was conscious but incredibly sore. She assessed her own injuries and thought she had two bruised ribs and maybe a concussion. All of us, minus Ariadne and Mei, headed to meet Yanus. On top of the exhaustion following the adrenaline rush of battle, I had a pounding headache from the earlier impact. Taha had briefly met with us, instructing us how we were to conduct ourselves in the carrier. I would've rolled my eyes would it not have been so painful. Omar started to voice an objection, but Huck shut him up and was right to do so. As much as it sucked kissing up to Yanus' gluttonous ass, we'd never make it to Kano without his help. Could we survive on our own? Maybe. But with the target painted on our backs, I didn't want Arjun to calculate the odds.

As we trudged through the camp to Yanus' carrier, I noticed that the men were nodding to us out of respect. It was the type of honor only earned by staring down death together. For that brief moment, I forgot about my headache. We hadn't escaped unscathed. Krista walked with a subtle limp, but with her attitude, she'd be damned before she'd tell any one of us. She was trying to hide it, but I could see the subtle grab of Omar's elbow for balance. Ciro had brought down a number of beasts with his arrows, but with the way he was cradling his arm, it must have been at some cost. The lengthy boat journey hadn't done our physique any favors. I prayed that we would have time to recoup and heal before the next ambush.

The rules for the carrier were pretty straightforward, just pretentious and annoying. We had to wear clean jumpsuits so as to not sully his furniture, though Taha couldn't promise we could sit. We could only eat if offered, but again, Taha couldn't promise that either. We had to remove our boots before entering, which was the least offensive. I looked forward to getting them off, though, in the tight quarters, I couldn't promise that the odor wouldn't be offensive to Yanus' delicate nasal passages. Since leaving the coast, my body hadn't touched water, so I was sure we all smelled ripe as a rotten potato, but I was used to it.

After slipping off my boots on a mat positioned on the carrier's rear ramp, I entered the ornate space. My jaw almost hit the decorative rug camouflaging the utilitarian metal underneath. The interior of the carrier, which I had seen enough of during our travels with the Misfits, had been painted in a detailed blue and white pattern with gold filigree. Furnishings were attached to the decking so that the motion wouldn't disturb them. Every surface had a lipped edge like we saw in the Lolade's boat to prevent items from rolling off of the edges. The space had a private head, a large table, two sleeping berths (one more lavish than the other), and a long, strangely-upholstered plush couch. Yanus must have seen my gawking.

"You like it?" he said, gesturing to the couch. "It's made from the exoskeleton of a spring tongue. The plates have to be laboriously worked until they are supple enough to be used. It's the smoothest material found on Earth—adapted to glide through the water to its prey with scary efficiency. Sometimes I have to be careful so that I don't slide off."

A laugh burst from his gut, jiggling his expansive belly.

"It's prey?" asked Omar, undoubtedly remembering the incident with Ade.

I could feel the tension radiating from Omar and casually put my hand on his shoulder. If one thing could ruin this cooperation, it would be his outburst, of which he was lingering on the cusp.

"It's… nice," I said.

"Nice?" said Yanus. "It's bloody incredible! This is why I don't invite cretins into my transport. You don't appreciate the finer indulgences in life."

Omar stepped forward. "Finer indulgences?! People died out there today. Your people! And you're sitting here in your fancy carrier bragging about your nice things. We should be mourning them instead of defending our right to passage. Speaking of today, where were you? I didn't see you out there in the chaos?"

"Careful, boy!" said an infuriated Yanus. "You are about to dangerously offend me. I want you out of my sight at once. You are not permitted to enter my carrier again. Am I understood?"

Omar turned on his heel and strode out, not bothering to answer.

"I warn the rest of you to tread lightly. You are under my good graces, but I will not tolerate another disrespectful outburst. Now, someone tell me what the hell you are doing here."

Huck stepped forward. "May we sit? It's been a long day."

Yanus sighed. "On the rug, yes."

What an asshole. Huck began, standing. He disclosed the generalities of Grand Major Leal's mission and our planned rendezvous with a scientist at Pod Kano, carefully avoiding disclosing details like Dieter's name or his Hive-busting bomb. Finally, he ended with our plan to journey to the proposed site of the Hive deep in the Australian Territory where we would attempt to wipe out the alien scourge forever. When Huck was finally done, Yanus reacted.

"Bwahahahahaha," obnoxiously laughed Yanus. He laughed so hard, that he could scarcely catch his breath as his face flashed through purplish hues. "You mean to tell me… that you eight… just you eight… can take down the Hive?!"

I watched as he fell over on his ostentatious couch again in a fit of laughter before finally regaining his composure.

"You guys are even more stupid than I thought," he said, wiping a tear from his eye. "Wow. Obviously, the inverts have it out for you, though I can't for the life of me figure out how they perceive you as a threat. I'm satisfied. I will continue to carry you with some stipulations. If nothing else, for the entertainment value."

Huck stood there perplexed at how to respond. Taha even seemed embarrassed.

"I will not have you endanger my men. You will all ride together in the cargo hauler at the rear of the convoy. You will drive," Yanus said, pointing to Huck.

"I don't know how to drive," Huck replied.

"Then learn. Taha will teach you," said Yanus, before returning to the comfort of his luxurious accommodations and ending the interrogation.

"Could you be a little more gentle with the bumps, Mr. Driver?" I asked Huck.

Huck shrugged with a smirk.

"You'll find it's much easier than you think," said Taha. "It simply takes practice and patience."

"Could we get some padding or something for those of us in the rear? It's miserably uncomfortable," I asked.

"I'll see what I can do," said Taha. "It's a little isolated, but you could take turns in the turret as well. It has a relatively comfortable seat and would afford you some fresh air. Just please don't use the guns barring an emergency. It attracts Arthropods like a magnet."

Then addressing Huck, "Get a good night's sleep. We'll start your training in the morning."

CHAPTER 8: ARIADNE

I found the third day of travel to be more challenging than the previous days. Taha, who I greatly appreciated, had scored us some sleeping mats from the men who had fallen in yesterday's battle. The battle that I completely missed. I only remember waking up with my head cradled in Mei's arms and finding myself looking at the hauler's floor where the wall should've been. Between the two of us, we speculated that I had bruised a few ribs in the collision and almost certainly sustained a concussion. Surface life was hard. It's no wonder so few made it to their destination pods. The terror of Release Day washed back over me. So many fallen candidates. Friends. All at the whim of Prime Minister Carvalho, who regarded us as nothing more than gladiators fighting for his entertainment. I stole a glance at Omar. I had to remind myself not to hold a grudge against him just because of his biological father. One day, Carvalho would get what he deserved, if he hadn't already.

I desperately wished humanity could still use communication technology. I'd give anything to speak to Professor Lucas and see how things were going in the pod. I wanted to see what the impact of Arjun's live-streaming of our Release Day had done on public awareness of the corruption in the Nucleus. Stupid inverts and their electromagnetic fields. Humanity used to be so much more advanced. The Arthropods had killed most of us, driven us underground, and reduced our quality of life to a fraction of what it once was. *We are going to change that. We'll give them something that would turn this war of attrition into extermination. We'll stick it right up their asses.*

"Ow!" I yelped, my vision went white with pain for a moment.

"Sorry!" I heard Huck yell through the cab's firewall.

You'd think having traveled back here he'd understand how important it was to keep the ride smooth for us. The difference was now with every bump, I felt intense pain radiate from my chest like white-hot lightning. Instead of our previous tactic of pinning each other across the bed, Mei had me from behind and was carefully holding me in place, herself strapped to the wall. A choice that was fine for now but would be an issue should the truck be toppled again. Being armored, the hauler had taken most of the transporters to flip back over. The most excruciating part for me had been being lugged around before and after the process. Huck was a quick learner, but the frequent massive jars, whether from ground conditions or gearbox mismanagement, were doing a number on my injured ribs.

Before departing, Taha had informed us that we would be reuniting with the ocean by sundown, an event the transporters would celebrate with a traditional feast. At first, I didn't understand the region's geography, but Taha patiently explained that we had left Freeport heading along an eastbound roadbed that eventually turned south toward another section of coastline. Going directly east to Kano would prove to be impossible through the dense jungle, so once the convoy arrived at the coast, we would follow it until we could turn northeast and head directly toward Kano. Dinner promised to be an affair—a specialty of this area that had survived the Arthropod infestation. I was already starving, so I was getting excited about the upcoming delicacy. I prayed that it wouldn't be anything too weird.

Unable to do much else, I let my eyes wander from face to face. Hemant had spent most of the morning up top in the turret, the rest of us opting to remain in our riding pairs. Judging by his occasional yelling, he was enjoying himself. The rest of us were trying to relax as best as we could with all the shaking and jarring. I watched enthralled as Arjun examined a stick, flipping it end over end. I had seen the same stick in his hands repeatedly and attempted to discuss it over the machine's boisterous tracks.

"Arjun!" I yelled before realizing how much pain a deep breath caused me.

Arjun uncoupled his legs from Ciro's and crawled to me.

"Yes?" he said.

"Can I see the stick you keep playing with? It looks familiar."

"It should. You were the one who identified it."

"Of course! You brought the neem!" I squeezed his hand.

"I grabbed it shortly after we killed the spine back. I'm hoping Dieter can help us weaponize it. In reality, Ciro and I have so many findings about the Arthropods to share with them. Otto was concerned that they only listen to other scientists, but I believe they will listen to us. We've been trained extensively in the sciences. We had already discovered inaccuracies in habitats, behaviors, and levels of intelligence as well as discovered a new species."

I loved Arjun's enthusiasm. He rarely shed his calm demeanor except when he talked about his studies. I listened intently as he went on for almost an hour about various observations and hypotheses that he and Ciro had come up with before he finally got too tired of balancing himself against the motion without help. Once Arjun returned to Ciro, I must have fallen asleep. The next thing I knew, we were stopping for lunch. I heard some frantic yelling and climbed out of the hauler to several slain hooks being dragged away and dumped down a nearby hill. I hoped that their carcasses wouldn't attract any unwanted attention before our departure.

Thanks to my head injury, Yanus wasn't forcing me to hunt, but Ciro and Mei volunteered for the hunting party. The transporters, while completely different from the Misfits, were growing on us. Initially, they struck me as cold in their demeanor, but during the time we spent with them proving ourselves, even with the language barrier, they had slowly warmed to us. After the hunters left, I made my way to where a small campfire had been lit. Huck gently helped me sit down on the ground with my back against a fallen tree that had been dragged over as seating. Once I had assured him I would be fine alone, he went off to help the men do some roadside repairs to the fleet.

"Every time I look at them I hate them," I heard Krista say.

I realized I was eavesdropping, but couldn't stop listening. I wasn't sure where she was, but judging by her candid speech, she didn't think anyone was listening.

"It's normal. They can be stuck-up bastards," replied Omar.

"Everyone's talking about Kano as if it's some haven, but they've forgotten I can't go. I'm marked as banished. And no one, not even Ariadne has brought up any plans regarding me once I get there. And she's the one I took the mark for!"

My heart leapt up into my throat. Banishment didn't mean anything outside of the pods. I had been so worried about survival, I had forgotten. Krista was right.

"I'm banished, too," said Omar.

"What?!" asked Krista for the both of us. "But you don't have the mark—the theta."

"I'm unofficially banished. Before I left, my father told me if I didn't ensure your deaths, to consider myself one of the Banished."

"But how would they know that at Kano?"

"Carvalho has ways of communicating. They might not know

it yet, but they'll know it soon enough. At the entrance, a pod will turn you away, but if they find a Banished inside, the punishment is execution. I'm not taking my chances."

"Then let's run away. Far away. There are survivors, remember? Hemant found them. We could too. We can live with them or make it on our own."

"No. We need these people to survive. We're targeted by the inverts for whatever reason. We don't know if the targeting would continue if we separated from the rest. I know you hate them, but we need to stay with them. I'm still holding out hope that if we somehow complete this fool's errand that our banishment will be repealed. I've spent my life training to defeat these assholes."

There was a long pause. Judging from the light impacts on the forest floor, Krista was pacing.

"Okay. But what do we do about Kano?"

"We have no choice. We have to make camp outside of the pod, maybe out of sight so as not to impinge on their chances of success. We'll have to survive on our own for however long it takes them to collect the weapon and depart. Hopefully less than a week."

"Whatever you think, Omar," Krista said, beginning to cry. "You're the only one on this god-forsaken continent that cares about me."

That stung.

•••••••••

All afternoon, I had barely been able to contain the melange of hurt and anger toward Krista. I continually caught myself staring across the hauler's bed at her. She must have noticed because she began to avoid my gaze. After all that we'd been through, she felt like Omar was her only friend. Acting like that, Omar would be her only friend. I wondered what Zeke would've thought about her personality change. They were both such kind and gentle personalities and had meshed so well. Everything that Zeke and I liked about her had vanished in mere weeks. Her glowing demeanor and bright personality had converted into a shadowed existence of open hostility. Omar wasn't my favorite person in our group in the first place, but he only encouraged less desirable parts of her new persona. I needed to share with Huck what had transpired.

Our evening's stop would be in a place Taha called Big Smile. If it lived up to his flowery description, the place would be gorgeous. Mid-afternoon, when we were getting close, Hemant dropped into the bed from the turret, encouraging us to check out the surroundings. The afternoon had been attack-free, so Omar and Hemant carefully lowered two of the massive armored panels of the hauler, so we could take in the sights. The fresh breeze blew through the bed, reinvigorating us. The place we found ourselves must have been quite a populous city before the Arthropod Landing. All around were the collapsed shells of skyscrapers and condominiums, all indicative of a thriving coastal city where numbers of humans I couldn't fathom must have lived. Though disintegrating, you could still make out the creative architecture and imagine the effect the artistic forms must have had on the coastal skyline. I couldn't imagine what the place must have looked like in its heyday. So free of worry that time could be spent not only building, but creating. The quality of human life before the Arthropod Landing must have been blissful.

Once the day's travel finally came to an end, I managed to get Huck's attention and pull him off alone while everyone else was out hunting or setting up camp. I had thought to confide in him what I had heard, but no sooner had he helped me down from the elevated bed, than I forgot about the pain and my plans. Turning, I saw the salty waters of the blue-green ocean spanning the horizon and it took my breath away. The pristine beach was layered in fine sand that looked as though it had taken its hue from the sun. Lining the beach were palm trees, adding to the serenity of the luscious paradise. Taha walked up with two cracked coconuts, one for Huck and me. I immediately burst into tears.

"I apologize, Mistress Ariadne," said Taha, falling back on his use of the honorific. "I meant no offense. This is one of many local delicacies I wish to share with you."

"It's not that, Taha," I said, wiping my eyes. "We lost a good friend before we left the Latin Territory. One of my last memories of Kurt was of him bringing me my first coconut."

Huck placed his arm around my shoulder and the day's emotions hit me like a bag of rocks. I collapsed into the sand, pain be damned, and started to bawl. Huck filled my ear with comforting things as Taha remained close by, unsure of what to do. When I finally composed myself, I apologized.

"You have nothing to apologize for, Ariadne," Huck said, sweetly kissing my forehead. I looked up at him and without thinking, kissed him on the lips.

Crap.

Taha rapidly excused himself, leaving Huck and me alone. I hadn't meant to do that. I liked Huck as a friend, but I didn't have the emotional capacity or desire to have a relationship when I needed to be focused on not only my survival but my mission.

"So, I needed to talk to you about Krista," I began, pretending that what had just happened—hadn't. "I heard her and Omar talking and—"

"What just happened?" Huck asked with a big dumb grin on his face.

"Nothing. Nothing just happened. I didn't mean to kiss you. You are going to forget that happened. About Krista and Omar—"

"I can't just forget it," said Huck.

Damn.

"I know. But this *isn't* going to happen, Huck, I'm sorry. It's probably lust anyway, since you've seen me without my shirt twice now."

"It's not lust," said Huck quietly.

Great. This is just what I need—a guilty conscience.

"I've liked you since the moment we graffitied that overpass together," he said, before getting up and walking away.

I looked over at the two forlorn coconuts sitting in the sand. I picked one up and took a deep swig. The liquid tasted amazing, but the sour taste in my mouth kept me from enjoying it. I hurled the coconuts into the ocean, one after another, hoping Taha didn't see. All I needed was to lose three friends today.

CHAPTER 9: DIETER

It took us all day to clean the lab after Rupert's grisly execution. With every squeeze of the bloodied rag over the bucket, I felt a vice-like compression on my heart. Making the correct decision by not giving Zabu the bomb didn't change the guilt I would forever carry. The pod's population desensitized themselves to Zabu's violent tactics, coping, and thus surviving, by ignoring it. As a result, Emile and I knew that no one would voluntarily help us with the cleanup. In a way, it felt appropriate for the two who cared most about him to be handling his remains, however gruesome they were. Neither Rupert nor I had significant others. Only Emile had a partner, so at least we didn't have to break another heart with the news of his demise.

We silently bagged the larger pieces of our friend's corpse and placed them with care into the lab's incinerator, saying a few inadequate words before igniting it. The exhaust would be cooled and filtered before feeding back into the pod's ventilation system. Cleaning the remaining bone, blood, and tissue proved far more tedious. In a way, the revolting act felt like penance for my choice. I felt a pang of guilt each time nausea reared its head. After we finally finished, we went our separate ways to mourn alone. Emile in the arms of his wife and myself with a bottle of stout hooch. While many chose the addictive effects of pheromones, or the more potent Dust, as their escape mechanism, I still preferred the less problematic buzz of alcohol.

If the rumors were to be trusted, some years back, a food scientist in Pod Pittsburgh had been studying Arthropod-based sources of sustenance. Arthropod pheromones, which were already trafficked by transporters, could be used orally and topically as a mild hallucinogen with tranquilizing effects, quickly detaching its user from reality. The scientist discovered that the pheromones could be further refined into what is now colloquially known as Dust. While her discovery had little benefit, its popularity was explosive among the struggling working class. Dust was quite addictive, making its users problematic for hours, if not days. It was easy to identify long-term addicts. They would meander aimlessly around the pod, uninterested in stimuli and usually muttering unintelligibly. From my communication with friends at other pods, Dust's grip was far stronger in Kano than possibly anywhere else. As tempting today as the idea of trying the softer pheromones was, my mission required me to be clear-headed by morning.

I made my way to the nearest recreation district where I knew I could find a decent hooch. In recent years, gambling and fighting had taken over as the primary form of vice. Where there are spectators—there's booze. I pushed through the sweaty, boisterous crowd up to the wagering and concessions window and ordered a bottle of their best hooch, which is to say, drinkable. In these wretched hives, the best stuff was tolerable, the worst stuff might put you in a coma. Nothing compared to the quality liquors that were so prized in Pod Munich. The vendor took my ration points hesitantly, observing that I was far from my element. The idea of profit eventually won out and he handed me my bottle, which I promptly took in the direction of the little corner of the pod I called home.

Upon nearing my apartment, I saw several women at the corner of the housing district proffering themselves for entertainment. I had had a few relationships over the years, none lasting, but I had never paid for a romantic interlude. I recognized one of the women as the one I had interrupted in the corridor earlier that morning. *Oh, what the hell. People do it all the time.* I waved her with me and she promptly followed, filling the air with promises of pleasure and gratification. By the time we arrived at the hatch to my quarters, we were energetically groping each other. My elderly neighbor, who had somehow managed to survive the purges, chose this time to emerge from her apartment. Normally filling my ears with the day's gossip, she simply dropped her head, shaking it in disappointment. I ignored the reaction and opened the hatch, barely pushing the woman in before she was ripping my clothes off. I held her at bay long enough to pour myself a drink. I wasn't going to do this sober.

After we each downed a few shots of the vile swill, she flung off my shirt and began kissing me sensually down my body. Within moments, her actions were sending electric bursts through every fiber of my being. Yet, I couldn't have been more emotionally detached. There was truly no connection between me and this woman. It was distraction and escapism in their purest forms. Not even the primal pleasure could fully grasp my attention. I began revisiting the events of the day, my inebriated mind flooding me with a melange of guilt, rage, and anguish. To the sounds of her inauthenticity, my movements became increasingly aggressive.

"Stop! You're hurting me!" she said loudly.

I froze. "I'm sorry," I said, pitifully.

She pulled herself away and I saw her for who she was. Another human simply trying to make ends meet, and here I was unintentionally taking out my anger on her. She threw on enough clothes to barely cover herself and exited quickly before I could change my mind. She left the ration points lying on the kitchen counter by the door. This wasn't who I was or who I wanted to be. I took a quick shower, so frustrated with myself that I slammed my fist into a tile, breaking it and my skin. After applying a bandage, I returned to the kitchen where I poured myself a large glass of the hooch before downing it. I plopped down on my tattered sectional and tilted my head back against the wall as I let the intoxicant wash over my brain. I wallowed in self-pity for a while before I came to my conclusion. *If I don't hear from Memo, I will carry to bomb to the Hive myself. Or die trying.* I had been a candidate and spent my time on the surface. I could do it again, albeit I was older and chunkier than I used to be. I got another glass of the foul liquor but passed out before the glass touched my lips.

•••••••••

I awoke later than usual with the alcohol's negative effects clouding my mind. The blood circulating in my head thrummed with a beat that made me crave darkness and silence. I had to go to the lab. Emile would be waiting on me, no doubt wondering where I was. I threw on some clothes and made haste to the lab, resolving myself to apologize and offer payment to the woman I had abused the night before if fate offered me the chance.

I arrived at the lab about the same time as Emile. Judging by the dark shadows under his blue eyes, he and I both would be spending the morning with a hangover. We gently nodded at each other before entering the lab that was filled with thoughts of both death and hope.

"Emile," I began, talking softly for my own benefit as well as his. "If Memo doesn't come through, I decided to carry the bomb out of here myself. I think you and your wife should consider leaving with me. It's no longer safe for you here."

"If that is what you feel compelled to do, I will help you in every way I can, my friend. But our home is here, and so we will stay—regardless of the cost. Maybe I will give Zabu a bomb that will blow him up instead," said Emile laughing, before grabbing me in an embrace. "For Rupert."

"For Rupert."

Working among the fumes of the astringent sanitizer made concentration all the more difficult. We quietly worked away, taking over where we had left off the day before when we were interrupted. We carefully filled the bomb's tanks with the chemical irritant we had developed years prior. We sincerely hoped that between the radioactive fallout and dispersed irritant, not only would we kill the Queens, but we would drive anything that survived permanently out of the Hive. The neem-based chemical compound was one of the first cooperative developments between Kano and Baghdad. I had proven successful in the field at deterring Arthropods according to the transporters we had supplied with it. After loading the irritant, adding the carrying straps was simple. The device was ready to be carried and only lacked one crucial component—the enriched uranium necessary for nuclear fission. As Emile and I returned the bomb to its home in the pipe, I realized I was going to struggle to carry it alone. I could worry about that on the surface, for now, I needed to concentrate on how to smuggle it there.

With the day's work complete, we parted ways. As I was returning home, I passed the same street corner and there *she* was again. She quickly gathered her things and began to hustle in the opposite direction.

"Wait!" I pleaded. "I want to apologize."

She turned cautiously and watched me.

"I'm sorry. I was not myself last night. I had just seen...." My eyes began to fill with tears. I held out my hand with the ration points.

"It's okay. We've all seen and done things we wished we hadn't. Giselle," she said, her soft hand closing mine around the points.

"Dieter."

I returned to my apartment feeling as if I had restored some of my humanity. I sat in my austere surroundings, continuing to think about the device I had helped create. Of all the destructive components we had access to, the pod's limited supply of enriched uranium wasn't one of them. It was under some of the tightest security in the pod on the lowest levels with the nuclear reactors that used it for fuel. I pulled down the unfinished bottle of hooch, feeling the label from the bottle's past life wrinkle under my fingers, and contemplated pouring another glass. I breathed out a deep sigh and poured it out into the sink, before filling my glass with the minerally water from the tap. Tonight, I needed a clear head. I needed to plan a heist.

CHAPTER 10: HUCK

I sat on the sand, distancing myself from Ariadne. The wind blowing in from the serene ocean tousled my hair as it filled my nostrils with the fresh smells of the sea. I watched as the sun set in a palette composed of orange, pink, and purple hues. The transporters to my rear had already unloaded and were making the final preparations for the feast. Whatever it was, Taha couldn't stop building it up in our minds. But none of that mattered. Not after having just taken a sucker punch to the heart.

It wasn't as though I had spent weeks pining over Ariadne, but I felt like we had grown close through our recent experiences. We'd been too busy surviving to think about something as trivial as romance. What started out as a glimmer of physical attraction had turned into a strong friendship—a friendship that I was beginning to think could be something more. Then, in that brief moment, I felt elated finding she felt the same way about me. No sooner than the elation bloomed, it collapsed as she thrust me away. And worse, treated me as though it was a matter of horniness. *She'd* kissed *me!* I felt my cheeks burning as the cool breeze did little to soothe them. It wouldn't do any good to sit around moping. Distraction had a tendency to get you killed. *What would Omar do?* Then I did it. I took all the feelings I had for Ariadne and shoved them deep down into a box before sealing it closed, then I put my best face forward and returned to the transporters to join them for dinner and revelry. By the time I arrived back at camp, our magnificent feast was already buried under a mound of sand for its slow roasting.

"Man, this is going to throw you for a loop," Hemant said, pulling me out of my head space. "I wouldn't be in a hurry to eat it, but Taha here says it will be the best meal I've ever had. I'm sure as hell going to try it."

"What is it?" I asked, but Mei and Hemant shook their heads, refusing to give in to my curiosity.

After an agonizing wait, a slew of men dug up dinner. I was entranced by the grains of sand whipping around on the air currents generated by the updrafts from the heat. Eventually, the men exposed the shape of our leaf-enclosed dinner. It was massive. Whatever it was, it was as long as two people and as wide as Kofi, the pump house attendant on the far side of the ocean. I glanced out over the sea, wishing I could see the Latin Territory wedged between the rippling ocean and twilight sky. Ariadne walked up to join us and diverted my attention back to the food. The men heaved the girthy package onto the sand and at Yanus' order, began to unwrap it. As the leaves splayed open, I saw what had kept Hemant and Mei tight-lipped. Inside was the largest lizard I had ever seen.

"What is that?!" I asked Arjun.

"It's a crocodile," Arjun said, laughing at my blatant stupefaction.

"It's the biggest freaking lizard I've laid eyes on!" I said.

"Not a lizard, but related," Arjun said. "It's amphibious. Somehow, it survived the infestation. Taha and I were just trying to figure out how."

"Arjun is right," said Taha. "It mainly lives below the surface of the water but can come onto land when needed. That's when the men hunt it. Once we got close—"

"Taha! Where are you, confound it?" yelled Yanus.

"I'm here, sir," Taha said.

"Well don't just sit there. Get my first-portions and bring them to the carrier. Get yourself something as well. Quickly now," said Yanus.

Taha nodded and began to collect Yanus' food.

"That guy's an ass. I'm not sure why Taha or the men put up with him," said Hemant.

"Me either," I said. "So how do we eat this?"

Omar stood, grabbed a plate, and walked over to where the transporters were already pulling bits of the crocodile's pale flesh from inside its tough, blackened hide. Krista quickly followed his lead and did the same. I watched as they emulated the transporters, ripping out a hunk of flesh each before finding a spot to eat.

I looked at Hemant and shrugged. We rose and trudged through the sand to the beast lying on the ground in front of us. In addition to the meat, the men had roasted what appeared to be yams and okra, both vegetables prevalent back in Horizonte, but here were significantly larger and more flavorful. I grabbed a small portion of each item and was about to find a seat when one of the older transporters stopped me, speaking to me in Arabic.

"I'm sorry. I don't understand," I said, looking around for Taha to no avail.

The man pulled me by my arm back to the beast and began to load up my plate several more times over what I thought appropriate, all the while motioning me to get more.

"Okay. Thank you," I said, inclining my head to him, a practice I had observed them doing regularly.

"I think he wants us to stuff ourselves," said Ciro. "This is a feast for them. Perhaps the largest meal they eat on each run."

"Don't forget, whatever isn't eaten can't be saved," said Mei. "And this thing's enormous."

"Okay then," I said, shoving the first, scalding bite into my mouth.

My awkward moment with Ariadne momentarily vanished as I collected an ample amount of food. My plate was stacked higher than I ever had. I felt like a glutton but noticed so many others in both groups were doing the same. I ate and ate, smiling and laughing as we all gorged ourselves on the tasty food. The crocodile's meat was firm with a fishy flavor, which I found delightful. The yams were soft and sweet, and the okra, though not my favorite, had just enough texture to round out the meal. After about a half-hour, once everyone was stuffed to the gills and blissfully satisfied, everyone dumped their uneaten food in the pit vacated by the crocodile and it was covered for the night in sand.

"That was amazing," I said. "I feel so good. I've never felt this good."

"Now I know what Taha was talking about," said Mei.

"We never had access to this much food at once, much less this nutritious," said Arjun. "It's no wonder we feel intoxicated."

The same older gentleman who had beckoned me to get more food came over to us with a tray of cups, motioning for each of us to take one.

"Coffee!" said Hemant, looking at Ariadne. "This is almost as perfect as that first cup of coffee with the Misfits."

"*Shukran.* Hemant," said Hemant, placing his hand on his chest.

"Khalil," said the man serving us, who smiled at Hemant's linguistic effort.

Ariadne nodded, taking a cup from the tray and sipping it politely. A film of tears formed over her eyes as she filled with sympathy for the Misfits we previously shared coffee with. Momentarily tempted to console her, I looked away not wanting to revisit the experiences from earlier. I sipped on the rich coffee. The Saharan transporters liked their coffee with a kick. It was thick and rich and the perfect accompaniment to our meal.

"When did you start speaking Arabic, Hemant?" I asked.

"I haven't. Ciro is picking it up. He's got a knack for languages. He taught me 'thank you' and a few others, but I only remember the one."

As we sat on the beach, I heard music emanating from behind me. We all turned to see its origin. The group of transporters had positioned themselves around in a circle and brought out various instruments. Most were chanting. Some were strumming stringed instruments, blowing on sets of pipes, and tapping small boards. The music was subtle and soft to avoid attracting the Arthropods but steeped in emotion and tradition.

"It's beautiful," said Ariadne, speaking for the first time since our encounter.

"It is," I agreed.

●●●●●●●●

I awoke to the sounds of the routine commotion that signaled breakfast. Groggily, I crawled out of my bivvy and grabbed a bite of the fresh fruit before heading down to the ocean for a much-needed bath. When I arrived, I met with Taha, Hemant, and Omar doing the same.

"I think you're ready to drive on your own today, Huck," said Taha as he rinsed his short, curly hair in the morning surf.

"Sure. I think I've got a feel for it," I said. It was true. Though I still needed a lot more experience, I felt competent enough to follow the tracks that led the way.

"Good, then you can train others as well," said Taha.

I looked at Omar and Hemant who were smiling. I wasn't sure if their bemused looks were from the potential excitement of driving or eagerness to watch me fail.

"Where are we going today?" I asked.

"It's going to be a long day," said Taha. "You'll be thankful for the big meal last night. We're traveling along a stretch of the coast that's rife with Arthropods, so we try to make haste and stop as little as possible."

"Awesome. I thought the reason we traveled the coast was to see less of the bloody things," said Hemant.

"I *am* talking about less of them," said Taha. "The Saharan Territory is inundated with them. The further into the hinterlands you go, the thicker the enemies and vegetation become. So when I say 'rife with Arthropods,' I mean they are numerous, but are unimaginably worse inland."

"Oh," said Hemant. "Listen to the man, driver. I don't care to veer north."

"Not to worry," said Taha. "We'll be going in and out of sight of the water all day. It's relatively easy to orient yourself. I hope to be done traveling by nightfall. We are going to be moving quickly until the afternoon. We need to drive through a particularly dangerous forest which is unavoidable. I urge you to be on your guard."

Thunk.

I turned to see where Omar had perfectly speared a spring tongue who'd snuck down the sand attempting to get the drop on us.

"I never let mine down," said Omar, withdrawing his weapon from the fuzzy ant-like creature's still twitching carapace and returning to camp.

Sneaky bastards, those toadies. On the verge of paranoia, I quickly finished cleaning myself and sat in the bright sun as it rose above the early morning clouds, drying myself off before donning the fresh jumpsuit I'd washed the night prior. When Hemant and I arrived back at camp, we collapsed our bivvies and threw them into the cargo hauler for the next leg of our journey. After everyone was loaded and ready to depart, I beckoned Hemant to join me in the cab.

"Why does Hemant get to ride shotgun?" joked Mei.

"I'm older and wiser," responded Hemant.

"Like hell you are!" she said, playfully shoving Hemant.

"Ahem," said Yanus, rounding the front fender of the hauler. "Are you two quite done?"

Hemant and Mei immediately dropped their arms to their sides.

"I hope you don't underestimate the need for your attentiveness on this particular journey. I don't trust you," he said, getting right up into my face. "I think you are a danger to my men and my gear, and most importantly, a danger to me. Get in the truck and stay close!"

The second his back was turned, I rolled my eyes, causing Ciro to snicker. Yanus turned around red-faced, but finding nothing obvious to fuss about, marched off in a huff.

"You heard the man," I said. "Everyone load up. Hemant, you're with me. Omar, I want you in the turret. It sounds like today could be pretty hairy. Ciro, I want you closest to the tailgate should the others need cover from your bow. Everyone clear?"

Everyone assumed their post as I walked the perimeter of the hauler, checking the panels, tires, and tracks.

"I think we're ready," I said to Hemant as I jumped into the cab. "Ready for your driving lesson?"

"I suppose," he said.

I saw the convoy ahead of us begin to roll out, and I started the engine. "Lesson one, let off the clutch pedal slowly as you press on the gas pedal to start moving." I began to demonstrate and promptly killed the engine as the truck bucked.

"That wasn't supposed to happen, was it?" asked Hemant.

CHAPTER 11: HEMANT

The morning progressed much faster once Huck regained his feel for driving the multi-ton vehicle. It was a struggle for him to manage all the controls simultaneously. I resisted the urge to poke fun at him, knowing when it was my turn, I might fare no better. I was pretty good with my hands, but never a quick study with written knowledge. I filed away each tidbit Huck shared about the gears, clutch, range, and locks, but after a while, I just started nodding absentmindedly. It would make more sense once I was doing it, I supposed.

After several hours of jostling across the relentless terrain, we finally stopped for lunch. Pulling out the dry stores, we gnawed on ration bars that tasted like the byproducts of a sawmill after the extensive meal we had enjoyed the night prior. Taha had escaped Yanus' reins long enough to explain that we were entering the riskiest part of the trip—the aforementioned forest. I choked down the rest of the tasteless bar and returned to the cab.

"You drive," I heard Huck yell from behind.

"Is that the best idea in Taha's forest of horrors?" I asked.

"Do you remember how to go?"

"Yeah."

"Stop?"

"Yeah."

"Turn?"

"Yeah."

"Then you're ready to go. Everything else is fluff."

"Alright, if you insist," I said, climbing up onto the bench seat.

I listened as the worn springs of the driver's side groaned, failing to effectively support my mass. I gripped the steering wheel like it was going to leap from my hands.

"Relax," said Huck, as the convoy began to pull out.

"They're leaving and I don't know what to do, Huck," I said through clenched teeth.

"Start the engine, then lift off the clutch while you push on the gas. Slowly. Not like I did this morning."

I started the engine and listened for the soft rumble that indicated the natural gas was turning the engine's crankshaft. I slowly let off the clutch, and the truck, despite its massive size, began to hop like a jackrabbit.

"Gas, gas," said Huck.

I gave it more gas, and it started to speed. In a panic, I let off the gas completely and it began to hop again. I gave it gas, but slower this time, the truck began to pull forward in a slow motion but immediately started sounding strange.

"It's over-revving. Remember, I explained that yesterday. You need to change gears."

I reached over to grab the stick, but Huck dissuaded me.

"You have to push in the clutch again."

"Again?"

"Yes! Clutch, change, gas, repeat."

I pushed in the clutch again, changed the gear, and pushed in on the gas. It wasn't perfect, but we were still going forward.

"Great job. You got it!" said Huck.

"I got it! I got it!" I said, smiling. "How many gears does this thing have?"

"I think Taha said ten."

"Ten?" I felt my smile fade slightly. *This was going to be a long day.*

After about twenty minutes of constantly up-shifting and down-shifting through the rugged terrain, I had finally gotten a feel for the machine. It was a pain in the ass, but also kind of fun. I only stalled out a handful of times. At the snail's pace we were moving, I never lost sight of the trucks ahead. Taha said we'd be moving fast through the forest, but what he meant was as fast the terrain allowed. I slowed as I saw the red brake light flick on each vehicle sequentially from the head of the convoy, the lights refracting in the raindrops that had accumulated on the windshield.

"Can you tell what's going on?" I asked.

"No idea. I don't see anything," said Huck.

"What's going on? Why are we stopping?" said a muffled voice from the bed.

"We don't know," I replied.

The rain picked up, further limiting our visibility.

"I'll go check," said Huck, locking a bolt into his crossbow before slinging the strap over his shoulder. The door creaked open and he descended the ladder as the mist blew into the cab. Huck vanished among the vehicles for what felt like forever but, in reality, was only a few minutes. He returned, soaking wet, mud-caked on his boots. Huck opened the sliding panel to the hauler's bed and spoke where the others could hear.

"Yanus' carrier got stuck in the mud. The men are digging it out now," he said.

"Tell them if Yanus would get his lazy ass out and push it might help," said Omar from the turret.

"Taha asked us to provide cover while they dig," said Huck. "Hemant, you and Omar stay put in case we need defensive fire and a quick getaway. Everyone else, with me."

I watch Huck and the others file out into the pouring rain, trudging through the thick, sticky mud that covered the abandoned roadbed. I sat for a while before boredom got the best of me and I was doing silly things like counting the gauges and finding how many positions there were on the shift lever.

"Hey, Omar, can you see anything?" I asked.

"No. It's hard to see anything through this rain. It's running right off my head and into my eyes. Remind me when we get to Kano to buy a hat."

"Will do. So, um, your dad, Carvalho. What was it like?"

"What was what like? Being the prime minister's son?"

"No, man. Like what was it like being someone's son?"

"I don't know," he said, pausing so long that I thought the conversation was over. "It was different, having something that no one else had. It wasn't exactly a warm relationship. It was mostly him telling me how disappointed he was in me. I was less his son and more a candidate being groomed for office. You know he had Lourenço beat me once?"

"He what?"

"Beat me. I failed some test. I don't even remember what it was. It wasn't important to me, but it damn sure was to my father," said Omar. "He had Lourenço set up a private training session, which was really him beating the crap out of me with a bo staff for several hours. I couldn't do anything comfortably for days. It only happened once. I suspect because Lourenço refused to do it again. I don't think it ever sat right with him."

"I wish Arjun and I had known our parents. I like to think they would've been nicer than your father. No offense."

"None taken. He was a belligerent asshole. While he's my

father, he's not important to me. I'm pretty sure he hung me out to dry when we were released. When— Hemant, we've got incoming! Can you honk the horn? Get the others' attention!"

I frantically searched for any button that could be a horn before finding one of the few buttons on the dented dash that still had a decal. I pushed it, unprepared for the noise it generated directly above my head. I'd consider myself lucky if all the Arthropods in the territory didn't hear that. It did the trick. Ahead, I saw the others moving about in response to the potential threat.

"I'm going to help! You alright up there?" I yelled.

"Yeah, but I won't start shooting unless things get ugly," said Omar.

"Good," I said, running towards Huck.

"What are they?!" asked Huck.

"I don't know! Hooks, maybe?" I said.

The rain was getting heavier by the second. We had to yell to hear each other over the sounds of the torrential downpour and heavy gusts as they blasted through the canopy above.

"Did you get Yanus' carrier out?"

"Yeah, but it won't help us much. The mud's too thick to make a run for it," said Huck. "We're going to have to stand our ground!"

"Great. I was getting too comfortable anyway," I said.

I slogged through the mud to where Arjun and Ciro were standing. The mud clung to my boots as if I was standing in a vat of glue. The slurp that followed each struggling step reminded me of eating a steaming noodle bowl—a reality that I couldn't be further removed from at the moment.

"Any idea what they are, Arjun?" I asked, having difficulty being heard over the rain.

"Their profile would indicate hook beetles," he said. "Remember to aim for their sides."

I watched as the hooks descended on us. I had trained in numerous conditions, even in rainfall. The arena had been set up to simulate rainfall, but the ground's substrate had always been sand to absorb potential blood. Having to fight with my legs damn near frozen in place would be a nightmare. It was my cold, wet, miserable reality.

The swarm of hooks washed over us like a tidal wave. The first transporter died instantly as a hook plowed him into the ground, spattering me with blood and mud droplets. All around me, the hooks performed kamikaze dives in an attempt to take us out. Fortunately for us, the impact alone killed many of them, but at the cost of human lives.

When one landed behind me, I turned and brought my hammer down on its carapace as hard as I could, almost falling over backward in the mud. I felt its chitinous exoskeleton crack under the blow and brimmed with success. *One down.* I lumbered over to where Ciro was firing arrows from his compound bow into the creatures' sides before Arjun would use his collapsed razor net like a monkey fist, bashing the hooks' heads in.

After taking out a few more, we started moving towards the commotion at the far end of the convoy where only a trio of hooks remained.

"Ow! What the hell was that?" I said, grabbing my arm. I pulled my palm away to see where my upper arm was draining blood from the front and back. "Ciro, did you poke me with an arrow?!"

Ciro, who had been focused on the mission ahead, looked at me confused.

"No! Of course not," he said.

The deluge wasn't helping stop my excessive bleeding.

"Arjun can you put a bandage—"

"Ouch!" said Arjun, looking down at his thigh where an identical injury just appeared. His saturated jumpsuit wicked the blood away from the injury, turning his leg crimson in seconds. Making eye contact with me he said, "This is new."

I heard Ciro yelp next to me as I saw another dot of red blooming on his shoulder. I rushed to him and held my hand on his wound's entry and exit.

"If one of these hits something vital, we're dead!" I said.

"Mashi! Mashi!" screamed a transporter.

In that instant, the word mashi transcended all language barriers.

"The blankets, Arjun. They're a defense against the mashi!" I yelled.

"They're in the truck!" he said. "I'll go get them."

Arjun sped towards the truck as transporters and candidates alike ran furiously for cover from the nigh invisible threats. All around me, transporters were throwing themselves into the icky goo that covered the ground and disappearing under the rough, protective blankets.

Zzzhhrrrp.

I looked down to see a tiny black conical Arthropod digging itself from the mud next to me. Its appearance looked harmless until I realized it had taken a chunk from the back of my leg, nearly grazing a tendon. Then the sharp pain hit. I struggled to keep pressure on Ciro's shoulder and the pain in my legs made me shudder. I unsheathed my dagger and sliced the minuscule invert in half.

Zzzhhrrrp. Zzzhhrrrp. Zzzhhrrrp.

All around, I saw the ground start to spring up with them. I looked in the direction they came from and my heart stopped. Coming straight for us was a black cloud maneuvering in harmony—a murmuration of mashi.

"Arjun!" I yelled.

"I'm right here," he said, throwing a blanket over Ciro and me. "It's not big enough for the three of us! There was only one! I'll see if I can find another one!"

"Like hell, you will! Get under here!" I screamed. "If anyone's being left out, it's me. Squeeze in with Ciro! I'll find cover."

I looked up to see the swarm was almost on top of me. I looked to the side and realized there was no way I could make it to safety. *This is it. No blaze of glory for me.* I was going to be impaled by a thousand tiny inverts. I closed my eyes and waited for the pain.

Whoomp!

I felt the wind knocked from my lungs as my face fell into the sludge. I spit out the muck and took a gasping breath. *That didn't feel like I thought it would.* I looked around, even in the limited light, I could tell I was under a blanket. I felt the distinct buzz of the mashi multitude bouncing harmlessly off the impervious shroud. It was followed by an agonizing scream behind me and realized my savior was being perforated by the minute phantoms. I winced as a wave of nausea hit me, not from the foul-smelling sludge I was submerged in, but from guilt. Someone had saved me at their expense, but who?

After a few agonizing minutes, I heard Taha yell, "All clear!"

CHAPTER 12: ARIADNE

After Taha yelled the all-clear, I peered out from under the blanket where I was hidden next to Mei. By the time the mashi attacked, Mei and I were close enough to the hauler to grab my blanket and imitate the transporters. The thick material must have either masked our presence or been resistant to their attacks. I escaped with merely a graze to my shoulder. The rain let up enough that we didn't have to yell and could finally see without difficulty. I joined the small group gathered around Hemant. By the looks of things, Ciro had taken a nasty hit.

"You lot are disastrous for my team!" yelled Yanus, so worked up that his body quivered with fury. "Now I've lost one of my best men to you numskulls."

"I didn't ask for this," Hemant said. "He sacrificed himself for me."

"It doesn't matter how it happened, Khalil was one of my best. He wouldn't be dead if it wasn't for you," he said, shoving Hemant in the chest.

I watched as Hemant forcefully repressed his anger, knowing he wanted to pummel Yanus almost as bad as I did. On closer inspection, I could also see the hurt in Hemant's eyes. Between Hemant and Yanus on the ground lay the corpse of the deceased transporter. Khalil. The same one who had shown us kindness on more than one occasion. His normally billowy clothing was a mass of tattered rags stretched over what was mostly now a skeleton. In mere seconds, the mashi had picked the flesh from his bones.

Yanus said something in Arabic to the men, and then addressed us.

"I instructed them that if you are found without your blankets again, they are to leave you to the mercy of the mashi, or I will do the same to them," he said before walking off in a huff.

"It reminds me of the piranhas Kebe told us about," Arjun whispered to Ciro.

"There are some medical supplies in the supply truck. You should be able to take care of Ciro's injury there," said Taha. "We won't be moving on immediately. Our culture dictates that funeral services must happen immediately for the dead, regardless of the inherent danger."

Taha left to help with the burial of the fallen transporters.

"Do you think we should help, Huck?" I asked.

"I don't know that they want to see our faces right now. In addition to bringing more invert attention to their party, now one died saving Hemant," said Huck.

"Can we not talk about that anymore, please?" asked Hemant. "I feel bad enough already without dredging it back up."

"I'm sorry, man," said Huck. "There's no way you could've known. I'm sorry that we lost him, but I'm glad we still have you."

Hemant nodded sullenly.

"Well, let me get Ciro patched up. Then I want to check the rest of your injuries. Everyone to the cargo hauler except for

Arjun and Ciro. I want you both in the supply truck. I'll treat the rest of you as I can."

•••••••••

The rest of us had suffered only minor injuries—nothing that would dramatically affect our chances of survival, at least. We'd all be sore and at risk for infection. A person can't have a foreign body go through them and not cause damage or contamination. Several of the transporters were injured as well, but when I offered to treat them, I was met with distrust and discomfort. I left the supply truck feeling confused. Taha was supervising the redistribution of personnel through the convoy and saw my dismay.

"Is something amiss?" he asked.

"I don't understand. I'm quite qualified to treat injuries, but the men acted as if I was a child," I said. "They shooed me out of the supply truck so that they could care for themselves."

"I'm sorry to hear that. You have to remember that the cultures of this area hold strongly to their long-held traditions—more than any other culture I've encountered in my travels," said Taha. Still sensing my confusion, added, "It's because you are a woman."

I scoffed.

"They have profound respect for womanhood and mean no insult," said Taha. "Those raised in the lower levels have traditional roles for the women of their society, but they hold no resentment for the role you possess. The men simply prefer to be treated by a male. That's all."

"I didn't like how it felt."

"Understandably so. You, Mei, and Krista are remarkable women. You'd have to be to survive as long as you have. If it makes you feel better, Pod Baghdad as a whole is much more progressive."

"Thank you, Taha."

"It's my pleasure to serve," he said, inclining his head.

I left his side feeling better. It amazed me how such a kind and wise young man had been raised by such a pretentious windbag.

Before long, we were back on the road, being once again thrown around like rag dolls in the cargo hauler's rear. Ciro's mashi injury had been through a muscle group, but he would recover well enough with adequate rest. He just might have to favor his shoulder for a while. I wasn't sure he would be able to manipulate his high-poundage bow until he recovered more. Fortunately, the transporters kept a vast array of spears and scimitars for him to choose from— at least until we arrived at Pod Kano. Every candidate had their preferred weapons, but we'd received training in all the common weapons. If the options were available, we could choose whatever weapon best suited our needs.

For the rest of the day, we stopped as little as possible. The rain let up and we made much more progress after passing through the dense forest. The remains of the road that lay ahead were overgrown but clear of obstacles and mud. We made good time, almost completely making up for our slow jungle passing. It was still a long day. By the time we made camp that night, I was exhausted. After a quick bite of dinner, I crawled into my bivvy still feeling the rocking from the day's motion and allowed the feeling to lull me to sleep.

•••••••••

The next morning, the dew that dotted the grass collected on my boots as I walked away from the camp for some privacy. When I returned to the camp, I took a deep breath through my nostrils. The fresh smells of dawn permeated my senses as I watched the sun clear the treetops. It was going to be a lovely day. Or at least until I saw Krista crawl out of Omar's bivvy.

I felt a ferocity rise from my abdomen and into my throat, a sensation that made my cheeks burn with fury. I forgot about all the pleasantness of the morning and stomped over to where she was stretching, a smile across her face for the first time in weeks.

"What the hell are you doing?" I said, not caring that my voice was loud enough for others to hear. "Do you have any idea what I went through when you were pregnant? You said you couldn't protect a baby. You couldn't endanger the team. You're barely over your miscarriage and you're sleeping with someone! Did you forget about Zeke that easily?!"

Krista's hand appeared out of nowhere, making a loud pop as it connected to my face. Her open hand stung my flushed cheek and my furious heart.

Barely restraining her pent-up anger, through clenched teeth she said, "You know nothing, Ariadne. You've never lost anyone you've loved. Not like me. You don't know what it's like to go to bed every night crying yourself to sleep, wishing you had died with him. I'm banished, Ariadne, or have you forgotten?!" She pulled up her sleeve to reveal the mark. "My life could be over any second of any day. I'm going to do what I please when I please. There's no need for you to concern yourself with me. Ever again."

Her words hit me much harder than the physical blow.

"I—" I croaked, but Krista had already turned her back.

Omar emerged from the tent, looking me in the eye.

"Nothing happened," he said. "She just needed comfort, but I'm sure what you announced to the entire camp helped immensely."

I turned and looked around, everyone in the camp had stopped to see what was going on. Omar was right, anyone who spoke United and didn't know about Krista's miscarriage did now. I was ostracizing my friends one at a time. I felt the heat in my cheeks again, but this time from embarrassment. I did the only thing I could think to do. I fled.

I darted off into the woods as my eyes blurred with tears. I knew going off alone was idiotic, but I didn't care. Maybe I didn't deserve to return. Krista hadn't even done anything. Neither had Huck. I finally collapsed onto my knees when my lungs burned with the same fire I felt in my legs. I was heaving sobs. I wrapped my arms around myself for the comfort that no one else would provide. I cried and cried. I finally caught my breath, sitting up against the moss-covered bark of a tree. Wiping the tears from my eyes on the filthy edges of my jumpsuit sleeves, I saw a small, green worm hanging down from the boughs above.

I let it lower to my knees, which were pressed tightly against my chest. I watched as it wiggled around aimlessly. *Why couldn't all bugs be harmless?* Not all bugs were from this planet. No one had any idea what planet the Arthropods came from. The records only showed that astronomers identified an asteroid shortly before it impacted in the Australian Territory. It was in the forthcoming weeks that the threat to humanity's existence began to emerge. I looked at the worm's silk as it inched back up to the tree. All it wanted to do was eat in peace. I'm sure that's all the Arthropods wanted, too, but they decided their food would be us. If we weren't able to plant our bomb in the Hive, the only chance we'd stand against the inverts would be to wait for them to exhaust whatever it was they were eating and die off. Too bad humanity would probably succumb first. Unlike the worm returning to the tree, I wasn't sure if the inverts had a way to return to their home. I guess they just spread and spread, and spread. *Selfish assholes.*

I heard the sound of leaves crunching and reached for the spear I'd been toting around. Damn! I didn't bring it. I grabbed the ever-present dagger at my waist, feeling woefully under-armed. Over a mound of dirt, I saw Huck's recognizable form coming toward me. I felt relief mixed with anxiety. He wasn't exactly the person I wanted to talk with at the moment.

"You okay?" Huck asked.

When does anyone ask if you're okay and you're actually okay? What a stupid question.

"I'm slightly better," I said, wiping the remaining tears from my eyes. "I'm not having a good week."

Huck sat pensively without saying anything for a few moments.

"That was a really crappy thing to do to Krista," said Huck.

"You think I don't know that?" I said. "Why did you come here, to piss me off?"

"No. Alright, I stated the obvious. Look. Krista's going to live her life. At the rate people die, long-term concerns like pregnancy aren't really on anyone's priority list. We're all just trying to enjoy what we have while we have it."

I think there was a little jab in there at me, but I tried not to read too much into it. Huck never made eye contact with me once.

"Yanus is bitching about us not being ready to leave," said Huck. "If you need a moment, that's fine, but can I talk you into having it on the truck? If you want, you can ride in the cab with me. I'm guessing you don't want to stare at Krista all day."

I nodded.

"Thank you," was all I managed.

CHAPTER 13: DIETER

What a dilemma. I racked my brain trying to figure out a way to steal a fresh rod of enriched uranium from the reactor storage but nothing seemed viable. Dying while procuring the rod would halt my plan; not to mention, it would attract Zabu's attention. He knew that we were developing a bomb, but he had no idea that it was a nuclear weapon. If he was aware of our true actual invention, he would tear the pod apart until he found what he wanted. I shuddered to think what he would do with it. It was of the utmost importance that the rod's theft went unnoticed. I desperately needed Emile's help, but I would protect him and his family. This was on me. After hours of deliberation, I surmised the only plausible way to steal a rod. I would go for a swim.

The reactors were at the bottom of the pod, where their operations posed the least danger to the residents. The fresh rods were located in a guarded and fortified room that only Zabu could unlock. Not even the reactor engineers could open it without him. Once the vault was sealed, the new rods would be wheeled to the reactors on hand trucks with a guard platoon of their own. Also untenable. I didn't stand a chance against the ruthless security guards on my own. They were highly trained and worse, savage. The used rods were placed into asbestos, lead-lined sleeves by nuclear engineers, who then rolled the escorted hand truck to the spent rod pool—known as the Pond.

The unguarded Pond was my access point. The pool's deep blue waters were unguarded because they figured no one would be stupid enough to handle spent fuel rods. The handling dangers posed by even ten-year-retired rods were plenty discouraging to would-be thieves. Between the heat and radiation, they were extremely difficult to handle. Just a few unprotected moments in close proximity to a spent fuel rod and lack of nutrition would be the least of your concerns. It had to be done.

The first task was to create a carrying container for the rod. Something that would keep me alive long enough to bring it to the lab, which fortunately was equipped to handle radioactive research. As a scientist, I had access to benign substances like lead and asbestos in ample amounts. I could load up on potassium iodide and wear the lab's radiation suit, though it wasn't exactly designed for swimming. It wouldn't do to drown during the heist. Possibly the most annoying aspect of the entire scenario was how little of the nuclear fuel I actually needed. Of the 18-kilogram rod, it would be condensed down to only one kilogram of material. Even a spent rod would have enough potential energy to irradiate the Hive and disperse the chemical irritant which would destroy their home and give us the upper hand.

With ideas darting back and forth in my mind, I make quick progress to my lab where Emile was already working.

"Morning," he said, looking over his half-rim glasses, his graying hair frizzing out to the sides. "You're looking chipper today."

"I am, brother. I know how to get the radioactive material, but I think it's best if you don't know. Plausible deniability and all that."

Emile stood and made his way over to me, clasping my forearms.

"We are partners, now and always. We started this together, and we will end it together. Now, enough hero talk. What do you need?"

I filled Emile in on my plan. He sat quietly, nodding as I explained each aspect of the heist. When I was finished, he vowed to help me in every way he could. First, Emile would fabricate the rod's insulated carrying tube while I retrofitted hazmat gear for underwater operation. During the theft, he would prepare our lab's radioactive measures for receiving and preparing the nuclear material. Then together, we would weaponize the enriched uranium. It was going to be a long day, so we didn't waste any time. Every day brought us closer to Zabu's deadline. And with Zabu, it really was a *dead*line.

Emile got to work on the tube, and I laid one of the lab's radioactive-level hazmat suits on the table. The suit was surprisingly flimsy given the amount of protection it offered. Even with thin material, the suit had considerable heft. The issue wouldn't be getting to the bottom of the Pond, but being able to return to its surface. The suit's breathing apparatus was self-contained and rated to work underwater, boding well for my mission's success. I trimmed out the unnecessary buckles and removed any superfluous weight the suit contained. I was able to reduce the suit's weight by 25 percent. It would have to be enough. Everything else was necessary to protect me from rapid death by radiation poisoning. I packed the suit, oxygen tank, and a few tools into a duffel and met up with Emile, who held the completed tube.

"It should withstand temperatures of up to 815 degrees Celsius, which I believe is more than enough. The lead content will protect against 99 percent of the radiation but adds significant weight to the tube, but I believe it's a worthwhile concession. I also took the liberty of disguising it as a damaged pipe. It seems to be our *modus operandi.*"

"Thank you, Emile," I said, hugging him. "With any luck, I'll be back within an hour."

"I'll have the room prepped and ready," he said.

I nodded and began my journey to the lower levels.

•••••••••

I arrived on the reactor floor without issue, having donned my hazmat suit in the elevator. Its reflective visor made it impossible for anyone to discern who I was. Acting like a competent worker, I made my way to the spent fuel pool. Security guards were prevalent around the level, but none seemed the least bit interested in an off-task engineer. I had no authorization or identification, not even a fake one, so it behooved me to not be caught and questioned. I followed the posted directions and easily made my way to the Pond.

The pool was eerily beautiful. Under the crossed catwalks above its surface laid a crystal clear blue lagoon surrounded by a hexagonal vessel. The walls doubled as mirrors, making the relatively small space feel falsely infinite. Under the catwalks was suspended the crane responsible for lowering the clusters of rods into place. The control panel for the crane was accessible, but seeing as the rods weren't being changed out in the near future, using it would be calling far too much attention to myself. I looked over the edge of the pool down into its depths. Meters below the Pond's perfectly calm surface was a honeycombed grid of cells, each holding a highly radioactive and extremely hot spent rod of nuclear fuel.

Taking one last look around to ensure that I was alone, I dropped the duffel, now only containing my tools, to the bottom of the pool. I watched as it slowly sank, drifting laterally as the underwater currents that cooled the rods carried it. Feet first, I lowered myself into the Pond. The water forced the excess air out of my suit, making it stick to my skin and sandwiching my perspiration between the suit and my body. I took a few deep breaths, knowing full well that I wouldn't have to hold them, and dropped myself into the glassy water.

I sank with surprising speed. Only the convex shape of the visor retained air inside my suit, leaving me literally feeling light-headed. My heavy tool bag had deceivingly led me to believe the currents underwater would be weak. As I fell, they forced me off course by meters from my intended destination, but no matter. The rod storage was somewhat circular, so where I landed was of little importance.

Once my feet made contact with the base of the pool, I took out my bolt cutters and began to snip the honeycombed casing from one of the rods. Even with the protection of my suit, I could feel the noticeable increase in the temperature. Too long down here and I would bake alive in my suit. I had to work methodically and rapidly.

After snipping off all the clamps, the panels hinged open, revealing the precious rod inside. I grabbed the tube that I had dropped with my duffel and opened it, watching the bubbles from its interior rise to the surface, making the rod twinkle as if the radiation it emanated was a visible phenomenon. With my bulky, heat-resistant gloves, I pulled the scalding rod from its chamber and lowered it into the tube before sealing it, the displacement of the water making it appear far lighter than it was.

When I was ready to swim up, I closed the panel so that the theft would appear less obvious, threw my duffel onto one shoulder and the rod on the opposite, and attempted to swim up. I barely left the ground. The duffel was too heavy. I would have to leave it on the bottom, calling attention to my work. I scooted it as close to the storage matrix as possible and again attempted to surface. Another failed attempt. I started to panic. I couldn't leave the rod. Making matters worse, my internal temperature was climbing to dangerous levels. *"What else could I leave?"* I thought. My tank! It was a terribly risky idea, but I could leave my tank. Though if it wasn't sufficient, my choices would be death at the bottom of a superheated pool or leaving the rod. I didn't see much choice. I pulled a small knife out from my bag and before I could second guess myself, I cut the hose, sending countless bubbles to the surface. I detached my tank, unclasping each of the buckles across my torso, and without the convenience of time brought by air, let it drop wherever it may.

Without the tank, I swam to the surface with the rod. I was unable to slow my ascent, desperately needing air. If I waited and passed out, I was dead. If I emerged in front of a guard, I was dead. It was a chance I'd have to take. I popped through the surface and feeling the water drain from the remainder of my breathing hose, took a deep gasp. Air never tasted so good. I looked around. Thankfully, I surfaced when no one was around. Whew. I pulled myself out of the tank and with the tube and made my way to the elevator. I quickly realized there was a gaping hole in my plan. All the water that had collected inside and outside of my suit was draining off onto the concrete floor, leaving bread crumbs straight to my abandoned gear. Dammit. There was always something else to consider. This was why I'd make a terrible criminal. I cut my losses and returned to the lab with as much haste as possible.

When I arrived, I donned a dry hazmat suit and we extracted the rod from our impromptu carrying tube. We then deposited it in our hermetically-sealed furnace where it would be super-heated into the gaseous form necessary to enrich it into the weapons-grade uranium we would need for the bomb. The process could take days, maybe even a week. Hopefully, we'd have enough time to finish our work before we were caught, cutting it far too close for comfort. I glanced at Emile and managed a weak smile. I hoped I wouldn't have to watch him and his partner perish in the same fashion as Rupert.

CHAPTER 14: HUCK

An awkward silence hung in the air like a morning fog as Ariadne and I watched the shrubby green landscape pass by our windows. I kept stealing glances at her reflection in the window trying to gauge her mood. After hours had passed, she verified that the panel to the hauler's bed was closed.

"Krista hates us," she said as low as she could, all the while digging the grime from under her fingers to avoid making eye contact.

"She doesn't hate us. She's just working through some things," I said. "It may take her a long time. Especially after this morning."

Maybe it was a mistake to bring up the morning's events. Ariadne was struggling to restrain her tears.

"She does. I heard her say it. I was trying to tell you before dinner, when we... when I... before we ate the crocodile. I know I shouldn't have been, but I was eavesdropping. Omar and Krista never suspected that I was there. They don't like us. They feel like outsiders around us. They're both banished."

"Wait. What?" I asked.

"Omar is too. Or he thinks he is. He said Carvalho told him if he didn't kill us, then he shouldn't bother returning to the pods."

My head spun. I knew Krista had been marked, but I was blindsided by the fact that Omar was, too. I had yet to determine the best plan for Krista upon our arrival at Kano, but maybe this could benefit us.

"When we get to Kano, they could stay outside together. Protect each other." I said.

"Sorry to break it to you, but they already decided that," said Ariadne. "Right after Omar convinced Krista that them running away together was a bad idea."

Wow. I really was out of touch with the group.

"Anything else I need to know about?" I asked.

"I think that's it. They need us like we need them."

"We need to talk candidly with them. We need to devise a plan so that they don't feel excluded. If we're going to survive, we need to repair some relationships. Maybe start with apologizing to Krista."

"It's none of your business, Huck!" Ariadne's cheeks grew flush. "What happened between me and her was just that, between me and her."

Just like that, silence once again descended on the cab. After what felt like ages, I broke it.

"You're right. I'm sorry. It's a matter between you and her," I said, shifting down a gear for the slight incline the convoy was ascending.

Ariadne nodded. "It's been a rough few days for me. I've made some poor choices and said even worse."

I hoped I wasn't one of the poor choices, but I let the idea pass before I could dwell on it. We rode along for several more hours, quietly again, but as if the fog had broken. There was notably less weight in the air between us. We put the cab's windows down and let the tepid breeze provide us with some refreshment. Hints of damp earth floated on the wind, brought forth by a passing rain. The beauty of the landscape made me want to recline in the grass and watch the wispy clouds pass over instead of operating the lumbering machine transporting us to Kano. I reminded myself that we were on a mission, not a vacation. By Arjun's reckoning, we had traveled more than six thousand kilometers and still had three-quarters of our journey to go. *"One step at a time,"* I told myself.

Eventually, the convoy pulled off at the remnants of what appeared to be a long-abandoned settlement. I pulled the truck up behind the tank truck and shut off the hauler's engine, absorbing the serene silence after the non-stop noise. As I stepped down from the cab, I stretched and meandered around, trying to work out the kinks that had built up over the course of the transit. I grabbed my crossbow from the rack behind the bench seat and watched as the others piled out of the bed.

"Can I ride in the cab next, Huck?" asked Mei, who was attempting to work a crick out of her neck.

"That's fair," said Ariadne. "Not that I'm in a hurry to give up the comfort."

"What are we stopping for, Huck?" asked Ciro.

"I'm not sure. I'll run ahead and check," I said, walking off.

I hadn't ventured far when I realized we'd arrived at a pump house. In typical fashion, Yanus was fussing at Taha. I still couldn't parse out why Taha put up with Yanus' behavior day after day. He was far more competent than Yanus.

"Good. I'm glad you decided to join us," said Yanus. "It's time your lot learned to refuel. Taha will stay and manage you. I want all the vehicles loaded with gas and water within the hour. We still have a long drive ahead."

Yanus stared at me as if waiting for a response. I had forgotten that he craved ass-kissing affirmation.

"Yes, Protector Yanus," I said, begrudgingly.

"I'll be taking respite from this devilish heat in my carrier. See that I'm not disturbed."

"Yes, Protector Yanus," said Taha.

I looked at Taha's eyes, waiting for them to roll but they never did. Taha was consummately professional, even when I was positive he didn't desire to do so.

"Let's get to work," he said.

•••••••••

A day after the pit stop, we ventured northeast, turning away from the safety of the coast. The feelings were melancholic. We were knowingly heading into more dangerous territory, but the change in direction also meant that we were getting closer to the next waypoint of our mission—Pod Kano. I'd take every success, even the little ones.

After several days of northbound travel, fending off mashi, midges, and another pair of multipedes, we arrived at a sprawling area of dense vegetation. The landscape was reminiscent of the jungle where we'd first encountered the mashi, which Ciro had dubbed dart beaks. Scattered on the terrain were high-canopied trees, layered boulders, and cool rivulets. Clear skies and comfortable weather made the locale ideal for camp. The vehicles formed a wagon-train arrangement for the night, which seemed unnecessary in the deceitfully peaceful setting. My hunger took a backseat to the child-like desire to explore the intriguing scenery. Once camp was ready and the hunting party dispatched, I joined Arjun and Mei for a late-afternoon jaunt. I grabbed my notebook in the hopes I could squeeze in a sketch or two.

"These rock formations are unusual," said Arjun.

"They're neat. I like their patterns," I said, quickly drawing a set of the large stones.

"I bet I could climb those. Maybe I can look around," said Mei.

"Go for it!" I said.

Mei climbed up a pile of the humongous, cracked boulders. The rocks looked as though eons ago, a giant had stacked them like pebbles, letting the wind and water carve them into their present shapes. Millions of years of erosion left a multitude of cavities for Mei to grasp to climb her way to the top.

"I can see for kilometers," she said. "God, it's beautiful."

"Any Arthropods?" I asked.

"Just antenna bugs. Maybe someone should keep watch up here. They're certainly eyeballing us. Or compound-eyeing us," she said, giggling at her own joke.

"That's not a bad idea," said Arjun.

"Hang on. I do see something," said Mei. "Walk to the other side of the formation, about the same distance you are from it now."

Arjun and I followed her directions up an incline before cautiously descending the rocky slope on the far side. We arrived at an area of flattened grass where Mei yelled for us to stop.

"What is it? I don't see anything," I said.

"Look around," Mei yelled. "It's all over the place."

Arjun and I looked around but still couldn't find anything. Then I saw it. Unlike the matte grass surrounding us, the flat grass glistened in the sunlight. At my side, Arjun was making the pensive sounds I had come to expect from him. We were looking at tracks. Slime tracks.

"Cave grub?" I asked Arjun, as Mei trotted up to us.

"Not likely. They prefer the complete opposite climate to this," he said. "This is something similar but nothing I'm aware of. There are many things we have yet to learn about the Arthropods."

"I don't like this territory," I said. "There's too much even you don't know. That scares me."

"The scientists at Baghdad clearly know only a fraction of the Arthropods that exist on the surface," he said. "I assume it's because so few make it back alive. There's another possibility though."

"Great," said Mei.

"We know that they aren't from here. We have no comprehension of their evolutionary timetable. It's probable, seeing that they are in many ways more advanced than us, that they may evolve faster, and may even be able to select desirable characteristics."

"Simplify it for the non-scientific people, bud," I said.

"Alright. You know how evolution takes a long time, right?"

I nodded.

"In a few hundred years, humans artificially selected amiable wolves, turning them into dogs. Are you still with me?"

I nodded again.

"The Arthropods in the Hive may be selecting desirable characteristics for this planet and encouraging speciation based on those mutations," said Arjun, then sensing my confusion, added, "They're speeding up the evolutionary process to thrive here permanently."

"Oh," I said.

"Crap," said Mei.

•••••••••

When we returned to the convoy, the hunting party had arrived with enough lizards and fish for everyone. After dinner, we shared our findings to Yanus, who wasn't alarmed.

"I've transported goods across this area for years. I've never seen anything leave a slime trail. You lot are imagining things," said Yanus. "You need to put that extra energy into something more useful. If there is something slimy that means us harm, my highly skilled men will take care of it before it gets anywhere near the convoy."

"That was productive," said Mei, once we were walking away.

"What do you think could leave a trail like that?" asked Ariadne.

"Since the Arthropods tend to share similar traits with the insects of Earth, my guess would be some sort of slug-like creature."

"That doesn't exactly inspire fear," said Hemant.

"I would've said the same thing about a cave grub and you saw how that went," said Mei.

"You got me there," I said. "I bet it would be alarming when your hammer just disappeared into its girthy mass, eh Hemant?"

"Shut up," said Hemant, smiling. "If worse came to worse, I'd go grab a box of salt from the supply truck. That'd take care of the thing."

"Yeah, but then you'd have the other slug to deal with," I said.

"What other slug?" said Hemant.

I nodded towards Yanus' carrier, and we busted out laughing.

That evening, as the transporters filled the air with their enthralling music, we heard a commotion emanating from Yanus' carrier. We could hear the voices clearly, though we couldn't see the interaction. Yanus was slovenly drunk.

"Please have a seat, sir," said Taha, letting his frustration slip through his words.

"I used da be someone, dammid! Now I'm shtuck in thish quagmire with you numbskulls. I was a fighder, and a damn good one. Women threw themselves ad me. Shpeaking of women, where's Fara? I haven't sheen her in ages."

"She ran away, sir."

"Well go get her, then! Shend five men. No make thad all the men. We need all of them."

"She's dead, sir. We found her body."

"Shuch a shame. She was so beaudiful. Why'd she run away, again."

"Sir, you really don't want to go there."

"Tell me, dammid!"

"She ran away from you, sir. You treated her very… poorly."

"Oh," Yanus, said pensively. "I shuppose I did. Do I treat you well, Taha?"

"You treat me fairly, sir," said Taha.

"Good. I thing I'll go da sleeb now."

"Good idea, sir. I'll just take this—"

"No, I'll keeb the boddle. It helbs me sleeb."

"Okay, sir. Good night."

Taha walked slowly out of the carrier and saw us staring. There was no point in trying to look as though we weren't listening in on their conversation. Taha rubbed the back of his neck as he walked to where we were seated.

"I suppose you heard all of that," he said.

"Yeah," I said.

"He's not the man he once was. That saddens him greatly. There was still a glimmer of that man when he took me in, but that side of him has all but vanished."

"Well, it's good to know he wasn't always an asshole," said Mei.

"Who was Fara?" I asked.

Taha immediately tensed up.

"I suppose you'll find out one way or another, though it's not something we generally speak of," he said, looking back at the carrier to verify that Yanus was passed out.

"Fara was one of Yanus'… involuntary concubines."

"Involuntary concubine, as in she was a *sex slave*?" asked Krista.

"I'm afraid so. Yanus regularly trades with the prime minister of Pod Kano. They don't always trade in the most ethical manner. Yanus has a penchant for young women, whereas Zabu desires a means of control, which Yanus supplies him with in droves."

"How does Yanus trade control?" asked Ariadne.

"Dust," said Taha. "One of the vilest discoveries by humans since the Arthropod Landing. It's been imprisoning people ever since."

"Is that like pheromones?" asked Hemant. "We've seen how *that* affects people."

"Dust is refined from pheromones," began Taha. "Pheromones can be harvested and used straight from the Arthropods. They put the user in a euphoric, detached state. When refined into Dust, it completely removes the mind from reality, putting the user in an emotionally numb state where they are remarkably open to suggestion. If everyone in Pod Kano was sober, Zabu would've been ousted years ago. There is still a resistance, but it's such a small fraction of the people, it only poses an inconvenience to him."

"Jesus," said Hemant. "I didn't think it was possible to like Yanus less. I see why Kebe warned Arjun about Kano."

"Master Kebe was wise to do so," said Taha, checking once again over his shoulder. "Interact with Zabu as little as possible. And whatever you do—don't offend him. His wrath is legendary."

CHAPTER 15: HEMANT

I found the recent insight into Yanus and Zabu's characters disconcerting. If it wouldn't be damn near impossible to get to the Hive without their help, I'd be urging Huck to find another way. I justified our risky company to make myself comfortable with our dependence on them. When Huck guided us up the incline and showed us the slime trails, it made me even more uncomfortable. I'd seen the inverts do some nasty stuff, and I wasn't ready for anything new. I sat by Arjun and put my arm over his shoulder.

"How's Ciro's shoulder?" I asked.

"It's better. He's regaining his mobility, but it'll be a while before he can properly fire his compound bow. Please help me protect him. I care about him."

"Of course I will. I know you do. And I love you."

Arjun gave me a questioning look before responding, "I love you, too."

"Hearing about how vile Zabu is reminded me of how important reminders of humanity's goodness are."

"There will always be people with undesirable characteristics. It's imperative that we never be those people," said Arjun.

"I couldn't have said it better myself. Good night, Arjun."

"Good night, Hemant."

I rose slowly, feeling the weight of the day lingering on my shoulders, and went to bed. We only had a few days left before our arrival at Kano. Even though it sounded like a rough place, I was looking forward to a sound night's sleep—one where I wasn't worried about a night attack.

I woke up the next morning to panicked yelling. I almost ripped the tent trying to get my oversize frame out of it quickly. I emerged, having torn half the bivvy up from the ground. I grabbed my war hammer and sprinted to where a crowd was forming.

"What is it?" I yelled, pushing my way through the candidates and transporters.

I was surrounded by foreign murmurs. Even in a different tongue, I could recognize the sound of confusion. When I managed to see what everyone was looking at, I understood. In the middle of the group was a pristine pile of human bones. Arjun was already crouched next to it, attempting to ascertain the cause of death.

"What happened?" asked Yanus, his face pale from the evening's overconsumption.

Arjun lifted one of the bones with a stick, stretching a thick, viscous slime between the elevated bone and the others.

"It would appear that whatever left the slime trails snuck through our camp last night and silently devoured the watchman."

"Preposterous!" yelled Yanus before grabbing his forehead and lowering his tone. "I've never seen anything like this. How did it penetrate our defenses unnoticed? How did it sneak up on… whoever the guard was?"

"There is a meter or so gap between each vehicle. If it squeezed through, it stands to reason there would be evidence on one of the vehicles."

"On it," said Mei, running off.

"As for the watchman, it must have been silent. Not only did he not anticipate the attack, but we all also slept through his death."

"Found something!" said Mei.

We left the pile of bones and moved where Mei was standing. Between the personnel carrier and the supply truck, the grass was flat and glossy. A film of slime-covered the tailgate and grill of the nearby vehicles, draining down slowly in transparent, colorless globules.

"I bet it was wider than a meter, but squeezed through," she added.

"Is everyone else accounted for?" asked Taha, then presumably repeating the question in Arabic.

Everyone began to check on everyone else. Moments later, a transporter began yelling.

When I arrived at the collapsed bivvy, my heart dropped like a lead weight. We were looking at Ciro's tent. Arjun knelt down next to the deflated habitat. On closer inspection, I realized that in addition to a thick layer of slime over the tent's surface, there was a vaguely human shape within, that had yet to stir.

"Arjun, don't," I said.

Ignoring me, Arjun tenderly dragged the zipper along its route, slowly revealing Ciro's pale face, looking straight up with unmoving eyes.

"Oh, Arjun," said Ariadne, falling to her knees and wrapping her arms around him.

"The creature must have passed over the bivvy and suffocated him," said Arjun. "He never had a chance to defend himself." Arjun reached forward and closed Ciro's eyes. "He was my closest companion. We dreamed of sharing our discoveries with the world."

I put my hand on Arjun's shoulder as the transporters offered their foreign condolences, before heading off to take care of their own fallen.

"I will never be the same," said Arjun, "but I am glad to have shared time with him."

"Damn cowards. They don't even have the dignity to kill us to our faces," Omar said, spitting into the shiny grass, still beaded with the morning dew.

"Welcome to the club," said Krista, before disappearing with Omar.

"I'll help you build a cairn for him," I said, boring holes through Krista's back.

"No. Ciro wanted to be cremated," said Arjun, then looking at me, "Help me build a pyre."

•••••••••

It felt unfair that we couldn't exact vengeance on the creature that had killed Ciro and the transporter. Taha described the fallen man to me, but I felt guilty for not being able to recall his face or name. The language barrier kept us from getting to know most of our hosts, but I could've at least learned his name. I swiveled the turret of the hauler as we pulled out to watch the dark plume of smoke cloud the horizon. It only took us a matter of minutes to find enough dead branches to construct the pyre. After gifting Ciro's bow to a reluctantly accepting Ariadne, she ignited the pile of branches with a blazing arrow in the traditional manner extending back millennia. Arjun stepped forward from where we'd gathered, a somber veil descended on our party as he began his mournful dirge.

> *"The winter it is past, and the summer comes at last*
> *And the small birds, they sing on ev'ry tree;*
> *Now ev'ry thing is glad, while I am very sad,*
> *Since my true love is parted from me ...."*

As the woeful melody repeated, one by one, the transporters began to hum with him in solidarity. Anyone who had made it through Ciro's death without tears now found them flowing freely. Arjun's piercing voice had cracked my heart asunder, draping each note with the fraying fabric of his loss. When he had finished, he turned and walked to the cargo hauler. I caught up with him and wrapped my arms around him, weeping into his shoulder, squeezing him so tight that I felt his armor cutting into my chin.

"I'm so sorry, brother," I said. "That was beautiful."

"Thank you," he replied, sniffling. "It was one of Ciro's favorites. He had an eclectic taste for ancient folk songs. Anytime he caught someone singing or humming an unfamiliar tune, he'd bug them until they taught it to him."

I hugged him again before he climbed into the cargo bed. I offered to stay with him, but he requested solitude. I knew if I was needed, Ariadne wouldn't hesitate to let me know. Omar was taking a turn in the cab with Huck, and I didn't mind the time alone in the turret to process what had occurred. I liked Ciro. I considered him a second brother, but I hadn't grown anywhere near as close to him as Arjun. Reading Arjun's emotions was a tricky affair. I had to trust him at his word, even knowing him as long as I did. The loss of Ciro would rock him to his core, but I didn't know how to help him. From past experiences, he would likely postpone grieving indefinitely, compartmentalizing his feelings so that he could focus on the present.

We rode for barely an hour before coming to a stop at a vast abandoned city. The horizon had no signs of the prolific skyscraper skeletons from cities past. The city was filled with small, squat structures indicative of homes and shops. The only structure still making an attempt to reach the skyline were shining twin towers, next to a second collapsed pair. I hopped down from the turret, checking in with Arjun as the others emerged from the bed. Arjun nodded to me as we gathered around Taha.

"What are we stopping for?" asked Omar. "We just got rolling."

"This is Golden Towers," said Taha, as the transporters fanned out, knowing something we didn't. "It was one of the larger cities in the vicinity and a hub for trading. Every time we pass through, we search a segment of the city for items of interest. Most of the goods we find are bartered in Pod Kano. My apologies to you. The found items will be packed into the hauler with you all."

That's Yanus for us. Always looking out for our well-being, I thought. "Why didn't we search in the larger port cities? I'd think they'd have more to offer than this dust bin."

"The abandoned mega cities are far too dangerous to split up our group. Due to the sprawling nature of this city, threats are more easily anticipated and dealt with. I should note that if anything special is found, Protector Yanus will keep that for himself, reserving it for his part-time home in Kano," Taha continued. "If Yanus deems anything worthy of his private collection, he will bestow a special gift on its finder."

"I'm not sure I want any special gifts from Yanus," said Mei.

"This is an area we haven't scoured yet," said Taha. "Fan out from here, but I urge you to stay in small groups and stay within four blocks of the convoy. Look for anything ornate or useful that's in acceptable condition. Things that might bring a profit in the marketplace."

"Arjun, I think you should stay with the vehicles," I said.

"Thank you for your consideration, but no," he said. "I would like to search alongside you. I would welcome the distraction."

"Only if you're sure," said Huck, overhearing his response.

Arjun nodded.

We split into three groups: Myself, Arjun, and Huck; Mei and Ariadne; Omar, and Krista.

"If any of you have any trouble, scream to high heaven," said Huck. "I don't want any more of us sacrificed for Yanus' self-interests."

"Let's go see what we can find for Captain Glutton," I said.

We meandered down a narrow side street with entryways still packed with signs of life, as though the owners would return any day. Nature had been slower to retake this one. The climate was arid, and the wind, brutal. The reddish eddies created by dust floating on the air currents carried a mystical beauty. I pushed forward, tripping on something. I looked down where my foot had pulled something out from its centuries-long hibernation. It was a kid's toy with three wheels.

"Do you think this is interesting enough to carry back?" I asked Huck.

"Doubt it. The handlebars don't turn, and I think the wheels are supposed to be softer than this," he said, pushing on the dry-rotted tires to illustrate his point.

I sat it carefully on a windowsill, shrugging, and we moved on. We ducked into a small house with low ceilings and even lower door frames. The fine dirt had dispersed itself into every nook and crevice in the home. Everywhere was a layer of the stuff, disguising what lay beneath. Arjun made his way to an ornately-carved armoire and dug into it.

In the corner of the room, I saw where our footsteps had revealed a bright red rug, peeking out from beneath the dirt's omnipresent uniformity. I pulled it up with too much force, filling the air with lung-burning particles, forcing the three of us outside.

"Why the heck did you do that?" Huck said when he was finally able to breathe.

"Sorry. Didn't think that through," I said, smiling between coughs.

"You find anything, Arjun?" I asked.

"Yes. The cabinet is full of small trinkets that appear to have been of great importance to the home's former occupants."

"Well, let's wait for the dust to settle and go back in and retrieve them," I said.

"I would prefer not to," said Arjun. "It doesn't feel right. I keep thinking about Ciro and how I'd feel if someone stole his belongings—not that he had any of note, but that's irrelevant."

"That's perfectly normal, Arjun. And it's okay. We'll leave the stuff in the cabinet," I said, squeezing his shoulder.

"We can't return empty-handed," said Huck.

"Let's get some half-interesting crap and say it's all we could find. Do you have any objection to me getting the rug, Arjun?" I asked.

Arjun shook his head. "Just leave the sentimental things, please."

"Of course," I said.

After hours of dusty, sweaty digging, we'd found enough things we thought would satiate Yanus' hoarding tendencies. In addition to the rug, we found a number of pieces of wooden furniture that had withstood the passage of time, multiple mirrors, and a number of moth-eaten books. It was the books that captivated my interest. The oldest ones were written with a language that just looked like squiggles and dots. The more recent books contained letters that looked like Universal English, but with extra lines and curls. I could sound out the similar letters, but the words felt strange in my mouth and sounded like little more than gibberish.

When we finally returned to the convoy and loaded the items into the hauler, we were exhausted and brown from the dust that had adhered to our bodies' perspiration. Yanus was in especially good humor, praising everyone for their findings. Though we received little more than a *"Hmmph."* Mei took the award for the day, having found a small bronze statue of a man holding a leaf-shaped blade and wearing a three-pronged crown. It was an interesting cultural find. I caught myself wondering if it depicted some famous leader from eras past.

Mei's reward wasn't anything exciting. As a matter of fact, I felt like we had dodged a bullet. Her reward was an evening with Yanus, which included dinner and an overnight stay in his personal vehicle. Taha assured Yanus would be respectable throughout and it was considered an honor. In Mei's own words, "He'd be eating his own snake for dinner if he tried anything." Mei didn't look thrilled when she was carted off by his royal highness.

While we took turns keeping watch, we each took a quick rinse in the murky river east of our search grid. Our exhausted group collapsed into our bivvies, forgoing dinner in favor of rest.

CHAPTER 16: ARIADNE

I rode in the cramped hauler's bed all morning, maybe I needed to learn to drive like Huck and Hemant so I'd have an excuse to sit in the cab more often. My concern was no longer keeping each other from flailing around the empty bed, but rather avoiding the shifting collectibles from our stop in Gold Towers. Arjun was taking his turn riding up front, while the rest of us were spread through the miscellaneous contents wherever we could find a comfortable human-sized gap. Yanus annoyingly still refused to let us share the space with his men in the personnel carrier, claiming the proposition held too much risk.

I gave up trying to communicate with Mei, who was closest to me, pretty quickly. Over the noise of all the vehicle's moving parts, it wasn't worth the effort. It was fine. I had a hand-carved wooden door to keep me company. I was going to have the reverse relief of its nature scene embedded in my arm by the end of the ride.

After hours of feeling like the candy inside a beaten piñata, we finally came to a halt. Climbing out of the bed, I saw that the transporters were again buzzing about as if on another collection run.

"We don't have any room in the hauler for more of Yanus' crap," I said.

Mei, who was climbing over the top of a tall-backed wooden chair, shrugged.

I surveyed the landscape. We had stopped just shy of a pair of bridges, only one still standing after centuries of disuse. Lying to our right was the edge of a town, much smaller than Gold Towers. The workers, uninterested in the town, were pulling out spears by the dozens.

"Do they know something we don't?" I asked.

Omar pointed over my shoulder, where I turned to see a large greenish-brown river dotted with islands and covered in water striders.

"Wow! That's a lot of striders! Why are there so many? And what do they need all the weapons for?" I asked Huck, who came alongside me.

"I don't know, but Yanus is walking our way. I'm pretty sure he'll tell us."

"Welcome to Harvest River," said Yanus with a grin from ear to ear. "It is here where we gather our most prized cargo. I'm excited because, with your help, we will likely double our profits this trip. You hear that, Taha?" Yanus slapped Taha on the back, making him wince slightly.

"What are we collecting now?" asked Hemant.

"Not collecting. *Harvesting*," Yanus said with a sickeningly crooked smirk as he waved his hand towards the idle striders.

"What? Them?" I asked, a pit forming in my stomach.

"Of course them. Not only are they the weakest of the inverts, but they also carry the most pheromones. Something having to do with how they attract mates. And you lot are going to help."

I squirmed as the pit in my stomach opened into an abyss. I hated the Arthropods as much as the next candidate, but I was not comfortable killing the relatively innocent ones. And worse, as Taha had explained, to help subjugate the most vulnerable populations under the yoke of addiction.

"What if we refuse?"

"Then damn that Lolade and her threats," said Yanus, getting so close to my face that I could feel the stench of his breath burning my eyes. "If you don't help me, I'll drop you all off at the next sign of the Demented. I think they still have a few camps west of Kano."

I shuddered, almost collapsing at the thought. My last run-in with the hemolymph-crazed humans almost resulted in things I'd rather not recall if I hadn't been rescued by the Misfits. Omar noticed my weak spell and came forward, putting his hand around my right arm for support.

"Alright," I said, dropping my head.

"Great! I knew you could be reasonable," Yanus said. "Taha will teach you the proper technique and we'll get started shortly. Don't spook them until we're all ready."

Yanus walked off and Omar leaned over to my ear, "Bastard. Anyone who says something like that has never set foot in a Demented camp."

I felt tears well up in my eyes. Omar could be such a hard person and his conversation with Krista left a bad taste in my mouth, but in moments like these, I was happy we were companions. After a few moments, I felt my breath return. After assuring Omar I was better, he returned to Krista's side.

"He had no right to threaten you like that," said Huck.

I nodded in appreciation. "Let's see what we have to do," I said.

"Yanus has never been good with guests," said Taha. "I apologize for his actions."

"It's not your fault, Taha," I said.

"Still, I feel the need to do so. I also want to apologize in advance for the instructions I'm about to impart to you. Please, everyone, gather around."

We reluctantly encircled Taha.

"This will be an uncomfortable experience for your first time, but it is part of our duties as Yanus' transporters. We've been using the same strategy for several months, and it continues to work. The creatures don't seem to catch on, making this almost seem unfair. The men you see unloading the spears will line up along the edge of the bank, as will you. Once in position, everyone will simultaneously spear the target directly in front of them, at which point the rest scatter quickly. It's imperative that your timing and aim be impeccable. Once the creatures are down, we will jump on the rafts we keep by the river and collect their bodies."

This feels about as gruesome as what they do to us.

"The harvesting is relatively straightforward. Your daggers will suffice. On the underside of the abdomen are white stripes. Simply cut along those lines the length of the abdomen. Inside, you'll find four kiwi-sized objects on either side. Those are the pheromone pods. Place them into the provided baskets and once everyone has finished, we'll be ready to move on. The next stage can be done in the carriers."

"Gross," said Krista and Mei in unison.

"Please, take your positions," said Taha.

Yanus paced up and down through the ranks, stopping at Arjun. "Too bad your friend didn't make it. We could have used every additional pair of hands."

Arjun burst towards Yanus, but with reflexes that could rival an eight, Hemant grabbed him by the waist, spinning him enough to divert his course.

"The tiny one has spunk," Yanus said, laughing as he walked away. "If he'd have hit me, I would've broken him in two."

It was the most emotion I'd seen from Arjun, but it was intense and swift. I'd heard the older citizens back in Horizonte talk about the ancient belief of karma. I had never been one to wish someone ill, but in my anger, I fervently hoped when Yanus' karma came back to haunt him, I'd be there to see it.

I walked to where the spears were being handed out, opting not to sully Ciro's bow with the perverse activity. As instructed, we each chose our intended targets. I watched as the striders interacted with each other almost playfully on the river, completely ignoring us. Their slender gray bodies glided along the surface of the water without breaking its tension, eating whatever aquatic lifeforms they consumed. I couldn't help but think about how harmless the one we petted a lifetime ago had been. You could almost sense it looking at you. There was some intelligence there that didn't appear to be malignant, making me feel all the more guilty when Leni killed it in anger. The only negative interaction we'd had with them was when they called the other, more violent Arthropods. Hopefully, something like that won't happen again today.

When the command was given, everyone let their spears fly. I watched as my spear sailed overhead, the tip twinkling like a star in the sunlight. After it hit the pinnacle of its arc, I watched it descend slowly and vanish below the surface of the water, harmlessly behind a strider. I was unsure how many others intentionally missed, but up and down the river, striders collapsed onto the water, releasing a collective moan of agony before resting still as the rest hastily retreated.

Startling me, one of the transporters behind me began to yell in Arabic, pointing and instructing those with the rafts to catch the corpses before they drifted downriver in the current. After about a half-hour of work, the rafts returned to the shore with the corpses and harvesting began in earnest. I split off into a group with Hemant. We flipped the first carcass over, and after a brief hesitation with Yanus' words echoing in my head, I began the first incision. I drew my dagger along the white line, feeling the tug of the friction on the blade. The abdomen's side separated slowly with the sound of ripping fabric that churned the breakfast in my stomach before revealing the pods inside.

Once the smell hit me, it was all I could take, I unsuccessfully stifled a gag before retching to the side of the carcass all over Hemant's right boot.

"I'm sorry," I said.

"It's nothing, really," Hemant said, holding his nose. "And I thought they smelled bad on the outside."

I laughed. At least I wasn't doing this alone. Hemant stretched the abdomen open as I tugged the first pod off of the tubule it was connected to, snapping off like an under-ripe grape from a vine.

"That's one," I said stuffily, trying to breathe through my mouth and doing my best not to look at the creature's compound-eyed face. I scratched the itch developing in my nose with the back of my hand in an attempt to keep the toxic black hemolymph off of my skin.

After twenty minutes, we had harvested an entire strider and went to grab a second, but they were already finished. We were the slowest harvesters of the bunch—not that I would lose any sleep over missing out on another.

Following Taha's instructions, we carried the basket to the supply truck where an impromptu processing station had been set up. In the bed, amongst the shelves of supplements, medical supplies, and dry rations, the men set up a small stainless steel table and chairs, attached to the bed to prevent movement. All in all, eight baskets of pheromone pods were harvested. Not the double amount Yanus anticipated, but enough extra that he was pleased with himself, continually rubbing his hands together in a despicable, miserly fashion.

"This is delicate work, my dears," Yanus said to Krista and me. "I prefer this to be done by the nimble and sensitive touch of ladies. I would like for you two to do it. I have determined after my dinner with your companion yesterday evening that she is far from delicate."

Krista and I glared at each other. We weren't on speaking terms and the idea of sitting alone with her for the next day squeezing pheromone glands struck me as excruciatingly awkward, activity aside. We climbed into the truck bed, sliding between the shelves, crates, and boxes. Taha climbed in after us and showed us what to do.

"I'll demonstrate how to milk a gland, but be mindful, right now, we are still. It will become significantly more difficult on the move," said Taha, sliding on a pair of rubber gloves and picking up a pod. The tubule hanging off the pod had already begun to dry and the fetid smell held hints of decay. Holding it over a metal container recessed into the table, he carefully, but adeptly massaged the pod, working his way from its more bulbous side to the more narrow. With a sickening pop, a burnt orange viscous goo slowly began to drain from the skinnier end, globbing down into the container. Once all the mucilaginous fluid had been persuaded out, he tossed the evacuated pod out onto the ground. "That's it. When the container is full, screw on one of those lid's behind you and place the filled container in the latched box next to you. Remember two things: One, these containers hold great value for Protector Yanus; Two, wear gloves so that you avoid letting the fluid come into contact with your skin."

Krista and I both nodded, but Taha had already turned. From outside the vehicle, we heard a loud cracking sound emanating from the forest. It was a sound that instantly transported me back to Release Day—just before the bone arachnids had burst through the forest.

CHAPTER 17: DIETER

I frantically paced the lab with little to do as the centrifuges whirred behind me, painstakingly processing the radioactive material. I decided to pass the time in our creature lab, two floors directly below our weapons lab. It had mostly been Rupert's territory, where we conducted our crossover research with Baghdad. Emile and I would periodically descend the dedicated, poorly illuminated staircase only as the need arose. The two of us preferred our nearly immaculate engineering lab where we could remain focused on our work without the distraction of clutter or untidiness.

I wasn't one to speak ill of the dead, but Rupert was the messier of the three of us. Due to the nature of the lab and its senior technician, the place wasn't only strewn with unorganized equipment, but between the unpleasant odors and the built-up grime, it certainly held a certain ick factor in my mind.

I unlocked the lab and pushed open the door, hearing it drag some rubbish on the ground behind it. The omnipresent formaldehyde odor burned my nose as it wafted on the outbound air currents. The room was dim, only illuminated by the specimen tanks scattered throughout the space. I fumbled for the light switch.

The bulbs blinked on, then immediately back off. *Bloody hell. Must be a short.* Like everything else in the pod, if lack of maintenance wasn't the problem, lack of replacement parts was.

I slowly made my way through the lab using the faint glow of the tanks to guide me, shuffling my feet on the floor to avoid tripping over anything unseen. Neither Emile nor I had been in the room since Rupert's death, so its condition was unknown. He would usually make the effort to tidy the place up if he knew we were coming down, but that wasn't the current case. I kicked a spare exhaust pipe and it skittered across the floor, bringing a few of the rodents and insects to life. I couldn't decide if their active presence made me more or less comfortable. All of them would need care soon.

I made my way to the back of the lab, past the column habitats dotting the center of the room, casting the entire space in a bluish-green spectrum. There it was. The terrarium I was looking for. I squeezed past one last habitat. *Wham!* I nearly jumped out of my skin when an immature hook beetle slammed so hard into the glass next to me that a small crack appeared. It was getting bigger and stronger. Time to dispatch. I reached up, fumbling among the buttons before I found the one I was looking for—the one with a safety cover. I flipped it up and depressed the circular button underneath. With a woosh, the tank's ceiling descended, driving the needle-like spikes down into place, impaling anything within. I felt a slight shiver rocket up my spine. This was unpleasant business. Arthropods would stop at nothing to eradicate us from the planet, but killing a defenseless one in a lab setting still didn't sit right. It was a shame we couldn't kill them more humanely. The Arthropods could survive in a vacuum indefinitely, thus the need for a radioactive solution to their existence. Better me putting it down than it falling into Zabu's possession. If Zabu knew of this one's growth, he would have likely used it in his sadistic gladiatorial ring—The Pit.

With any luck, the Resistance would take him out before long. My goal was to buy them time. Since the loss of Bogota, we couldn't take a single day for granted.

I turned away from the gruesome scene, avoiding the black hemolymph beginning to drain down into the collector from the deceased creature's body. Situated in the furthest reaches of the lab was Radar, our token antenna bug. He had been with us for a number of years since a group of transporters stumbled upon him injured and brought him to us for research. Rupert had named him after the way his head steadily followed our movement in the lab. Being one of the few Arthropods we could allow to grow to full size, he had the largest tank in the room. The half-cylinder sat against the wall, extending floor to ceiling, part of which had a large fan that ran constantly, allowing him to hover for extended periods of time.

Because of the unaggressive nature of the aerials, he'd taken on a pet-like status as we studied him. We had tried all manner of experiments on him in an attempt to develop a method of jamming or disrupting his communication, with no success. His electromagnetic disruptions eventually resulted in the lab having to be specially insulated just to ensure nearby equipment could run properly. Ultimately, we had stopped subjecting him to semi-ethical experiments, relegating him to lab mascot.

I walked up to the glass and stared at him as he floated instinctively in the artificial wind, his compound eyes taking me in. We had never been able to ascertain what signals he could still transmit to the network from this depth. I regularly wondered if the Queens were watching our every move through his eyes. All I needed was to walk up to the Hive with the bomb and the Queens be like, "It's *you!*" It was easy to inadvertently consider Radar a friend, but I had to constantly remind myself, pet or not, he was the enemy and wouldn't hesitate to share any information he gleaned. It was an uncomfortable thought, but before I left for the Hive, I'd have no choice but to put him down as well. The near-instantaneous death would suit him far better than one of Zabu's cruel schemes, though the justification wouldn't make it any easier. *Why can't war just be black and white?*

•••••••••

On my way to check in on Emile and the centrifuge's process, two of Zabu's men rounded the corner ahead of me. After my theft of the rod, I was constantly on edge, but I forced myself to walk normally. I wanted to doubt they were in the research district for me, but there weren't many other reasons for them to be here. *They don't know that you've done anything wrong. Don't give them any reason to think otherwise.* I keep my pace consistent, minimizing eye contact and walking as if I had pressing duties needing attention. They passed me and I let out an imperceptible sigh of relief.

"That was him," one of the guards said to the other.

Damn.

I heard their steps pursuing me from behind.

"Technician Dieter?"

I turned to face them, still clinging to hope that they weren't here to arrest me. "Yes?" I said, hoping they didn't notice the lump in my throat.

"Prime Minister Zabu requests a private audience with you," the taller one said, his olive-drab beret imperceptibly dotted with blood from a recent violent encounter.

"When would he like to see me?" I asked.

"Now. We are your escort," said the shorter one.

I followed them to the elevator and stepped in, the armed guards standing in front of me acting as a physical barrier keeping me from leaving the elevator at my own discretion. The weapons slung over their shoulders were a composite of ancient wood and over-burnished metal. Relics of ages past, but no less deadly for it. Due to their excessive wear, the rumor was that their accuracy was terrible, but unless I could outrun a supersonic bullet, a shot would be no less lethal. I ran my hands nervously through my hair, flinging off the strands that clung to my hand.

As the elevator clicked through the floors, illuminating the buttons that still functioned, I couldn't help but think how the bomb would ever get to the Hive if Emile and I were executed for our crimes. Memo promised help, but even if they came, without the weapon, their arrival would be fruitless.

The elevator opened and we walked across the narrow well-maintained executive catwalk to the Nucleus where the minister's office was located. I rested my hand on the railing, my hand clammy not from the significant heights but from the looming threat of death at the end of Zabu's machete. I gulped so loudly, that I swore it echoed down the pod's central chamber.

Before I knew it, we stood at the large double hatches of the prime minister's office. Each door was painted to depict a biased retelling of our pod's history, characterizing Zabu as our pod's savior. The tall guard knocked softly, before opening it with a squeal that carried through the vacant corridor. There was a day when the pod bustled with life. The now-empty halls served as an unpleasant reminder of the loss of life. The interior of Zabu's office was quite dim, the numerous candles barely illuminated the large space with a tepid yellow glow. I heard the hatch squeak closed behind me, leaving me alone with him. I searched the room for a moment before I recognized his broad-shouldered form. I apparently had interrupted his ritual prayers.

He ceased his recitations and stood from his kneeling posture, revealing the shrine hidden by his torso. Murmurings throughout the pod had long carried gossip of his twisted beliefs. Seeing the statue of Ala raised my concerns even further than before, his choice from the Odinalic pantheon being telling. The traditional goddess of death stood off-centered in the cabinet, displaying a python wrapped around her extended arm. Her hyper-realistic nude figure was only clothed in a draping golden necklace and sheer shawl, her vacant eyes forever watching. Zabu turned and slowly closed the cabinet's doors, latching with a soft click as the wood panels nested in their place.

"She's beautiful—Ala," the prime minister said. "It is said that she would cause the ground to swallow those who sin against her. This is why I want this bomb. The people of Pod Baghdad are *weak* and *sinful*." Zabu collapsed into his tall-backed chair, stroking the emerging live python that had been concealed by the darkness. I gasped.

"She scares you, no? Do not fear her. You are doing the goddess' work. You know that the last messenger on his return tells me they fornicate with their kindred—and with the same sex. The *same* sex. This is against nature—against *Ala's* nature. It's is my duty to give this bomb of yours to them, so that they might be swallowed by the ground."

"If Ala wished, wouldn't she smite them herself?" I asked. It was risky pushing back, but I couldn't help myself. Since swimming with the radioactive rods, I felt a newfound strength.

"I like the way you think," he said, tapping his temple with his index finger. Even in the dim light, the body language of his silhouette was readable. "You scientists are a clever bunch. Perhaps too clever, sometimes."

I swallowed. He paced around his desk towards me, I stiffened up, bracing myself for the unexpected. If my time in Pod Kano had taught me anything, it was that Ndulue Zabu was impossible to predict.

"You are thinking, who am I to carry out the goddess' wishes, no?"

I nodded.

"Wise beyond your years. I like you. I would prefer not to kill you. But do not mistake my sentiment for weakness, should you fail me. To my point, death is a tool. Perhaps the oldest tool since creation. It motivates us. It rids us of the excess. Excess weakness. Excess sin. Excess apathy. It is cleansing. And I am her cleanser," said Zabu, as the glimmer from his teeth reflected a wicked smile.

I'm working for a deranged lunatic with a messiah complex. I need to get the hell out of this pod.

I wrestled my response. He said nothing to imply that he had discovered the rod's theft. Maybe I was safe.

"How is my bomb coming?"

I mentally scoffed at the notion of it being *his* bomb.

"We are on schedule to finish by your thirty-day deadline, Prime Minister. We have started assembling the components."

"That's good to hear—for your sake. I shall make a trip down to examine your work soon," he said, before turning back towards the makeshift altar.

I turned to leave, assuming I was dismissed.

"There's been a theft," I heard him continue from behind me.

I turned to face him once again, but he still spoke with his back turned to me.

"I fear it is the Resistance moving against me. They do not wish for me to remain in power. They fail to understand that without me, there would be chaos," said Zabu. "If you have any insight into the Resistance you will come tell me immediately, understood?"

"Yes, Prime Minister," I said.

"You are dismissed."

As soon as I was back in the elevator on my way down alone, I collapsed in the corner, consumed by intense relief and unsuppressed panic.

CHAPTER 18: HUCK

I felt nothing but discomfort at the idea of killing all of these innocent water striders. If not for Yanus' likely empty threats to leave us with the Demented, which had visibly shaken Ariadne, it would've been tempting to push him into the river and say to hell with his entire operation. I didn't fight it, reluctantly opting to participate for the good of the mission. The second I fired the bolt from my crossbow into an innocent water strider, a tidal wave of doubt flooded my mind. As the strider I had targeted collapsed onto the murky water from the direct hit, I mumbled an apology, grasping for forgiveness from the deplorable action.

Harvesting the glandular pods was the easier part. Having already inflicted the death blow, I was able to detach myself from the work, removing one pod at a time from the corpse of the Arthropod before moving on to the next. I glanced over at Ariadne to check on her. Despite the tender wound I still carried from her words, I still cared deeply for her. They were harvesting slower than we were, but she seemed to have come to terms with the task, and I wasn't going to interrupt.

Once the revolting work was completed, Taha collected the

glands and loaded them into the supply truck for Ariadne and Krista to process. We had begun to load our equipment back into the vehicles for departure when a familiar sound echoed from the vast forest opposite the town, sending a familiar chill down my spine. Without bothering to assess the threat, I sprinted back to where I'd laid my crossbow, shouldered it, and sprinted for the cover of the hauler. Peering around the large tan vehicle, I waited for my eyes to focus on the dark green tree line in the distance. Accompanying the thunderous cracking, I could see the treetops in the distance toppling as a multitude swarmed the forest floor below. I knew what they were before the first one broke through.

"Eights!" yelled Omar as the first wave burst forth.

Damn the aerials! Part of me understood the resentment the inverts felt towards us for our last deplorable action. Moving with lightning speed, they closed the gap and the battle began in earnest. I loosed a few bolts, making successful hits, before realizing I would soon be in the middle of the fracas. I jumped on top of the hauler and crouched next to the turret, laying my bolts on the roof next to me. One by one, I fired at the eights swarming the others. Already, scattered on the ground were the bodies of several transporters. We were vastly outnumbered. I risked a glance at the forest and saw wave after wave of ceaseless reinforcements. Survival was looking bleak, but I continued to fire. I scored a direct hit through the eye of an eight, sending it careening into the dirt, just long enough for one of the whirling transporters to finish it off with their razor-edged blade.

I reached down and grabbed my last bolt. *Bloody hell, they went quick!* I surveyed the landscape. There were still so many! I fired my last bolt, which missed, alerting the eight to my presence. Focusing directly on me, it plowed through those in its way, slinging and slashing them to ribbons with its saw-toothed legs.

As fast as I could, I dropped into the turret and used the pedals to swing the double-barreled machine gun to face the bastard. *Screw waiting for clearance to fire! If I wait any longer, there won't be anyone left to fight. It's not like there are more inverts to attract. They're all here!* I wrapped my fingers around the handles and depressed the trigger tabs, opening fire. The large-bore weapons' slow rate of fire pounded mercilessly on my unprotected ears. With each of the repeating *doom, doom, doom,* I watched as the beasts in the distance blew apart, showering the others around them in hemolymph-saturated chitin. As I centered the next group in my targeting reticle, I heard the other vehicle's external weapons chiming into the symphony I had begun, each playing its own part. As if orchestrated, the enemy gradually fell one after another, littering the ground with their viscera as the closest creatures were finished off in hand-to-hand combat. When I finally stopped firing, the barrels glowed cherry red and smelled of super-heated steel. The other weapons subsequently stopped firing, sensing the lull in attackers.

I climbed down from the turret, dropping directly into a puddle of the creatures' black lifeblood. The dire situation had turned around into another win for the humans but at the expense of numerous transporters, whose billowing ivory outfits now rested stationary and crimson on the earth. Hemant walked up to me, grasping me in a bear hug, covering me in the residual entrails that had adhered to his jumpsuit during the fray.

"Gross, dude," I said, slinging the goop from my hands.

"I don't care," he said, laughing. "We did it thanks to your quick thinking with that turret!"

Suddenly, Yanus appeared from between the vehicles, looking clean as a bride on her wedding day.

"What the hell were you doing, firing without my explicit order?!" he yelled.

"If I didn't do something, we all would've died!" I yelled in response. "I didn't see you out here giving the orders! As a matter of fact, I didn't see you out here at all! Where——"

Yanus' fist met my face and, for a moment, all I could see were stars. For a guy who never fought, he packed a helluva punch. As my vision returned, I put my hand on my cheek to assess the damage. My jaw was tender, maybe even broken.

"How dare you impugn my noble character! I am your protector, and you would do well to remember such!"

"And how exactly were you protecting us?!" asked Hemant, getting into Yanus' face, daring him to strike. "By cowering in your vehicle?!"

"I… I… I have provided you my vehicles, my men, my food and this is how you return my favor?!" said Yanus.

"You want the favor returned?" asked Hemant, nodding. "Okay, I'll return the favor."

Hemant walked to the back of the supply truck where the harvested glands were. *Don't do anything stupid, Hemant.* After a moment, he returned carrying a shovel and walked over to the nearest body of a transporter, and began digging. After looking at each other, Taha and the rest of us went to grab more shovels. The remaining living transporters stared at us as we began to dig graves for their fallen, their faces brimming with respect at our defiance and appreciation for our efforts. Yanus stared with his mouth agape before eventually sneaking off to his cozy carrier.

Unlike the Misfits, the Saharan transporters hung closely to their burial traditions. Once the group of us had interred half of the bodies, I began running on fumes, the battle's exertion already weighing heavily on my physique. Sensing this, the local transporters joined us to help complete the task.

"Arjun, we've got to do something about those bloody aerials," I said. "We can't kill a damn midge without them alerting the Hive and sending reinforcements. It's only going to get worse as we get closer. You saw the attack today, we can't continue at this pace. We're dropping like flies."

Arjun froze momentarily.

"I'm sorry, Arjun," I said. "That wasn't my best analogy."

"It's okay. I know you meant nothing by it. Your assumption is correct," said Arjun. "We are operating at an unsustainable pace. I've already lost Ciro. I can't lose you. You remember how they reacted when we shot down the last one. We almost lost Mueller to those multipedes. Our only chance to take down the antenna bug network is all at once. We need to confer with the scientists at Kano."

"What about finding where they roost or whatever?" asked Hemant, leaning on his shovel. "We've seen them rotate out. They can't all fly back to the Australian Territory. Where do they sleep? They do sleep, right?"

"Yes. All creatures need rest and fuel. In that respect, they are no different from the indigenous species."

"*If* we could find their nests, we'd still have the same problem," I said. "If we dispatched a bunch of them at once, we'd still have all the ones in the sky reporting our attack."

"What about jamming their signal?" asked Ariadne, attempting to clean the accumulated grime from her forehead with the back of her gloved hand, only smearing it instead.

"That would be a viable option if we knew how. Most machines with the ability to accurately analyze their output waves ceased to function upon their arrival," said Arjun. "After the Arthropod Landing, humans had to revert to antiquated technology to do rudimentary communication. Depending on what equipment Dieter has in Pod Kano, we might be able to detect what frequencies they broadcast on. Maybe we can create a counter wave of sorts and broadcast it into their midst. Their jamming garbles our communication, but it does not stop the actual transmission."

"That's it then," I said. "Let's do that!"

Arjun smiled for the first time since Ciro's passing, an event that already felt like weeks behind us. Death was getting to be a fact of life I was growing too comfortable with on Earth's surface. I wasn't sure what was more frightening: being killed by an enemy face-to-face or being killed defenseless in my sleep. I forced myself to return the smile and was reminded of the condition of my jaw. I'd have to have Ariadne look at it when she had time. It was nice to have a shorter-term goal than the Hive, even if it was as daunting as disrupting an entire global alien communication network. I picked up my shovel to resume digging, then I saw familiar forms in the sky.

"Dusters!" I yelled.

Would this day ever end? Everyone scrambled into the vehicles, leaving the few remaining dead where they lay. We couldn't risk our lives to properly care for them. I hoped that it didn't interfere with the transporters' beliefs too seriously. I jumped into the driver's seat and watched the others through the side mirrors, making sure everyone was accounted for. I looked forward in time to see Ariadne and Krista jump into the supply truck and I started the engine. In my agitation, I killed it immediately.

"What's wrong?" shouted Omar from the seat next to me.

"I killed it!" I said, watching the other vehicles begin to pull away.

"Do something!"

"I'm trying!"

"We need to leave!" he said pointing to the larger powder moths, now close enough to see the pill bugs grasped in their talon-like appendages. "Get. Us. Moving!"

Finally, the engine started again and with a bucking start, we were off. The first of the vehicles in the convoy made it to the intact of the two bridges and the realization hit me like a blow from Hemant's hammer. The dusters weren't targeting us, they were targeting the freaking bridge! I looked at Omar, who'd had the same realization.

"Go!" he said.

I could only go as fast as the vehicle ahead of me. The tank truck's driver was oblivious to the urgency of the situation. I honked, willing him to move faster. Through the dust generated by the convoy, I could see him looking back at me, struggling to discern what I was trying to communicate. I pointed, motioning to go as obviously as I could. Taking the hint, he increased his speed but was still weighed down by the compressed gas he carried.

"Go around!" Omar yelled, "He's not going to make it."

I hated to admit it, but Omar was right. Passing him would be cutting it awfully close to the bridge's guardrails, which if misjudged, passing could result in both vehicles crashing into the river below. It was risky, but seeing no alternative. I nodded, pushing the pedal to the firewall.

"Hang on!" I yelled to those in the back.

I left the rough, cracked tarmac for the even rougher earth. We bounded alongside the tanker as the driver looked at us with confusion.

"Get over. Get over. Get over. Get over! Get over!" yelled Omar.

At the last possible second, I swung in front of the tanker, barely missing the rusty mangled guardrail.

"Whew!" I sighed.

"Don't rejoice yet," said Omar, leaning forward to look up at the looming dusters, who were already filling the air with their sporish poison.

With my foot firmly against the floor, we were catching up to the others just as I heard the first explosion from behind. With a slam, the hauler's rear tracks returned to their contact with the bridge's aged concrete, lurching us forward with their increased speed. I checked my rear view in time to see the flame-engulfed tanker falling through the damaged bridge into the waters below.

The driver's death weighed on my conscience, but our mission could continue as a result of his sacrifice. The dusters continued to drop the polies, but they detonated in the water or behind us, their heavy wings unable to keep up with our speed. One thing was certain, the transporters would not be coming back this way.

Empty of their armaments and unable to suffocate us with their biological agents, the dusters returned from whence they came. We had survived the attacks of the day and had a plan for taking down the aerial network. If only the elation wasn't overshadowed by the day's high death toll. Too many people were dying for us. I desperately hoped we would make it worth their while.

•••••••••

"What's your plan, man?" Omar asked after we'd been rolling for a while.

"I'm guessing you're referring to Kano," I replied.

Omar nodded. I knew this moment would come, but I had been unsure how to broach the subject.

"Taha tells me that Pod Kano is surrounded by old structures, some of which are still intact. I doubt we'll have time to find you a perfect hideout. You and Krista could focus on survival. We'll try to be in and out. I know it's not optimal, but it's all I could come up with."

"Not optimal?!" Omar yelled, smacking his hand into the metal dash. "Huck, you're going to boot us out in the middle of nowhere and say 'Good friggin' luck.'"

"What do you want me to do?! Anywhere we've already seen is too far from the pod. For all I know, the dusters are still after us. *Every* second up here is a gamble with the unknown. You think we want to be alone with this unhinged Zabu guy? If I could scrub away your sentence, I would. You and Krista both have proved yourself time and time again."

"Thanks, Huck. Sorry I got on your case. I'm… actually afraid."

"You?" I asked, receiving a harsh glare. "If anyone can survive, it's you. You may be the most suited out of all of us. Before Ade lost his leg, you guys were a force to be reckoned with. We'll drop you off with everything we can spare. With any luck, we'll be out of the pod lickety-split and on our way to Baghdad with the weapon."

Omar nodded, taking in the idea.

"Okay," he said. "Try not to take too long."

CHAPTER 19: HEMANT

Before I could see our destination from the hauler's turret, I heard the excited yells float back through the convoy from the vehicles ahead. After the air had cleared from the duster attack, I had climbed up into the unoccupied perch for the remainder of the journey.

"I think we're here!" I yelled down.

I heard whoops and hollers drifting up from the other candidates. Then the realization hit me. *Citizens. We were about to be citizens.* We had survived the prerequisite journey from one pod to another, automatically making us citizens! *"Whoo-oo!"* I yelled into the air.

Ahead, I could barely discern the bumpy terrain created by the long-collapsed edifices of the pre-Landing city of Kano, whose lifeless ruins encircled the pod. As the train of vehicles pulled into the clearing. Huck must have realized the significance of our proximity and gradually slowed the truck to a stop. *Omar and Krista.* Krista was officially banished and could never enter the pod. We were operating on the assumption that Omar was as well. This would be the end of the road for them—at least temporarily.

I climbed down to the already empty bed and jumped out onto

the ground, puffing a cloud of dust into the dry air. Our drive inland had seen the gradation from the forested regions of the coast to the scorching climate near the Sahara Desert, for which the territory was named. The flat ground extended like a desiccated ocean from horizon to horizon, allowing me to see for kilometers until the dust-saturated atmosphere obscured it. Aside from the city's skeletal remains, the only variation in the landscape was ridges of stone.

"I'm sorry we have to rush our goodbye, but we have to catch up to the others," said Huck.

"I understand. Don't worry about us, we can take care of ourselves," said Omar, pulling Krista into a side-hug. "Lickety-split, right?"

"Lickety-split," echoed Huck.

Krista seemed flippant about the ordeal, even smiling every now and then—something I hadn't seen her do since Zeke's death. Omar was resigned to the idea. He was a survivor. I was confident upon our exit of Kano, they would be ready in the wings. They pulled their packs and gear from the hauler, as Huck passed them a carton of dry rations. Krista crossed her dual katanas across her back as Omar spun his naginata restlessly.

"I know neither how nor when we'll leave the pod, nor do I know how we'll notify you," said Huck. "Just be ready at a moment's notice and keep an eye out for us. If what everyone says about this place is true, we may be leaving in a hurry."

"Understood," said Omar. "Arjun, do you still have those survey binoculars?"

"I do," he said, rusting in his pack. "Here you are."

"Thanks, man. We'll keep a lookout. Good luck," said Omar, embracing Huck and patting him on the back, before embracing each of us.

"Love you," said Krista to Ariadne, giving her a quick embrace.

Huck and I looked at each other with the same confusion. They must have reconnected while they were milking the glands in the supply truck.

"Take good care of my friend," said Ariadne, more effervescently than I would have expected.

"Will do," said Omar.

We all looked awkwardly at each other before Huck stated the obvious, "Well, we need to get moving before the others ask too many questions. See you soon. Promise."

We piled back into the truck and drove off, leaving Omar and Krista to fend for themselves for days, maybe even weeks. With any luck, the inverts would ignore them. This landscape was far too open for good cover. It would be hard enough for them to survive the heat, let alone repeated attack. We left them with as much water and goods as they could carry. *"Godspeed,"* I thought as I watched them vanish in the dust left by the hauler.

•••••••••

The final stint of our journey passed by in mere minutes, the roads having been well maintained by the transporters as each trip held the landscape's encroachment at bay. There was an eerie uniformity to the sprawling, inanimate city. The dry climate and fine dust offered some modicum of protection, preserving the structures' condition as the years meandered by. The resulting uniformity made the terrain appear as though the gods had sifted the land with a gossamer coating of dust.

I couldn't fathom what life must have been like on the surface before the arrival of the inverts. I felt the drop in the engine's revolutions and rotated the turret towards the cab. We turned into a colossal open square of ground where no evidence of buildings betrayed the area's purpose. Spread like a juggernaut over the earth was the slightly convex dome of Pod Kano. I felt my heart flutter.

The last time I was outside of a pod, almost everyone around me had perished. The sight I expected to be comforting was anything but. My mind struggled to grasp the massive scale of this feat of humanity in the absence of trees and homes for comparison.

As Yanus' private carrier pulled up to the entrance, I saw the city's great gate, flush with the dome's surface, begin to open. Sprinkling dust like a coastal rain, the doors parted and receded into the superstructure, revealing the ramp down to the staging area. I took a deep breath. This was supposed to be exciting. It was the moment I completed the requirements of citizenship, but somehow it felt… off. More like I was being swallowed by a beast than embraced by my peers. I never was much for folklore, but the place brimmed with bad juju. Something was amiss in Pod Kano.

The convoy pulled to a stop with a cacophony of brake squeals at the ramp's base while the steel gate sealed behind us with a muffled *whump*. I'd spent all of my life in a pod save for the last few weeks, but suddenly, I felt a tidal wave of claustrophobia. I confronted Huck as he descended from the cab, my eyes slowly adjusting to the darkness.

"I don't like this place, Huck. I'm already in a hurry to get out of here."

"I know what you mean," he said. "This place gives me the heebie-jeebies."

"You guys, too?" asked Mei, approaching with Ariadne. "That's not good."

"Let's just find Dieter, get the device, and get out of here," said Ariadne.

"Speaking of which, where—"

"Yanus, my friend," a voice boomed from the shadow, carrying easily throughout the vast chamber.

I turned to see a handsome, broad-shouldered black man

flanked by two guards and approaching Yanus, his arms open for an embrace.

"Prime Minister, so good to see you once again," said Yanus to the man, having to crane his neck to look the minister in the eyes.

"And you as well," said the minister. "And I see you've brought me some new faces, no doubt here because of the prestige of my pod. Welcome citizens! Unofficially, of course, until the ceremony. I am Prime Minister Ndulue Zabu. Pleased to make your acquaintance. I look forward to adding your distinctiveness to our own, making our pod even greater."

Huck and I eyed each other. I didn't know if now was the time to tell him we weren't staying. I didn't want him to have the wrong impression.

"Thank you, Minister Zabu," said Huck. "I'm Huck of Pod Horizonte. This is Ariadne; Hemant; Hemant's brother, Arjun; and Mei, also from Horizonte. We appreciate your hospitality, but this isn't our final destination. We plan to move on as soon as we have recovered from our travels."

For a split second, a hint of anger darted across his face, but it vanished as quickly as it had appeared, replaced by his wide smile.

"Of course, of course. I think you may change your mind once you take in all our pod has to offer. It is a great place where candidates, blown to us like seeds on the wind, can land, plant roots, and thrive. You will find our pod is *alive* with possibilities."

If the pod gave me bad vibes, this guy's were worse. I'd been around him for less than ten minutes, and I was already uncomfortable and distrusting. He and Yanus seemed like perfect bedfellows. I would bet all my ration points that Master Kebe was right about him. We needed to get what we came for and get the hell out of here. I looked around for our contact, Dieter, but didn't see anyone aside from Zabu's escort. It may not have been a safe time to meet us. I hoped he wouldn't wait too long.

"You all must be weary from your trip," said Zabu, "My men will show you to your quarters. You will have the pleasure of staying in our luxury apartments so that you can see what we truly have to offer. You will join me in the morning for breakfast, yes?"

"Of course," said Huck, glancing at us.

"Me too?" asked our ass-kissing friend, Yanus.

"Yes, my friend. You too."

After the minister had departed, we collected our gear and weapons.

"You won't need any of that here," said one of the guards in an accent I struggled to understand. "We will provide you with everything you need."

I reluctantly replaced my pack into the hauler before turning back to the guard.

"And your weapons. Leave them here."

Every red flag I could imagine was being raised, but we were powerless. Each guard was armed with some old-fashioned automatic weapon and neither one looked friendly. I reluctantly removed my dagger belt and laid it in the hauler, as did the others. After bidding goodbye to Taha, we parted ways with Yanus, Taha, and the transporters. Then wearing only our scratched and dented light armor and filthy, odorous jumpsuits, we followed the men from the Nucleus into the apartment district of the third floor.

As we walked across the catwalk, I kept an eye out for our unknown friend, Dieter, looking for anyone who might look interested to speak with us. The pod, while almost identical to Pod Horizonte, was filthier and appeared far less populated. All of a sudden, my nasty jumpsuit didn't seem so out of place. Litter, sand, and rust abounded in the pod. Everywhere my eyes fell were signs of unmitigated degradation and disrepair. For a man who bragged about his pod, it looked like junk. If this had been my destination, I would've been disappointed.

We arrived at a hall of identical hatches, bathed in white and leading to private residences where the guards divided us up between rooms. I was given a suite with Arjun and Huck. Ariadne would share with Mei. It was instantly obvious that the guards weren't going to leave until we had locked ourselves in for the night.

"You guys going to be alright?" I asked Ariadne.

"Sure," she said "We'll see you guys at breakfast."

We each headed into our apartments as the guards locked the door behind us with a clank.

"For invited guests, I sure feel a lot like a prisoner," I said, turning to face Huck and Arjun.

I perused the apartment, taking in our accommodations. The place was fully furnished and quite nice, given the condition of the pod lying just outside the door. There were three bedrooms and a common bathroom branching off from the living room and kitchen. Along the far wall was a light panel covered in moth-eaten curtains, giving the illusion of a window.

"I don't know about you, but I'm about to crash," I said. "I'll try and figure this crazy place out in the morning."

Huck and Arjun grunted their agreement.

We were a mess. Huck's jaw was still swollen from the encounter with Yanus. Arjun, though hiding it well, was still a wreck after the loss of Ciro. And as tired as I was, I didn't expect to sleep in this unnerving place. I thought about how our quarters differed from Krista and Omar's and immediately felt some guilt. After checking on Arjun, I headed into my room, pulling the pocket door closed behind me. The room was fairly spartan. In addition to the bed, there was a bedside table with a lamp, a chest of drawers, and a succulent plant—probably all that could survive here. All said, the space was the nicest I had ever slept in, but its near-perfect appearance left me with the distinct feeling it was set aside to impress visitors. I was certain that if we were able to explore, we'd find a much different experience elsewhere in the pod, perhaps one of the reasons we were contained. I stripped off my gear, planning to sleep in the buff, but surprisingly found several different sizes of clean jumpsuits in the drawers.

"Alright, it's not *all* bad," I said to no one.

After taking the single most appreciated shower of my entire life, I slept in clean clothes for the first time in over a month.

CHAPTER 20: ARIADNE

I was disoriented when I came to in the small apartment bedroom. Everything was foreign. After tossing and turning for hours in the strange comfort of an actual bed, I eventually dozed off. The night had been fitful, plagued with nightmares of Krista and Omar being overrun by inverts while the five of us were imprisoned in Kano. I dragged myself from the cool sheets, supremely groggy and fuzzy-headed, unsure what had woken me—

Bam! Bam! Bam!

That. It sounded as though someone was beating down our door. Must be time for breakfast. So much for a leisurely morning. I felt like crap warmed over. What was wrong with me?

I exited my room and shouted, "We're up. Give us a minute."

The banging thankfully ceased. I wasn't sure how long we had, so I went to check on Mei. I slid open her door to find her about as alert as me, sitting up in bed with her hair matted to one side of her head and her deep night's sleep evident from the trail of drool on her cheek. If the surface had taught me anything, it was the value of a good night's sleep. At least one of us had gotten one.

"They're not a patient bunch, you may want to get dressed," I said.

Mei flopped back into bed.

"Mei, I'm serious."

"So am I," she said, covering her face with a pillow.

With hostility, I pulled the pillow down, yelling, "Now!"

"Jesus, Okay," said Mei.

"I'm sorry, I don't know what just came over me," I said, attempting to calm her disheveled hair.

"It's okay. Is everything alright?"

I nodded. I wasn't usually an angry person. Mei wanting a few more minutes of rest wasn't any reason to get bent out of shape. I took a deep breath as I threw my hair back into a ponytail. I wondered what was for breakfast. I was starving and a massive headache was beginning to radiate from the back of my skull. I picked up my armor, debating whether to put it on when another banging on the door came.

"We're coming!" I yelled.

This time the anger was justified as a result of their impatience. I left the armor on the bed and joined Mei in the fluorescent-lit hallway, waiting for my eyes to adjust to the brighter light. Huck, Hemant, and Arjun looked equally groggy as the guards steered us back to the Nucleus.

"I wouldn't mind some coffee right now," I said to Hemant. "I've got cravings like you wouldn't believe."

"Don't get my hopes up," Hemant said. "I don't want to be disappointed if they only have tea."

"I like tea. Ciro and I—" Arjun paused.

"It's okay, brother," Hemant said, putting a hand on Arjun's shoulder. "Talk about him all you want."

"He'll never truly be gone if we keep his memory alive," I said.

"Thanks, Ariadne," said Arjun.

I felt a burning sensation as my eyes began to water. I still hadn't had time to fully process Ciro's death. The downtime in the pod would undoubtedly bring suppressed emotions to light.

•••••••••

As we passed under light, after light, after light, my mind flashed back to the gland processing in the supply truck. As Krista and I had scrambled to evade the dusters in the battle's aftermath, we ran for the cover of the supply truck, our newly assigned vehicle. Once the convoy had escaped the sky-borne threat, we reluctantly began the gross work of milking the Arthropod glands for their pheromones. As we rode along in silence on the rutted road to Kano, we would squeeze pod after pod with our gloved hands into the table's receptacle. The orangish goo reeked of iron, sulfur, and death. The second we were sure we had exited the poisonous fog of the powder moths, we had the vents open, giving us some reprieve from the god-awful stench.

After filling up several containers and depositing them into the chest, we started getting into the groove of the monotonous work. Krista and I still weren't talking. Between Zeke's loss and the accusations I'd thrown at her, there wasn't a lot of love between us. With nothing else to do, I threw myself into the work at hand. While working on a particularly difficult pod, massaging it just as Taha had illustrated, nothing was effective. I laid it on the table and used the palm of my hand to bust its internal sack. When it popped, it did so with great force, spraying the noxious goo all over Krista's face.

"Gross! Get it off me!" she screamed.

I grabbed a clean towel, and after wetting it, began to rub the sticky substance from her skin. She jerked it from my hand and began doing it herself.

"If I need your help, I'll ask for it!" she said.

What a bitch. It was an accident and I was trying to help you.

Taha had insisted that we wear gloves to avoid contact with the substance, but never explained why. I heard about pheromones going as far back as Horizonte, but was innocent as to how they worked. Were they ingested or absorbed? Who knows. Krista cleaned herself up, and I lowered my head, returning to the work, infuriated by what had transpired. I could feel the anger seething under my skin. How had she gone from being my best friend to someone I hated so much? I heard the pop of a gland and felt the warm sticky spray on my face.

"Really?!" I said, reaching for a towel.

"Screw you, Ariadne," said Krista with a vile edge to her tone.

I began to cry. Krista rolled her eyes and resumed her work as I cleaned up. I didn't know if the tears were from sadness or anger. Probably both. If I didn't hate her before, I was starting to now. I put my head down even further, tuning out everything but the work, praying the awkward trip would be over soon. As time drifted by, the work became a repetitive blur and I began to care less and less about Krista's actions. I topped off another container and sealed it, before turning to place it in the chest. As I turned, the world blurred, the truck rotated like a planetary sphere with me at its core. Every aspect of life unfolded in slow-motion. The flies buzzing, attracted by the odor, flapped their wings only a few times per second. The light illuminating our work radiated warmth like a campfire on a cool night. I set a new container into the table's recess and tingled at the satisfying clink as it fell into place. The rough canvas of the seat felt so smooth to the touch as I dragged my fingertips along its weave, satiating my senses.

With some effort, I focused on Krista across from me who was flipping her hand back and forth in front of her, mesmerized by its movement. I smiled at her and she returned it.

"What's happening?" she asked, slowly.

"I think we might be high," I said, feeling the words struggle to leave my parched mouth.

"I feel so… good," Krista said.

"But I'm a good girl," I said, the warmth moving down to my toes. "I don't do pheromones."

"Chill the hell out, Ariadne. One squirt won't make you an addict like Akhil," said Krista, slurring many of the words. She laid down on the bench, folding her legs against the shelf next to her.

Mirroring her pose, I let the rocking of the truck lull me into a deeply relaxed state.

"Maybe you're right. I'm too uptight."

"Hell yes, you are," Krista said sluggishly. "You're an asshole when you get all high and mighty."

"Well you're a bitch when you're angry," I said, then added, "even if it is for a good reason. And I can't believe you wanted to run off with Omar."

"You knew about that?"

"I wasn't dropping no eaves. Eavesdropping?" *Whatever. My mind is a muddled mess.* "I happened to overhear your conversation."

"I felt like you forgot about us. I felt neglected every time you all talked about Kano."

"I'm sorry. We'll get something figured out, even if I have to ask the inverts politely. Could you imagine?" I asked, putting on a posh, upper-level accent. "Please Mr. Eight, would you be so kind as to leave my friend alone whilst I entertain myself in Pod Kano?"

I laughed as if it was the funniest thing ever said. Krista convulsed with laughter so hard at my stupid impression that she fell in a heap off the bench. I rolled down onto the dirty, cramped floor with her.

"I'm sorry about Zeke," I said, gently tucking her thick, wavy hair behind her ear.

"Thanks," said Krista. "I'm sorry for spraying you with this stuff, even though it feels pretty awesome."

"I'm sorry about yelling at you and Omar. I was hurt. It hurt to think you would sleep with Omar so flipping, flippar… flippantly," I said, struggling with the fog obscuring my thoughts.

"Nothing happened," said Krista, wagging her finger at me.

Hypnotized by the movement, I could almost hear the air currents as her finger moved backward and forwards through the stuffy air.

"I know. Omar said as much. You are important to me. I love you," I said, kissing her on the forehead and feeling her warmth radiate through the hyper-sensitive nerve ending in my lips. "I've been under a lot of stress. It's a lot. Taking care of wounds. Making sure we're all eating the right nutrients. Not dying."

"Well you do a good job, sister."

"Thanks. Speaking of care, we can't do this ever again. This isn't good for us. We shouldn't do drugs," I said, doing my absolute best to sound serious.

"Thanks, Matron Ariadne," said Krista, giggling. "I love you, too."

I held her hand and we laid there until the peak of our stupor wore off as the vehicle trundled along unnoticed beneath us. Groggily, we moved back to the benches, finishing off the few remaining pods as the last traces of our high dissipated. When the time came to drop Krista and Omar off on their own recognizance, we were sober, finished, and friends again.

●●●●●●●●●

I arrived with the others at the Nucleus' grand dining hall, having made the short journey on autopilot. The hall was a space I'd never laid eyes on in Pod Horizonte. It was reserved only for the pod's prime minister and his regents. When we entered the grand room, there was only Zabu, Yanus, Taha, and one other person aside from the guards who lingered on the periphery. The room was illuminated primarily by natural light, streaming in through circular portholes in the ornate, curved ceiling. Our escorts took their positions with the other guards standing at attention and bracketing each entryway. The minister, Yanus, and the stranger approached us. Taha's presence seemed to be only that of a supportive role to Yanus, not a guest of the minister.

"Welcome citizens of Pod Kano," he said, intentionally ignoring our plans to leave. "Please stand shoulder to shoulder."

He stood back, taking us in.

"Yes, you would make a fine addition to our people," said Zabu. "My apologies for detaining you last night. It was a... *necessary measure* until we could properly orient you to our home. I would ask that for the time being, you don't wander the pod unaccompanied. But enough about that. I forget my manners. This is Chattar, my loyal advisor."

"A pleasure," said Chattar, pushing his round glasses tighter onto his chestnut face. "If you have any needs, please ask your escorts to relay them to me."

"Thank you," said Huck.

"And I believe you are all well acquainted with Yanus," said the minister. "Now it is time."

Chattar walked away to pick up a diminutive antique wooden box from a side table before returning back to Zabu. A third of a meter shorter than the ebony-skinned Zabu, Chattar's typical Bhopalese stature was almost comical next to the giant. Chattar opened the carved box, revealing its aged crimson velvet interior to Zabu. Inside was a collection of small pins.

"We are honored to bestow the gift of citizenship to each of you. Following this ceremony, you will be free to choose surnames, petition jobs, and produce offspring," said Zabu, making uncomfortable eye contact with me on his last bullet point. "Chattar will see to the completion of your tattoos."

Walking over to Huck, he removed a pin from the box.

"I pronounce you Citizen…

"Huck, sir."

"I pronounce you Citizen Huck. I confer to you all the rights and privileges therein."

"Thank you, Minister," said Huck, shaking his hand.

Zabu worked his way down the line, giving each of us our pin before inviting us to be seated for breakfast. The food wasn't to the degree of freshness we had grown accustomed to, but the menu was expansive and made with the highest degree of opulence. We each ate from gold-rimmed plates and drank from crystal stemware. And the coffee—the coffee was to die for. Hemant and I looked back and forth smiling as we sipped the dark, rich brew. When we all had sufficiently stuffed ourselves, my headache had calmed, though not as much as I had hoped. I still felt on edge, slightly nauseous, and still craving something that felt just out of reach. Then it hit me. It was the deleterious effects of the pheromones I had absorbed. *Of course!* If this was the detoxification period. I couldn't imagine what it must be like after Dust, its much stronger cousin. I felt a cold shiver from the realization. I still couldn't believe I had used the vile substance, even inadvertently.

Gradually the conversation shifted from small talk to more serious matters. Huck inquired about the pod's population, to which Zabu dodged smoothly, but not without raising my suspicions. I asked about the nutritional quality of the food, and Chattar suggested I accompany him down to the horticultural levels for a tour. Arjun asked about the weaponry developments, to which Zabu said "were exciting," but made it clear that the scientists were far too busy to be bothered.

After breakfast, we all rose with the prime minister. My curiosity was far less satiated than my appetite. In reality, we hadn't learned any more about the pod than when we started. It seemed as though they were obscuring something, though I couldn't discern what. We would need an unescorted tour of the pod for answers. Maybe then we could find Dieter. Maybe even Kebe's friend, Ekon.

"Thank you for breakfast, Prime Minister," I said, feeling the courtesy as a necessity. "We appreciate your hospitality while we're here."

"You are most welcome, Citizen Ariadne. That sounds incredible, does it not?" said Zabu. "I, of course, would naturally encourage you to choose our pod. I intend to show you all of its fine merits over the coming months. If you still want to leave after I have done so, you will be free to do so—on our next Release Day."

CHAPTER 21: DIETER

I was fortunate that the Resistance movement against the prime minister was taking the brunt of the blame for the fuel rod theft. If Zabu traced the rod back to me, I would probably have been lying dismembered on the floor of his office as his henchmen hunted down Emile and his partner. I was living day to day with my intestines in a bowline knot from anxiety, making eating nigh impossible. Despite the meticulous care I'd taken in the cooling pool and the radiation lab, I was already showing signs of radiation poisoning. The exposure level was uncertain, but I needed to smuggle the bomb out before becoming incapacitated by the sickness' complications.

In a fortuitous turn of events, the rumor was spreading of some new arrivals with the regional transporters. I desperately hoped that it was the aid Memo promised. It had to be. If I had absorbed enough grays of radiation, I couldn't make it to the sea, much less the Hive, on my own. "And I always thought the food would do me in," I muttered. I pushed the plate of cold eggs and potatoes away from me, their pale uniformity making it impossible to tell which was which.

I needed to surreptitiously contact them. I held the best chance of catching the newly-minted citizens in their apartments in the evening, but time was of the essence. I desperately needed the arrivals to be the team I was hoping for. If it wasn't, well… I didn't want to dwell on that. I looked at the time through the cracked glass of my wristwatch. It was just after breakfast. If Zabu was following his usual tradition, he would wine and dine them, encouraging them to commit to staying before they saw the real Pod Kano. Sneaky bastard. If candidates knew what Kano was really like, they wouldn't even use this pod as a rest stop.

I left my apartment and made my way up to the upper levels. The citizens would be guarded, but maybe I could play it off as gleaning them for information regarding Horizonte's energy research. It was a weak excuse, but the guards weren't chosen for their intelligence. I arrived at the third level just in time to step off the elevator right into the midst of Zabu, his entourage, and the new arrivals. *Scheisse.*

"Technician Dieter. So good of you to join us," said Zabu.

In the blink of an eye, I saw a wave of suppressed excitement pass through the citizens. It was enough to provide me with a modicum of relief. I knew I'd found them.

"Dieter has been working on a… project for me," said the minister. "It promises to help change the world. I hope whatever brings him up here is more important than his work."

"My apologies, Prime Minister," I said, stumbling to think of a plausible reason. "It's just that Horizonte has been doing some fascinating work in the field of energy research. I was hoping that maybe our guests could share with me what they know. It may… err… help us with our project."

Zabu arched one eyebrow, cautiously mulling over my reasoning. "Good idea, Technician Dieter," said Zabu, turning to the citizens. "I have the pressing duties of administration. Take the next few days and reinvigorate yourselves. We will discuss job placements first thing next week so that you may contribute to our glorious society. Temporarily, of course."

Zabu turned on his heels, whispered something to one of the two remaining guards, and walked away back towards the Nucleus. I let out a sigh of relief. The Resistance could only take the blame so long if I continued acting suspiciously. I opened my mouth to greet the citizens.

"Release Day?! Are you freaking kidding me?!" said a fair-skinned female, her lightly curly hair pulled back into a tight ponytail.

"I know. Who does he think he is?!" said the more muscular of a pair sharing the same Bhopali ethnicity as Zabu's advisor, Chattar. He didn't continue his angry line of thought when he realized that the guards were still present.

"I thought we'd be able to—" a dark-haired male said, looking warily at the guards, "to *rest* and leave when we chose."

"I can't do another Release Day. I can't!" said a girl with Wuhanian features as sharp as the knives she undoubtedly carried in her currently empty sheaths.

"And what about Omar and Krista?" asked the fair-skinned one.

The smaller of the Bhopali pair looked pensive. He stood there looking at me, not contributing as the other four of them squabbled amongst themselves, forgetting I was there.

"Hey!" I said interrupting their squabble more forcefully than I had meant to. "Sorry. I've been a little on edge lately. It seems as though you have matters to discuss, so I won't keep you. Do you bring any *news* from Pod Horizonte?"

"I'm sorry," said the young man with dark hair, taking a deep breath. "We're all kind of in shock at a surprise the minister dropped on us. We've been here less than a day and things aren't going remotely as planned. I'm Huck."

"It's good to meet you, Huck."

"This is Hemant and Arjun. They're brothers. This is Ariadne, and Mei."

"A pleasure to meet you all," I said.

"To answer your question, yes. We came here to…" Huck began, glancing at the guards. "To *resupply* before heading further east."

"How far *east*?" I asked, determined to find out if these five people in front of me were the hope I had dreamt of for so long.

"Pretty far," said Arjun. "We are hoping to bring an end to this interminable war."

A massive grin crossed my face. Memo's reinforcements were here.

·········

I reluctantly left the group to rejoin Emile in the lab and inform him of our companions' arrival. I had so much to discuss with them, but it would have to be out from under the eavesdropping ears of the guards. Zabu wasn't an idiot. We would be fools to think otherwise. Flat-out secrecy seemed to be the best choice as opposed to fabricating fictitious reasons for meeting with the citizens. As the elevator's lights flicked from each grease-rimmed button to the next, I ran through potential contact methods. Messengers were out, they'd be interrogated. Hard lines were out, they'd be monitored. I needed to meet with them face to face, but how? When I entered the lab, Emile dropped the act of slaving over his workspace.

"How'd it go? Did you see them?

"I did."

"And…?"

"We couldn't talk freely, but it's them. They're here to help us!" I said.

"Thank the stars!" said Emile. "How do we proceed?"

"I have a plan, but you're not going to like it."

Emile sat stone-faced.

"We're going to need Zhen's help."

Emile's face reddened as he ranted in a hodgepodge of French and United and paced to and fro, an action I only observed when he was intensely upset.

"Pourquoi? Why would you risk her in this?" Emile asked, his accent made stronger by his anger.

"We have to communicate with them and we can't be seen doing it. She's a medic. She can operate under the guise she's seeing to their health. Think about it, Emile! She could guarantee us repeat visits."

Emile stroked his goatee, another nervous habit. Then he let out a breath of defeat.

"Okay. I will have her rearrange the staffing assignments so that she will be their attending medic. We will do this. We will put our lives at risk for the greater good."

"Thank you, Emile," I said as he slumped into his workstation, dismissing me and my thanks with a subtle wave.

•••••••••

That afternoon, Emile brought Zhen to the lab. Zhen was a beautiful, proud woman for her age. Emile often made jokes comparing her to a fine Cabernet, growing richer in body and flavor with each year that passed. In the meticulously clean room, for the first time, she appeared out of place. Her normally regulation appearance was disheveled and her makeup was running. The prospect of her involvement had shaken her considerably. Zabu made it no secret what happened to those committing seditious acts against the pod. Doing so would expose not only you to potential torture and death but your family and friends as well. Emile, still upset, comforted her by rubbing her shoulder.

"I wouldn't be asking this of you if there was another way, Zhen," I said. "I've known you as long as Emile has. The time has come to stand up to evil. The weapon is almost ready and Memo's couriers have arrived. If we don't do something, no one will."

Zhen nodded. "I know," she said, her voice cracking. "I want to do this for Rupert and everyone who's died under that bastard's reign."

"This is for all of humanity, Zhen. We could take out the inverts! Once and for all!"

"I don't care about the inverts," she said, placing her hand over Emile's on her shoulder. "I don't have the capability left to care about the devil out there when we face the devil in here. I'm doing this to return the suffering to Ndulue Zabu."

I nodded. "Good. Here's what you need to do."

CHAPTER 22: KRISTA

Huck dumped Omar and me out at the southern edge of the city. It was too late in the day to follow the convoy into the city with the dangers that emerged at dusk. We needed to find some semblance of shelter and set up camp in the few hours before nightfall.

We trekked up the road the convoy had traveled, easily tracking their route with the trails the vehicles had left in the dust. Provided it didn't blow away, it wouldn't be difficult to find the pod in the barren cityscape. Less than a kilometer into the city, we were surrounded by building-shaped mounds of rubble, edges rounded by the accumulated sand. As far as the eye could see were the ruins of civilization's past. Since the trucks had already passed out of hearing distance, an eerie silence left me unnerved as we made our way through the crumbling, lifeless city.

A short walk into the city, we stumbled upon a squatty octagonal building, its brick structure still intact after the centuries. Omar recognized the potential shelter as well.

"What do you think?" he asked. "It looks like its still got most of its roof."

"It's fine," I said, making a beeline towards the structure.

In reality, it was far better than anything we'd stayed in recently. I was in a really grouchy mood. Maybe it was because we'd been dropped off like rubbish. Maybe it was because we were sleeping on the ground while our friends slept in beds. Maybe it was because my stomach was growling like a cave grub. Or hell, maybe it was because I was coming down from a bloody drug high. What a hell of a day.

"Everything okay?" asked Omar, knowing for damn sure that it wasn't. "You and Ariadne seemed to have made up, right?"

"Yeah. It's not that. I'm pissed that we got the short end of the stick. I suppose that I should have gratitude and yada-yada for the safety and achievement of my companions, but right now, I'm here and they're there, so I have the right to wallow in self-pity."

Omar thought better about answering and left me alone. I set down my stuff in the central space of the building. The construction was solid, though it was hard to figure out the reason for the unusually shaped building's existence. It didn't matter. It was our place for the night. The cool evening wind whipped in through the openings, but at least there weren't any signs of Arthropods. For the moment.

"What do you want to do about dinner?" asked Omar.

"Do I look like your wife?" I asked. "Want me to go hunt and cook your supper?"

"What the hell, Krista? I was asking what are you thinking might be a good plan for dinner?"

"I'm sorry. I'm just… I'm on edge right now, okay?"

"I get it. It feels pretty crappy, being left out here," Omar said, examining the gaping holes in the roof where the weather had laid waste to the metal and wood. "It is what it is. I was really pissed when we first left Horizonte. I don't know that my father was ever serious about the appointment he promised me, but I often catch myself wondering what it would've been like. Then I remember the pod, and the world, are going to hell."

"Don't forget that your father is a narcissistic asshole," I added.

"That too. I'm just saying I think my place, our place, is here. Do I still hold a few grudges against the others? Sometimes. I'm allowed. Sometimes I think anger helps keep me going. Anger with Carvalho, the inverts, and them," Omar said, pointing with his dagger in the direction of the convoy.

"I guess. Anger keeps me going, but it clouds my judgment and distracts me. At the same time, letting it go feels like giving up. I suppress it during the day and let it breathe at night."

"Aren't we a bunch of shiny, happy people," Omar said, chortling.

We heard a rustle outside the walls and instantly fell silent. I listened closely for any sound so that I could determine the threat and location of the noise. I could hear Omar's breathing, and then a subtle rattling. I glanced at Omar, realizing he'd heard it too. We crept to the window and peered out. Just feet beyond the perimeter of the building was a dark gray animal with quills extending from its back.

"What is it?" I mouthed to Omar.

"Dinner," he said, pulling his dagger from his belt.

With a practiced flick of his wrist, the dagger nailed the animal through the throat, pinning it to the gnarled tree behind it. After listening to verify the coast was clear, we collected our prize.

"My question still stands."

"It's a porcupine," he said, picking it up gingerly. "Careful with the barbs. They're nasty if they get into your skin."

"And we can eat it?" I asked.

"Yup. They're supposed to taste pretty good, too," answered Omar.

"And how do you propose we prepare it?"

"I saw a pot in the hut thing. I can make a small fire and roast it without attracting too much attention. It's a pretty big animal for the two of us. We can salt what's left and carry it with us."

"I'm glad I have you out here with me. It seems like you paid more attention in class than I did."

Omar smirked.

"What?" I asked.

"You can fight, I'll give you that, but you don't know squat about surviving on your own, do you?"

"Not really. I knew I wasn't fully prepared. I skated along through the courses supported by Ariadne. We'd always figured we'd travel together and could count on each other."

"And how has that been going?"

I lowered my head. Until today, we'd both been pretty hostile to each other. Not exactly the dynamic duo of our dreams.

"Not well," I said.

"Nope," Omar agreed. "The only person you can count on out here is yourself. It sounds selfish, but it's reality. So from now on, our survival will depend on you."

"Wait. What?"

"Just what I said. You don't need to be depending on anyone but yourself. What would you do if you lost Ariadne? Or me? I'm going to teach you, but you're going to do everything."

"What if we starve?"

"Then you'll have my death on your conscience too," Omar said, grinning. "More incentive to keep us alive. I know this stuff, and you have to learn it. The porcupine will last us at least two days. You've got that long to find us our next meal."

After dinner, which was actually really good, we put our sleeping pads together and curled up next to each other for warmth while the meat cured overnight. I laid next to Omar with my head on his chest.

"Thank you for offering to teach me. You're right. I wouldn't survive more than a few days without help."

"We'll get you up to speed. You can't have forgotten everything you learned in class."

"You'd be surprised."

Omar kissed me gently on top of my head and through my arm, I felt a subtle throb from his waist, causing me to sit up and scoot away.

"So… Can I ask you a personal question?"

"Umm, I suppose."

"What happened to your girlfriend in Horizonte?" I asked.

Omar paused for a moment, staring out through the window at the twinkling stars that inundated the night sky.

"Celeste. She was killed on Release Day," said Omar, his eyes beginning to water. "I was so busy keeping an eye on Huck and his friends that I wasn't paying attention when a hook mauled her. When I realized what was happening, it was too late. The damned thing ripped her apart like tissue paper. In every moment of solace, I mourn her. I loved her."

"Omar," I said. "Why didn't you tell me this sooner?"

"Because I'm not like Huck, whining about every little feeling I have," Omar said, growing more defensive.

"I'm sorry you lost Celeste," I said.

"Thanks," he said, wiping his nose on his dirty sleeve. "It means more coming from you than it would anyone else, after Zeke."

"Mmmhmm," I muttered, feeling a little guilty at the mention of Zeke after the close contact with Omar. Our perceived isolation from the others initially had caused an alliance of necessity. But lately, that alliance had transitioned into a friendship. A chilly wind blew through the place reminding me of the cold, and I rejoined Omar.

"Just for warmth, okay?" I said.

"Just for warmth," he said.

CHAPTER 23: HUCK

I wasn't sure what I had been expecting when I met Dieter, but the man who stepped off the elevator wasn't it. Years younger than I expected, his hair was thinning and grungy. He sported circular glasses like Chattar's, but with a lens diameter not much larger than his eyes. The stereotypical lab coat looked baggy on his thin frame. He looked disconcertingly gaunt, the bags under his eyes adding notable age to his face. Regardless of his health, he was key to our success.

Our excitement for crossing paths with him had been tamped down by Zabu's surprise announcement that we would be held until Release Day. I wasn't sure what crap he was trying to pull. In what universe was it fair to make us, now citizens, endure that horrendous bloodsport again?! Screw that! We would be leaving with the weapon long before then. We just needed to figure out how to do it without getting caught. This city might be similar in layout to Horizonte, but functionally, it was an entirely different world.

Carvalho had been better at masking his corruption—at least to the general populace. Once we uncovered his atrocities, it was clear.

Zabu was less discrete, running the pod with an overt authoritarian approach. And where were the regents? I had been under the impression that all pods had the same hierarchy, but Zabu clearly wasn't tolerant of other people's opinions.

"Where do you think they are taking us?" I asked Hemant as the guards led us down the hall away from where we first encountered Dieter.

"I'm not sure," he said. "If this place has the same layout as Horizonte, it would be to the medical district."

"Maybe it's for the tattoos," said Ariadne.

I nodded. It seemed like as good a guess as any. We were still in the upper levels, but we were starting to see the myriad differences from the pod of our birth. Everyone walked around unsmiling, weighed down by invisible burdens. Whenever they noticed our escort, their eyes fell to the floor as their pace increased, always giving us a wide berth. The heat in the pod was stifling, and with the trace accumulation of sand in every corner, it felt as though we hadn't left the desert at all.

We rounded a bend and came face to face with a haggard man sitting cross-legged on a rough-spun blanket, pleading for ration points. Instantly, one of our guards was on top of the man, dragging him up to his feet as the other guards blatantly attempted to divert our attention. Ignoring their distraction, we watched as the attacking guard plunged the butt of his rifle into the man's ribs over and over until the man collapsed on his face, spitting blood on the stained concrete.

"What have we told you about begging?!" the guard yelled, landing a swift kick in the man's ribs. "You either work, or you walk! The next time I see you, it better be with a tool in your hand!"

The guard gave him a final kick for good measure, then looked at us, having forgotten all about our presence.

"Sorry you had to see that miserable wretch," he said. "The prime minister has no tolerance for weakness. If you see any beggars, you are welcome to do the same."

Ariadne's eyes were filled with concern for the fallen man. It must have taken everything in her to leave the gravely injured man at the prodding of our escort. When I saw her face again, she was doing her best to conceal her tears. What had we gotten ourselves into?

We arrived at the medical district, as Hemant predicted. Entering through the hatch, I was pleasantly surprised by the cleanliness of the space compared to the dingy corridors only a door away. An amiable older woman with a thick head full of curls and deeply understanding eyes came out from behind a desk and introduced herself.

"I am Medic Zhen. It's a pleasure to make your acquaintance."

Looking at our escort, she cleared her throat and gestured towards the door with her pupils. Taking the hint, they evacuated the space, leaving us alone with the doctor. Once the hatch had sealed behind them, she continued.

"Officially, I'm here to check your overall physical condition and complete your tattoos," said Doctor Zhen.

"And unofficially?" asked Mei.

"I'm a go-between of sorts for Dieter. He works in my partner Emile's lab."

I looked at the other excitedly.

"That's great!" I said.

"Great only if we aren't caught," she said in a matter-of-fact tone. "Zabu's not one to tolerate indiscretions against him. I'll be doing some follow-up visits, but after that, you guys are on your own."

"Understood. What do you need?" I said.

"First, to examine you," she said. "Open or closed?"

"I'm sorry. What?"

"The curtain. Open or closed?"

"Umm… How intensive is this exam?"

"Relax. Just to your skivvies."

"Open is fine. We've seen most of each other anyway." I said.

"Some of us more than others," added Ariadne.

I was worried she was still taking my accidental reveal of her to the Misfits personally, but I heard her snicker as the doctor lifted my arm, palpating my ribs.

"Dieter wants to confirm you are who he thinks you are. Why are you here?" she asked, continuing her check.

I looked back at Arjun, who nodded approvingly. "We were sent here by Memo— err, Grand Major Leal, to pick up a device from Dieter and carry it to the Hive."

"That's what I wanted to hear. Dieter wasn't sure what all to expect from Memo, but I think that's exactly what he was hoping for. Now, aside from your bruised jaw, you're good to go. You next," she said, motioning to Ariadne. "The Hive, huh?"

"Yes ma'am," Ariadne said.

"That's quite the trip. And no need for ma'am here. Zhen, please," she said, looking closely at Ariadne's hand. "This was good fieldwork, whoever did this.

I saw the look of sadness pass over Ariadne's face as she thought of Kurt. Zhen inspected Arjun and Mei, who each received a clean bill of health, but had some concerns for Hemant's knee, which hadn't healed as well as she would've liked.

With the exams out of the way, she completed our tattoos which gave us ample time to chat, encircling the letters "HZ" on each of our arms with the gear-like symbol representing the pods.

"Well, Dieter has the device you are looking for, but it's not ready just yet," she continued, wiping the excess ink from Mei's forearm. "He says maybe a few more days."

"Well, we can't leave in a hurry. Zabu's planning to hold us until Release Day," said Ariadne.

"What a bastard," she said. Then leaning over closer and smiling, "We'll see about that."

•••••••••

That evening, I lay in my bed unable to dispel the distraction of our predicament. I was thrilled we had connected with Dieter and Zhen, but I couldn't shake the feeling that our duration within the pod could prove just as perilous as the surface. If we continued our mission, we would be stealing and escaping from a tyrannical dictator. *If* we managed to accomplish it without any harm coming to us, we would be leaving an enraged foe in our wake, not to mention the risk of potential collateral damage. I finally drifted off to a nightmare-plagued sleep.

Bam! Bam! Bam!

What was it with the banging? Was it too much to ask for a gentle morning knock? Or maybe have some hot caffeinated beverages waiting for us? Probably. I heard Arjun answer through my bedroom door.

"Yes," he said.

"There will be a gathering in the central forum," I heard the muffled voice say as I slid my door open. "Your attendance is requested. We will escort you down in a half-hour."

"Why do I get the feeling requested means required?" asked Hemant, still groggy from his lack of morning stimulant after the door slid back into place.

"Probably because it does," I said. "Arjun, you want to get some hot water going?"

"Sure."

I returned to my room to get dressed, resisting the urge to climb back into bed for the next twenty-nine minutes. When I returned to the kitchen, Arjun had made tea for himself and coffee for Hemant and me. While I wasn't quite the addict Hemant was, I appreciate the robust flavor of coffee to the subtle notes of tea.

"Thanks, Arjun," I said with Hemant grunting his agreement.

Arjun nodded, sipping his scalding tea through the steam escaping the cup.

At some point, our kitchen had been stocked with food, all similar fare to what we'd find in Horizonte. Despite holding us against our will, Zabu supplied us with food of the highest quality available. He still naively hoped that by threatening us with Release Day and showering us with gifts, he'd force us into staying.

Arjun prepared eggs and potatoes for breakfast, topping them with onions and even infinitesimal specks of bacon. After our time on the surface, the simple act of turning a knob to produce a gas flame and cooking without fear of attack was cause for gratitude.

"This is amazing," Hemant said with his mouth full.

"It is pretty awesome, Arjun," I said. "I could get used to living here if it wasn't for the nut job up top."

"I agree," said Arjun. "I don't trust him one iota."

Bam! Bam! Bam!

"We're coming," Hemant and I said in unison.

We rinsed our plates and threw them in the sink before ducking through the hatch. In the corridor, Ariadne and Mei were already waiting for us.

"If you please," said one of the guards, gesturing the way.

I led the way to the central forum for whatever gathering Zabu had planned. We could hear the murmuring of the multitude long before we reached the catwalks to cross to the space. When I walked in, I felt a wave of false familiarity. The vast room looked almost identical to the one in Horizonte, down to the walls' mossy plant growth and inescapable musty odor. The last time I had stood in a central forum was just before our Release Day, a memory flaring my already high anxiety.

All around me were upset bystanders who quieted as our armed escort led us through to the front of the scarred-up main platform, not pristine like the well-maintained one of Horizonte. This one had seen more action. What type of action, I avoided pondering. The crowd of a few hundred stood silent, save for a handful of whispers passed around just beyond the ears of the guards.

On the platform, a panel slid aside as ten guards marched just as many people out in chains, poking and prodding them with bayonets as they clanked along the stage. As they passed in front of me, I saw where the shackles rubbed their skin. Several legs were scarred with open wounds and broken blisters, weeping blood onto the stage as they made their way across. Their clothes looked worse for the wear than those of the beggar. Once the prisoners were lined up and the guards positioned behind them, Zabu marched out triumphantly, stopping next to a small table.

"Welcome, vested citizens of Pod Kano, to another Gathering," he began. "This morning, before we begin the sentencing, I would like to introduce you to our newest arrivals."

"Come, come," he said to us, leaning over the stage.

We ascended the stairs to the platform's side and crossed over to the prime minister.

"These are our new citizens. They come to us from Pod Horizonte in the Latin Territory. They crossed an ocean to join our prestigious ranks. Please, give them a round of applause."

There was forced scattered applause. Again, Zabu was promoting the idea that we were staying. He obviously was used to getting his way. After our introductions, we were ushered back down to the floor to watch the Gathering's proceedings.

"The residents you see before you are convicted criminals. I have found them all guilty of violating The Code from supplied evidence and testimony."

I looked at Hemant in my periphery as he returned the look. *Who does this guy think he is?*

"Four are guilty of aiding the Resistance. Three are guilty of being active members of the Resistance. Two are guilty of stealing. And the last… we will get to the last. First, those guilty of aiding the Resistance will be participants in the coming Release Day."

There was a murmur in the crowd and a lone wail. Zabu flicked his eyes out over the crowd, causing everyone to freeze and silence to descend. The four people that aided the Resistance lowered their heads. Resistance against Zabu seemed like a good thing.

"Second, the members of the Resistance, your punishment is death," said Zabu.

Again, I heard crying members of the crowd, but Zabu was too focused to notice. He withdrew an ornate dagger from a canvas wrap from the table, raising it up in an offering to some unknown deity. *Oh, he means now!* Without pomp or hesitation, he approached the first member. Grabbing him by a clump of his curly hair, he lifted the man's head and slit his throat, spilling his blood down the man's body allowing it to puddle on the stage.

"No! No!" the woman next to him pleaded, as he did the same. Her last words emerged as a gurgle.

The next two were dispatched as quickly as the first with methodical proficiency. This was not a man I wanted to anger, yet here we were about to do just that. Would it be my blood on that stage next? I looked at Hemant, who was forcing back tears of anger. Mei just stood there, mouth agape. The two accused of stealing each had a hand removed by the same dagger. Lastly, he came to the remaining man.

"This man defies not only me but sins against nature," he said. "He will bear great pain and great affliction."

I watched as the man was turned away from the audience and stripped of his clothes. Next to me, another man pushed between Hemant and me to the edge of the platform. His face was twisted in horror with tears streaming down his face. He looked ready to jump on the stage and intervene. On the platform, a guard brought Zabu a multi-tailed studded whip.

"It is said that this man is guilty of lying with another man," said Zabu. "He is a disgrace to his humankind."

Zabu reared back with the whip and made the first strike. The man buckled screaming as the rents in his flesh began to seep, but he was lifted again by the indifferent guards. The man standing at the edge of the stage started to climb, but Hemant subtly retained him.

"Let me go! I have to help him!" he pleaded in a whisper.

"He'll do the same to you," Hemant responded.

Recognizing him for who he was, Arjun walked up to the man's side and held his hand. With new resolve, the man looked on, watching his beloved take blow after blow. Finally, Zabu turned and faced the crowd, and I saw both men relax.

"Now for his affliction," said Zabu, taking his knife and slicing at the man's groin.

The man screamed in agony as Zabu held a bundle of the man's flesh high in the air, blood draining down his arm. It took all of Hemant's strength to hold the heartbroken man back.

CHAPTER 24: HEMANT

As we filed out from the appalling display of the Gathering, none of us could bear to look at each other. The shame shrouded me with a clingy disgust that no amount of bathing would remove. Zabu was a disgrace to humankind. I filed into the elevator amongst the others, surprised that the guards had selected one of the mid-levels of the pod. My stomach dropped with the plunge of the elevator to its unknown destination. The level was far more populated than the one we'd left above. Waiting for us was Zabu's advisor, Chattar, his unreadable face giving us no hints as to why we were there.

"Welcome, citizens," he said. "I took the liberty of finding you some more appropriate long-term lodgings for the duration of your stay. If you'll follow me…."

"What was wrong with the lodgings we had?" Mei asked.

We followed Chattar around the railings looking out over the central shaft, filing past each of the floor's various districts on our left. Chattar was perfectly manicured, his hair slicked down and his high-collared, coffee-colored suit neatly pressed. We arrived at the level's housing district. Holding a handkerchief over his face, Chattar led us down a narrow corridor similar to the cohabitation levels many of the couples had in Horizonte, but far less opulent than our previous lodgings. We stopped at the entrance to a stale, dimly lit common room at the dead-end of passage, the once red paint making the space resemble a body cavity rather than a place of respite. The room held a number of circular booths around its perimeter with a gigantic, elevated cushion in the middle, ripped and patched from many cycles of use and repair. The hatches lining each side of the corridor were patinated with a layer of oxidation and filth.

"These two rooms will be your permanent homes," said Chattar, dropping his improvised filter. "I apologize for their lack of comfort, but times are hard. We must all make sacrifices. Each apartment is laid out for two people. This common room is yours to use as you see fit. Aside from the occasional squatter, this corridor is uninhabited."

"What happened to the other residents?" I asked. "I thought over-population was a big problem in all of the pods."

"Very astute, Hemant. Perhaps I misjudged you," said Chattar. "Our demand on resources is a problem, but space isn't a noteworthy issue here."

"If space isn't the problem, why couldn't we stay where we were," asked Mei.

"My dear," Chattar said, looking annoyed. "The prime minister needs those apartments to reward those most deserving of it. You all were rewarded for your survival, but now you must earn the right to be so honored again. Now, if that's all the questions, I have your work assignments."

"Work assignments?" asked Mei.

"My, aren't you a precocious one," said Chattar, pulling out a list. "You weren't expecting to rest on your laurels, were you? This is a functioning city and workers are a necessity. Refusal to follow The Code is dealt with most severely, as you no doubt observed. Your work assignments are as follows: Huck, we have no need of your recycling abilities here. You will report to the Dust processing plant on level 91 where your specific duties will be assigned."

"What?!" asked Huck.

"Dust. Processing," said Chattar, over-enunciating. "I have other matters to attend to and don't have time for your impertinence. Now, please remain quiet until I have read your assignments. Ariadne, your strengths in comestibles would be a welcome addition, we would like you to present yourself at the horticulture district on Level 80. It is our experimental district. Mei, you will accompany Ariadne to the test farm. We appreciate your specialized battle training, but traditionally we only allow males into our armed forces."

Mei didn't have any desire to be part of Pod Kano's armed forces, but the discrimination left her notably pissed.

"Arjun, your intelligence is obvious. You will report to our non-lethal weaponry lab on Level 35. And lastly, Hemant, we could use your brawn in the Muskrats, our prestigious security force. You may rendezvous with them on Level 65. All of you need to be at your assigned posts at 0600 in the morning. Being tardy will result in punitive measures. Here are enough ration points to get you through the next few days. I wish you luck in your future endeavors."

With that, Chattar was off.

"I get the feeling Zabu is no longer trying to impress us," said Arjun.

"Anyone else think he has no intention of letting us leave?" Huck asked.

"All the more reason to get what we came for and get the hell out of here," I said.

"Let's go see what the apartments look like," said Ariadne. "Anyone opposed to Huck getting the solo room?"

No one said anything, so that was that. It made sense. I wondered if it would be weird for him to be alone for the first time, well, basically ever. Back in Horizonte, everyone had a dorm mate from the moment they left the matriarchs' care and transitioned to independent living. Thinking about his isolation made me miss Zeke. In the few weeks we had known each other, he had been an excellent companion and generous to a fault—even when it meant death. When all this crap was over, I wanted him to have a permanent memorial, even if that meant building it myself.

Arjun and I claimed the first door on the left leaving the common room. Ariadne and Mei took the first on the right. Huck took the next door on our side. Figuring they were all the same, we stepped into the girls' dark room. The first thing we noticed was the odor. After weeks of living on the surface, we instantly recognized the smell of death.

"*Gah,* what is that?" asked Mei with her nose pinched shut.

"I'm afraid to turn on the lights," said Huck. "I don't know what we'll see."

As it was, the dim light from the hallway barely illuminated a few meters into the room. I felt for the panel controlling the lights and depressed the switch. The lights blinked for a few moments before glowing normally. The room was about as nasty inside as it was outside and was similar to the layout of the posh apartment in the upper levels, but far more compact in design. The origin of the smell must have been the bloody spray pattern left on the far wall of the main space.

"So how many of the hallway's residents do you think left of their own volition?" asked Mei.

"I don't want to know," I said, feeling the irritation begin to ignite under my cheeks.

"Let's make the best of this. Hopefully, we won't be here long anyway," said Huck. "I'll get cleaning supplies and we'll get both rooms habitable. Then we can grab something to eat."

It turned out that the gruesome stain was a fair representation of the condition of both apartments. By the time we had finished, there wasn't a shower long enough to make us feel clean.

●●●●●●●●●

I choked down a handful of macadamia nuts and two overripe nectarines before bustling out of the apartment. After the night's cleaning work, the fatigue had caused all of us to oversleep, leaving us only minutes to arrive at our work details. As we emerged, Huck was slamming his hatch shut, waving as he ran off to work. Out in the corridor, we bumped into the girls.

"It's good to know it's not just us," I said, zipping my jumpsuit the rest of the way up.

"Nope!" said Ariadne. "I haven't felt this rushed since the Misfits, but at least then, there was coffee."

"Don't remind me," I said, starting down the hall. "At least you probably won't be doing PT."

"Shoveling dirt is plenty tiring, trust me," said Ariadne.

"You never said we'd be shoveling dirt," said Mei.

"Honestly, I have no idea what we'll be doing," said Ariadne. "For all we know, we'll be slave labor giving the minister's nature."

"God, I hope not," said Mei.

"The neem, Hemant!" said Arjun. "I forgot it!"

"You're going to make us late, Arjun. You don't know if you'll meet Dieter today anyway."

"I'm getting it regardless."

"We need to get going," said Ariadne. "See you this evening."

Ariadne and Mei took off down the hall, leaving me standing in the dank corridor waiting for Arjun to hide a tree branch in his jumpsuit. The odd duties of brotherhood. We stayed together until we arrived at the elevator and had to split up.

"If you talk to Dieter, ask him to develop a mask that can protect us from those damn dusters," I said.

"I will," Arjun said, nodding.

I gripped Arjun's forearm and he clasped mine in return. "Stay safe. Keep your head low. We can't afford any attention."

"I will, brother," he said as he stepped onto the up-bound elevator.

I rode the elevator down to Level 65 as I had been instructed. When I arrived, the scene that greeted me was unexpected. Dedicated to the guards, the floor was a hive of uniformed men. There were men everywhere, but instead of rigorous training and organized operations it was like walking into a level-sized seedy bar with thousands of patrons. Directly off the elevator was a group laughing, seated around a metal table on food drums and tossing dice around a heap of ration points and shiny baubles. Walking between the tables were scantily dressed women, revealing their wares to the inebriated troops enjoying far too much R&R.

Someone pushed me from behind, "Gawk somewhere else."

It was probably already past 0600 and I still had no idea how to find the Muskrats. I walked to a solitary guard, leaning against a wall. Smoke from his cigar plumed out of his nostrils.

"Excuse me," I said, feeling unnecessarily polite. "I'm looking for the Muskrats."

Filling the air between us with the noxious odor of stale tobacco, he pointed to the next corridor over. The opening was flanked by two guards, each occupied by women caressing and teasing them. I nodded my thanks to Smokey and headed toward the pair.

"What do you want?" asked a guard as a woman chewed playfully on his ear.

"I've been assigned to the Muskrats," I said.

"By who?"

"By Chattar."

The guard gave a forced laugh. "Chattar is an old fool. No one is *assigned* to the Muskrats. The Muskrats anoint members into their ranks—*if* they are worthy. Are *you* worthy?"

I didn't know how to answer that. I knew nothing of the group's reputation or assignments. I had minimal exposure to gambling and despite my single romantic experience being with a complete stranger, it still wasn't the same as a prostitute. *What I wouldn't give to be back in that idyllic village again.*

"Are you deaf?" the guard asked again, changing to a more offensive posture and shoving the woman aside.

"I have what it takes," I said.

It was true. I was in great shape and I was an experienced warrior. Though I wasn't sure what I'd be tasked with doing, I was pretty sure I could handle it. The guard seemed satisfied enough with my answer and directed me back.

"Talk to Saif," he said, pointing to the far end of the corridor at what had been a cooking establishment in decades past. I walked down the hall, ignoring the questionable activities playing out on either side of me. When I reached the dining area, I scanned the room. Off to the side, a band played smooth jazz, filling me with nostalgia for Professor Graça's record that she played occasionally during class. Seated in the far corner was a pile of a man, looking as though he'd been poured into the booth more than sitting in it, the rolls of his face broken up only by a pencil-thin mustache. His formal military dress was striped in appearance from the additions of fabric to accommodate his copious girth. Making eye contact with me, he motioned me over with a subtle two-finger movement.

"You wish to join the Muskrats," the man asked in a barely audible voice.

It was more of a statement than a question. The bald uniformed man to his right stood and began to assess my muscle mass with hard random pinches around my body. I looked at the fat man, feeling far over my head, and wondering what had caused my life to end up here.

"You have potential," he said. "Are you of sound mind?"

I nodded. *Although someone of sound mind would run from here screaming.*

"I'm Commandant Saif," the larger man said as I strained to hear over the din. "The man next to you is Captain Abbas."

"What is your weapon?" Abbas asked.

"I use a war hammer, Captain," I said.

"A war hammer is not suited for close-quarters combat," said Abbas. "Can you handle a one-handed mace?"

"Yes, Captain. I had training with fixed and chained maces in Pod Horizonte," I said.

"It's settled then," whispered Saif. "You will accompany Captain Abbas on his next mission to further quell the Resistance against Prime Minister Zabu. It is then we will see if you have the capabilities of a Muskrat."

CHAPTER 25: ARIADNE

Mei and I stood alone in the elevator taking us down to Level 80. As the cab dropped, I feared what our tasks would entail. Would my supervisor be like my previous mentor, Greenskeeper Chun, or would they be more akin to Yanus? I tried not to allow anxiety's iron grip to take hold. I took a deep breath to settle my nerves.

"I kept feeling like the pod was missing something," said Mei. "I think I just figured out what it is. There aren't any old people."

"I've been too busy stressing about other things, but now that you point it out, you're right. Come to think about it, aside from the beggar we saw the other day, I haven't seen any unabled."

"Or failed ones! What do you think happened to them all?"

"I'm afraid to ask. We've already seen how Zabu deals with infractions."

"Do you think he kills them?"

I didn't respond. Every second we were in Kano was another second keeping us from our true goal of ending the war.

"We have to get out of here," I said.

"How are we going to do that with these stupid work details?" asked Mei.

"Every spare second you have, look for things that could help us. Just don't put us at risk. I don't want any of us to be publicly punished, but let's see if we can smuggle out some food. Anything small. Stuff that's durable and has a long shelf life."

"I'll do what I can."

We stepped out onto the receiving area of Level 80. Hints of earth wafted on the air currents, flooding me with nostalgia for my time apprenticing in Horizonte. So much had changed since then. I had changed so much. The smell varied from that of the surface, which was fresher, cleaner. This was the metallic smell of stale dirt intertwined with the decay of compost. We followed our noses through the bustle of occupants, making our way to the section of the floor allocated to horticulture. A large balding man stopped us at the gates, his undersized moth-eaten vest barely covering the filth on his undershirt.

"You are strangers," he said. "You can't come in."

"Oh, do let them in Cesar," a stern, middle-aged woman said. "They don't look like hooligans."

"Thank you," I said.

"Don't mind Cesar," she said. "He is as strong as a hook beetle but has a simple mind. Zabu lets him stay because his strength is immensely helpful to me in the farms."

"I'm sorry, Zabu lets him stay?" asked Mei.

"Ah, yes. You're definitely the new arrivals I've heard about. Chattar said he'd be sending someone down. I'm Greenskeeper Miranda. I'm sorry to disappoint you…"

"Mei."

"Ariadne."

"I'm sorry to disappoint you, Mei and Ariadne, but Zabu is not a kind man," said Miranda. "Anyone who can't cope with the daily demands of life in Kano is released at the first available opportunity."

I looked at Mei. That explained a lot.

"But how is that right?" I asked.

"Zabu's sense of morality varies from that of most people. The years have taught us long-termers to avoid causing a stir. Keeping your head low and doing your work is the only way to remain in the pod."

"How do you live like that?" asked Mei.

"We all have ways of coping, right Cesar?" she said with a sly grin.

"Right," Cesar said, pulling a bulbous finger from his ear.

"Speaking of which, nothing's going to get done with us idly chatting. I assume you were sent to me because you have strong plant skills and green thumbs, is that correct?"

"She does," said Mei. "I was just assigned with her, but I'd like to help."

"That's alright dear, we could always use extra hands and willing minds. It's hard but rewarding work. The problems of the world vanish when your fingers are in the earth. The only bugs you'll find here are the ones Earth has always possessed. Without them, we would cease to exist. Puts things into perspective, doesn't it?"

I liked this woman already. Judging by Mei's smile, she did too. Miranda led us back to rows and rows of raised beds, illuminated by wide-spectrum lights suspended from the high ceilings. We stopped at her workbench, an old wooden surface marred by decades, if not centuries of use. Scattered across its top were myriad gardening tools, most of which I recognized and a few I didn't.

"Surprised?" Miranda asked Mei. "All of our research and development can be done with the simplest tools. You'll find no fancy gizmos here, and that's the way I like it. It forces us to be more creative. The majority of our experimentation is done by varying compost, growth media, cross-pollination, and hybridization. The exponential possibilities through those alone are more than I can accomplish during what's left of my lifetime."

"What can we do to help?" I asked.

"Today, we are splicing the hazelnuts. We've found that one varietal is far more productive from the same amount of nutrients when grafted onto the rootstock of another. I'll have Liesel demonstrate the process and get you started. We have beaucoups to do, so we best get busy. Cesar will follow behind you with the fresh compost mix."

"And how do we apply compost, Cesar?" she asked the gentle giant as a girl roughly our age joined us.

"Gently," he said, mimicking a gentle spreading with his hands.

"That's my good boy. Mei, Ariadne, this is Liesel," she said, turning towards the girl. "They will be joining our farm. Now, you all run along. I'll be attempting some new strains at my workbench. Just yell if you need me."

I looked at Liesel. Her face and hands were covered in dirt, as was her gardening apron. A twig stuck out from the long hair hanging over one of her shoulders. Even beneath the layer of grime, I could see that she was gorgeous.

"It's good to meet you. It'd be nice to have someone my age down here. I don't get to hang out with girls much, just Cesar and Miranda. They're wonderful people, but sometimes I just want to talk about something other than plants."

"What about your training cohort?" I asked. "Don't you talk with them?"

"My training cohort?" Liesel laughed. "You guys really are from another pod. Zabu nixed the cohort program before I was born. Only select males are combat-trained now, and then only for Zabu's militia, not for anything top side. The rest of us apprentice in the pod's various districts based on demonstrated aptitudes. You heard what happens to the rest."

"Sadly, yes. So you've never left the pod?"

"Nope. Not me nor Cesar. Miranda came from Pod Munich, up north, before things got really bad here. She remembers what it used to be like."

The differences between Kano and Horizonte were immense, even down to the levels of corruption. Had all the pods strayed so far from their original intent? It's not as though there was any global government maintaining them. Any remnants of the UTE were scattered once everyone outside of the pods was killed. The pods were left at the mercy of their leadership. It was assumed they would follow protocols, but in front of me was evidence to the contrary. Liesel guided us back to two long beds of hazelnuts, each of the hundreds of green sprigs only centimeters tall.

"These are the hazelnut beds. We're basically taking all of the tops, or scions, from the bed on the left and applying them to the rootstock on the right."

"How do we do that?" asked Mei.

"We make a matching angled cut with a razor on each plant. Then we apply the scion to the rootstock, matching the stems. Last, we wrap it with some plant-based tape that falls off once the graph takes hold," said Liesel. "Relax, I'll show you."

Liesel demonstrated the process with ease. I had practiced it a few times during my internship, but not enough to be an expert. By the time all these plants were finished, Mei and I both would be.

"Let's get busy," said Liesel. "This is going to take a while,"

Hours later when we sat down for lunch, my back was sore, my hands were cramping, and my fingers were covered in micro-cuts. Miranda prepared a vegetarian lunch of fresh garden vegetables, fruit, and nuts accompanied by fresh-baked bread and a fizzy drink she made herself called kombucha. The produce, while fresh, still couldn't match the quality of the surface, but I appreciated it nonetheless.

"How do you get fresh-baked bread down here?" asked Mei.

"That one is easy. All the produce is supposed to go to the top to be divvied up level by level, but there's always some side-bartering. I trade a basket of fresh produce and an alluring wink to the baker a few corridors over and he keeps us stocked in bread."

"You shouldn't lead him on like that, ma'am," said Liesel.

"Who said I only lead him on?" said Miranda with a demure smile.

"*Agh,*" said Liesel, laughing and clasping her hands over her mouth.

Mei and I both cracked up. Cesar chuckled, unsure of what we found so funny.

After lunch, we returned to the tedious work. But now, soreness flooded my hands, making the delicate work all the more difficult. Making matters worse, the plethora of tiny cuts on my hands stung with every twitch of my fingers.

"How long does it take your hands to get used to this," I asked Liesel.

"A few weeks," she answered. "You'll have calluses, muscular hands, and won't even feel the occasional nick. You'll never get the dirt stains out of your fingernails and your hands will always be useless in the evenings."

"A warm salt-water soak is the answer to many ills," said Miranda, walking by to check the progress. "Great job, all. Especially you, Cesar!"

"Good job, Cesar," I said as Mei echoed.

Cesar bared his unkempt yellow teeth in a big grin. The lumbering giant had hauled heavy burlap bag after bag of compost all day without complaint.

Once the greenskeeper was out of earshot, I spoke to Mei. "I can't imagine living here with my head in the sand my whole life. If we weren't leaving, I'd have to do something."

"You guys aren't staying?" asked Liesel.

"We weren't planning to," I said. "We were just going to stop here before we continued on to… another pod. Zabu won't let us leave."

"That's how he is," she said. "People are just cogs in his machine. If a cog isn't doing its job, it's replaced and the old one, discarded. When you walked in, all he saw were new cogs."

"Surely not everyone just rolls over for him," said Mei.

"That's where the Resistance comes in," whispered Liesel, after verifying no one was listening.

"Zabu forced us to watch the public execution and sentencing of several members of the Resistance," I said. "It was terrible."

"I know," said Liesel, tearing up. "We lost three good people that day."

"Wait, you said 'we,'" said Mei.

A look of terror crossed over Liesel's eyes.

"Oh, God! Please don't say anything. I beg you! I beg you! He'll torture and kill us!"

"It's okay. It's okay," I said, trying to calm her down.

I wrapped my arm around her as she sobbed.

"I'm the worst at keeping secrets," she said. "Thank you."

"It's okay. We're kind of a resistance ourselves," I said.

"Really?" Liesel said, sitting up and looking at me.

I looked at Mei, who nodded in consent.

"We were secretly sent by a regent from our pod to infiltrate the Hive," I said. "We stopped here to pick up a device. We're not much, but we're hoping that's just the tactic this war needs."

"Just you two?" she asked.

"No, we came in with three others," I said. "And there are two more waiting outside."

"If that's the case, I want to do everything I can to help you," Liesel said, the glimmer of optimism returning to her eyes. "I need to run it by the leadership, but I'd like you to join the Resistance."

CHAPTER 26: DIETER

Zhen had come through better than I could've hoped. After examining Memo's reinforcements, she made her way down to the lab to share everything she'd learned. A wave of relief washed over me, knowing that the radiation sickness was progressing faster than I'd predicted. Despite the efforts to protect ourselves, both Emile and I were suffering its ill effects. My head hadn't been full of hair to begin with, but every morning, I would wake to find more of it left on my pillow. It was only a matter of time before more serious symptoms started to rear their head.

I didn't fear death. Not that I was in a hurry to reach it, but I had come to terms with the concept long ago. I was hoping to die of old age in my sleep, but given the turmoil in Kano, I would settle for something quick. The lingering demise of radiation poisoning wasn't what I had in mind. The real kicker was Emile. My choices had impacted him in a way I didn't foresee. While his exposure had been less than mine, he was also experiencing hair loss. I hoped Zhen would be able to forgive me.

It was just like Zabu to make the new citizens stay until Release Day. He was such a prick. Luring citizens in with the promise of a good life, then pulling the rug out from under them the moment they had committed to staying. Though in Huck's case, no commitment had been made. It was tantamount to imprisonment. I looked over at the pipe containing the bomb. I hoped this crazy idea would work out.

After hearing a knock, I checked through the viewport before opening the door for Zhen and Emile. Zhen's eyes were red, and Emile looked pale. I helped him to his seat. I wasn't sure why, but he seemed worse for the wear than I was.

"Well," said Zhen, sniffling. "We're whole-heartedly committed to this, aren't we?"

I let out a nervous laugh. "That we are."

"Then let us do it right," said Emile. "What do we need to do next?"

"I was just thinking about that," I said. "The radioactive material is sufficiently concentrated. The centrifuges finished last night. We need to seal it into the bomb. Once we do, there's no turning back. It cannot fall into Zabu's hands. We'll have to sneak Huck and the others out with the bomb, supplies, and a vehicle if they are to have any chance of crossing the distance that lay ahead of them."

"What do you suggest?" said Zhen.

"The transporters are still here, are they not?" I said.

"They are," said Emile through a cough.

"If memory serves, their leader, Yanus, rides in a customized vehicle. There are rumors that due to his paranoia, it's fully equipped for long-term solo survival. His fear will be our gain. I propose we hide the bomb on his carrier. The vehicle should already be stocked with fuel and provisions. If we could help Huck and his friends escape in that…"

"There will be many hurdles," said Emile. "The vehicles are heavily guarded for exactly this reason. And where would we hide a package of this size on his carrier?"

"What about the gas cylinder?" asked Zhen.

"It would cut their fuel in half. Not to mention, altering the cylinder would be time-consuming and make a substantial amount of noise," said Emile. "The idea has merit."

"I can make it work," I said. "For added measure, I can disable the other vehicles so they can't immediately follow."

"What about the gates?" asked Emile.

"What about them?" I asked.

"They have dual controls. Both guarded, again for reasons like this."

"We'll have to find a way to take out the guards," I said. "Then you and I can each flip the switches. Maybe even temporarily disable the panels too."

"Dieter. Have you looked at yourself? At Emile?" asked Zhen. "Neither of you are in any condition to climb the ladders to the control towers, much less fight."

"We have to find a way!" I said. "We've risked too much to stop now. We can bring Huck and the others into the plan. We will have to stay behind to man the switches, but they can handle the guards. They are young, and have proven themselves in battle."

"Against Arthropods, Dieter, not humans. Violence against one isn't the same as the other," said Zhen. "And are you willing to give your lives for this? Because if you flip those switches, that's what you'll be doing."

"We're already dead, Zhen," said Emile. "Look at us. We're falling apart. At least I'll die for something."

Zhen began crying. "I know. I just can't bear to lose you."

"We do this for everyone. Not just those in Kano but everyone on Earth," Emile said, standing.

I rose to help, but he waved me off. He walked over to where Zhen was sitting and slipped something small into her hand.

"If we are executed, promise me you'll take this," said Emile.

"Your death will be quick and painless. Far less than anything Zabu would do to you."

Zhen let the pill roll out of her hand where it hit the ground softly.

"No. If he kills me, I want to look into that bastard's eyes when he slits my throat."

●●●●●●●●●

After some convincing, Zhen left the lab so we could transfer the radioactive material to the device, transforming the low-grade bomb into a nuclear weapon. Though it felt like a futile gesture, we donned the protective gear and entered the radiation lab. After collecting the concentrated material from the centrifuge, we used a hydraulic press to form it into a perfect sphere. The powerful physics behind the nuclear reaction that would occur from such a seemingly innocuous ball humbled me.

"This is the key to destroying the Arthropods at their source, Emile," I said, presenting the potent sphere in my gloves, the material's warmth seeping through to my hands.

Emile only nodded. He was suffering. We removed the bomb from its hidden compartment, opened the casing, and deposited the uranium into the sphere of charges that would initiate the reaction before permanently sealing the mechanism shut. Emile struggled to screw the panel into place, continually slipping the screwdriver across the device's painted surface. I gingerly placed my hand across his shaking fingers, calming him just enough to complete the task. Then we replaced the completed weapon into the pipe.

"It's finished," said Emile. "Don't forget to teach them how to arm it."

"Thank you, Emile," I said, pulling him close. "We will do this. It will make all the difference. Now, go rest. I can handle it from here."

Emile shuffled out of the lab. I found myself sitting at my table for several hours, staring at the wall. Contemplating various scenarios and dwelling on Emile. I could only assume his age had played a factor in his more advanced poisoning.

A light rapping on the door pulled me from my thoughts. I scurried to the viewport and saw the young man from before, instantly recognizing him as one of the twins. I jumped to the hatch, swinging it open.

"Come in, come in," I said. "I'm sorry, I have forgotten your name."

"Arjun," he said.

"What brings you here, Arjun? How did you escape your work detail?"

"This," he said, pulling a bent and withered tree branch from the interior of his jumpsuit.

"That must have been quite uncomfortable, carrying it around like that."

"It was not pleasant, but it is important," said Arjun.

"The colleagues I'm assigned to have yet to appreciate my practical abilities and are using me as a courier," he said as I examined the familiar wood.

"*Azadirachta indica.* I'm not much of a botanist, but I know this one. Sometimes the transporters bring us enough to concentrate. In return, we supply them with aerosolized canisters, but we can't ever make any substantial amount."

"So you know it! We've found even in its natural state, it's quite effective at repelling the smaller Arthropods like hook beetles and bone arachnids. We think it may be how the survivors have lived so long unmolested. How does it work?"

"Fascinating! We could use more field data like that. Neem is the trifecta. It acts as an antifeedant, repellent, and egg-laying deterrent. It's like gold. The catch is it only works in close proximity and high concentrations," I said. "Wait. Did you call bone arachnids small? Forgive me, you've been outside far more recently than I have. Are hook beetles and bone arachnids not the larger Arthropods?"

"They should be reclassified as medium-sized. We have come across one that is far superior. We believe we may have been the first to interact with it and live. We coined it the spine back. My companions refer to it as the Nightmare."

"Dear God," I said after Arjun had described the creature to me. "And it wasn't fazed by the neem?"

"Not at all, but I believe the neem holds great value against the others. I thought it would be helpful if you were unaware of it."

"It was helpful. It brought us together," I said, smiling. "The bomb we've created is a chemical-nuclear hybrid. It uses a neem-based repellent, the same that we've shared with the transporters. Anything that survives the radiation and explosion, we're counting on the neem to repel. We don't want the Hive to ever be inhabitable again."

Arjun stood there, staring at me.

"Is there something more?" I asked, curious.

"I believe the Arthropods perceive our group as a threat. I find this encouraging. They seem to be targeting us using new tactics that are alarming the transporters. As a result, I think it is imperative that we destroy the network of antenna bugs."

"I've never known the Arthropods to feel threatened. And in my experience, it takes a lot to alarm a transporter. If what you say is true, this will be a challenging mission indeed. As far as the network, that's a daunting request, my young friend. I'm afraid my lab partners and I have been trying to crack their system for years. We've had one in captivity that we—"

"You have one here?" asked Arjun, breaking from his deadpan manner of speaking.

"Yes, would you like to see it?" I asked.

"Please."

Arjun followed me down to Rupert's former lab, his curiosity like that of a school child. I led him to the rear of the lab where Radar's enclosure was located. He stared for a long while at the creature through the glass.

"What do you feed it?" he asked.

"Rats," I said. "There are plenty to be found in the city."

"I hate to rush you, but are they going to be missing you on your work detail?"

"I suppose you're correct. I should return. Have you tried jamming their communications?"

"We've tried everything you can imagine. All of the equipment is under that plastic tarp over there. You're welcome to try anything."

"You said this lab is abandoned," said Arjun. "Could I use it?"

"I…um. I suppose there's no harm in that."

"My partner," Arjun said, pausing and resting his hand on the glass. "My partner and I used to debate about how best to stop the network. I always leaned toward jamming. He always thought a virus would be more effective."

"Both seem valid. We tried mild viral strains to ascertain effectiveness, but we were limited to non-lethal methods having only one subject. In the closet, you'll find a shoulder-fired rocket launcher and a handful of payload rockets. We borrowed them from the armory as a potential delivery system, but never tried it. The scientist this lab belonged to was executed."

"Oh," said Arjun. "Were you close?"

"Very," I said, feeling the burn in my eyes. "Zabu hacked him to death right in front of me."

"I'm sorry."

"That's part of the reason we have to get this bomb out of here. I've got a plan, but I'll need your help," I said. "The weapon *cannot* fall into Zabu's hands. He wants it to annihilate the residents of Pod Baghdad. He's under the auspices that he's some mercenary of death, cleansing the Earth on behalf of his deity, Ala."

"That's extremely disconcerting," said Arjun. "I'll share your plan with the others and we'll get to work immediately."

CHAPTER 27: KRISTA

Omar and I left the squat octagonal building at first light and followed the convoy's trail into the city. We walked down the road, only our footsteps echoing between the few standing dilapidated walls. Each footfall kicked up another swirl of dust behind us. The temperature was already climbing. Without shade, sunstroke would pose as much of a danger as our hidden enemy.

"You need to find breakfast," Omar said, reminding me of his sadistic little plan to teach me survival. "The cured porcupine we need to save for emergencies. I know it'll be hard, but we have to balance hydration and water rations. There are no pump houses outside the pods, so unless we find some surprise source, what we have has to last however long they're inside."

"How long do you think it'll take?" I asked, thrilled about adding another concern to my list.

"I figure a day to get settled in. Maybe a day to become citizens. Another day to find Dieter. A day to plan. A day to execute the plan. Maybe throw in two more days for good measure… a week."

"A week?!" I asked. "We don't have enough water for that."

"We do if we keep our heads," said Omar. "We need to avoid

doing anything in the heat of the day. Early mornings and late evenings are the best time to roam. At night it's the reverse problem with the cold."

"This sucks," I said.

"It'd suck less if you'd catch us breakfast," said Omar, smirking.

I continued walking and kicked at the dirt. *If he wants breakfast, I'll give him breakfast. Then maybe he'll shut up and quit playing teacher.* I pulled a single katana from my back, wishing I was as adept with a bow as Ariadne. The katana was great for battle, not so much for hunting. I strode down a promising alley where a branchless tree had dropped its fruit which lay rotting on the ground. I crept along, looking for little scurriers. I slid through the disintegrating remnants of human occupation, carefully moving them with my free hand, keeping an eye out for a nest of something that might resemble breakfast.

Suddenly, a fat rodent darted across my feet. I swung my blade down, but not in time. The tip sparked as it impacted a rock nestled just below the dirt's surface.

"Dammit!" I said.

"They're quick little bastards," said Omar.

"It's not just that. This is going to dull my blade."

"I have a better idea," he said, pulling a long ancient piece of wood from a crate, a few nails still curled out from the end. "Use this."

"A board?"

"It's wider and has sharp points. Best of all, it's trash."

I returned my katana to its sheath and taking the board, I returned to my previous strategy of gently flipping the items. In a matter of minutes, I uncovered a nest of cane rats. Six of the large rodents darted away as I swung the board down with as much speed as I could muster.

"Caught one!" I yelled.

"Great!" said Omar, who'd effortlessly pinned a second with his naginata. "We live to see another day."

"Smart ass."

We ducked into a small concrete house that had withstood the years and located the home's fireplace. It was strange. Aside from the wind-accumulated dust, I could almost imagine the home as being recently inhabited. Charred wood still filled the pit below the fireplace, waiting for the family to return from their excursion for dinner.

"You think we can get away with a small fire?" I asked. "If I'm going to eat rat, I'd appreciate a sear. Arjun taught me how to minimize the escaping odors."

"This is your show," said Omar, spreading his hands.

"You're no help at all," I said.

I piled nearby dry kindling under the grate. Reigniting the hearth established a connection with the absent family that spanned the centuries. I hope it brought us some luck. The grating glowed bright red by the time I had finished cleaning the cane rats. With each kill, I was becoming more proficient at cleaning my prey. I buried the offal outside and seared the meat before covering it. Even protected from the day's heat, I was already dripping with sweat. As the meat cooked, I joined Omar, keeping a watch out the door. Once the meat had cooked, we consumed everything I had prepared. Cane rats were surprisingly edible, though they had an aftertaste I could only describe as funky.

Not wanting to linger where we had cooked, we immediately departed, heading deeper into the city in our search for the pod where our friends were. After crossing a few kilometers, the sun cleared the tops of the rubble, bathing us in its oppressive heat. We pushed forward, determined to find decent shelter until the evening when we could make more progress.

"Look up there," I said, seeing looming towers in the distance. "Can we stay there? Part of it is still standing."

"Maybe," Omar said, squinting. "There's a lot of trees clustered there. If it's uninhabited, the shade could give us some protection. If it's inhabited, well…."

We picked up the pace, anxious to arrive at the potential destination. Impeding the direct path was a cluster of overpasses in various stages of collapse. *Is that a tunnel?* I looked back at Omar with concern.

"I see it. We could circumnavigate it, but that would take hours. With all the rubble, the chances of an ambush could be worse off the main thoroughfare. At least here we can see the blind spots and avoid them."

"Then let's do it," I said.

I pulled the katanas off my back and we pressed forward. Laying just ahead was a fallen road, its supporting columns standing like sad soldiers at attention with no duty to perform. Climbing over the debris didn't present a problem, but the triangular pockets created by the accordioned road provided perfect alcoves for hidden inverts. Running under the road, shrouded in darkness, was the ominous tunnel that we'd have to brave to reach our goal.

"I don't like this," I said. "I kind of wish we'd gone the other way."

"Too late now. If there's anything in there, they already know we're here."

"Great."

"See that bend ahead," Omar said, pointing. "Make for that. The second you see any inverts, sprint for those towers. Fighting here in the open would be suicide."

"What if it's barred closed?"

"Let's worry about one thing at a time, shall we?"

I nodded. It wasn't a great plan, but he was right. A fight here would be asinine. I cautiously pressed ahead, katanas at the ready. I rotated the blades to keep the beaming sun from reflecting into my eyes. A rock fell, bouncing down a small incline, snapping my gaze to its origin. Nothing. I was on edge. When I was thirty meters from the bend, that's when it happened. An omnidirectional hissing flooded the air around me with no discernible source. Suddenly, looking to my right and left, the sun revealed the recognizable beaks of hook beetles slowly protruding from every crevice. Coming from the tunnel directly ahead was the loudest hiss of all.

"Run!" yelled Omar.

I didn't need any encouragement. I sprinted as fast as I could towards the gap. Jumping the crushed barriers in one leap, I bounced my feet back and forth between each side of the angled concrete. The hissing, having turned into a roar, was gaining behind me. With a leap, I misjudged the gap and felt a pop in my ankle. Pain rocketed up my spine, but I had no choice—painfully continue or undeniably perish. I risked a glance back at Omar, who was right on my tail.

"Don't worry about me! Just go!"

I darted under the trees and through the brush blocking the path to the towers. Heart pounding, lungs burning, ankle electrified with tingles. Just ahead, the building's function was immediately clear. A mosque! I plunged through the open door, long since destroyed by time. The building stood, but the walls were dotted with gaping holes. I frantically looked for cover, finding the entrance to one of the two towers was wide open, offering no cover. The second tower had the only remaining door, but curse my pessimism, it was locked.

"Dammit!" I said, seeing no sign of Omar.

I heard the swarm and leaped to the door. Shoving my katana through the chain locking it, I pulled back with as much force as I could muster. The old chain sheared off and the door swung on its hinges.

"Omar!" I yelled, just as he flew through the air into the lobby, landing on his back with a thud.

"Go!" he yelled, "I'll hold them off!"

"Like hell, you will!"

I grabbed him by the collar and all but threw him towards the tower's stairwell. The hooks were on top of us. With our backs to the door, we slashed and cut through the attacking inverts. We couldn't hold them off, there were too many. With no way to lock the door, we were done for.

"I have an idea!" I said. "Get in the tower and shut the door behind us!"

"But there's no—"

"Do it!"

We did everything we could to keep our attackers at bay as we perilously backed into the tower. Once inside the opening, the close quarters made defensive movement near impossible. The door became impossible to shut, the hooks relentlessly pushing through, gnashing at our faces. With beaks only centimeters from my face, I could smell the odor of death on their wicked tongues.

"Omar, do you still have any of Otto's smoke canisters?"

A look of surprise crossed his face. "Hold them off!" he said, twisting to wrench one from his pack.

No sooner than he had it out, he pulled the key and dropped it at our feet. The smoke-filled the tight space, blinding and gagging us. Over the welcome hiss of the canister, I heard the welcome sound of the enemy retreating. With my eyes closed and stinging, I felt my way through the caustic fog until my hand reached the door. I pulled it to and jammed my katana through the empty hole where the deadbolt had once been and into the time-softened concrete of the wall. With a signal to Omar, we ran up the tight, spiraling staircase to the top of the minaret. Acting like a chimney, the tower drew up the fumes, choking us for the entire ascent. We finally reached the top, gasping for air through the narrow viewports as the attacking hooks snapped fruitlessly beyond them.

"We're safe!" I said, hugging Omar and coughing.

"For the moment at least," he said. "Though I have no idea how we're getting out of this."

After a half-hour, the smoke cleared and the inverts, unable to attain their prey, lost interest. I stood at the rusted iron railing surrounding the narrow shaft encapsulating the corkscrew staircase. I listened as my lingering cough echoed off the curved walls. The tower was a miniature analog to Pod Horizonte—to the extent of trapping me inside. Omar had collapsed to the rough sandstone floor between where two stalagmites had begun to develop over the centuries of the mosque's vacancy. Attempting to cross the few steps to him, I collapsed, wincing in pain. The adrenaline mask, removed. Omar was immediately at my side.

"What's wrong? What happened?"

"I sprained my ankle on the overpass. In the excitement, I forgot all about it."

Omar raised my jumpsuit leg and took in a quick breath before another fit of coughing.

"That bad, huh?"

"It looks worse than it is. Shame we don't have any ice."

Omar pulled some meds from his pack. I took them from his hand, my fingers running across his calloused palm, and dry swallowed the tablets. Omar pulled a carved stone from the wall and dropped it at my feet, raising a cloud of dust.

"It won't be comfortable, but you need to elevate your leg. I'll let you take the night off from hunting," he said, winking. "We'll eat the cured porcupine here tonight. Maybe by morning, I'll have some idea to get us out of here."

He started to turn and I grabbed his hand.

"Thank you," I said. "I couldn't have survived today without you."

Omar smiled subtly, forming dimples in his cheeks. "Yeah, you could have. You don't give yourself enough credit. You thought of the smoke and barricade. You're a badass."

I felt a flutter of pride in my chest, and for the first time since Zeke had died, I felt like things might be okay.

CHAPTER 28: HUCK

I reluctantly hit the button for level 90, already sweating profusely, though whether from nervousness or the heat, I wasn't sure. Like Horizonte, I'd need to take the lift down to 90, then the stairwell to 91. The societal divisions in Kano were different from Horizonte, but inequality still reigned. It was as though the First Builders subconsciously encouraged it with their design. I stepped off the elevator and followed the signs leading to Dust processing. When I arrived at the entrance, I was greeted by eight men guarding the twin hatches.

"What is your business here?" one yelled, lowering his weapon from his shoulder. "No one is allowed down here without explicit permission!"

"I was ordered to come here!" I said, holding my hands out.

"By who?!" the guard said, racking a round into the gun's chamber.

"Uh, Uh, Uh… Chattar! I promise!" I said, the threat of violence making it difficult to think.

Before the guard could interrogate me further, we were interrupted by the squeal of the hatches' under-oiled hinges. The leftmost hatch swung open, revealing a corpulent man with a mask resting in his unkempt thinning hair and sporting an equally ratty beard.

"What is the problem, gentleman?" he asked.

"This man was claiming he was sent here. I don't believe him, so I was about to shoot him."

"Thank Zabu we don't pay you to think, numskull. He was sent down here."

The guard stood rigidly at the affront, then skulked back to his post. The bulky man waved me through the door and into the small lobby. The first thing that hit me was the intense heat radiating from beyond the security station directly in front of me, where another handful of guards loitered, playing a card game. One of the guards jumped up, but the man motioned for him to remain seated. The second thing I noticed was the odor, not coming from the space as much as the man guiding me deeper into the dungeon.

"Call me Foreman Oskar," he said. "You will do everything I say, without question, is that understood?"

I nodded, though my participation would only be through coercion. As I followed in his wake, I resisted the urge to gag from his offensive fumes.

"What's your name, kid?" he asked.

"Huck. Citizen Huck," I added for good measure.

He turned and leaned down to stare me in the face. His crooked yellow teeth looked and smelled of death. "Do I look like I give a rat's ass whether you're a citizen or not?"

I shook my head.

"There'll be none of that here. I am the be-all end-all. *Everyone* answers to me."

We walked into a huge sweltering room, glow from the heat lamps bathing the space in an orange-hued umber. The room was filled with a number of workers, varying in age from young children to older adults, all working by lines of strange equipment. If not for the uniform coating of the fine brown Dust on every surface, the facility would've seemed dedicated to food production. Oskar slapped me in the chest with coveralls and a mask as he lowered his apparatus into place.

"Put these on," he said in a muffled voice. "They're hot as hell, but will keep the deleterious effects from messing with you. Otherwise, you'd be a worthless lump in about twenty minutes."

I slipped the rubberized suit, cinched on the hood, and pulled the mask into place. I felt the sweat begin to pour down my back, the encapsulating suit refusing to let the heat of my body dissipate.

"You'll learn the ropes from Midge over there," said Oskar, pointing.

"Midge?" I asked.

"Yeah, that little skin-headed urchin over there. Named after those damn surface bugs, the ones that constantly buzz around you, draining the life from your body."

"You've been on the surface?" I asked.

"What are you implying?"

"Nothing, I just—"

"You just what? You didn't think I had what it takes? I'll have you know I set a record time from Munich to Kano. Impugn my honor again, *boy*, and I'll strap you under the heat lamps and leave you overnight. Now, get the hell out of my face," he said, picking up what appeared to be a riding crop.

"Yes, sir," I said, struggling to enunciate through the mask.

I walked over to the short worker Oskar had pointed out.

"Excuse me, Midge?"

"That's me!" said a high, childish voice. "I'm Midge, well not really. Everyone calls me Midge. My name's really Zauna. I like Midge, it suits me well enough. I've never been to the surface though. Working down here isn't my favorite but—"

"Midge…!" yelled Oskar.

"Sorry, we should get to work," said Midge, talking so quickly it was hard to follow. "You and I will be working the vats. That's these things here. We're about to start a new one so I hope you got a good night's rest. You're going to need it today. What's your name? I didn't even think to ask. I forget things like that all the time."

"I'm Huck. I don't know anything about what to do. All I know is that Dust messes people up."

It was the first time Midge had been silent.

"We don't talk about that," whispered Midge.

I didn't know how to respond, but Midge immediately returned to her normal momentum.

"We fill the vat with distilled water, then add the raw extracted pheromone fluid and add a reagent. Is it true you brought us this batch of pheromones?" asked Midge, without giving me the chance to answer. "Don't ever, ever add the raw pheromone to the hot metal. It will render it worthless. The reagent will cause the product to crystallize, but we have to heat it up really, really slowly. The waiting is so hard. I'm not tall enough to stir, so you'll have to do that. You have to stir the whole time. It can't start to crystallize until it's in the pans. You can't stop stirring, whatever you do or Oskar will make you regret it."

"The pans?" I asked.

"Enough chatter! Get to work!" said Oskar as he collapsed into a tiny little chair, the unlikely juxtaposition of the two almost made me laugh.

Midge gave me a worried look, and we went to work. I recognized the similar canisters from Ariadne and Krista's work in the supply truck. We carefully scraped the goo from the tins into a large pot, making sure to not miss a drop. According to Oskar, it was worth more than "our pathetic little lives." Once the pot was full to Midge's contentment, we added purified water and Midge readied the bottle of reagent.

"Grab that paddle on the wall. And whatever you do—"

"Don't stop stirring. I got it, Midge," I said. "How long does this take?"

"About twelve hours," said Midge, squirting in the reagent.

·········

When I finally got back to our common area, I could barely feel my arms. The idea that I would have to repeat the process tomorrow felt like an impossible proposition. I walked into the crimson room and collapsed onto the central cushion. The cool faux leather feeling comforting to my filthy aching body. Ariadne rose from where she was sitting with Arjun and Mei and leaned over my face, her hair hanging down to my shoulders. I felt a stir in my chest from her smile and playfulness but dismissed it when I remembered the embarrassing incident at the beach.

"Rough first day?"

"The worst. Dust not only ruins its consumers' lives but also the lives of those who refine it."

"I just got back too," she said, offering me a bandaged hand. "It's nothing. My fingertips are torn to shreds. Arjun, Mei, and I have been comparing assignments."

I set up and felt like I was going to black out.

"You need to eat," she said. "Thankfully Arjun whipped up something. I'll go get you some."

"Thanks, and a shower." I said. "Well, how was your day, Arjun?"

"It was pleasant enough. My assigned lab thought I was best suited for errands. I suspect their doubt of my intelligence stems from racism. Lucky for me, Dieter appreciates it. He loaned me a lab," Arjun said, turning his head as Ariadne returned with some yellow and green food for herself and me. "Between the free time I am allotted and the resources available, I believe that I can find a method to bring down the antenna bug network."

"That would be fantastic, Arjun," I said with my mouth full. "This is pretty good, by the way."

Ariadne echoed the sentiment.

"Where's Hemant?" I asked.

"I don't know," said Arjun. "Considering each of our tasks has different expectations, I am not sure when to expect him."

"Maybe they have barracks of their own," said Ariadne. "Like the laborers back in Horizonte."

"It's possible, though I will miss him," said Arjun. "Not to mention, it would make our escape slightly more challenging if he proves difficult to communicate with. Speaking of our escape, Dieter needs our help."

"How so?" asked Mei, scraping the last of the food into her mouth.

"The weapon is a chemical-nuclear hybrid. It's—"

"Nuclear?!" I said. "Like destroys cities? That nuclear?"

"Yes," said Arjun. "It's the only way to ensure the destruction and irradiation of the nest."

"And of us," I said, shaking my head in disbelief.

"Are you unable to continue," asked Arjun.

"No, I can do it. I just didn't expect to have a device of that potential strapped to my back."

"Not *your* back," said Arjun. "Hemant or Omar would have to carry it. The device is quite heavy."

"I didn't mean that literally, Arjun."

"Sorry," he said. "Dieter proposed that we hide it in one of the fuel tanks of Yanus' personnel carrier. It would cut our fuel in half, but it would be unlikely to be found."

"*Our* fuel?" asked Mei.

"Yes. The plan is to steal Yanus' carrier and the attached buggy."

Each of us grinned from ear to ear. I forgot all about my need to shower.

"I love that idea. Serves that blow hard right!" I said. "We could gradually stock the carrier with food Ariadne smuggles out from the farms. Hemant could supply the arsenal. Arjun can work on the antenna bug problem. Maybe I can track down Ekon and see if he can help us get to our next milestone, Baghdad. Ariadne, could you obtain some medications?"

"Maybe," Ariadne said. "Though I'd rather take my chances with plant-based cures than getting my arm amputated for thievery."

"Don't do anything you're not comfortable with," I said. "I would prefer that we get out of here unscathed. How were the farms? Other than jacking up your fingers."

"Actually, it was enjoyable," Ariadne said as Mei nodded enthusiastically. "Our supervisor, Greenskeeper Miranda, is a really nice lady. There's a helper named Cesar who's extremely strong and friendly, but not very bright. Then there's Liesel, she's really cool too."

"And really pretty. She taught us how to hybridize trees to make them more productive!" said Mei. "It was tedious but rewarding."

Ariadne leaned in, whispering, "And she's a member of the Resistance against Zabu."

"Maybe they can help us escape. Anyone who's against Zabu is good in my book. Either way, I'm glad you guys had fun," I said, chuckling. "I can't echo that. Dust processing sucks. I'm not sure what's worse, the work or the result."

"Could you sabotage it?"

"I doubt it, we're watched closely. And under armed guard. Not to mention, I don't want anything to hurt its users. It's not their fault Zabu uses it to imprison them, nor do I want any fallout for the other workers. They're good people. Just today, I met a little kid who works in the facility. What the hell is a little kid processing drugs for?"

"Everything about this pod is wrong," said Mei. "It's worse than the corruption in Horizonte. I feel bad leaving the people like this."

"At least they have the Resistance," said Arjun.

"You know what?" said Ariadne, smirking. "There is something we can do. Maybe we can stir up a little trouble before we leave."

CHAPTER 29: HEMANT

The crappy bunk groaned under my weight as I sat up on the pock-marked mattress. After a night of little rest, I felt groggy as hell. Around me, the Muskrats snored on, sleeping off the previous night's inebriation. The day before had been a bizarre one, filled with emotions.

After being introduced to Captain Abbas by Commandant Saif, Abbas led me to a common area, rife with gambling, consumption, and erotic displays.

"This is the Den," Abbas said in his deep voice. "With diligent work comes ample reward. Prove yourself as a Muskrat and you will have a life that you'll find most pleasurable. Go ahead and have a little taste, but stay clear-headed. Your first excursion will be in a few hours."

With a squeeze on my shoulder, the contemplative man was off. No sooner had he left my side, than two women with ebony skin as deep as Grace's clung to me. Their hands ran up and down my body, eliciting a primal response. With great difficulty, I declined their offers and left them to their pursuits. For an eternal second, I second-guessed the decision. Shaking my head, I made my way to an empty built-in bench behind a table and had a seat on its moth-eaten surface. I laid the new mace at my side. *What was I going to do for a few hours in here?* Devoting so much time to my brother and training had left me with little time for myself. It hit me that I didn't know that much about myself. *What do I enjoy?* What a strange feeling.

"Drink?" a woman with a deep cleavage asked.

"Umm… tea, please," I said.

The woman arched an eyebrow but said no more as she walked away. I scanned the room, looking from card games to groping sessions to drinking competitions. *What was I doing here?* I might not truly understand my own desires, but this wasn't it. Again, I felt the tug to return to the group of survivors who had cared for me after my leg injury. Maybe I could have a simple life on the surface after all this mess, if that would be possible during my lifetime. The woman returned with my tea, smiling, stooping to offer a teasing view. The tea's color was off-putting, and the sachet appeared moldy. *Not many requests for tea around here, I guess. Maybe I'd pass on the tea.*

"I wouldn't drink it either, man. Here, this won't flatten you out nor does it taste like dog piss," a blond-bearded, squat youth said, placing a stein matching his own in front of me. "Not that any of us Neanderthals would know what dog piss tastes like. I've never even seen a dog. I hear they keep them in some pods as pets. Imagine that. Not here. It'd get eaten here. Mathias."

I looked down at his offered hand before placing mine in his grip. "Hemant."

"It doesn't take a genius to see you're new here. Word of advice, only drink the alcohol. Everything else is more of a gamble than those tables. More free advice, they'll all cheat you so don't bother. Lastly, unless you want it to burn when you pee, I wouldn't touch a woman here without protection."

"Umm, thanks," I said.

"I like you, Hemant. Stick with me and you'll be alright. Where you from anyways?

"Horizonte."

He whistled. "Geeze. Long way for this crap hole."

"I was aiming for Bhopal," I said, reticent to provide him with my true reason. "I stopped for a resupply and they're not in a hurry to let me leave."

"Candidates check-in, they don't check out!" he said, slapping my back hard enough to make me sputter.

"Welcome to the Muskrats! Where everyone's a degenerate."

•••••••••

Mathias and I spent the next few hours chatting in the Den until Abbas returned.

"Muskrats, gear up!" he commanded.

In a flurry of activity, everything dispersed, some soldiers more haphazardly than others due to their inebriated state. Mathias led me to the platoon's staging area nearby where we stood waiting for everyone to assemble. The entire force, who moments before were sloven and drunk, was surprisingly rigid and raring to go. I found their ability to flip between work and play so rapidly impressive. Once in formation, the captain made his address.

"At ease," he said, the men relaxing their tension. "Our assignment today comes from the prime minister himself. The Resistance has been hoarding food and medications, for what reason is unknown. As you are aware, this is an act against The Code and a direct offense to the people of Pod Kano. We cannot allow any group to interfere with our food allocation system, lest the pod fail. It is an act of sedition that will not stand! They will be punished! We will raid the warehouse and bring the supply back into the chain—the people's chain!"

"Oorah!" yelled the force.

Zabu was a nasty piece of work. While I didn't have any beef with the Resistance, the idea that they were absconding with everyone's food was wrong. I had no issue helping take it back on behalf of the pod's hungry residents. I had already seen evidence of food deprivation. Maybe the Resistance wasn't as innocent as I had imagined. After providing us with the location of the warehouse, we stormed out of the staging area and into the freight elevators by the dozens.

After our arrival on the desired floor, innocent residents scattered, feeling the upcoming conflict. Through the stagnant air, we marched down a wide corridor to the locked bay doors of our intended target.

"Intel says their storage facility is under minimal guard," said Abbas. "Consider anyone inside to be a traitor. Permission to dispatch on sight."

I glanced at Mathias, who nodded. I wasn't ready to kill anyone. Up until now, I'd only slain inverts. I would avoid human encounters once inside. A burly Muskrat stepped up. With a blow of his short-handled ax, Sparks flew as the lock broke free. Abbas threw open the door and the men piled in yelling. Caught up in the surge, the mob pressed me forward.

My eyes took a moment to adjust from the well-lit hallway to the dim warehouse. As far as my eyes could make out, the room was filled with two-meter cubes, marred from excessive use and presumably full of food. The men dispersed between the cubes, clearing the space. First, a shout erupted, followed by a gurgle. With the element of surprise lost, the sounds of rifle discharge permeated the air.

With Mathias at my side, we rounded a corner and came face to face with a Resistance fighter. A look of fear passed across his face before he turned and ran. No sooner than he had escaped around the corner, I heard a sickening thud. His body fell to the ground just ahead of us, his skull crushed, the remaining lifeless eye staring back at us. His assassin, a club-toting, broad-shouldered Muskrat, glared at us suspiciously before rolling his eyes. We began to hear cries of "All clear," and rejoined the others in a clearing.

"Good work, Muskrats! That's another notch in our belts. Work's not over yet. Get these crates on the elevators and back where they belong, save for one. Surely the Resistance would've eaten through a few," the captain said, winking.

The men cheered. Not that we hadn't rescued the twenty-some-odd containers and restored them to the masses, but keeping one for ourselves? There was something about that that put me ill at ease.

"Tonight, we feast," said an excited Mathias, his eyes twinkling.

•••••••••

Returning the crates had proven far more difficult than I had imagined. Each must have weighed 700 kilos or more. *What was the Resistance doing with all this food?* Further alarming me was my lack of strength. Each crate was conducted back to its origin by a single Muskrat, making the work go by quickly, but no matter how hard I pushed, I could barely scoot mine. Even Mathias, barely over half my height, wasn't struggling as much as I was. I was a big guy. Stronger than a number of those around me, or so I thought.

"Must be heavier than the others," I mumbled.

I didn't know how my strength had waned during my time on the surface. I fought invert after invert and was always exercising or sparring with the others in my downtime. I desperately needed to get more in shape if I was going to train in Bhopal for the last leg of our journey. Maybe I would train to pass the time in lieu of debauchery.

"Having trouble?" a voice boomed behind me.

I turned and saw the club-wielding Muskrat from before. I didn't want to answer honestly, but truthfully, I was. I nodded.

"I must have lost some of my muscle mass on the surface," I said, holding my head high.

"Try this," the man said, placing a small apparatus over my mouth before I could object.

Having no alternative, I breathed in. After my exertion moving the crate, it was a deep breath too. The fiery vapor burned my lungs. When the man removed the device, I had a fit of coughing.

"Welcome to the club," he said, patting me on the back.

When the fit subsided, I stood erect, my head spinning.

"What the hell was that?" I said to myself.

Feeling light-headed, I went back to pushing the crate. Again, nothing much. I don't know what I expected, but after a moment, it felt as though the crate had grown lighter. Before I knew it, I had pushed it into the elevator unassisted, ascended a few levels, and was passing it off to some logistics twerp.

With my head still in a fog, I returned to the Den where everything seemed a little less offensive than before. The gambling was just good-natured fun; the flagrant intercourse, only natural activities; the over-intoxication, simply letting loose some steam. I plopped down next to Mathias at what had become our booth. When the waitress returned, I struggled to pull my eyes from her breasts.

"Something strong, honey," I said, resting my hand on hers, surprising myself.

"You're really going for it, man," said Mathias. "Must have been a good hit."

"A good hit of what?" I asked.

"Dust, man," Mathias said, looking at me as though I was stupid. "How the hell do you think my tiny ass pushes a damn-near-metric-ton crate across a room?"

"Dust?!" I asked. "But Dust is… bad."

"Don't act like a freaking saint. It's a tool, like anything else. We're not like the foggers who can't live without it. Sit back and enjoy the ride," he said, then mumbling to himself, "And it makes the less desirable things we have to do easier."

The waitress returned with my drink, and I downed it in one gulp. The next few hours were a blur, passing by without perception. When I came to my senses, I was laying in a strange bed, my head clear aside from a slight headache. I sat up abruptly and heard a faint moan next to me. I looked down to find the striking waitress from the Den, fast asleep. Her voluptuous naked body was only half covered by the thin sheet.

"Oh my God," I stammered. "Oh my God."

Trying not to disturb her, I donned my jumpsuit and left her tiny apartment as quickly as I could, and found myself just down the corridor from the Den. I needed to rejoin the others and reorient myself. I had been with the Muskrats for hours and had forsaken my morals—and I didn't like who I was becoming. I was starting to see one of the myriad reasons Dust was so vile. *The elevators!* I could see them gleaming just on the other side of the Den. With my jumpsuit partially zipped, I scurried toward their sanctuary.

"Hemant," I heard a wispy voice say and turned to see Commandant Saif and Captain Abbas standing together. "I am hearing good things about you from the captain. It seems like you are fitting right in."

That was the last thing I wanted to hear. I wanted no part of any of this any longer.

"Hemant the Muskrat," he said in his wheezy voice, a toothy grin on his pudgy face.

"Get some rest, soldier," said Abbas, pointing to the barracks. "We have another mission, first thing in the morning."

CHAPTER 30: ARIADNE

We spent our second day in the farm transplanting tender new sprouts into the raised beds. I found the work to be quite delicate, but it was much less injury-prone than working with the razor on the frail stalks. I found the work pleasant and therapeutic. With each disturbance of the earth, my nostrils filled with the pleasant organic smells, bringing me a sense of peace after weeks of stress and fatigue. I caught myself wishing I could stay here on the farms, but then reality would set in, and I would realize the notion's stupidity. Our mission was vital. Humans didn't belong underground. *How wonderful would it be to have a garden on the surface— my only concern, the frosty chill of winter?* My thoughts were interrupted by yelling at the entrance to the farm. Liesel, Mei, and I stood to discern the source of the sounds.

"Leave him alone!" shouted Miranda.

"Stop it. Stop it," Cesar pleaded.

Two guards were harassing Cesar, laughing at his distress. I confronted the guard, pushing him back and surprising him. Instantly, I felt the pain radiating from my cheekbone as it made contact with the back of his hand.

"You dare to interfere with the minister's work?" he said.

Miranda stood between me and him.

"Forgive her, she's new. Our ways are unknown to her. I will see to it that she knows her place in the future."

"See that she does!" he said, spitting at my feet. "Insolent little bitch."

The guards gave one more shove to Cesar for good measure, grabbed some of the day's harvest, kicked over Miranda's tool table, and left. The instant they vanished around the corner, Liesel was at my side.

"Are you okay?" she said.

"Yeah. The only thing they did was piss me off," I said, rubbing my sore cheek.

"Are they always like that?" asked Mei.

"I'm afraid so," said Miranda.

"Gone?" said Cesar, crying.

"Yes, Cesar," Miranda said. "They're gone."

"Can't we do anything to stop it?" I asked, looking at Liesel.

"Liesel told me that she slipped our little secret," said Miranda. "I recognize genuine souls when I see them. Our group, shall we call it, exists for precisely that reason. Alone, we cannot compete with tyranny, but together, we stand for all. We endure the daily shakedowns, but it's at night that we thrive. If you wish to be proactive, perhaps you could join our plight. We're meeting to address an incident tonight. Would you care to join us?"

"Please say you will," said Liesel, tugging on my arm. "We need everyone we can get."

I looked at Mei, who was enthusiastic.

"We're in," I said.

•••••••••

By the time we completed the transplanting work, it was late evening. My mind had spent the day spinning with excitement and nervousness at the prospect of joining the Resistance. We were supposed to be flying under the radar, and yet, it felt wrong not to help those along the way. Maybe in return, they could aid us in our escape. As we tidied up, Miranda drew the rolling door to the farm closed and we huddled around the righted tool table.

"There are rules you must know," she began. "We don't arrive together. I'll give you the location. Your familiarity with the pod layout will be sufficient. Everyone staggers their time and varies which entrance they use. And you'll only meet a fraction of the group. We never meet in full, nor are all the leaders present at any one meeting."

"Miranda, you've been forthright with us, so I want to do the same," I said. "Our interest in the group isn't completely altruistic. We aren't planning on staying at Pod Kano."

A look of surprise crossed Miranda's face. Liesel, already aware, shifted in her seat. We told Miranda all the details of our mission and our need for supplies and escape. Miranda sat stone-faced for a long time before responding.

"I believe we can help you," she finally said. "Our cause is great, but your cause is greater. There will be a significant risk to this endeavor. Do you understand this?"

We both nodded.

"Good," she said. "Tonight's passcode is 'Loxley.'"

•••••••••

I later found myself walking through one of the pod's market districts, doing my best to appear uninteresting. It was a perfect location for a meeting given all the traffic already present. I arrived at the designated vendor and asked for pomegranates—an extraordinarily rare delicacy in any pod. The vendor showed me to a hatch behind her stall, but before opening it, halted and stared at me impatiently.

"Loxley," I said under my voice.

With a sharp tug, she pulled back the bar locking the heavy metal in place, and swung the door open. I ducked through the entry into a room reeking of grease and sweat, all the earmarks of the working class. The bodies we crammed together in the relentless heat. I pushed my way towards the middle where I could see, and to my surprise, everyone was gathered around Miranda. She and a curly-haired male wearing a hand-woven vest over a linen shirt sat next to each other. Across the room, I saw Mei and Liesel and smiled.

"I think this is everyone," Miranda announced, winking at me. "We have two new faces joining us tonight. This is Ariadne and Mei. They come from Pod Horizonte, in the Latin Territory."

Miranda gestured toward each of us with muted encouragement and sporadic gasps.

"They have already witnessed Zabu's tyranny and happily joined our cause. As lucky as we are to have them, they are imprisoned here. Their destiny is leading them further than Kano. They have been tasked to deliver a destructive device to the Arthropod Hive, which could potentially bring an end to this never-ending conflict."

Boisterous cheers of excitement from the attendees exceeded their notions of secrecy.

"After talking with Pyotr, we have decided we will do everything in our power to help them. In return, they offer their abilities to use for the duration of their stay."

More cheers.

"Now, for the business of the night. The rumors you have heard are true. The Muskrats, Zabu's anti-Resistance squad, attacked our warehouse yesterday afternoon and confiscated the food under the auspices that we were hoarding it for ourselves. All four attendants were killed. Months of work, gone. I'm afraid that as a result, hundreds could starve by month's end."

The room's reaction was mixed. Heads dropped in sorrow. Others were filled with a defiant rage. Tears glistened in the lamp light.

"Excuse me," I said, every head swiveling towards me. "I don't understand."

"Zabu claims that his network equally distributes the food among the residents," said Pyotr. "Deaths from starvation are supposedly due to *other* causes. But the truth is that his *egalitarian* system funnels the food to those he deems worthy. Zabu wields starvation, addiction, and oppression just like he does his infamous machete. We steal the food from the system. A crate here and a crate there, and truly distribute it equally."

"Tonight, we are carrying out one such raid," said Miranda. "Pyotr and I have been planning for several weeks. We have the potential to collect five crates, enough to feed several hundred people for a few days. It won't restore our loss, but it will get us back up and running. At great personal risk, Pyotr has offered us his textile warehouse as a temporary storage facility."

A few hands patted Pyotr on the back as he nodded his thanks.

Miranda explained the heist, taking the time to clarify each detail. Once everyone was ready, we moved out.

•••••••••

Mei and I crouched down against a waist-high bulkhead. Like the other Resistance fighters, we were armed with a random assortment of short, bladed weapons. Ahead, two others flattened themselves against the wall in front of the storage bay, our evening's target. A guard stood on either side of the wide roll-up door. Miranda and Pyotr's orders were clear—no one dies unless it's unavoidable. Using a stolen container of sleeping gas, the advance team took out the guards. A second team bound, blindfolded, and gagged the men as the first team raised the door and pushed forward into the space.

The unoccupied room was relatively small. The room was lined with pitted concrete walls. Deep grooves shined up from the regular crate movement. In total, ten fighters moved into the cramped quarters.

"Start moving the crates," said our leader, the only one of us armed with a cartridge weapon.

Several of the stronger men and women paired up to shift the loaded crates to the waiting elevator.

"I don't like this," said the leader, his bushy beard disguising his mouth. "They know we're desperate and this place only has two guards?"

The man pondered for a moment, sniffed the air, then with an impulsive blow, broke the lock off one of the crates. Inside was a cluster of weights and a lifeless body.

"It's an ambush!" yelled our bearded leader. "Retreat!"

Before we could move, guards flooded in from the corridor, blocking the exit and forcing us to our knees. More guards escorted in the four who had taken the crates and the two guarding the elevator as the unconscious guards were awoken. I looked at Mei, in desperation, fearing that we'd just screwed up Memo's mission. I should've stayed out of local politics. *But how could I stand by while innocent people suffer?* One by one, we were raised to our feet and restrained. As a guard cinched the cuffs around my wrists, there was a loud burst of pops and all the guards fell, save for the one at my back. Grabbing me painfully by my hair, the guard pulled me back into the recess behind the door where he was safe from the enemy fire.

"Let me go!" I pleaded, the captivity dredging up my trauma from the Demented.

I felt the cold metal of a gun barrel pressed deep into my temple.

"Do as I say and you might live!" he said in his harsh local accent.

I could hear the Resistance fighters clamoring down from their posted lookout. I hadn't been aware that snipers had our backs, but was flooded with thankfulness for their existence. Mei came around the corner and I felt the painful pull of my hair.

"No further!" he yelled as Mei halted.

Dropping her hand to her side, she subtly touched her waist. Her eyes met mine as she tried to wordlessly relay her intention, then it hit me—she smuggled in her knives. I gave an imperceptible nod. As her hand flicked, I dropped like dead weight, feeling locks of hair rip from my scalp. By the time my butt hit the floor, the guard's body slumped next to me, Mei's throwing knife deeply embedded in his right eye socket. As I took gasping breaths, Mei rushed to my side.

"You're okay," she said. "You're okay."

I sobbed. I was terrified. My head was on fire and my butt was badly bruised.

"We have to go, Ariadne! They will have heard the gunfire."

I nodded and let Mei lead me to where the fighters were hustling into a vacant elevator. The bearded man let us off in random groupings floor by floor before Mei and I departed remarkably close to our apartment. Once I felt safe, I collapsed onto a bench and the tears came in a deluge as Mei embraced me. After what seemed like hours, I regained my composure.

"Look at me," I said. "I'm a wreck. How can I slay inverts and break down around humans?"

"I don't think you ever get over the Shock," said Mei. "What happened to us will stick with us our entire lives. We have to learn to cope with it and face it, just like Grace said."

"I know. To top it off, I endangered our whole mission. What was I thinking?"

"You were thinking of others like you always do. It's why we do everything. Hell, it's why we are on this mission. The point is, that we are doing the right thing on both counts. Now, let's go home."

"No," I said. "Can I have some time alone?"

"Are you sure you don't want to do that back in the apartment?"

"No. I don't want to be anywhere claustrophobic."

"If you're sure..." Mei said.

I nodded. She reluctantly disappeared in the direction of our apartment.

"You are wise beyond your years," a voice said from the darkness. "You can never do wrong when you place others before yourself."

I spun, having thought I was alone, and saw a lone man crouching against the wall in homemade clothes, a scraggly gray beard hanging from his face. There was a kindness in the deep brown eyes recessed in his dark, skin-tagged face that made me relax.

"Sorry to eavesdrop. When a soul is lost in the bustle of life, one has a tendency to ignore all others," he said, amusing himself. "Sometimes it is hard not to listen. Why are you so restless, young one?"

I wiped the tears from my face, feeling strangely at ease with the stranger.

"I'm a liability to myself and my friends," I said.

"Doubtful," he said. "You put your life down to protect others. Your friends are aware of the risks that accompany you."

I felt my heart lighten. I wasn't sure where this mountain-top guru had come from, but I appreciated the serendipitous moment.

"Ariadne," I said.

"It is a pleasure, young Ariadne. They call me Ekon."

CHAPTER 31: DIETER

"Technician Dieter?" the guard asked from my apartment doorway.

"Yes."

"Prime Minister Zabu would like a word with you in his office. He instructs you to bring evidence of your progress."

"I'll be right there," I said, gathering my things.

I waited for the guard to leave but turned to find him still there. An escorted trip then.

"I need to stop by my lab on the way," I said.

"Whatever you need, Technician."

I had anticipated this scenario. Planning the escape was taking a significant amount of concentration, but I made sure to set aside time to develop a realistic decoy. One Zabu couldn't see right through, like my stupid stunt that brought about Rupert's death. The bomb would look authentic even upon a deep inspection but would be completely inert. Its only explosive device would function solely to destroy the bomb with limited collateral damage.

I arrived at the corridor to my lab with the guard in tow and was confronted by Zhen, who was clearly shaken.

"Oh, Dieter," she said, burying her face in my chest. "It's Emile."

"What is it? What happened?" I asked, gesturing to the guard she seemed oblivious to.

"He died last night in his sleep. It must have been…" she said with a quivering voice before taking notice of the guard, "his heart."

"What?" I asked, feeling as though I was being swallowed whole.

"I woke up this morning and found him like that. Cold. He was so cold."

I wrapped my arms around her, patting her on the back. Damn that radiation! I had more exposure. I deserved to die, not him! I was furious with myself. I wished I had been at Emile's side as he passed. I wanted to be there for Zhen, who was like a sister to me. But no, I had to entertain Zabu's megalomaniacal urges while secretly trying to save humanity. At the moment, I wanted to show humanity rather than save it.

"I'm so sorry, Zhen," I whispered. "Tell me whatever you need."

Zhen looked me in the eyes.

"Finish what he started," she said.

Pulling herself into her ever-composed manner, she wiped the tears one eye at a time, held her head high, and walked away down the corridor. Behind me, the guard cleared his throat impatiently. I took a deep breath and continued into my lab. With the guard's help, I loaded the spurious device vertically onto a two-wheeler, strapping it down with ratchet straps, and carted it down the hall to the elevator.

I felt a nervous flutter in my stomach as the elevator rose, but I was no longer concerned with my well-being. For one, I no longer cared about my own life except for how it fit into the grand plan. The more Zabu took from me, the more dangerous I became. And two, with Emile gone, Zabu couldn't finish the device without me. I was indispensable. There were a handful of other scientists in the pod who hadn't run afoul of the minister, but few with the knowledge of explosives I had.

Before I left Pod Munich, my specialization was in the explosive arts. I became quite adept. Sticky grenades of my own invention were a major contributor to my successful journey to Kano, where I believed my skills would be used to overcome the Arthropod threat. I didn't realize I'd be working under a morally-twisted narcissist hell-bent on global domination.

The ding acknowledging our arrival sounded as the elevator doors slid open. I wheeled the dolly out from the cab and through the security checkpoint outside of Zabu's office with a helpful nod from my escort. After the guard knocked at the door, the prime minister showed me in. Before departing, the guard whispered something in the minister's ear.

"Thank you," Zabu said, dismissing him and shutting the hatch. "I am sorry to hear of your friend's early departure. It is funny. I wasn't aware of him having problems of the heart."

"Err… thank you. He'd been hiding it for years. If I may speak freely…," I said, wheeling in the device.

"Of course," he said, escorting me into the office and motioning for me to take a seat.

Already seated in front of the desk was Yanus, the leader of the local transporter team and a supremely unlikeable person. I'd had minimal interaction with him but enough to find him to be a pompous wretch of a man. Situated towards the back of the room was Yanus' personal attendant, whose name escaped me.

I continued, "Emile was afraid if his heart problems were known, he would be expelled from the pod."

"A logical man and a fair assessment. Now, how is this bomb of mine?"

"It's mostly ready, Prime Minister. It only lacks some final adjustments and the addition of the explosive compounds. I've taken the liberty to include shaped charges, which would open up your intended target like a tin can."

"Yes. Yes. Yes!" said Zabu, grinning widely. "I knew you would see the way of Ala. I was just telling our friend Yanus that our new development has the potential to deal out the justice of Ala, doubling the wealth of our people."

"Speaking of wealth…" interrupted Yanus.

I watched as Zabu's eyes rolled back into his head, his back to the transporter.

"You'll notice our most recent shipment of pheromones is not only of superior quality but also higher quantity," Yanus said, steepling his fingers. "We were fortunate to have the candidates from Horizonte aid us in the hunting as well as the processing."

"Thank you, my friend, you will be compensated appropriately," he said, forcefully patting the fat man on the back.

"There is another matter…" said Yanus, taking a draught of the dark liquor in his hand.

"Please," said Zabu, growing impatient.

"It would appear that my most recent… companion… has run off. A pity really. She was quite a beauty. We searched for her an entire half-day, ultimately finding her eviscerated by some pack of inverts. So unlucky. If only she'd remained in the comfort of my protection. You see, she leaves me without… a sensual escape from my burdensome worries."

"And why is it you can't seem to hold on to your… companions?"

"They don't seem to enjoy my presence as I do, theirs."

"I see."

"As a matter of fact, I was so desperate that I even considered my attendant, Taha!" said Yanus laughing, clearly loosened from the intoxicant's effects.

"Let us hope not, Yanus! Ala has no tolerance of sins such as these!" said Zabu, leaning over his desk in Yanus' cowering face.

"I jest! I jest, of course! I would never. Yes, never," said Yanus, all traces of inebriation vaporized.

"I will supply you with two pleasing companions of delicate age and demeanor, lest you be once more tempted by any ungodly instincts."

"Why thank you, Prime Minister. I find your generosity most appreciated."

I sat stone-faced through the interaction. Burying my disgust for the pair deep inside so that it didn't reveal itself at an inopportune moment.

"I'm sorry, Technician Dieter," said Zabu. "Yanus doesn't understand the boundaries between business and unsavory conversation. I wished to bring the two of you together because I would like you, Yanus, to carry Technician Dieter to Pod Baghdad in an advance team. My army will follow a day behind. When my forces arrive, I want you both to be ready to crack Baghdad like the weak, rotten egg it is."

The second I had been dismissed from their presence, I resisted the urge to flee from Zabu's evil sanctuary. Those two humans each were foul creatures who deserved no better fate than being fed to the Arthropods. Together, they were a vile blend.

The departure of Memo's mission was of paramount importance. I needed to help Huck and the others escape before Zabu could exercise his twisted vigilante justice under the guise of his macabre deity.

After stashing the dummy device in my lab, I removed my lab coat and donned a dark sweater to accompany my black slacks. When I was satisfied with my inconspicuous appearance, I took the elevator most of the way up to the pod's primary entryway and staging area.

Stepping off the elevator a few levels early, I took the unlit stairway the remaining distance. The cavernous room was dark, save for the halos of scattered sconces, under which roamed four guards. Even in the obscurity, I could smell hints of the surface still lingering on the air of the expanse. Making my way along the curvature of the vast surrounding wall just beyond the sight of the guards, I rolled under Yanus' private carrier. *"I'm not quite as limber as I used to be,"* I thought as I came to a stop under the chassis.

To enact our plan, I had to empty one of the two natural gas tanks completely before it could be converted into a hidden storage compartment. I disabled the system's equalizer and opened the bleed valve as slowly as possible, so as not to alert the guards. Sweat dripped down my face into my eyes. The slightest rush would create a loud hiss, bringing about my discovery and likely death. I cracked the valve until I heard the faintest of hisses. *Done! Now the wait begins.* It would take hours, maybe even days at its present rate to thoroughly evacuate the tank and achieve the same pressure as the atmosphere.

I rolled out the same way I came in, crouching by the tracks of the carrier, and saw that I was directly behind the back of a guard. Without thinking, I held my breath, freezing every muscle. The guard, only a meter or so away, seemed oblivious to my presence. I thought for sure he would hear the adrenaline-spiked heartbeat emanating from my chest. After what felt like ages, the guard finally continued along his route. Letting out the slightest relieved sigh, I crossed back the way I'd come, stepping onto the staircase and coming face-to-face with a returning wide-eyed guard.

CHAPTER 32: KRISTA

My back was killing me. Even with the pad from my pack, the hard stone floor of the minaret was unforgiving. I stretched, hearing the crack of my joints as the night's tension dispersed. Rolling over, I saw Omar already awake and staring out of the tower's narrow window.

"Any sign of the bastards?" I asked.

"Not a hint," he said.

"Think they left?"

"Maybe, but I don't trust them. Let's stick to the shadows today. With any luck, the aerials won't give us away. We can't survive an open confrontation. And we have to get to the pod."

"They wouldn't leave us, would they?" I asked.

"They absolutely would, and I couldn't blame them. If they come out of that pod, and we're nowhere to be found, at most, they'd give us 24 hours. Any longer and they'd be sitting ducks. We're alone out here. They'd probably figure we didn't make it. I wouldn't take it personally."

"We've come this far together. I feel like they'd at least owe us a search."

"Don't forget these monsters eat the dead. If we'd fallen, there'd be nothing to find."

"Good point, I suppose."

"Right now, let's eat what's left of the porcupine and see if we can't escape this hell hole."

After I choked down breakfast, I was glad that the desiccated meat was gone. I had enough porcupine for one lifetime. We descended the winding stairs, stopping abruptly at the steel door frozen into place by my katana. In the faint light that filtered down the staircase, I could see where rust had begun gnawing at the door's edges. Omar rustled in his pack before pulling out the only other smoke grenade in our possession.

"I hate to waste it, but I don't want to open this door to an ambush," said Omar.

"I think it's worth it," I said.

I grabbed the hilt of the katana and at his signal, yanked it from the disintegrating concrete, throwing ashen dust into the air. Omar jerked the door ajar to fling out the grenade before slamming it shut as I replaced my sword. We listened closely as the smoke dispersed, hearing only the hissing of the pressurized canister.

"On my mark, run left. If they chase us, find the nearest shelter. Ready?"

I nodded. I grabbed the katana and ripped it from the wall as Omar slung the door out of our way. Holding our breath and ignoring the sting in our eyes, we darted through the cloud, hugging the wall to our left and emerging from the building unscathed. Sticking to the shadows, we threw our backs against the nearest building.

"There's not a one," I said, tearing up from the irritant.

"Don't let your guard down," said Omar.

Silently, we crept along the buildings and rubble, keeping the road in sight. The tracks we followed were disappearing as the wind-blown dust erased the signs of the convoy's passage. Protecting us from the sun's looming rays, stalking through the shade allowed us to travel further without the ill effects of the heat. By mid-morning, we were desperate for food and getting snappy with each other. We still carried the ration bars, but we were saving those for dire emergencies. More concerning, our meager water supply was running dangerously low. When the tracks took a turn to the south, we were elated to discover a small reservoir.

"Is that what I think it is?" I asked, poorly containing my excitement.

"Unless it's a mirage, I think so," said Omar.

"Don't even joke."

We jogged to the small lake, praying the water wouldn't be stagnant. The placid blue-green water looked promising as we neared its narrow shore. Using a cloth, we filtered the water into our bottles before dropping in purification tablets. After the tablet had dissolved, I risked the first sip. Though it was tepid and foul, it was safe and hydrating.

"It tastes disgusting," I said to Omar as he emptied his flask over his head.

The little rivulets beaded down his hair, once closely cropped, now several inches thick, matching his developing beard. He was starting to resemble the Saharan transporters more than the clean-cut, untried candidate he'd been when we first met. As Omar shook the excess water from his scalp, I grinned, feeling a deepening fondness for him. I guiltily suppressed the feeling, knowing it had only been a matter of weeks since Zeke's death.

"You think there are fish in there?" I asked.

"One way to find out," Omar said, gesturing towards my pack where I had some of Kurt's old tackle.

"At least I'm more comfortable with fishing than hunting, though this'll go faster if you help."

Omar groaned as he rose and stretched. Within the hour, we caught five under-sized fish, but enough to keep us alive another day. I wasn't looking forward to the raw meat.

"Let's find someplace cool to eat these minnows," said Omar, sarcastic on both counts.

We settled for the closest nearby shelter, not wanting the fish to spoil in the excessive heat. It was another mosque, much smaller than the previous one, but built like a vault.

"God, if only we could see the pod from here," I said. "This place looks impregnable."

"It's as sturdy as it must have been centuries ago. They knew their craft. It even has a lookout tower," said Omar, pointing to the squatty minaret, a fraction of the previous pair's height.

After breaking the aged lock on the door, we barred the entrance from the inside with some twisted iron rubble and explored the ancient structure. The feeling of security was delightfully refreshing even in the region's extreme heat. In the back of the place, we found a small kitchen.

"You think we could cook the fish?" I asked.

"I wouldn't risk it. We're getting closer to the city center. We don't want to attract the inverts to where we'll be hiding for an extended period."

"Damn. I just really wasn't looking forward to sashimi."

"The bloody things are so small, you could swallow them bones and all."

"Hard pass."

"We can build a fire. There's enough wooden furniture in the next room to burn for days. The smoke isn't near as attractive as food. We could even boil our water. It might make it more palatable."

"I'm definitely up for that. It tastes like an eight's armpit," I said.

"And how would you know what that tastes like?" Omar said, smiling.

"You know… How they smell, I guess," I said, feeling my cheeks flush from embarrassment.

Omar gave a deep resounding laugh, a sound completely new to me.

"An eight's armpit…" he said, shaking his head.

After devouring the tiny meal, which hadn't been near as bad as I built it up to be, we lit a small fire using readily available parchment and the dry wooden furniture. As each piece of wood was laid on the fire, we watched, entranced, as the coating bubbled off before the wood underneath combusted. With water boiling, we pulled it from the embers to cool. Sitting on the floor next to Omar, I watched the steam evaporate into the air as the sun dipped on the dusty horizon. The last thing I remember was my eyelids beginning to droop.

"Wake up," Omar said gently.

My eyes fluttered as I woke.

"How long was I out?" I asked.

"Few hours. You looked like you needed it."

I looked toward the tiny windows, high in the wall. Judging by the light, it was past dusk.

"We need to move," I said.

"That's not wise. The light's fading and those inverts have far better night vision than we do."

"But what if they come out of the pod, and we're not there?"

"Doubtful. It's still awfully early."

"Please, let's go. You said yourself that we must be getting close."

"Fine. But the second it gets dark, we take shelter wherever we can. That may mean uncomfortable accommodations, princess."

A glared at him. I wasn't a damn princess. I could hunt. I could kill. Was I ready to walk off into the sunset on my own? No. But then again, going solo wasn't wise for anyone who valued their life, including Omar.

"Fine," I echoed. "But don't call me princess again."

"Whatever you say, princess."

"Ass hat."

Once we'd left the security of the building, I started to second guess my decision. We were losing daylight and leaving a solid sanctuary. Regardless of the indecision, I pressed on. No sooner than we'd left sight of the shelter, we came upon a bloom of polies.

"Dammit," Omar muttered.

The pill bugs weren't a huge threat on their own, they were unintelligent scavengers but usually found hot on the heels of the larger Arthropods. Their sickening gnawing echoed off the walls that remained standing around us. Whatever it was they were eating, it was too disintegrated to tell. Only the dark red spatters indicated an Earth-based life form. Omar gestured how to proceed around the bloom and I followed him, being careful to stay close and silent. The detour spent the precious remaining light, putting us at severe risk of being caught blind.

In the dim light, I didn't see a mangled piece of rusty steel protruding from the ground. After stepping off of it, the tension released, making it bounce into the air with a *sproing!* Omar glared at me, appalled. We froze, no longer hearing the polies smacking. After a tense, breathless moment passed, the chewing continued and we ventured forth as rapidly as we dared. Breathing a sigh of relief once back near the road, we picked up our speed. Moments later, I saw a familiar shape in the distance, protruding slightly above the flat surrounding terrain.

"Is that what I think it is?" asked Omar.

"That's the pod! We made it!" I yelled.

"*Shhh,*" said Omar, a wide grin across his face. "Be happy, just do it… quietly."

"Sorry, I'm just so excited!" I said, hugging him.

Omar returned the hug tightly. When I pulled back, he looked me in the eyes, wrapped his firm hand around the back of my neck, and pulled my lips to his. First was a shock, then I relaxed into pleasure. I passionately kissed back, feeling a fire igniting in my chest. Under the glow of the rising moon, I opened the top of his jumpsuit revealing his taut body. He kissed down my neck as I ran my hand up the side of his torso, feeling the undulation of his muscles beneath.

Grabbing me under the thighs, he hoisted me into the air and carried me into an intact nearby building within eyesight of the pod. I pressed my lips firmly onto his as he smoothly drew my zipper down, fumbling to remove my pack and shut the door. As he laid me down, the fire in my chest roared into an inferno as Omar's blaze joined my own. The flames continued through the night, leaving neither of us longing for warmth.

CHAPTER 33: HUCK

After the obligatory search in the lobby, I staggered into the Dust facility on my second day, barely able to slip on the rubbery suit after the previous day's exertion. Midge was looking as confident and content as ever, already laying out the receiving pans and setting the large steel pots on the burners.

"I don't know how I'm going to stir today," I said. "I can barely lift my arms above my elbows. I'm so sore. I thought I was in better shape than this."

"No worries," said Midge. "Hey Oskar, can we shift to the ovens today?"

"Foreman Oskar, you little runt! I don't give a rat's ass as long as you're pulling your weight."

With that Midge waved the oven workers over to our station. I felt a wash of relief.

"Don't get excited, greenie," the bald worker said, so tall she towered over me. "You'll be begging for this spot back tomorrow."

I nodded my thanks as Midge, and I headed to the ovens. In a matter of minutes, the ovens were roaring, and I realized why the others had abandoned their post so quickly. The intense heat radiating from their open ends steamed me inside my suit like a crustacean.

"Make sure you drink plenty of water," said Midge. "If you pass out, Oskar will piss on you until you wake up."

I rolled my eyes in jest.

"I'm serious. He's done it before. He has no sympathy for falling due to dehydration."

"Jesus," I said. "Remembering to drink won't be a problem with that image stuck in my head."

"That's the idea," Midge giggled. "Once the boilers are up and running, they'll fill the trays like we did yesterday. As they hand them off, they'll start crystallizing. We run the trays through the oven to bake off the moisture. Got it?"

"Got it," I said through the muffling mask.

"And don't drop the trays or passing out will be the least of your worries."

Once the first tray was ready, I carefully balanced its precarious weight as I cautiously approached the ovens, the steaming liquid sloshing back and forth. I quickly realized the trays were as taxing to my arm muscles as the constant stirring had been. I fully appreciated the ancient cliche about frying pans and fryers. The rigid metal trays were cumbersome as well, the decades of heat had warped them, making carrying them laden with the Dust solution a daunting task. I finally made it to the oven's receiving end and gently loaded the tray onto the metal conveyor belt, somehow managing to not spill a drop.

"Now only a few hundred more," said Midge, positive as always.

I carried ten or so more with no loss before I had my first little bobble. My foot slipped on the dusty floor and I had the slightest bit of spillage, but once the liquid in the tray began rocking back and forth, there was no stopping it. Before Midge came to the rescue, about a quarter of the tray's contents had sloshed onto the floor.

Oskar was on me quicker than I thought the fat man could move. He jerked the tray from my hand and slapped it into the oven, spilling almost as much as I had. Spinning me around by my shoulder and kicking me in the back of the knee, he had me on the ground before I could react. I felt the first impact of his crop across my upper back, burning hotter than the oven's heat. Then again. And again. Every time I made the motion to stand, the blows would come across my ears. With each blow, the rage inside me grew. When Oskar finally stopped, Midge was there to help me up.

"Don't do anything," Midge whispered. "Trust me. I know."

Midge helped me rise to my feet and face Oskar, who was millimeters from my nose.

"Maybe next time you'll be more *careful*," he said, his fumy breath nearly toppling me once more.

I seethed but trusted Midge's guidance. The notion that I could take the washed-up oaf gave me some comfort. With my upper body in a frenzy of pain, I worked ceaselessly until our first break was called. As I choked down the provided gruel, I couldn't help but stare at the back of Oskar's obese frame desiring nothing more than to show him up at his own game.

"It's not Oskar you have to worry about," said Midge. "Dust is how they subjugate the people. Standing against the supply line is a great way to wind up in the Pits. Zabu knows you can survive, so he's not about to banish you."

"You're wise beyond your years, Midge."

"I'll be ten soon enough, you know."

I smiled. I would miss this kid when we left, but someone Midge's age had no place on the surface, though I'm sure Midge would insist that survival wouldn't be a problem. Hell, Midge had survived this long in this nonsense.

"You said 'the Pits.' What are those, exactly?"

"I don't know. It's one of those things that no one ever comes back from."

I nodded, struggling to find an end to Zabu's tyranny. Midge and I finished working the day without another incident. When I left the processing floor, I was rigid with pain and inflammation. The surface of my skin felt swollen and irritated from the oppressive heat. My back was covered in raised welts from the beating I had sustained. My arm muscles were numb from the repeated strain. The thin woman was right, I wanted my old place back. I wondered if the pulverizing station was any less intolerable.

Ignoring the disgusting conditions of the facility's locker room, I stripped down and took a cold shower to rinse away the sweat, dust, and misery. I was caught off guard when I was joined in the shower by Oskar. I didn't figure he was one for showers, reeking the way he did. Thankfully, he passed me with nothing more than a grunt. As I closed the water valve, I saw his back was covered with evidence of uncountable whippings, and I felt the faintest wisp of pity. When he turned to look back, I quickly diverted my eyes and exited the area. I didn't feel clean, but I felt better.

Taking time to clear my head, I meandered back to our apartments. As I was passing through the level's market district, I caught sight of a group of junkies wedged between two vacant stalls. There were four of them, all in tattered clothes and piled atop one another like old laundry. A quick glance revealed a state of bliss, but closer inspection showed behind the smile was something more ominous and dissociated. Someone shoved past me walking towards the group.

"Sorry, guy," he said. "Hey, since you're here, it's been a long time since I ate anything. Can you spare any points?"

I fumbled in my pockets, looking for some of the tokens Zabu had provided, pulling a few out.

"I'm actually pretty hungry too if you want to go get something," I said. "My treat."

The man looked at his companions, then returned his glance to me.

"Sure, guy."

Not wanting to take him too far from his companions, I found an establishment close by that looked relatively appetizing. Aside from the obscenely loud upbeat music and a strange blue lighting bathing the patrons, the place looked promising.

"You again?" the host asked, her hair formed into a badass faux-hawk. "Do you have points this time?"

"He's with me," I said, struggling to speak over the music.

She gave a look of indifference and escorted us to a back table where we had a seat.

"What's your name?" I asked him.

"Everyone calls me Tang. You?"

"Huck."

"Thanks for taking me out like this."

"Sure. Will your friends want anything?"

"Not for several hours, they won't."

"What can I get you?" the waiter said, interrupting.

"I want an *asaro empanada*. At least three of them," Tang said.

"I'd like the same, maybe just two for me," I said, as the waiter disappeared. "You sure your friends wouldn't like anything?"

"They're up for the next few. No need. It'd be nasty by then."

"Up for the next few?"

"Yeah, guy. I mean, Huck. They've found their way out. Who am I to interrupt it?"

"You mean to the surface?"

"No, guy," he said, looking at me questioningly. "You new here?"

"I just arrived from Horizonte."

"Wow. Judging by your dust stains, I figured you for a rezzy. That explains your accent."

"What'd you mean, a way out?" I asked.

Tang arched his eyebrow. He was about to speak when the waiter dropped our plates off unceremoniously with the delicious-smelling stuffed entrées.

"Dust, guy," Tang said, shoving the food into his mouth while explaining. "Kano's only got a few types: oppressors, oppressed, living, and dead. The powder may not change our lives, but it makes us feel free again. At least for a bit."

I thought about Akhil and what divided the addict from the teetotaler. A grimace must have passed across my face.

"If you're going to judge me, you can keep your damn *empanadas*," Tang said, dropping his second helping on the plate.

"No, no," I said, waving apologetically. "I'm sorry. I've just… I've had some rough experiences. Please stay."

Tang reluctantly picked up his food.

"Wouldn't you rather change your life?"

"Look around, Huck. How are we going to change this?" Tang said, starting on the third. "The second anyone stands out, they are destroyed by the oppressors."

"What about the surface? It's beautiful, fresh, and—"

"And full of freaking inverts, Huck! God, and I thought my brain was addled."

"I've been there! It's gorgeous. Of course it's dangerous but probably no more than inside here. The Arthropods congregate around the pods, something fierce, but get through that and it's livable."

"I don't know, guy. Look, I work, I buy some powder, and I enjoy myself. It's not a great life, but it's my life. And I'm certainly not on the run from a bunch of dang Arthropods."

There was nothing more to say. It was clear Tang was done with me and the food. I looked down and saw where I hadn't touched mine. I left the points on the table and walked with Tang back to his friends. I handed him the two wrapped portions.

"Thanks, Huck," he said. "It was nice talking to someone again."

Tang, pulled a small inhaler from his thigh cargo pocket and charged it.

"Sure you don't want to escape, too?"

"I'm sure."

"Suit yourself, Citizen Oppressed," he said, smiling.

I watched him take a heavy hit and lay down slowly on the mound of blankets next to his friends, thinking about the irony of his words.

•••••••••

When I arrived back at the apartments, I found Mei and Ariadne waiting with a strange bearded man. As soon as Ariadne saw me, she lit up excitedly.

"Huck, we found him!" she said, tugging on my arm.

"Hi," I said to the stranger. "I'm Huck."

"Ekon," he said.

I looked at Ariadne dumbfounded.

"I know," she said. "He was just… there."

"She makes it sound as though Ekon appeared to her like a mystic," he said, chuckling. "It is far simpler than that. Isn't it obvious? Fate has wound our destinies together. Young Ariadne has kindly explained your mission. Ekon serves at serendipity's pleasure. Ekon will embark immediately for Pod Baghdad and alert them to your needs."

My mouth fell to the floor.

"Do not be surprised, young Huck. Master Kebe wouldn't refer you if your intentions weren't pure, nor would fate have been so accommodating. No, this is of the utmost import, methinks."

"How will you travel," Mei asked. "It's an invert-filled desert from here to there."

"About that, worry not, young Mei. Ekon is of an ancient line of people, who have roamed the desert for millennia—since long before the strange worms. Rest easy. Ekon will find you help. We have something special. Just for you," he said, making an unusual bowing motion and departing with a laugh.

"Is it just me, or is he a little crazy?" asked Mei.

"Oh, he's crazy," I said. "But something about him puts me at ease."

"I think we can count on him too," said Ariadne.

"That's amazing you found him when you did," I said. "I haven't had a chance to look for him. Have you told Arjun?"

"I don't want to burden him further. He's pretty worried about Hemant," said Ariadne. "We haven't seen or heard from Hemant in days. You know how Arjun is with his work when he's like that."

"We need to make sure he eats," I recalled.

"Absolutely," said Ariadne. "On another note, we were almost captured today."

"Do what?" I said.

"We helped the Resistance with a food raid," said Ariadne, sheepishly. "We didn't think anyone would get hurt, but it was an ambush, Huck."

"Dear God!" I said. "We aren't supposed to be making waves, Ariadne."

"It was the right thing to do, Huck. These people are hurting. Our mission to the Hive would be pointless if there was nothing left to save.

"I suppose you're right," I said. "Is everyone alright?"

"We escaped, but there were casualties on both sides. Zabu's going to be in a rage."

"I'm glad you guys are okay," I said.

"What about you?" asked Mei. "Was your second day any better?"

"No," I said. "I was beaten."

"Oh, no!" said Mei, as Ariadne sucked in a breath.

"It's nothing," I said, dismissing it. "My day has put things into perspective. You're right. We can't leave Pod Kano like it is. We can't emancipate the entire population, but we can remove one of the regime's pillars and break the addictive cycle in one fail swoop."

"How do you propose we do that?" asked Ariadne.

"You're in with the Resistance now. We help them destroy the Dust plant."

CHAPTER 34: HEMANT

Why am I so hot? I slung the blankets off only to feel a sharp chill. *Damn fever again.* My head was pounding. I palmed my eyes as I set up on the edge of the bed. *What the hell did I do last night?* I stumbled out of my bunk, grabbing the wall for stability. The rest of the platoon snored around me, many with the evening's companionship. After releasing the nightmarish pressure in my bladder, I found my way to the water station and glugged down an ungodly amount before I felt sated. Leaning against the counter, I took a few deep breaths, trying to relive the events of the previous night, but only glimpses flashed in my mind.

Then I felt the raging hunger. Raiding the cold locker, I threw together a sandwich of whatever was convenient and inhaled it. *Better.* I felt better. Still, the massive headache persisted as though Commandant Saif was resting his heel on my temple. *What did I— Oh. That.* I hustled back to my bunk and dug around in my side table drawer, the one place we were allowed to keep personal effects, and scattered its contents on my mattress. I shoved Arjun's photo out of the way, superstitious that he could somehow sense the person I'd become. That line of thought was for another day. My fingers felt the coolness of the textured metal grip and the soft rubber mask.

I pulled the breather out and took a deep inhalation. The device would need to be recharged soon. I felt the flow of chemicals flood my brain, electrifying each synapse like the neon sign over a seedy pub. Instantly, the headache dissipated. The tingling started in my chest and worked its way towards my extremities. I felt invincible again. God, it felt good! I looked down again at the photo, still out with my other belongings. *Was this who I'd become?* I shook the voice from my head. *Not now. Later.* Captain Abbas filled the doorway, his shadow stretching across the floor.

"Muskrats! Attention!" he yelled.

I pulled my jumpsuit zipper to and stood at attention, watching as the others groggily rose from their bunks. Many of them took hits as they rose and threw on their uniforms. Barely up and we were already basking in the warm glow from the empowering Dust. *I'm just using it to be more effective. I could go without—*

"The Resistance is getting bolder in their attacks. They were able to outmaneuver us in the ambush we set. They killed some of our own," he said, gesturing towards the empty bunks, their forlorn mattresses rolled up. "The Prime Minister is tired of their subterfuge. With his permission and the blessing of Commandant Saif that we are going to, shall we say, shake them out."

"Oorah!" I yelled with the others, my earlier concerns slipping away as the drug's effects took hold.

The Resistance was proving to be problematic for the pod's infrastructure. I sure didn't agree with Zabu's methods, but he had an organized system to keep the pod afloat and the Resistance was messing with it. I looked at my assignments as fighting for the people's wellbeing, not as being one of Zabu's tools. Following Abbas, the other Muskrats and I filed out the door and headed to the mid-levels.

"What the hell are we doing in a residential area?" asked Mathias, pushing through the others to join up with me.

I shrugged.

"There's a rumor we're taking out someone essential," he said. "I hope it's worth it. That asshole Abbas interrupted my beauty sleep for this."

"You'd need a lot more sleep, man," I said, laughing.

"Shut up. Hopefully, after this, we can eat breakfast. I'm so hungry, I could choke down a polie."

"That's disgusting, man."

It was his turn to shrug.

We filed down a corridor lined with apartments. Resistance fighters could be anyone. If they'd identified a cell in an apartment, who was I to judge? Anytime a resident would open their door to the hallway, they'd immediately shut it again when they saw our approach. Towards the end of the corridor, Abbas stopped at an unmarked hatch, the number plate having been removed long ago. With a whirl of his hand, Abbas gave the command to ready our weapons. I raised the cold metal of the mace to my shoulder level, the augmented adrenal response surging in my veins.

With a gesture to the ram crew, they battered the hatch open, and the entry team flooded through. Breaking dishes and muffled screams washed out in the hall and within moments, an innocuous-looking older couple were brought forth from the apartment and forced to kneel at Abbas' feet. Granted, I didn't know much about the Resistance, but the elderly pair didn't seem like fighters to me. Abbas crouched to their level, pulling the woman's face up by her chin to look him in the eye.

"Tell me," he said in almost a whisper. "Who are the Seven?"

The woman muttered what sounded like a prayer in Chinese.

"The Seven? I don't know what that means," she said, crying. "We are vendors. We make carved hand tools. We know nothing outside of our trade."

"Your trade? Your shop is a front for Resistance fighters," he said, stroking the matted gray hair from her face. "If you wish me to spare both of your lives, you will tell me the names of the Seven. If you can tell me the names of your cell's leaders, you will walk away from this encounter."

All the woman's innocence vanished, her face becoming a hardened mask.

"You will never get what you want from us. Zabu is a blight on Kano. We won't stop—"

Abbas slowly drew a pistol and fired it point-blank into her husband's head, splattering his brain all over the far wall and his wife's face. Even through my Dust-softened emotions, my stomach plunged in reaction. *They did something very wrong. Yes, they must have. Surely this was an appropriate punishment.* Captain Abbas wasn't ruthless. Still, there was something about the exchange that felt wrong.

"What are the names of your cell leaders?" he repeated with the same flat intonation.

The woman held up her hands pleadingly and whimpered, unable to speak. Her husband's blood dripped off of her fingertips. She slowly shook her head, and Abbas leveled the pistol at her face. Suddenly, a messenger sprinted up to him and said something into his ear.

We will finish this conversation later, yes?" he said, leaving the woman alone with the corpse.

"Muskrats, there is a Resistance attack underway. We've been reassigned! Everyone to level 93!"

•••••••••

When everyone had arrived on 93, there was already a thick layer of smoke billowing overhead. The acrid veil clung to the ceiling, drafted toward the central shaft where it would give the air filters hell. My eyes burned from the fumes. The smell of singed Dust permeated the air.

"What's going on?" I asked Mathias.

"This is where they refine our powder, man. The Resistance must have hit it," he said.

"But there are more facilities, right?"

Mathias shook his head. "This is where they stored everything, too. Enjoy your last few hits, they're probably all we're getting for a while."

I unclipped the breather from my belt and took a sparing hit, feeling the yin and yang of power and relaxation. Already riding a buzz, everything took on a surreal quality. Colors more vibrant. Sounds more distinct. Some emotions enhanced while others numbed. Next to me, Mathias also took another hit as Abbas addressed us.

"They've hit us hard. The facility has been destroyed along with our Dust stockpiles and raw pheromones. You boys are high on the priority list, but cherish what you have. We'll likely have to go months without more."

An audible groan and varying expletives joined the lingering pops and crackles from the unextinguished fires.

"But I also have good news. Many of the fighters are holed up in there," said Abbas, pointing. "They've trapped themselves. This is your chance. Take revenge as you see fit, but spare anyone who you think is a leader. Zabu will deal with them personally. Anyone else, eliminate at your discretion. Mask up and move out!"

"Oorah!" we yelled.

Next to the entrance, a platoon member was dealing out masks. I donned the face covering, which reeked of sweat and mildew, and proceeded into the facility lit orange by the sporadic flames. Marching past the vacant security checkpoint, I headed deeper into the factory floor. Despite the tall ceilings, the smoke hung lower, trapped between the beams supporting the space's ceiling. In the distance, I heard the distinctive pop of gunfire and clutched my mace more tightly. The Muskrats fanned out among the stations in an attempt to root out stragglers. Mathias covered my back. I pointed towards a storage room that had yet to be cleared.

"Let's check it out," said Mathias.

"What if they have projectile weapons," I asked. "This mace can't stop bullets."

"It's doubtful. Their entire force only has a few," he said. "That's why they only arm us with these."

We pushed towards the hatch. After counting down on my fingers, Mathias kicked the door in. For his small frame, he packed a punch. The door swung wide on its groaning hinges as we listened for any sign of life. Nothing. I risked a glance inside. Just like the main area, the room was filled with contaminated air. We pressed forward, crouching behind waist-high storage cabinets, still listening for any movement. I peered over the countertops to the rear of the room where shelves or pheromone containers lined the walls, their contents bubbling out all over the floor, ruined by the intense heat. Seeing no one, I stood. Mathias followed.

I walked to the rear of the room, struggling to maintain my balance on the slimy floor. I walked through the aisles of shelving scanning for any sign of movement. The room seemed abandoned.

"Clear—" I began to say, turning towards Mathias.

I heard the sickening crunch of a skull as I saw an unfamiliar gaunt face centimeters from mine. The man's eyes rolled back into his head as his body crumpled to the floor. Mathias stood behind with his mace, now covered in a thick pink slurry.

"What was that you were saying?" he said.

I could hear the smirk behind his mask.

"Don't say 'clear' until we've checked every damn nook and

cranny, dumbass," he said. "I don't like killing people, but he was about to eviscerate your kidneys."

"Thanks, Mathias."

"Now, before you go off all half-cocked again, check behind those crates for any more of these bastards. Then you can yell 'clear.'"

The body, now bleeding into the orange goo, turned the floor to an icky brown sludge that stuck to my boots. I held onto the shelf for balance as I shuffled to the dark, far corner of the room where the crates obscured a potential hiding spot. As I approached, I heard movement and readied my weapon. I couldn't hesitate. I had to strike before they did. As I peered around, I swung, then struggled to halt the strike midair.

After spending months together, even masked, I recognized Ariadne's frame. I was pretty sure one of the two behind her was Mei. If not held up by my mask, my mouth would've hit the floor. Ariadne's eyes burned as they stared into my soul. They were filled with hurt, agony, and anger. I deflated. Everything wrong about my actions hit me like a blow from my own war hammer. *I'm on the wrong side.* Everything I had been told about the Resistance had to be wrong. My soul filled with doubt and despair. I started to move my hand towards Ariadne, who jerked back in shock. My world warped with a clarity that pierced through Dust's veil. *What had I done?* I turned back to Mathias, who looked impatient.

"All…," I choked, my throat dry as a bone. "All clear."

Mathias raised an eyebrow before shrugging his shoulders. We left the room, shouting the all-clear. The rest of the skirmish had concluded. Near the entrance, Abbas had two figures: a vested man with short curly hair and an older woman with long gray hair.

"We've got their leaders!" Abbas yelled. "Two of the Seven!"

Hoots and hollers rose from the Muskrats as I stood frozen. I turned to look at Mathias, who surprisingly, was frozen as well.

CHAPTER 35: ARIADNE

After Huck's suggestion to destroy the Dust refinery, we had taken him immediately to meet Miranda and discuss his idea. Miranda led me, Mei, and Huck to a Resistance hideout. Coming in Miranda's tow, the others had been quick to accept him. In consideration of the recent ambush, Pyotr and Miranda planned the clandestine meeting in a space never used by the group. Through antiquated maps, Pyotr had located an old archive room that appeared forgotten. With a blow from Pyotr's staff, the antiquated lock shattered. The door swung wide, filling the hallway with the odor of mildew and rat feces.

"Are you sure this is sanitary?" Huck said, looking at me.

I grunted uncertainly, pulling my shirt over my nose.

"At least the guards won't want to come in after us," said Mei, smiling.

We filed into the dank room, illuminated only by a handful of candles, trying our best not to trip over the disintegrating heaps of paper—decades of the pod's history—rotting into oblivion. After the last person entered, Mei closed the door and more lit candles were divvied out. Even in the undesirable setting, there was something oddly comforting about being surrounded by friends and the warm glow of candlelight.

I missed Hemant and Arjun. With Hemant stationed elsewhere, when Arjun wasn't working, he holed himself up in his newly-acquired lab. Huck would periodically find traces of food in his apartment, so at least we knew he was eating and, hopefully, sleeping. I was excited to make a difference for the pod's residents, but I was also anxious to be back on track with Kano growing smaller in the distance.

"If you can find something sturdy enough, have a seat," said Pyotr, his face bathed in a subtle glow. "I apologize for the conditions. Zabu is becoming relentless in his pursuit, and we must mitigate risks wherever possible. We have it on good authority that guards have been given free rein in all matters involving us. That means harassment, death, and possibly even torture until the Seven are identified."

"In light of the escalation in hostilities, some of you may no longer feel comfortable being part of the Resistance," added Miranda, in her soft but commanding presence. "Rest assured, we understand. If the risk is too great for either you or your families, you may leave now and none of us will think a modicum less of you for it."

No one stirred.

"I am pleased you all recognize the importance of what we are doing," said Pyotr.

"We have an unexpected objective to discuss tonight," said Miranda. "For the first time, we have someone inside the Dust facility willing to aid us in its destruction. All of our previous attempts to place a mole in the facility have failed. Removing the drug's power from Zabu's iron grip will force the residents to face the reality they've been avoiding. This is a chance to change things! Huck, would you please share what you told me earlier?"

I turned towards Huck, who even in the orange cast of the flames, had paled from the sudden attention. He slowly stepped forward into the midst of the group, his footsteps softened by the floor's residual moisture.

"Um…I guess most of you don't know me, that is unless you were at our presentation. Which, err… wasn't a good moment for you all," began Huck.

I cringed. He could face the most terrifying of Arthropods but not a room full of Resistance fighters. If he was going to win people over to his idea, this was an awkward start.

"So, I've been working in the plant for a few days. I know it's not much, but it's been enough to get a feel for how things are run and what the place's vital components are. It's basically a four-part process. First, the raw pheromone is mixed with a reagent to encourage crystallization. Second, excess moisture is baked from the crystallized material. Third, the dry material is carefully collected. Finally, the crystals are pulverized and dosed out into inhaler capsules for distribution."

"None of that is new to us," said a scruffy middle-aged man. "What are you proposing we do to stop it?"

"Rickson, please let the young man continue," said Miranda.

"Yeah, uh… For one, the raw pheromone is extremely sensitive to high temperatures. They keep it shielded in a 'cool room,' but any spike in the refinery's temperature, from say a fire, would be more than the room's insulation could handle. A fire would also activate the fire-retardant systems, destroying the exposed powder, leaving only the equipment to be destroyed."

"Between the guards and the civilians, we've never been able to openly attack the facility," said Pyotr. "What are you suggesting to circumvent that?"

"The workers are all there under duress. This mission cannot be completed unless their safety can be guaranteed. I've—"

"Nothing is guaranteed in Pod Kano," interrupted Rickson.

"I've got a proposal. We take a daily break for lunch, but the foreman staggers the time. The Dust can't be left unattended in certain stages, so we break when it's possible. If I could somehow get a message out to you when that time comes, the civilians would be safely away in the break area. I could bar the door and you could conveniently not enter."

"Your proposal is sound," said Miranda. "With small incendiary charges, we could render the equipment useless and limit casualties. The fire caused by the explosions should be enough to overheat the raw pheromones and activate the fire suppression system, destroying the Dust."

"How's he going to get a message out?" asked Rickson.

"I have an idea," I said as all the attention turned to me. "Huck went on a mission back in Horizonte and used short-range radios. Does Kano have anything like that?"

Miranda's head swiveled towards a thin-haired man leaning against the wall, who spoke as if on cue.

"It's possible," he said. "We have those same transistor radios. It would be hard to hide the headset and system. And he'd have to get close to us. Real close. Are you familiar with Morse code, Huck?"

"I'm afraid I'm not," said Huck. "I've heard of it, but aside from that, no."

"I can teach you enough. 'GO' and 'NO.' Three letters," he said. "The problem is still overcoming the Arthropod-generated interference."

"How far apart can we be?"

"Six feet at the most."

Rickson snorted.

"I could take up smoking," said Huck, forcing a laugh. "The smokers go out to the lobby for their drags just before lunch."

"That could work," he said. "The thick wall is liable to interfere, but if you could cut the distance to say, three feet, it should work."

"There's one other hangup," Huck said. "We're searched on entry and exit."

"Let me deal with that," volunteered Liesel.

The group divided up into squads to plan the attack, which would take place in the morning. Mei and I were assigned to the demolition team. I craned my neck over the huddle of fighters to watch Huck with Liesel and the techie, whose name I'd since learned was Uri. Uri was removing components from a small device to make it lower profile as Liesel was testing the hidden placement of the radio around Huck's thigh. *Did she really need to touch him to put it on?*

"Ariadne?" Rickson said as Mei dug her pointy elbow into my ribcage. "Care to join us."

"I'm sorry," I said, feeling my face flush. "What did you say?"

"I said, 'Are you comfortable handling explosives?'"

"I will do whatever it takes. I'm trained with various weapons, but explosives are new to me."

"That's fine. They're foolproof," said Rickson. "Well, provided you don't hang around after you place them. They're magnetic. Huck tells us that all the equipment is metallic enough for the bombs to adhere to."

Rickson held out a small device, which looked similar to a bell you would use to grab a host's attention at an eatery.

"Turn the dial as far as it'll go. That puts it in 'chain mode.' Basically, when another detonation is nearby, it'll give this little booger permission to do the same. Attach it somewhere critical on each piece of equipment, push the center button to arm, and get out of the way. They're small, but that doesn't mean you want to be nearby when they go."

"Understood," I said.

"If everything is metal, how will it cause a fire?" asked Mei.

"Huck told Pyotr that half the stuff in there has rubber coatings to reduce static discharge. Trust me, if rubber gets hot enough, it burns like you wouldn't believe. Our forward team will take out the external guards and station Uri where he can pick up Huck's signal. Assuming we are a 'GO,' after a three-minute count, the forward team will force entry into the lobby, and when it's clear, we move in to place charges."

Rickson pointed to a crude sketch of the factory's interior.

"Here are the lines of equipment, you each should see your name. You are responsible for explosive placement and personal withdrawal. The last two charges I place will be on a timer. One of which is for redundancy. Once your charges are down, withdraw. We don't have time for a roll call. Once the place goes up, we'll scatter into the wind. Understood?"

Mei and I nodded.

·········

The next morning, Huck left with the radio hidden high on his inner thigh. I wasn't sure what exactly he and Liesel had planned, but Huck seemed assured that it would work. Funnily enough, what had him the most nervous was his first experience smoking.

Before leaving, I hid a note for Arjun warning him to escape just in case anything happened to us. As planned, Mei and I met up with the others and stationed ourselves around the corner of the facility at the chosen rendezvous. We watched from a distance as the forward team advanced on the guards. With practiced precision, eight men rushed forward, each slamming a guard into the wall and shoving a knife up through their skulls before any of them could make a sound. *It's necessary. They are the bad guys, Ariadne.*

I took a deep breath, trying to calm my nerves. Somehow, this subterfuge was more intimidating than operating on the surface. At the silent command of Rickson, we lowered our provided masks into place. Huck had warned us that the air was thick with the concentrated intoxicant, which was far stronger than the pheromones Krista and I had experienced in the truck. Next to me, Mei's knives were out and at the ready for the ensuing confrontation.

Listening closely to his headset, Uri gave the motion for "GO." The forward team entered as we advanced on the hatches. There was a small scuffle from inside the lobby, followed by shouts of "All Clear."

Miranda and Pyotr pushed into the room next, refusing to sit out of combat. Miranda had said that people wouldn't look up to leaders who would send troops into combat without being willing to go themselves. She and Pyotr both would be far better leaders of Pod Kano than Zabu. To our left, we could hear several fighters playing at breaking down the door to the break area if only to keep the occupants out of harm's way.

As planned, the demo team followed and dispersed amongst the equipment. Huck was right, even before we lit the place up, the heat was oppressive. I ran along my assigned production line setting each dial on the palm-sized explosives and arming them. By the time I finished the line, having laid demolitions from the stirring pots to the packing rooms, an echoing *boom* rocked the chamber. I looked alarmed at Mei, who was just as confused as I was. It wasn't an explosive, but the sound was concerning. Then we heard the shouts and gunfire.

"Hide!" I yelled.

"Where?!" asked Mei, searching for respite from the conflict.

"There!" I yelled, pointing at the cool storage room from Rickson's rudimentary map. "Huck said something about it being protected!"

We sprinted towards the door, encountering Liesel and beckoning her to join us. Two guards had already entered the space and blocked our way. I dropped into a slide and hamstrung the man with my dagger. As he fell, I reversed my knife sending it up through his kidneys. Mei had simultaneously taken down the other guard with a knife to the temple. We ran into the room, closing the door and pausing to see what was unfolding. In the central area, Pyotr and Miranda were on their knees and bound.

"Dammit!" I said, panicking.

"Look at Rickson!" said Mei.

Liesel whimpered.

Rickson stood, a smug grin on his face from having placed the last explosive. With a defiant yell, he thundered towards the nearest guard, who stopped him with a superhuman kick to the chest. Rickson rocketed back and crumpled next to the vats of his assigned line. He looked up, crossing eyes with me, grinning through his bloody smile and subtly motioning me to go as his body was engulfed by the first explosion. Behind me, Mei squeaked.

"We have to hide," I said, holding back tears as I shut the door.

Before I could pull the door to, Uri ducked inside with us.

"Take cover," he whispered. "I'll try and distract them. Escape when you can!"

Liesel and I followed Mei back to the far wall of the storage space, the contents of which I now saw only as revolting. I could already feel the heat rising in intensity through the shielded walls and hoped it would be sufficient to destroy the pheromones and make our mission worthwhile. Mei found a cluster of crates with a gap that, with luck, would conceal us from detection.

Mei hunkered down as we followed suit, trying to remain as quiet as possible. We heard the door open and the footfalls of multiple guards. I suppressed my panic, knowing there was no way

I could defend myself against armed guards from this tiny alcove. My only opportunity would be to surrender.

When I heard the sickening squish followed by a conversation between the guards, I knew Uri had fallen and I stifled a silent cry, praying the guards would pass us by. The last of my hope fleeted as I heard footfalls advancing towards the crates. *We're dead.* I readied to pounce, hoping maybe, just maybe, an opportunity would present itself. Then, when he came around the corner, I saw—*Hemant?!* My anguish began evaporating from the heat of my wrath. I stared at him, dumbfounded, my heart breaking asunder. *How? Why?* After trying to touch me, he backed away, lied to his companion, and disappeared among the crackling flames leaving us alone in our suffering.

CHAPTER 36: DIETER

Glaciers moved while the stairwell guard and I locked eyes. Finally, he raised his rifle and shouted for the others. Moments later, I was surrounded by weapons leveled at my head.

"What are you doing here?" asked the senior officer.

"I… I will be traveling on the convoy when it leaves," I stammered, trying to sound more sure of myself than I was.

I slowly pulled out my identification badge. The guard snatched it from me, holding it under the nearest light to read.

"Why weren't you escorted? Why did you not announce yourself?"

"I just wanted to have a look. I've never seen the vehicles up close."

The guard eyed me suspiciously.

"You're coming with me. We'll see what Chattar has to say about your intrusion."

A guard placed me in restraints, and I was escorted towards the administrative offices in the Nucleus. The more I thought about it, the more plausible my excuse seemed, providing me with some measure of relief. It was a perfectly acceptable reason to be there. More worrisome was if they decided to closely inspect the vehicles, would they find the fuel leak I had created? Then I would be mincemeat. I tried not to dwell on that.

We walked down the corridor, our figures passing from sconce to sconce in the low sodium light of evening. As we neared the offices, I saw a familiar face running toward me across the Nucleus' retractable catwalks, looking as vibrant as ever.

"Oh, Dieter! You said you would only be a moment!" Giselle said, pausing to take in my escort. "Tonight was supposed to be *our* night."

Behind me, the guards chuckled. Giselle ambled over to them, caressing their upper arms and the scruff of their necks as she maneuvered felinely through them.

"Gentlemen, I'll be disappointed if I can't have him all to myself," she said, pouting. "But I'd hate to leave you two *all alone.* Let me have him, and you two go down to Dame Adaugo's. Tell her Giselle sent you. You'll be happy you did."

She blew them a kiss.

"Consider this your warning," the senior officer said in a stern voice, trying to conceal his excitement. "If I catch you in a restricted area again, I may not be willing to take you to Chattar. Are we clear?"

"Yeah…yes, sir," I said, as the guard released me from the restraints.

Giselle took my hand and led me away as the guards almost bounded away.

"I really don't know why that works so well," I said.

"Control the human desires, and you control the humans," she said. "Zabu figured that out a long time ago. I'm just using his own weapons against him."

"I'm glad you did," I said. "Could I get you dinner? You know, as a thank-you."

"I'd love to."

•••••••••

I woke to the foreign sounds of cooking in my cramped apartment. Normally I grabbed something on the go, rarely preparing anything more complicated than a wrap. When I stumbled into the kitchen, Giselle already had breakfast ready and was pouring a cup of coffee for each of us. She had a way of bringing warmth to the normally cold space.

"You didn't have to do all of this," I said.

"I wanted to," she said. "And before you ask, you don't owe me anything for last night. That wasn't business."

She came around the bar and seated herself next to me, her figure plainly visible through the thin shirt she'd chosen from my closet. She held my hand.

"I really like having you around," I said.

"I'm sure you do," she responded, smiling. "Treats at night and in the morning. Considering where I found your spatula, I knew you didn't cook often."

I laughed. "It's not just that. I like your company," I said, pausing. "I'm sick, Giselle. Nothing contagious, mind you. My lab work has… poisoned me. My lab partner died yesterday from the same illness."

Giselle's hands flew to her mouth.

"Oh, Dieter," she said, resting her hand on my leg. "I'm so sorry. I didn't know."

"You couldn't have. You gave me comfort when I needed it most. For better or worse, I'm not taking time to grieve right now. I have to finish our work before something happens to me. Emile's death can't be in vain. Our existence is just so… fleeting. I don't have a ton of time left, but if you are willing, I'd like to spend it with you."

She squeezed my hand tightly. "I'd like that too," she said.

"You wouldn't have to work anymore. I have more than enough points to last you the rest of your life. When I'm gone…" I said, choking up. "When I'm gone, everything I have is yours."

"I might take you up on that," she said, leaning over to kiss me on the forehead. "The work has been good to me. Obviously, there are intolerable clients in any industry. It's provided for me when I had nothing. I'm not as young as I once was so my clientèle is waning. The idea of settling down is… honestly, a relief. I wish we could have longer. It's not fair that I find someone I like just in time to lose him."

"To be honest, I've been so enamored with my work, it took Emile's loss to make me realize the importance of other things. Had we found each other earlier, I'm not sure I would've valued it near as much as I do now."

Giselle straddled me and kissed me.

"Then let's not waste any more time," she said, our food untouched on the counter.

•••••••••

That afternoon, I reluctantly left Giselle in the apartment to meet Arjun in the lab. I had managed to concentrate his neem sample into several vials of oil, though without more source material, it couldn't be much.

As I approached the central shaft, there was a frenzy of activity. The military presence was on high alert. Over the course of my commute, I was stopped at four separate checkpoints for ID verification. *What in the world is going on?* I finally managed to get to the lab and found Arjun anxiously waiting for me in the hallway.

"You're late," he said, pacing back and forth. "You said you'd be here at 13:00 and you weren't."

"Arjun, it's okay. I promise. I was stopped at a number of checkpoints. Something's got their attention, but it's not us."

Arjun nodded, keeping his eyes low.

"You'll be pleased to know I got the neem concentrate ready," I said. "There are only a few vials, so you'll have to use it sparingly."

Arjun seemed to perk up.

"That's good news. I've found something as well. When my intelligence isn't being squandered on mundane errands, I have been experimenting in the lab. Back during our release from Pod Horizonte, I felt sure that something was being used to attract the Arthropods. I—"

"Wait, what?" I asked. "Attracting Arthropods on Release Day?"

"We were pretty confident that Prime Minister Carvalho was luring Arthropods in to create more of a spectacle for himself and his coterie. We were the first group to survive a release in untold years, though it took some cheating the system on our part."

I stood there with my mouth agape while I collected my thoughts.

"Is all pod leadership corrupt?" I asked, running my hand through my hair and ignoring the loose follicles. "Memo never really spoke much of this."

"I am inclined to think many of the leaders, without oversight, succumb to the natural corrupting tendencies of power."

"Wow, that's… that's troubling. If my previous communication with Baghdad is to be trusted, it seems to be far better ruled than Kano or Horizonte. Or so I hope. You guys could use a stroke of luck."

"In my experience, there's no such thing as luck."

"Well, how about I hope that you find more favorable conditions when you arrive at the next step on your journey."

Arjun cracked a rare smile.

"As far as my initial comment, I suspected that they used some sort of attraction signal. Based on the assumption that there must also be a repellent signal. I've been toying with a large range of low-frequency bands, but still well above the human hearing range. That's when I found it. There's a desirable range around 41 hertz that would repel Radar with regularity. I think it's plausible that the same frequencies could have a similar effect on the other Arthropods. The frequency has to be significantly amplified in wattage to be effective. The external speakers on Yanus' private carrier should be sufficient. I have modified a portable transceiver to emit this frequency. It should enable us to make excellent time to Baghdad should my theories hold."

"You are something else, Arjun," I said, shaking my head.

"Yes," he said. "That's what people continually tell me."

"So would you like to see the neem?"

"Please."

We walked into my lab, and I escorted him to my desk where I withdrew a large wooden box. I cracked open the lid, revealing the numerous glass vials inside, and watched Arjun's eyes light up.

"I'm sorry. They aren't all neem. Just these four on the top right. The rest are various chemical concoctions that we tried on Radar, many of which proved useless."

"Could these be loaded into those payload rockets?" Arjun asked.

"You'd need a tiny charge to optimize the oil's spread, but yes!"

"I believe that the concentrated delivery could be more effective than the aerosolized deterrent we currently have should we run into another spine back. Used in tandem with the auditory deterrent, we should have a chance of arriving at Baghdad unscathed."

"Then let's load up some rockets!"

•••••••••

Once we had gone to Rupert's old lab and modified the rockets, Arjun left to make his obligatory appearance in the non-lethal lab before heading home for the night. I meandered over to Radar's cell, watching him hover in the updraft as he eyeballed me with curiosity. In a way, he had become a friend, a last remnant of Rupert.

As Arjun and I loaded the neem cartridges into the rockets, I had warned him of the ever-increasing security. Though I wasn't sure what it was in response to, the implications were obvious. Arjun and his friends needed to leave with the most haste. Once the bomb was loaded into the carrier's fuel tank, Zhen and I would all but force them out.

I reached up and toggled off Radar's air current, watching him scurry off back to his cozy little nest of reeds in the corner. I looked down in my hand at a cluster of sticky bombs I had created for Arjun and laid them next to his transceiver where he'd be sure to find them. I hoped they'd prove valuable for him on the next stage of his journey. I placed my palm on the glass separating me from Radar.

"Thank you, buddy," I said. "You've helped us in more ways than you could imagine. While I've never cared for your friends, you've been enjoyable company."

I watched as his antenna twitched.

"I hope you fly for eternity," I said, depressing the button.

CHAPTER 37: KRISTA

*T*hunk went the spear as it nailed its target to the wall. I walked over to the crumbling edifice to reclaim my spear and prey, proud of how far I'd come. By now, I was getting used to the taste of cane rat, enjoying it more than porcupine and especially more than bony reptilian meats. With a jerk, I pulled the spear from the wall, cleaned the carcass, and carried lunch back to what Omar and I had dubbed "The Hut."

The Hut was a squat little building. Like the others, what had made it endure time also made a secure shelter. Conveniently, it had a second level underground with a cooking pit recessed into the floor in which we could cure meat safely. Piles of rubble and detritus surrounded the Hut, making perfect nesting grounds for the oversized rats. With the ample food, we'd had access to enough meat to last however long it would take Huck and the others to return.

The area surrounding the pod's low-relief cone was wide-open land, offering little protection for wildlife and therefore few inverts. The cane rats seemed to abound in the area, likely multiplying faster than the inverts could pick them off. With a little cunning, I could snag one in a matter of minutes. Omar had been right. I needed to learn to depend on myself, and that's exactly what I had used the time to do. Old, weak Krista had been blown away by the harsh winds of the desert. She wouldn't have survived long anyway.

Omar still hadn't returned from his scouting excursion. He had been prowling around the nearby rubble looking for helpful items, like the spear I had been using for hunting. I went downstairs and placed the rat next to the little pit and started a fire, the smoke drawn out of the building through a chimney in the pit. With the fire burning hot, I smothered it, placed the rat over the coals, and covered it. If it wasn't for the looming threat from the inverts, the Hut would almost feel like I'd made a cozy little home. We were like the frontiersmen from early American Territory history.

"Krista!" yelled Omar excitedly, bursting through the door. "Krista!"

I had my katanas out and ready, fearing that I had somehow attracted unwanted attention by the food preparation.

"It's okay," he said, gasping. "There's someone out there!"

I ran out the door, scanning the horizon. Sure enough, off in the distance was a figure. I ran back in to grab Arjun's binoculars. Through the dust that had somehow wormed its way into the body, I could tell that he wasn't one of ours.

"Here, look," I said, handing them to Omar. "No one we know. Should we get his attention?"

"I don't think that's necessary," said Omar. "He spotted us. He's coming this way."

I didn't want to appear threatening, but I also didn't want to be caught off-guard. In the bright sunlight, my katanas would shine like a second sun, so I left them sheathed, but drew my dagger and held it behind my back. We waited patiently for the man to cover the distance between us, which was considerable. Finally, he arrived, beaded with sweat from the exertion under the scorching sun.

"Ekon is a friend," he said, extending his hand.

I recognized the name as Omar shook his hand.

"Ekon was sent by your friend, young Ariadne. Ekon would also love some tea," he said, inviting himself into the Hut.

I looked at Omar, who shrugged, and I put my dagger away before following him inside. Staying on the ground level where a dry breeze blew through the house, we ignited a small second fire to heat an old metal pot full of treated lake water with some added herbs. Ekon had remained in quiet contemplation since entering.

"Mr. Ekon?" Omar prodded, offering him a cup.

Ekon's eye focused on Omar.

"Oh, yes. Of course. I'm sure you wish to know about your friends."

"Please," I added, excited.

"They are well, the ones I met at least," he said, pausing.

"Which were…?" I asked.

"Young Ariadne, Mei, and Huck," he said. "They wished Ekon to alert those at Baghdad who might be sympathetic to your cause. Young Ariadne fears that escaping the pod in the transporters' carrier might not be sufficient to cross the extensive dunes to your next destination. She was hoping Ekon could dispatch an escort to meet and guide you."

"Escape in Yanus' carrier? I asked. "What's going on?"

"The prime minister decided they should remain permanent residents of Pod Kano."

"Then we have to help them escape!" I said. "What can we do?"

"Nothing, my child. I'm afraid there is unrest in Kano and your friends have fallen into the thick of it. But worry not, they are strong of will and mind. They will escape, but they will do so in a hurry. You must be ready to depart at a moment's notice," he said, laughing. "They are causing quite a stir! If they don't escape soon, the prime minister will have them in the Pits!"

"What?!" I asked. "Why is that so funny?"

"Because he will never catch them! They are doing the work of the gods!"

"How long will they be?" said Omar, taking a sip of the tea.

"Not long, Ekon assures you!"

"Then how are you going to get to Baghdad in time to be of service?" I asked.

Ekon laughed deeply.

"Because Ekon is a Tuareg!"

Over several rounds of tea, I learned more of our friends' plight and the evils of Zabu's tyrannical reign. Afterward, Ekon rose and dismissed himself.

"Ekon is afraid his time for idle chatter is at an end. Ekon must go," he said.

"Are you sure you don't need anything more than that," I asked, gesturing to the small pack he carried on his back. "You're welcome to stay until the morning. We have plenty to eat."

Ekon shook his head as we followed him out the door. Ekon bowed in thanks to our servitude and began his walk across the desert.

"How in the world is he going to get to Baghdad before we do?" I asked. "That's got to be thousands of kilometers."

"I don't have the slightest idea, *but he's a Tuareg!*" said Omar, mimicking Ekon's accent.

I laughed and turned to watch Ekon's figure receding and saw nothing but the heat waves coming off of the open kilometers of flat, dry surface.

"Wait. Where'd he go?" I asked.

"Okay. Now that's freaking weird," said Omar.

EKON'S INTERLUDE

Arising through flecks of the universe,
Swirling on currents moving nowhere,
Infinite energy dormant below soles,
Relentless, grains shoot on the air.

Rising and setting, souls ever incessant,
Always more or less, never none or many,
Dripping through one into another,
Leaving everything and nothing—bare.

Ancient wisdom in granules abounds,
Enduring millennia to wisp into minds,
Finding no respite in the shadows,
Lost forever to that which comes after.

A lone mote shuttled by indifferent tides,
Finally resting on the stoop of destiny,
Unfurling power to uncharged forms,
A wisp departs, rocketing into the air.

CHAPTER 38: HUCK

After a slew of interrogations, the guards released all of the facility workers. Having been barred in the break room with the others, they had no reason to suspect my involvement. Oskar even went as far as referring to me as a hero for having the presence of mind to bar the door. *It helps when I know what's coming.* Once released from custody, I overheard the guards bragging about having caught two of the Seven and, though the mission had been a success, I questioned the high cost.

"Zauna," I said, using Midge's real name. "There's nothing left for you here. What are you going to do next?"

"I'm pretty clever," Zauna said. "This isn't the first job I've ever had or the last. I'm pretty good at staying out of harm's way and ducking off the radar when needed. What about you? Where are you going?"

"I'm going to leave the pod with my friends," I said. "Would you like to come with me? It's not safe, but it's not here."

Zauna's mouth dropped.

"Thanks for considering taking me, Huck, but my place is here. Too many people that depend on me. I'm small, and I don't eat much, so I share my points with those who can't work. Without me, I'm afraid they'd starve. I'll really miss your company. You're one of the very few people who doesn't complain about my excessive chattiness."

I understand," I said. "You are a hell of a person, Zauna."

"Thanks, Huck. You're not so bad yourself," Zauna said, winking. "And call me Midge."

•••••••••

"We have to find Cesar!" Ariadne pleaded upon my arrival back at the common room.

"Okay. Where is he?" I asked.

"He would be on the farms," said Liesel. "We've never been able to get him to live anywhere else. Without Miranda, he'll be confused and scared."

"Let's go," I said, speed walking to the elevators. "Tell me what happened en route."

By the time we stepped off the elevator on Level 80, my head was spinning. How could Hemant have betrayed us? He was our friend.

"Does Arjun know?" I asked.

Ariadne shook her head.

"We haven't seen him in days," said Ariadne. "Only signs that he comes back to eat and rest. I wouldn't know what to tell him. First Ciro and now his brother—he'd fall apart."

"Is it possible they're forcing his hand?" I asked as we arrived at the farm's wide rolling door.

"He didn't look very forced to me," said Mei, crossing her arms across her chest.

"I know him too well," I said. "I can't believe he's on their side. There has to be some reason for his actions. We can't just leave him here."

"What do you propose?" asked Ariadne.

"A rescue," I said.

"How do we know he'll even come?" asked Mei. "Or worse, rat us out?"

"He's still in there somewhere," said Ariadne. "He lied to his partner to protect us. There was something in his eyes, too. Like a realization. Huck's right, we should rescue him."

"Cesar! Cesar!" yelled Liesel, running off between the artificially lit beds.

"Aren't you forgetting something?" asked Mei. "He's in a freaking guard platoon! How the hell are we going to *rescue* him?"

"We—" I held my words as a platoon of yelling guards ran by outside. "What's going on?"

"Lockdown!" said Liesel, arriving with Cesar. "We've got to go, now!"

"Ariadne," said Cesar, moving in for a hug.

"Cesar, we have to leave," Ariadne said. "Come with us."

"Miranda?" asked Cesar.

"She'll come along later, okay?" said Ariadne.

Cesar nodded and tagged along. We went straight back to the elevator, keeping our heads low as we headed for our apartments. By the time we stepped off, an announcement was coming over the central intercom.

"Good day to you, residents of our glorious Pod Kano. This is your Prime Minister Ndulue Zabu. It is with great sadness, I place the city under a mandatory lockdown. An act of terrorism has occurred in our home. The Resistance bombed one of the essential farms, putting a great strain on our food supply—your food supply. Until the lockdown has ended, the punishment for being outside of your homes will be execution. Punishment for affiliation with the Resistance will be execution. Lastly, failure to report knowledge of the Resistance will be punished by execution.

We cannot rest until this threat is vanquished from our home. This is all."

"The farms?!" said Mei. "Who does he think—"

"Get back to the apartments!" I yelled.

We broke into a run, Cesar doing his best to keep up. We made it back to the common room without incident. Cesar, more confused than ever, was gasping for breath.

"How are we going to rescue Hemant now?" asked Ariadne. "For that matter, how are we going to do anything?"

"I need time to think," I said, pacing.

"What are they going to do with Miranda and Pyotr?" asked Mei.

I glanced at Cesar, who was busy absorbing his new surroundings.

"Probably what you think," I said. "Zabu is desperate to track down the other five. The only ones who have that knowledge are Miranda and Pyotr."

"Miranda?" Cesar asked again, on the verge of hyperventilating.

"Shh," said Liesel, patting his hair down. "Soon, okay?"

Cesar nodded, moaning quietly to himself.

"Can we rescue them?" asked Mei. "We could get the rest of the Resistance and—"

Ariadne was profusely shaking her head. "They would be under the highest security. Zabu's going to fail to get what he wants from them, then dispose of them—probably dramatically," she said. "There's nothing we can do. I hate to say it, but they knew the risks when they took up their mantle. We still have our own mission to finish. We can't do that if we're dead."

"No!" said Liesel, burying her face in my chest.

I gently wrapped my arms around her and patted her back.

"Let's focus on what we can do," I said. "Let's rescue Hemant, get the bomb, load the supplies, and get the hell out of here."

"What about me and Cesar?" asked Liesel. "We can't stay here.

Miranda took care of us. Without her, the guards would have taken advantage of me long ago. And Cesar…"

"You're coming with us," I said, making the decision. "It's a hard life on the surface, but you'll have our help."

Liesel nodded, returning her head to my chest. I looked up at Ariadne and could swear there was a momentary scowl.

"Thank you, Huck," said Liesel.

"Arjun!" yelled Mei.

I spun around, inadvertently almost knocking Liesel to the floor.

"Are you okay?" I asked.

"I'm fine," Liesel said, wiping her face. "Go talk to your friend."

"What are you doing here?" asked Ariadne.

Arjun looked around. "I *live* here," he said, confused.

"How'd you get out?" asked Ariadne. "How'd you get down here?"

"Arjun, I think what she's trying to ask is 'How did you get through the lockdown?'"

"There's a lockdown?" asked Arjun.

"Arjun, geez!" said Mei. "Don't you pay attention?! It's pod-wide. Those caught without permission will be executed!"

"Wow," said Arjun. "Um… I am glad I avoided any unpleasantries. That would have been less than desirable."

"That's a bit of an understatement, Arjun," said Ariadne. "We've got a lot to talk about with you."

"I do as well. Can I talk freely in front of them?" he asked, pointing.

"Of course," Ariadne said. "Arjun, this is Liesel and Cesar. They worked with us on the farms. They are good people, and they are going to come with us."

"Okay," said Arjun, drawing the word out.

"You said you had something to tell us," Ariadne said, distracting him.

"Of course. Dieter was aware of the neem. That's how they developed the transporter's smoke canisters. He concentrated my sample into an oil that we added to several rockets. We believe they can be used for last-line defense against another spine back. I also discovered an Arthropod-repelling frequency and created a device to generate it. It will only work when plugged into the carrier's speakers. Regrettably, I didn't have time to create a mask to protect against the Powder Moths."

"Arjun, you're amazing!" said Ariadne.

Arjun smiled sheepishly.

"I've got the masks covered," I said, pulling out several masks I'd stolen from the plant. "It's only four, but it's some protection.

"Where is the equipment now?" asked Mei.

"In my lab, relatively close to Dieter's lab with the bomb," he said. "We'll need to haul everything to the convoy, but I am not sure how with a lockdown in place. Dieter must have anticipated the lockdown. He was practically begging us to leave."

"We were hoping to get help from the Resistance to leave, but there was an incident," I said. "Our cell is scattered and our contact is probably going to be killed."

"What type of incident?" asked Arjun.

"I think you should sit down," I said.

"Does this have something happened to Hemant?" Arjun asked, his brow knotting up in concern.

"He's okay," said Ariadne. "He's been—"

"Captured!" interrupted Mei. "His guard unit is holding him against his will."

"We have to do something then!" said Arjun, growing animated.

"We are, Arjun," I said. "We were just planning something when the lockdown happened."

"We need to consult Dieter," said Arjun. "He and Zhen—"

"Good day once again, residents of Pod Kano. In one

hour, there will be an execution ceremony in the central forum. Attendance is mandatory for those of age. This is all."

"There's our opportunity," I said.

"That is not possible," said Arjun. "We haven't had time to plan appropriately."

"What choice do we have?" asked Ariadne.

"She's right," I said. "We have to act while we can. Mei and I will get Hemant. Arjun, Cesar, and Liesel retrieve the stuff from the lab. See if you can't round up Dieter and Zhen. Ariadne, grab food and medicine and meet us at the incline. If you come across any Resistance members, we're going to need their help to overpower the convoy guards. Everyone clear?"

Everyone nodded, save for Cesar who stared vacantly up at the ceiling.

•••••••••

Mei and I split off from the others and ran towards Level 65 against the throngs of people heading to the execution. We hoped that we could find Hemant in all the chaos and prayed we could rescue him. With great difficulty, we pushed forward, avoiding the guards mixed in with the crowds.

"How are we ever going to get down?" asked Mei, when we paused in an alcove. "We aren't making any headway and the elevators are too congested."

"Aren't there stairs?" I asked. "There are always stairs. I doubt many people would be in a hurry to climb so many flights."

"That way," Mei said, pointing.

We forced ourselves back into the current of bodies, making our way to the floor's less populated medical district.

"There should be stairs at the far end of this corridor," she said. "Or at least there were in Horizonte."

"Good enough for me," I whispered, as we snuck past one of the guards.

Once we were clear of his view, we sprinted down the vacant corridor, not worried about the slaps of our boots over the numerous feet thundering behind us. We arrived at the door, cautiously opening it. I held my head inside and heard no sounds coming from within.

"Let's go," I said.

Mei and I flew down the flights, jumping from landing to landing, not worrying about the inevitable ascent which would undoubtedly be far more arduous. Between the adrenaline and excitement, the first twenty levels flew by, having only encountered a handful of others, none of which were guards. When we arrived at Level 62, I knew we were getting close. It was unlikely the most prestigious guard platoon of the pod would have the rear entrance to their level unguarded. I slowed down, coming to a complete halt, and put my finger over my lips. We took the remaining flights silently. When we were on the level directly above our target, I could hear the guards conversing.

"…don't mind not going. Abbas thinks it's some right of passage for the newbies to guard the stairway. Gotta protect that handrail," someone said.

"I've seen enough violence to last me a while," said a familiar voice. "Honestly, I appreciate the time to think."

Mei looked at me in surprise. I nodded. It was Hemant. The issue was the other guard. We'd have to take him out before we could escape with our friend. I gestured to Mei, who was quick on the uptake. We carefully unsheathed our daggers and pounced over the railing. In an instant, we had the unprepared guards against the wall, each with a blade at their throat, initially not knowing which was Hemant in the low light.

"It's me! It's me!" I said as Hemant wrestled free of my grip.

"Don't hurt him!" Hemant yelled to Mei, whose blade had already drawn some blood from the guard's neck.

Mei reluctantly dropped the short figure to the pavement but kept her weapon ready.

"She's a feisty one!" said the short guard. "I like her."

"Ugh," said Mei, rolling her eyes.

"Mathias, these are my friends," said Hemant. "Well, I hope they're still my friends."

CHAPTER 39: HEMANT

"**D**amn. Y'all are the last thing I expected to see," I said, escorting Huck and Mei into the Muskrat's hangout. "I figured you'd leave me for dead given my actions."

All around us were the trappings of vice, making my inexplicable behavior even more exposed. I cringed, suddenly feeling naked.

"How could you, Hemant?!" Mei blurted, crying. "We trusted you!"

"I'm sorry, Mei. I'm so sorry," I said, lowering my head in shame. "Look, something happened down here. Something I'm not proud of. Mathias can attest to it. We're fed propaganda by the truckload. They told us that the Resistance is hurting the people of the pod… that they are claiming everything for themselves."

"You know better than that, Hemant!" she said. "You saw what Zabu did our *first day*. Then how he changed his promises. Is that the type of man you trust?"

"Mei, I made a mistake! They brainwashed me! They got me addicted to this," I said, holding up an inhaler.

Mei gasped. Huck's face was a mix of sadness and anger, though I was unsure who it was directed towards.

"That's how they control us, keep us from feeling, make us strong," I said. "I made a mistake. It was my fault. I'm ready to pay for that mistake."

"We've all done really stupid stuff," said Huck, as Mei's looked torn about his acceptance. "I know you can't earn back everyone's trust overnight, but I trust you. Now, we have to get out of here!"

"Your reunion is touching," said Commandant Saif, coming around the corner. "When I choose my men, I choose those who have something to offer and are obedient to a fault."

Saif dropped into a chair which groaned in complaint. Taking a pause to catch his breath, he continued.

"You have invited strangers into our midst. Trespassing in the Den is strictly forbidden. Your punishment will be execution when Abbas returns, unless…"

"Unless what?" I asked.

"I find your female friend to be quite… soothing," said Saif. "Leave her to me. Dispatch the other. Do this and you will live, albeit a miserable existence for your traitorous behavior."

"I have a better idea," said Mei, slinging one of her knives directly between his eyes. The *thunk* of the knife reverberated like a pumpkin being split. "How's that for soothing, you bastard?! Now, can we *please* get out of here?"

"She just, um, did that," said Mathias, dumbfounded.

"That's Mei for you," I said. "Since we're here, there's a weapons cache in the corner!"

After loading up with all the gear we could carry swiftly, we embarked on our 65-floor upward journey. Mathias chose to come with us. With my vouching, Huck allowed it. There wasn't anything left for Mathias to return to. He would have to answer for Saif's death. If all went to plan, there was ample room in the carrier.

Each of us wore fresh light armor over our jumpsuits, an assault rifle over our shoulder, hand weapons, and a bag of miscellaneous goodies. All courtesy of the Muskrat armory. Even multiple floors before Level 30, the location of the central forum, we could hear the rage of Zabu's amplified voice thundering through the pod's superstructure. We climbed on in silence as our legs burned from the ascent.

"…before you. They are traitors to the pod, traitors to the residents, and traitors to me! May Ala judge them for the swine they are! They have refused to share with me the rest of the Seven, so they will suffer an agonizing death in the Pits as I bear witness. If I have the remaining five of the Seven within the hour, I shall grant them a lenient execution at the edge of my blade. Until then, we will wait."

I heard Mei whimper behind me.

"We can't just leave them," she said.

"They're too strong," I said. "Almost the entire Muskrat force is up there, hyped up on Dust. Not to mention, Zabu's personal guard, Chattar's personal—"

"Hemant, shut up," said Mei.

Silently, I returned to my somber hike.

"He's right, Mei," Huck said. "Miranda and Pyotr believed in our mission. The best thing we can do is take advantage of the opportunity they are purchasing with their lives."

"I know we can't do anything," she said, rubbing a tear from her cheek. "I feel like a coward running off and leaving them. Nothing will change that."

I rubbed her shoulder.

"We'll honor them as soon as we can," I said.

"You guys haven't really told me what's next," said Mathias. "I know you don't exactly trust me, but what's next? Anything you could tell me would be quite helpful."

"We're meeting the rest of our group at the incline, where we are likely to encounter resistance," Huck said. "We need to dispatch said resistance surreptitiously so we can escape without half of the pod coming after us. That sufficient?"

"I believe it is," Mathias said.

We continued upward, each step serving as another second in the countdown to Miranda and Pyotr's demise. I didn't know what the Pits were, but if having my throat slit was favorable to them, I didn't want to know. When we finally arrived at the top level, we had to make the most harrowing portion of our journey, and our fresh suits were drenched with sweat. The only entrances to the incline were across the catwalks to the Nucleus. The same catwalks that loomed far above the central forum and would most certainly be guarded.

I cracked the door at the top of the staircase and looked out.

"It appears to be clear," I said.

"Hemant-clear or clear-clear," Mathias said, chortling.

Huck and Mei looked confused.

"Sorry, inside joke," said Mathias.

We filed out into the hallway, thankful for the limited ambient light, moving to the far end where the platform circled around the central shaft. The area, more apartments, looked virtually identical to the nicer apartments Zabu had used to lure us in.

"They live a little bit nicer up here, don't they?" said Mathias.

"All a bloody illusion," I said, nodding. "Masking the fact that like Horizonte, Kano's leadership is no longer interested in winning the war. The 'haves' just want to continue having, war be damned."

"And you guys are going to change that?" Mathias asked.

"That's the plan," I said. "If we can get out of here."

We stopped shy of the catwalk behind a half-wall, peering over the top at what appeared to be two guards circling the platform around the far end.

"How are we going to get past them?" asked Mei. "We'll be visible on the catwalk."

"We need a distraction, but one that won't cause any attention from below," said Huck.

"Dammit!" said Mei.

"What? What's wrong?" Huck asked.

"I had an idea that I think'll work, but I don't like it."

"What is it?" I asked.

"*Arrg.* I'll do it, but I need some promises from you all first," she said.

We nodded.

"First, this never happened," she said. "Second, if I see you leering, I'll kick your asses."

Mei started slipping off her jumpsuit and we turned away, giving her some modicum of privacy, though turning Mathias took some encouragement.

"When I lure them down here, take them out as quietly as you can," she said. "Count to five and then you can turn around. If either of them is gay, we might be in trouble."

Surprisingly, in moments, she had lured the two guards away from their duty, both following her like puppies, both more than pleased to escort her to the holding cells. They didn't even know what hit them. As we dropped their bodies to the floor, Mei threw her jumpsuit over her naked figure.

"Men can be such pigs," she said. "Good thing it's something we could count on."

"I'm not a pig," Mathias said, standing upright.

"Then turn around and let me get dressed," she said.

When Mei was all zipped up, we crossed the catwalk in a crouch. I couldn't help but stare at the vast numbers, trapped below for the duration of the prime minister's macabre countdown. As we arrived at the Nucleus, we froze, hearing footsteps on the opposite side. I motioned for a halt and raised my weapon. Around the corner came Ariadne. I lowered my weapon, breathing a sigh of relief.

"Ariadne, boy I'm glad to see you," I said.

"The feeling isn't mutual," she replied, fuming. "When the danger is passed, you owe me an explanation and an apology."

I nodded. That I did.

"Any sign of the others?" Huck asked.

Ariadne shook her head.

"I was trying to figure out how to get across when the guards disappeared," she said. "I'm guessing your work?"

"More Mei's actually," said Huck. "The guards found her to be quite alluring."

"You didn't," she said to Mei.

Mei grinned. "It worked, didn't it?"

Ariadne shook her head, grinning. "Who's this?"

"Mathias, *encantado*," he said.

Ariadne gave Huck a look.

"He's a strange one, but Hemant vouches for him," Huck said. "He's coming with us."

We plowed up the winding stairs to the staging area and incline where the convoy vehicles were kept. When we neared the top, we could hear a struggle. After waiting patiently for a few minutes, the place grew quiet and we could hear the voice of Taha and Arjun. We slowly emerged from the darkness.

"Arjun?" I shouted.

"Hemant?" I heard replied from the far side of the vehicles.

Disregarding all danger, I broke into a run around the frozen convoy. When I saw my brother, I picked him up, twirling him around above the ground.

"How have you been, brother?" I asked, laughing.

"Far better than you," Arjun said, smiling. "They said you were captured and forced to do unimaginable things. I'm so glad you are safe."

I looked at the others and mouthed, "Thank you."

"It's so good to see you, Taha," said Ariadne. "I missed you!"

"And I, you, Mistr— Ariadne," said Taha through a sly smile. "Arjun informs me of your intent to steal my master's carrier and buggy. You have my blessing, provided you never speak of it."

"Do we have everything?" Huck asked. "Not only did we find Hemant, but we also brought his friend Mathias and a bunch of stolen Muskrat gear."

"I have the food and medicine," said Ariadne.

"Liesel and I didn't find any Resistance fighters, but we found Taha, Dieter, and Zhen," said Arjun. "Cesar carried the bomb up on his shoulders, and the device on my back is the signal generator I was telling you about."

Dieter and Zhen said "Hi," from under the carrier.

"They were three sheets to the wind when we found them, too," said Liesel.

"I can't say I blame them," I said. "Let's load up before Zabu's hour is over."

We all worked quickly to load everything into Yanus' personnel carrier, including our belongings from the cargo hauler. With Taha's help, it was accomplished in minutes. With the irreversible modification to the fuel tank, Dieter still suggested hiding the bomb inside, saying it would be more protected from road conditions and less likely to contaminate us with ambient radiation. The downside was we'd have to stop at pump houses even more frequently. I preferred that to a long slow death from poisoning, but then I remembered that would be Dieter's fate. When everything was prepared, we hastily said our goodbyes.

"Are you sure you won't come with us, Taha?" Ariadne asked. "You deserve better than Yanus."

"The transporters are a rough bunch, but they are my family. They look up to me and respect me," he said. "While I may not see eye to eye with Protector Yanus, he is my master and I will respect him as such. I'll tell him I tried to stop you."

"I admire your devotion," I said. "If you ever get tired of that blow hard, you know where to find us."

Taha nodded.

"You ready?" asked Dieter, the hangover causing him to wince from the bright sconce.

Huck nodded.

"It's been a pleasure," Dieter said. "Zhen and I will ascend those ladders to the gate's manual controls. Once those doors open, you need to barrel through them. I don't know if the bridge can override them. If that's the case, we're all dead."

"Are you sure you'll be alright?" Arjun asked Dieter.

"Not even a little," he said. "Zhen and I are doing this because it's right. If that means our death, so be it. This is for Emile and Rupert."

Below we heard Zabu's muffled voice booming unintelligibly, signaling the end of our time.

"And Miranda and Pyotr," said Ariadne.

I jumped in the front seat as Dieter and Zhen climbed. Huck and I watched mesmerized as the doors slowly slid open on their massive casters, bathing the staging area in the sun's radiant light.

"Feels weird, going back out, you know," I said.

"Sure does," said Huck. "Ready back there?"

"We're all strapped in!" replied Mei. "Tailgate's on the way up!"

"Here we go!" Huck said, mashing the accelerator and steering us towards the opening.

Then there was *tatt-tatt-tatt* of gunfire followed by ear-piercing screams.

CHAPTER 40: ARIADNE

"What happened?!" Huck yelled from the cab. "Is everything alright?"

"Mei's been shot!" I said, holding pressure on the wound as tears flooded my vision. "Don't stop!"

"How bad is it?!" yelled Hemant.

"Shut up and let me work!" I yelled back.

The bullet wound in Mei's neck was hemorrhaging blood all over Yanus' decorative rug, spread across the floor of the carrier. I was holding pad after pad to the wound, but nothing was stopping the flow. She was going to die unless I closed the wound. I panned the carrier, watching everyone and everything shake as we hit the rough terrain. With the people chasing us, we couldn't stop. How was I going to operate like this?

"I spotted Krista and Omar!" said Huck. "We're only going to slow down. Someone open the hatch!"

Liesel jumped up and hit the controls for the tailgate, which began to drop over the hitch attaching the buggy. Huck slowed the carrier to a crawl and in hopped Omar and Krista, whose eyes grew wide at the scene of carnage.

"Go!" shouted Omar, banging on the side.

Liesel hit the panel and the gate started to rise as Huck gunned the vehicle. Reunions and introductions would come later. We were so close to escaping without a hiccup. The tailgate was on the way up. The sporadic gunfire was plinking fruitlessly off the armored exterior, then right before the gate closed, Mei dropped, clutching her throat. A bullet had squeezed through the narrow gap and gone clean through her neck before lodging itself in an article of furniture.

"Liesel!" I yelled. "Get the suture kit from my pack!"

"You can't be serious," said Omar.

"She's going to die if I don't!"

I snatched the kit from Liesel, ordering Omar and Liesel to hold Mei steady. In his seat, Cesar was screaming, rocking back and forth. Liesel cradled Mei's head and Omar held her torso firmly in place. When I took away the pad, there was so much blood. I directed one of the ceiling lights to the laceration and began to work, sewing the wound from the inside out. Cleaning was damn near impossible given the conditions. One false move and I'd slit her carotid artery. I'd just have to rely on the small supply of antibiotics we had on board. Gradually, the loss of blood slowed, but she had already lost too much to survive without a transfusion. It was a piss-poor job, but it had calmed the bleeding.

I leaned back on my haunches and examined my work. *It'll have to do.* I applied a topical antibiotic and heavily bandaged the wound. We had barely left the pod and I'd already run through half of our emergency medical supplies. I looked at the ornate rug, now saturated with Mei's blood.

"Omar, help me lift her to the bunk," I said.

Omar helped me carefully move Mei into the swaying cabin where we set her down gently. Mei's already pale complexion looked stark white after the fluid loss.

"Will she be okay?" asked Krista.

"I don't know," I said, fighting back tears. "We need a blood donor."

"I'll do it," said Krista, rolling up her sleeve. "Mei would do it for me."

"It's not that easy," I said. "We have to find who among us has compatible blood. If we don't, it could kill her."

"Oh," Krista said. "How can we check?"

"I have a kit, but I'll need a sample from everyone. Including Huck and Hemant. We can't waste any time," I said, opening the hatch to the cab. "We need to stop for a moment. Is there anyone following us?"

"I can't see any signs of followers through the dust," replied Huck. "Dieter and Zhen must have jammed the gate. I'll stop, but it can't be for long. Our pursuers already have too many advantages over us."

I felt the vehicle's motion slow and grabbed a handful of syringes and labels. As soon as the tailgate was down, I had Omar toss the rug out the back. I didn't need a constant reminder of how little blood remained in Mei's fragile frame. With Liesel's help, I took samples from each team member and gave Huck permission to start moving again.

Back inside the rocking vehicle, I tested each person's blood with a gel kit. Mei was O-positive, fortunately, a common type. The second I had a corresponding donor, I grabbed the syringe and inspected the label.

"Mathias!" I said. "You're a match. Get over here!"

Mathias reluctantly came over and had a seat on the bunk next to Mei's, paling as I withdrew the transfusion kit.

"This may surprise you, but…" Mathias swallowed. "I'm afraid of my own blood."

"That explains why you kept your eyes shut so tightly when I retrieved the sample, then," I said. "Lay down and close your eyes. I'll take care of everything. I promise."

Within moments, the viscous, life-giving fluid was rolling through the tubes to Mei's body as Mathias forced himself to breathe calmly. For the first time since we'd left the pod, I surveyed the interior of the carrier. It was a packed space for ten people. Undoubtedly, some would be sleeping on the floor, but it was far sturdier than any of our bivvies and offered much more protection.

Arjun had already set up his repellent signal and informed us that it was broadcasting from the external speakers of the carrier, though I couldn't hear anything. The cabin was crowded with bodies and supplies. As soon as we stopped, Yanus' furniture and decorations would have to go. It was taking up too much valuable space. Thankfully, the carrier still had its fold-down bunks positioned behind Yanus' elaborate wall hangings.

"How are you holding up?" asked Krista, sitting beside me.

I looked down at my hands, which were still caked with dry blood.

"I'll be okay," I said. "I just need some time. I can't rest until I know she's okay."

Krista wrapped her arm around my shoulders.

"It's good to have you back," I said. "I missed you guys. How did you manage on your own?"

"It was rough at first, but Omar taught me how to take care of myself. He's a good guy, you know?"

"I do. You're not such a bad girl, yourself."

"Get some rest, Ariadne," she said. "I promise I'll wake you if anything changes."

I nodded. I sat next to her for a long time, trying to keep my eyes open, but eventually, I succumbed to sleep. When I woke, there was far less light coming in through the narrow viewports. I checked the transfusion's progress and saw that Mei's uptake had slowed. It was complete. I disconnected the tubes and woke Mathias.

"You're all done," I said. "Thank you."

"How is it I just woke up, and I'm so tired?" he asked, shaking his head.

"You just donated a lot of your blood. You're going to feel weak until your body replenishes it."

"How long does that take?"

"Weeks. But you should feel fairly normal in a day or two."

"You could've mentioned that before."

"It wouldn't have made a difference. I was taking your blood regardless," I said, smiling.

I crossed the cabin to where Liesel was cradling Cesar, who in the crammed personnel carrier looked even more like a giant.

"How's he doing?" I asked.

"He's okay, all things considered," she said. "He doesn't comprehend what's going on. Everything and everyone is new to him. While you were asleep, Omar introduced himself and Krista. Cesar didn't like Omar. I'm not sure he cares for Mathias either, but he seems fine around the women."

"Miranda?" Cesar asked.

"Shh," she said. "I don't know what to tell him or even if I should."

"This is new to me, too," I said. "In Horizonte, they kept the unabled isolated before releasing them with the rest of us. Before Cesar, I'd never spent any real amount around someone with his particular needs."

"Despite his needs, he's one of the most helpful, caring people I've ever met," she said. "I don't know how you can protect us out here. Neither of us has any battle training. We're liabilities."

"Don't say that," I said, looking her in the eye. "You saw what we did for Hemant. We don't leave friends behind."

"Thanks, Ariadne."

I felt the vehicle slowing to a crawl as Hemant opened the panel to the cab.

"We're in the middle of some small town. Huck pulled a good way off the main road into a little forest where we can set up camp for the night," he said. "There's a river. It seems isolated enough."

We lowered the tailgate and milled around the area under Arjun's assurances that his device would be running all night. I caught up with Liesel and Cesar as they stepped down the rear ramp of the carrier.

"Wow!" she said, dumbfounded at the first stars poking through Earth's atmosphere. "Is it always this beautiful? Cesar, look!"

Cesar slowly raised his head before wrapping his arms around himself.

"It's a big place when you've lived your entire life inside," I said. "What's weird is if we ever go into another pod, it'll feel cramped."

"It's going to take some getting used to, but I already want to stay up here forever. It's like another world."

"You may change your tune when we have our first run-in with the Arthropods. We're going to need to teach you to defend yourself."

"I can't promise I'll be a good student, but I'll try my best."

"If it makes you feel better, we haven't seen any evidence of Arthropods since we left," said Arjun. "I know the device is working, but until we can confirm how effective it is on the various Arthropod species, I think it would be wise to sleep inside."

"Do you think it's safe enough for a fire," I asked, shivering in the cool air.

"We have plenty of that asshole's furniture," said Omar.

"I'm fine with it," said Huck, shrugging. "Keep it small though. If they're following us, I'd hate to give away our position."

After about fifteen minutes, the pile of Yanus' furniture was ablaze in the waning light. Huck frowned seeing the gargantuan bonfire, but we didn't care. It had turned into a celebration. Not only had we escaped the pod but did so with the explosive device that was paramount to our mission.

"I don't suppose anyone has some hooch?" asked Mathias. "It doesn't seem right to be out here again without something decent to drink!"

"Not unless there's some in the carrier," said Huck.

Mathias trudged off to look.

I sat staring into the fire, feeling the warmth blast through my bones. After a few minutes, I went to go check on Mei again, who was still sleeping soundly, her color slowly returning. I heard a strange knocking sound and looked over to find Mathias laying in the corner convulsing next to an open cabinet, foamy drool accumulating at the corner of his mouth.

"Help!" I screamed.

Huck was the first one in, followed shortly by several others.

"What's happening?" he asked, seeing Mathias shaking.

"Hemant, was he prone to seizures?" I asked, hearing no response.

"Hemant?" I asked, turning.

Of all the people crowded behind me, none of them was Hemant.

"Where's Hemant? I need Hemant!"

Arjun and Huck ran to go find him. In moments, Huck returned.

"He's lying by the fire doing the same thing! Arjun's with him," he said. "What's going on?"

I thought for a moment, struggling to recall what the two would have in common.

"Dust!" shouted Huck. "He said the Muskrats were all forced to use Dust!"

"Dammit," I said. "They're going through withdrawal."

"That's a good thing, right?" asked Krista.

"Not if it's deadly," I said, kicking myself. "If I'd thought of that, I never would've allowed him to give the transfusion. Does anyone know if they brought their inhalers?"

"They didn't," said Huck. "They both left them in the Den."

"Arrg," I said. "Check the carrier. Search everywhere!"

A few agonizing minutes later, we'd found a container of the raw pheromones. Apparently Yanus kept a secret stash of his own.

"It might work," I said.

Using my dagger, I applied a generous smear of the translucent goo to the forearms of the convulsing team members. Within minutes, the shakes had ceased and both appeared to be sleeping, however fitfully.

"That was quick thinking on your part, Ariadne," said Krista. "Do you think it will happen again?"

"I don't know. I don't know enough about Dust."

"I watched this happen to my parents. Unlike you, in Kano, we lived with our families. Or at least I did until I lost them. That's when Miranda took me in. People could break the addiction, but it was difficult. My parents tried time and time again. They were good people. They always fell back in when the withdrawal became too strong. They always had to taper their doses. The night they died, they had been clean for weeks. For whatever reason, they decided to do it again. When they did, they used their normal dosage and overdosed immediately."

Liesel began to sob. Huck reached out and held her hand.

"Do you think the pheromone will work as a taper?" I asked, ignoring Huck's proximity to her.

"I think so," said Huck. "But I saw how concentrated Dust is. It's numerous times more powerful. The pheromone might keep them from seizing or dying, but they are going to have one *hell* of a withdrawal."

CHAPTER 41: DIETER

As soon as the carrier and its trailer were through the gates, I motioned for Zhen to close the massive doors. The staging area at the base of the incline was inundated with armed soldiers. *So much for fading into obscurity.* I frantically searched the room, looking for something—anything to destroy the controls. Along the wall, I found an old fire cylinder, decades past its useful cycle. Well, it would be useful to me. I hefted the metal container over to the switch, and let its weight do the work. By the time the guards swarmed the room and forced me to my knees, the station's panel was nothing but sad fragments and mangled wires drooping from the wall. Hopefully, I had bought some time for the group's escape.

"To the minister's office with them!" said Chattar, waiting next to the convoy, perfectly groomed as always. "He'll want to deal with them *personally.*"

With gun barrels prodding my back, Zhen and I were practically shoved to Zabu's office. No sooner had we entered his lair than Yanus was on us.

"Do you have *any* idea what lengths I went to have my carrier made?!" screamed the impish man. "It was one of a kind. One of a kind! My artifacts are priceless I tell you! It took me years to collect them all! Your miscreant friends better not put a single scratch on anything of mine or mark my words, heads will roll!"

"Calm, my friend," said Zabu, turning from his discomforting shrine. "Heads will roll, you are correct, but not for the reason you think. Technician Dieter, Medic Zhen, please have a seat."

I hesitated, but Zhen held her head high as she strode forward to be seated. I followed, forcing myself to emulate her example.

"I am in a foul mood, you see," said Zabu, barely retaining his composure. "I wished to obtain information from two captives today, but they refused my… *charms*. There are still five Resistance leaders unaccounted for, and this does not please me. I tell you this because if I doubt you are telling me the truth, I will be *very displeased*. Today, I am not a patient man."

Zabu walked to his desk and picked up a beige piece of paper, tattered from extensive handling.

"This is a letter sent to me from the Prime Minister of Pod Horizonte. Somehow," he paused, glaring at Yanus, "its delivery was not prioritized."

Yanus gulped.

"Had it come into my hands sooner, many undesirable events could have been avoided," said Zabu, clearing his throat. "I want to read part of it to you. 'Should they succeed, regard your newest visitors as a threat to our way of life. And Ndulue, please don't do anything foolish with your new toy.' Now, since my friend Davi has little concern for the workings of transporters like Yanus and his ilk, I have to assume he is talking about the latest arrival of candidates. That would be the very same candidates you aided in escaping my pod."

"And in my vehicle!" said Yanus, who hushed with a glare from Zabu.

"This infuriates me more. Davi said they are a 'threat to our way of life.' Do you know what this means?"

I shook my head.

"I think you do," said Zabu. "And this 'new toy.' I admit this puzzled me. At least it did until I discovered that one particular scientist had shared a number of communiques to one of Horizonte's regents."

I shifted nervously in my seat.

"You see, he begins to sweat," said Zabu to Yanus. "Yes, you, my friend. You had a good relationship with this Grand Major Leal, no?"

I could see no point in denying it. After everything, I was as good as dead.

"Yes," I said.

"And this 'new toy' Davi mentioned, it was my bomb, no?"

"Yes," I repeated.

"But you just completed this bomb recently, or so I thought. I said to myself, 'Zabu, you have been played for a fool.' Dieter, you've had the bomb for far longer than you've let on. If Davi is worried about it, that means it must be far more powerful than you've let on. How powerful? I wonder. Then I connect the dots. The stolen fuel rod was not stolen by the Resistance as I suspected. You, my friend, created a nuclear weapon, didn't you?"

I nodded. Zabu did a single enthusiastic clap.

"My boy," he said, grinning from ear to ear. "Ala could not have gifted me anything better!"

Zabu waved his hand and Chattar walked in, carrying Giselle, who was twisting against her restraints. *No! How could he have known? How could he bring her into this?*

"Your face carries surprise," he said. "I keep track of the vices of those critical to my success. I never figured you for one who enjoys the company of prostitutes."

"Leave her alone!" I said.

"I have struck a nerve, I think. Now, I need you to answer my next question with *complete* honesty. How you answer will determine my leniency for you and your friends. Where is my nuclear bomb?"

"It just left on its way to the Hive," I said, hoping they would be long out of reach by the time Zabu's engineers pried the doors open.

The gut-wrenching scream that escaped from the prime minister was unnerving. Zhen turned her head away. Even Yanus was cowering. Zabu angrily picked up the ceremonial knife from his alter to Ala and opened Giselle's throat without a moment's hesitation.

"No! I screamed. "Giselle, I'm sorry!"

I watched as Chattar let her fall to her knees, blood cascading down the front of her dress. I held her in my arms as she caressed my cheek. Then the life vanished from her deep brown eyes.

"You said you'd be lenient!" I said, choking up.

"My friend, that was leniency," said Zabu, turning to Yanus with clenched teeth, "Go. Get. Them. Or you will join Dieter and Zhen in the Pits."

•••••••••

Brash guards escorted Zhen and me down to the holding cells while Zabu's staff prepared the Pits for our arrival. Ceaseless rumors abounded as to what they contained. The public only knew that their use was saved for the most heinous of crimes as defined by the prime minister. However, people could only speculate as to what lay inside. Most assumed Arthropods. The only thing I was certain of was that our deaths would be slow and painful. You didn't piss off the prime minister and simply get your throat cut.

The political holding cells were located near the base of the

Nucleus and were supposedly unsoiled, a condition which I blamed on their short use. The death sentences of the Pits were not procrastinated, nor were they subject to appeal. Prisoners guilty of minor crimes were sent to the cells on the lowest levels, patiently biding their time until the next Release Day. Horror stories abounded about the conditions below, which, unlike our cells, allowed visitors to the condemned. Not that either of us had anyone left.

Giselle. The look in her eyes flooded my mind. She was so innocent of all of this. If I'd had any idea of what would befall her, I would have avoided her. She didn't deserve to be punished for my actions. As I thought about the friends I'd lost, I realized I'd never had the chance to properly grieve them. I'd never been one for religion, but I longed for a peaceful place on the other side of death's veil where I would be reunited with them.

I arrived at our shared cell. The space was spartan, offering only a toilet fused to the wall and two benches. It didn't even have a bunk, very telling of its nature. We each had a seat before we felt the door's reverberation as it swung closed.

"I'm sorry, Zhen," I said.

"Dieter, would you shut up?" she responded. "I knew what I was doing the moment I stepped into Emile's shoes. Don't act like you got me into this. You didn't. I chose to stand up to Zabu on my own, and I will damn sure face the consequences."

I nodded.

"Then can I thank you for all you've done?"

"That you can."

"Then thank you. I couldn't have accomplished what I did without you."

"You're welcome, Dieter. I'm sorry about your friend. I regret that I never got a chance to get to know her."

"To be honest, neither did I. Our meeting was… fortuitous, but there was something there. Something I hadn't encountered before."

"I know that feeling well. Emile and I had it. Did you know that I hated him when I met him?" she said. "He was a cocky son of a bitch. Thought he knew everything. Kept explaining things to me as if I had no clue. I was a trained medic, dammit. Finally, I'd had enough and told him off. In his eyes, nothing could've been more attractive. He pestered me to no end until I agreed to go to dinner with him. It was then I found out he was a stand-up guy, and *really* good in bed."

"I could've died without knowing that last tidbit," I said, laughing.

Zhen chuckled deeply.

"He could be ornery, but I loved him more than anything else in the world."

"I wish I could say I understand. I didn't have enough time with Giselle to feel love with that depth."

"I'm just glad you got to experience it. Some people go their whole lives without feeling love."

Just then, the lights went out.

"I guess it's time to sleep," I said.

"Mmmhmm," said Zhen.

I laid there for the next several hours, restlessly tossing and turning on the frigid, uncushioned metal. I was unable to sleep, plagued with the thoughts of whatever waited for us in the morning. Somehow Zhen was sleeping peacefully, apparently having come to terms with her death. When the lights returned, I had maybe slipped off for an hour all night. A guard appeared at our door, and saying nothing, gestured us out.

We were escorted by four silent guards to the elevator, then down to Level 55, the old training levels. I looked at Zhen, who carried a look of complacency. I struggled to recall what would be located on the level in my home pod of Munich so many decades ago. *The training arena! The Pits are the training arena!* I shivered thinking about what threats waited for us there. Zabu had a fondness for fighting Arthropods for sport. It didn't take a genius to realize what we'd be up against.

"We don't have to fight," I said to Zhen, not caring what the guards thought or overheard. "We can stand our ground and take death with dignity."

Zhen nodded.

When the elevator opened, we were greeted by Zabu, Chattar, an unfamiliar child, and several other high-level civilians—Zabu's loyalists. They were some of the few who still supported and cowed to him, largely because they knew what happened to those who stood against him. Hell, the man slaughtered his own regents. It was the child's presence that concerned me. The prepubescent boy was filthy in appearance, obviously unrelated to the others.

"Dieter. Zhen," Zabu said. "Always a pleasure."

Zhen spit in his face. He removed Chattar's handkerchief from his pocket and dabbed his face.

"That feisty spirit will make for great entertainment," he said, escorting us to the large double doors of the arena.

Inside, the area looked much as it did in Pod Munich. It was surrounded by rusty red corrugated walls, the floor coated with a thick layer of blood-soaked sand. A hint of fresh death still clung in the air. The Resistance leaders. I hoped that their deaths didn't deter the others from continuing their fight. Zabu's men closed the doors, locking us all in. Chattar handed us each a spear.

"You might think, 'I will not fight,'" said Zabu, resting his hand on the boy's head. "This is a common thought. I assure you, you will fight. If you do not, this child will join you in the arena. You will fight to save his life."

We're fighting then. Save for Chattar, Zabu and his entourage climbed the ladder to the viewing balcony above. Chattar yanked on a semi-concealed lever in the wall, before darting up the ladder himself.

Slowly, a massive steel cube lowered from the ceiling, angry noises emanating from inside. When the rusty crate landed with a puff of dust, I lowered my spear. Through the cloud of airborne sand, I could faintly see two creatures emerging from the open lid. I felt the sweat pouring down my arms as I looked at Zhen, who was shaking but staring defiantly towards the threat.

I stared into the dust, trying to make out its form. If I knew what it was, I could fight it. Within the particles, all I could see was an absence. A vacancy. There was the shape of an invert, but no visible invert. My mind raced. The researchers at Baghdad regularly shared our findings. They never mentioned anything about an invisible invert!

I grabbed a handful of sand and flung it at the displaced dust. For a fraction of a second, I saw the creatures' forms. They had long, prowling, mantis-like forms. With a rapid gyration, they slung off the revealing sand, once again becoming invisible to my naked eye.

"How are we going to fight that?" I asked.

Zhen shook her head.

The sly creatures' light bodies skated across the sand, leaving nearly undetectable footprints. I closed my eyes and focused on the subtle clicking of their mouths. When I felt as though I had one of the creatures targeted, I dashed forward, spear extended ahead of me.

I felt no resistance and knew I had missed. I heard a whistle through the air, then the room spun. When everything came to a standstill, I saw my body several meters away as the world faded to black.

CHAPTER 42: HUCK

I barely slept the first night back on the surface. I checked on Mei, Hemant, and Mathias so often that Ariadne was ready to knock me out. The withdrawal seizures had stopped, but they feverishly tossed and turned as they lay unconscious. Hemant filled the night with his disconcerting moans. Mathias, who we assumed had been addicted to the Dust far longer, continually stopped breathing. Ariadne tended to them tirelessly through the night, jostling Mathias every time an episode of apnea occurred. Mei was sleeping soundly but was as pale as the sun-bleached rocks surrounding us. When the light of morning broke over the trees, I was thankful I could give up the feigned attempt at sleep and made coffee on the carrier's gas burner.

"How are they doing?" I risked asking Ariadne.

"Mostly the same," she said. "I just don't know enough about this, Huck. I'm giving them a low dose of pheromones and praying that it keeps the fatal complications at bay. Mei has barely shown any signs of improvement since the transfusion. I'm praying she's not septic."

She started crying from exhaustion. I reached out to comfort her, but she avoided my contact as she stepped away, returning to her patients. I stood there awkwardly for a moment before addressing the others.

"Anyone willing to help me catch breakfast?" I asked.

No one was excited, but Liesel, Arjun, Krista, and Omar joined me down at the murky water's edge to cast out our lines. I let myself relax, focusing my attention on demonstrating to Liesel how to fish. Aside from the background hiss of Arjun's signal from the vehicle's speakers, there were only the sounds of nature. I listened to the running river, the buzzing of insects, and longed for sounds of birds, few of which still existed. After about twenty minutes, the four of us had caught enough large catfish for breakfast.

"Is your device strong enough for us to cook these over a fire?" I asked Arjun.

"I wouldn't risk it," Arjun said, the deep concern for his brother etched on his face. "It should provide us with a safety net, but I don't completely understand its strengths and weaknesses. I would operate the same as before. I can't guarantee that it would stop a determined Arthropod."

I nodded. Sashimi it was then.

Liesel loved the sashimi, having never had fresh fish of this caliber before. The real humor came from Cesar, releasing our accumulated tension. He ate the fish willingly, but his facial expressions as he ate had everyone splitting our sides with laughter, even Ariadne. After breakfast, we cleaned up the campsite and prepared to embark once again. I was slightly disappointed that the smell of coffee hadn't awoken Hemant from his stupor.

I pressured Arjun into joining me in the cab on the next leg, knowing he needed the distraction as badly as I did. As we drove east, I leaned close to the dusty windscreen to stare up at the aerial network, omnipresent in the clear blue sky above.

"What do you think is going through their minds right now?" I asked. "They have to see us. Do you think they are like 'It's you!'?"

"By 'their minds' do you mean the antenna bugs or the Hive?" he asked.

"I don't know. Either one, I suppose."

"I would imagine that they do. At the very least, they consider us a threat. Otherwise, they wouldn't have done so much to impede our progress. We've encountered less resistance on this continent than I would've suspected, but that's concerning. The last time they stopped showing interest in us, they had the spine back waiting for us."

I shivered. The prospect of an attack from some other super invert was terrifying. We'd barely escaped the last one with our lives. Many didn't.

"All the more reason to take out their eyes and ears. Did you make any progress on it in your lab?"

"If I'd had more time, I might have. The non-lethal lab kept me on a long leash, but they required my services for several hours a day. In the cabin is a shoulder launcher with rockets Dieter and I rigged up with neem, but I doubt it would have much of an effect on more than a handful of the antenna bugs. I tried to develop something to jam their signals, but stumbled upon the repellent signal first."

"Could you experiment more with your transceiver?"

"I don't think so. For one, I would have to disable the current signal, which might be the only thing keeping us safe. Secondly, it doesn't have near enough power to affect anything other than what is relatively close."

"I was really hoping that we could knock out their surveillance," I said. "I'm afraid if we don't, they'll have something nasty waiting for us around every bend."

"That may be the case," said Arjun.

I waited patiently for a "but," but Arjun just stared out the window in contemplation.

"Huck, I may be overanalyzing, but the roadbed ahead looks more recently traveled than it should."

I looked at the roadbed. I had become so accustomed to driving the vehicle at the rear of the convoy that following tracks was almost an afterthought, but in this case, no one should've been ahead of us. Any doubts I may have had vanished when I saw some fresh invert carcasses on the side of the road.

"You're right," I said, opening the panel to the back cabin. "Omar, we need to armor up! I think we're about to have company of the human kind."

Omar crowded himself into the tiny pass-through to the vehicle's cabin.

"Please tell me it's not the Demented," he said in a hushed tone.

"No, like transporters."

"You sure?"

"I followed those tracks for days. Trust me, I recognize the tread pattern. They must have snuck past us during the night."

"Ambush?"

"Almost certainly. According to Yanus' map that I found, we're coming up on a pump house. I'd bet my ration points they're waiting for us there."

"Your worthless rations points?" chuckled Omar. "I'll pass, but you're probably right. Can we avoid them?"

I looked down at our fuel gauge.

"No," I said. "We have to stop unless we want to hoof it. Losing the driver's side canister cost us precious fuel capacity. Even if we raided the buggy, its supply would only get us slightly further."

"Even if we could take the transporters, should we fight them?" asked Arjun. "They accompanied us for thousands of kilometers. While I wouldn't go as far as to call them friends, they were not enemies."

"He's right," said Omar. "What do we do, dear leader?"

I sighed. "You think Zabu's troops are with them?"

Omar thought for a moment.

"There's no way to know. If we are running out of fuel, we have no choice but to stop. We'll just have to face them when the time comes."

"Okay," I said. "Prepare the others. This could be dicey."

•••••••••

When we rode into the next town, abandoned like all those before it and immediately saw why it was labeled as Archton on the map. Towering over most of the ruins on the landscape was a large metal arch, echoing the town's glorious past. Though most of its facade had blown off over the centuries, the rigid construction still towered defiantly over the landscape. We followed the road and its ominous tracks directly into the city. As we came upon the bridge to cross the river, we saw Yanus' convoy and gradually pulled to a stop.

"Are you ready, Omar?" I asked.

"Locked and loaded," he replied from the single machine gun emplacement the carrier had for defense.

"I don't see how shooting them will have any positive outcome," said Arjun. "We're out-gunned and out-manned. May I remind you that Yanus was paranoid enough to load his carrier with weapons, but it is not a tank."

"I know, Arjun," I said. "But I can't die without fighting back. If it comes to that."

Both sides stayed frozen in place like the town around us, each daring the other to make the first move. After a half-hour standoff, Taha emerged and slowly crossed the dusty plateau, a large parasol protecting him from the incessant barrage of the sun's rays.

"It's good to see you again, Master Huck," he said, neglecting to drop the honorific.

"You too. I wish it was under better circumstances," I said, gripping the steering wheel. "How'd you find us? How did you beat us here?"

"You forget, my people have been doing this for a long time. Much longer than either of us has been alive. We stumbled upon your tracks off the road and pressed on, knowing the pump house would be your next stop. It wasn't difficult for Protector Yanus to suss out. It if makes you feel better, I offered no help."

"So… what now?"

"Protector Yanus is demanding your unconditional surrender. From here, he will escort you back to Pod Kano where you will be tried and likely executed."

"What reason do we possibly have for cooperating?"

"You don't," said Taha. "He's furious with you. He saw his bloodied rug as we left the pod. He doesn't hold you in the highest regard."

"What do you suggest?" I asked him, betting on our relationship. "We can't go on without fuel."

Taha thought for a moment.

"I have come to a conclusion. It is one I have been wrestling with for days, so do not take my decision lightly. I believe your mission is far more important than anything I have done or will do in the service of my master. If I do this, I will be betraying my people and risk dying a traitor alongside you."

"Taha, you are one of the noblest humans I know."

"I believe my path is clear," he said. "May I use your intercom?"

"I can make it happen, but we cannot broadcast the protective signal at the same time," said Arjun.

"If we don't, we might not be around long enough for it to matter," I said.

Arjun flipped a few red switches on the panel and handed Taha a microphone.

"I hope this works, inshallah," he said and began speaking in Arabic to the rival convoy.

As I listened, I could hear the passion in his voice and even excitement. Ariadne, Krista, and Liesel huddled up to the pass-through to listen as I explained what had happened.

"What's he saying?" asked Ariadne.

"You know I don't speak Arabic," I replied.

"My guess would be he is attempting to turn the transporters to our side," said Arjun.

After ten minutes of passionate speaking, Taha returned the mic to me.

"It's finished," he said, exhilarated.

"What'd you say?" asked Ariadne.

"I simply told them the truth," he said. "Whether they choose to act on it is ultimately up to them. Either way, I have broken the contract with my master, which is punishable by death."

"Thank you, Taha, from the bottom of my heart," I said. "You always have a place with us. You wouldn't be the first of us carrying a mark."

"I am honored, Master Huck."

Minutes slowly ticked by as we waited for a response. Finally, doors on the other vehicles began to open as the transporters filed out, curved blades in hand.

"It would appear they have chosen to ceremonially fight," said Taha.

My heart sank. There was no way we would outlast their number or skill. It would be shameful and dishonorable to mow them down with our guns. After all, they had helped us when no one else would. I hit the button to lower the tailgate before climbing down from the cab myself. Save for those of us who were incapacitated, we filed out and stood in front of the carrier. The Saharan transporters let out a loud choral yell, held up their scimitars, then let them clatter onto the ground.

"What?!" I said, looking at Taha.

"Fortune has favored us! They have sided with you, Master Huck!" said Taha with a wide smile.

I started screaming and jumping up and down with the others. Immediately, we heard screaming from across the field. Yanus spilled from the carrier, bubbling over with rage and yelling at the top of his lungs in Arabic.

"What are you doing? I am your master," Taha translated. "How could you honor these ingrates? When we get back to the pod, I will have you all flogged. I hope fleas infest your beds. Pick up your swords and fight if you have any honor. How are you going to listen to that child, Taha? Do you have any—"

Then Yanus disappeared, leaving a meters-long blood splatter across the pristine sand.

"What the hell just happened?" I asked.

"The signal!" screamed Arjun, jumping into the cab and furiously flipping buttons on the dash. "I have to reactivate it!"

Taha and I searched the skies and quickly identified the offending creature. Hurtling aloft was something narrow and black with a screaming Yanus clutched in its legs. A swarm of identical creatures headed directly for us.

"Got it!" yelled Arjun as we watched the mysterious creatures immediately divert from their strafing run.

"That was too close," I said. "What the hell were those things?"

"I don't know," answered Arjun. "If our journey is teaching us anything, it is that we still have much to learn of the Arthropods."

"I too am unfamiliar with them," said Taha. "The Arthropods seem forever full of surprises, especially when it comes to this crew."

"And we still have so far to go," said Ariadne. "I'm scared to think of what else we might come across."

Before she could continue her thought, something unusual happened. The transporters started chanting Taha's name. At first just a few, then eventually, all of them. We reemerged from the vehicle to, "Taha! Taha! Taha!"

"It would appear they have chosen a new leader," said Taha, looking at us with a satisfied grin.

"What's next, Taha?" asked Ariadne.

"I'll resume Yanus' route as their new leader, though I won't refer to myself as protector," he said.

"What about Boss Taha?" I suggested.

"I enjoy the sound of that," he said. "Regardless of my title, a beneficial legacy is of great importance to me and my beliefs. I will no longer trade in pheromones or slaves."

"Won't Zabu be pissed?" I asked.

"Prime Minister Zabu depends on the transport system. He can't function without it or our knowledge. As you're aware, surface survival is not something just anyone can do. I think that's why my men respect you so. The carrier and buggy are yours, may they aid you on your mission. I can request new vehicles from Pod Monterrey, though you might defeat the Hive long before I acquire them."

I laughed as I pulled Taha into an embrace.

"I wish you well, Taha, and hope our paths cross again."

"I'm sure they will, Huck."

CHAPTER 43: HEMANT

The air was thick with the smell of sulfur and the horizon dark, save for the dim glow of the volcanic peak in the distance. The heat from the lava rivers surrounding the wide island made me drip with sweat. The ground pounded with the march of a million feet. I frantically scanned the perimeter of the rocky island for the others, but as far as the eye could see were just more inverts, pouring down the hills and lining the far sides of the molten flows.

"Arjun!" I screamed. "Arjun!"

"I'm here!" he yelled, pinned underneath a rocky outcropping.

"I got you!" I said, trying to lift the jagged boulder from his torso.

I tried with all my might, feeling the strain on every tendon and muscle, but couldn't get the rock to budge.

"I can't, Arjun," I said.

"We'll find another way," he said, taking my hand.

The drumming stopped. I looked over the island and saw it, the Nightmare, but unlike the first one we encountered, it was incandescent, glowing from within in the same vibrant hues as the surrounding lava. It was as though it had climbed through the cracked Earth itself.

At the beckoning of the spectating inverts, the looming creature let loose a terrifying roar and charged toward me. The Nightmare crashed through the boulder, trampling Arjun under its spindly feet.

"No!" I screamed as I rushed to his side.

Arjun lay in the blackened earth, soot covering his innocent face and mixing with the blood he sprayed with his cough.

"It's going to be okay," I said, crying. "Everything's going to be okay!"

The tears burned as the ash fell from the sky. I could hear the monster roaring triumphantly behind me. I gazed over Arjun's mangled body. The weight of the creature had pulverized his bones from the waist down. Arjun hacked, covering me with a red mist.

"Kill them, brother," he said. "Kill them all."

Then his convulsions stopped and he was still.

I defiantly stood in a fury, holding out my hammer at arm's length towards the enemy. I ran towards its towering bulk, letting out a scream from the bottom of my lungs as I raised my weapon to strike.

"*Aaaaaahhhhhh!*" I yelled.

"Help me hold him down!" screamed Ariadne. "Omar hold him tighter! Huck, he's coming loose! Grab his legs."

"Where?! What?!" I yelled, throwing my body against the restraint. "Where's Arjun?! Where's my brother's body?!"

"Hemant, look at me!" said Ariadne. "Arjun's fine! He's outside! I need you to listen to me. You're okay. You were hallucinating."

"Arjun! I have to see Arjun!"

I felt a prick and looked down to see Ariadne withdraw a syringe from my arm.

"I need to… see… Arjun," I said.

Arjun walked in and held my hand.

"He was going to give himself a heart attack if I didn't," Ariadne said to him as I drifted off into unconsciousness.

When I woke, it was nighttime again. I felt different and wrong. I tried to raise my arm to check if I was still restrained. When it wouldn't budge, I knew. I looked to my left to see if I could undo the clasp on my own. But where my hand should've been, I saw the fuzzy, saw-toothed leg of an eight. I felt the bile start to rise as panic set in.

"What the hell?!" I attempted to say, but only the clacking of mouth parts emanated from my head.

I looked to my left side and saw that it matched my right. Tears formed in each of my numerous eyes. The bushes ahead parted as a figure emerged, bathed in the firelight from behind my arachnid form, which cast a bizarre shadow. When the figure came closer, I recognized it for what it was—a Demented. *I have to warn the others!* I thought, senselessly. The vile humans would kill me long before I reached them.

"They'd never believe you anyway," the figure said in a familiar voice, putting her face so close to mine, I could feel her heat radiating through the fine hairs spanning my body. *Ariadne!*

"Help me!" I tried to say.

Everything was wrong. Ariadne wasn't one of the Demented. This wasn't real.

"If it's not real, then why does this hurt?" she asked, slicing open my abdomen with her wicked blade.

I screeched in visceral, searing pain. Ariadne tugged length after length of intestines from my body as she began to consume them raw with her mangled teeth, the black hemolymph staining her face gray in the orange firelight. As I pleaded for mercy, I hoped the rivulet of my tears would soothe the burn in my belly. I wrenched my eyes closed against the spreading pain, when I opened them, I saw Huck.

"Hemant, are you okay?" asked Huck, his eyes sunken from lack of sleep.

"I've got to go!" I said, breathing hard.

"You can't leave until Ariadne clears you."

"No, I mean I got to go!"

"Oh, uh…"

Huck fumbled with the straps. As I stood, I almost lost all sense of balance. How long had I been out? With Huck's help, I made it to the edge of the woods, barely getting my jumpsuit down in time. After sending Huck on, I had one of the single most uncomfortable experiences of my entire life. It was no wonder that the abdominal sensations had painfully permeated my dreams.

"Hemant, do you need anything?" Ariadne yelled from the edge of the woods.

"Only for everyone to stay the hell away," I yelled.

I finally hobbled back to camp, where someone had built a roaring campfire. Despite the intense heat radiating from my gut, the rest of me was cold. I trudged my way back to the fire. Omar, who was seated on a downed tree trunk next to Arjun, relinquished his spot for me.

"Do we have anything soft to sit on?" I asked.

Within minutes, Krista was back with a cushion from the carrier.

"Thanks," I said.

"How do you feel?" asked Ariadne.

"Like I've been to hell and back again," I said, wrapping my arm around Arjun. "And I'd give that area of the woods a wide berth for the rest of the time we're here."

Omar snickered.

"Sorry about fighting you folks whenever that was. I was having some pretty rough nightmares. Where are we? What'd I miss?"

"Mei is still in a coma," said Ariadne. "She's improving, but it's slow going. Mathias is having similar issues as you, but they're worse. We're assuming it's due to his longer usage."

"I can't imagine worse. I feel like I've been running marathons the entire time I was out. My belly's on fire and my head is pounding like never before. If I ever see Dust again, it'll be too damn soon."

"The last time Mathias woke, he thought the carrier was crawling with Arthropods. Floor, ceiling, everything," Huck said. "Issue was we were the Arthropods. He fought so hard he broke one of his straps and gave Omar that shiner before we got him sedated."

"To your other question, we are a hundred and fifty or so kilometers east of the pump house," said Arjun. "Taha's transporters got us all fixed up. We stopped all of our movement when we realized you and Mathias were worsening."

"Taha's transporters?" I asked, arching an eyebrow. "I really did miss a lot."

"Get some rest, Hemant," said Ariadne. "We'll fill you in in the morning."

●●●●●●●●●

When the sun pierced through the open ventilation slats of the personnel carrier, I rolled out of bed to find Mathias already up and piddling around. He was sitting by the fire as Huck tried to stoke the embers from the night before and rekindle it. When I sat down next to Mathias, his eyes were glazed as he stared into the early flames.

"How are you holding up, man?" I asked, sitting next to him.

"Like I can't tell up from down," he mumbled. "I'd wake up, and I couldn't tell what was real and what wasn't. That's some scary stuff, man. I felt like I lost… myself. Now that I'm back, I mean, this feels like reality. I feel like myself, I suppose, but I also feel like I'll never be happy again."

I sat pensively, unsure of how to respond. Huck sat listening, but quiet.

"I hallucinated too, but these guys were there every time I woke up to guide me out," I said, gesturing to Huck and those sleeping in. "I don't know if I would've made it without them. I can't promise you happiness, but we're here for you, okay?"

Mathias nodded. With everyone up, Huck and a few others managed to pull some palm-sized fish out of a nearby shallow lake. After begging for Arjun's consent, we grilled them over the fire, the tantalizing smell luring everyone close. As we devoured the oily fish whole, everyone licked the tasty grease from their fingers, relishing in one of the tastiest breakfasts we'd had on the surface. Even Mathias looked content. As we packed up our gear for another day of driving, I pulled Ariadne aside.

"I'm concerned about Mathias. He seems really… down," I said.

"You know him better than I do," she said. "Regretfully, the majority of my experience with him has not been a positive one."

"He's a good guy, just like I am. We just made some serious mistakes."

"I know, Hemant. I can forgive you, but I can't stop reliving that moment in the plant. Those feelings hit me like a truck, and just like a truck, they run me over every time I see your face."

"I'm sorry, Ariadne," I said yet another time.

"I know. I'll be okay. I just need time to deal with some things," she said, glaring over at Liesel and Huck palling around.

I got the distinct feeling I wasn't the only issue she needed to work through. Even having been unconscious for the last few days, I could tell Liesel was into Huck. With Ariadne having spurned him, who could blame him for being interested back?

"About Mathias," Ariadne continued. "I have some antidepressants, but they would likely just postpone the underlying issues. His body needs to readjust to the absence of the drug. It has to find its old homeostasis, which applies to emotions too. The best thing for him is to wait it out."

"He'll love to hear that."

"Be there for him. Guide him through the struggles. Like Grace and Mei did for me," she said, squeezing my hand.

At the mention of Mei, Ariadne's shoulders drooped.

"Can we go see her?"

Ariadne nodded. We made our way into the carrier where her still form rested peacefully on the fold-out cot.

"How's she doing?"

"Stable, but that's all I can say. I've cleaned and restitched the wound, treated her for infection, and given her a transfusion. There's nothing else to do but wait," Ariadne's voice began to crack. "That could've easily been a fatal wound, Hemant. She barely survived."

"You've done all you can for her," I said. "You did great."

She leaned over into my arms. We stood there for several moments before she pulled back.

"Thanks, Hemant," she said as we walked out of the carrier.

When we came out, I saw Krista and Omar holding hands. I can't say I was surprised, having spent all that time alone together while we were in the pod. Ariadne was far less enthused and all but ran around to the other side of the carrier. It was no secret what all she had done for Krista in the past. I was glad Krista had found happiness again, something that was so fleeting on Earth's hostile surface. I just hoped that whatever they were doing, they were careful about it.

Once the physical and emotional baggage was loaded into the carrier, I got Mathias situated in the gun turret where I thought the fresh air would benefit him more than that of the stifling cab. Then after no one else showed interest in riding up front, I climbed into the cab with Huck for the next leg of our journey.

CHAPTER 44: ARIADNE

As the personnel carrier lumbered along, the tracks rumbling beneath my feet as they passed over the rocky terrain, my insides overflowed with turmoil. I stared at Mei, willing her to wake from her prolonged slumber. Cesar was in the corner, whimpering again. Liesel was doing everything she could to calm him, but the truth was he hadn't been alright since we'd left. Everything familiar to him—his work, his caregiver, his environment—had all been inexplicably stolen. I had been worried about his survival before, but my concern continually mounted. The only solace was that I knew leaving him meant his certain death, so I had no regrets about bringing him. I fought the desire daily to overreact to Krista and Omar's intimacy, but always stopped shy when I considered the damage I had done the last time. Then there was the budding relationship between Liesel and Huck. I told him off, so he had every right to happiness without me, but that didn't mean I wasn't second-guessing my actions.

"What I wouldn't give for a restful night's sleep," I said to Arjun who was adding to his copious notes.

"Surely you have medication for that," he said as I rubbed my eyes.

"I do, but I need to be ready for when Mei wakes up. I can't be of any help if I have medically-induced grogginess."

"I suppose you're correct. If you'd like, you can rest now. I'd be happy to wake you should the need arise."

"No, thanks. I had a bunch of coffee already this morning. I'd rather chat with you. It's a welcome distraction."

Arjun closed his notebook, suppressing his mild annoyance at the interruption.

"How do you think Ekon is fairing?" I asked.

"I have been wondering that myself. We're obligated to take a more circuitous route that can accommodate our vehicle. He seemed intent to travel on foot, following his people's roots. If he takes a more direct approach, he could shave more than a thousand kilometers off the distance. However, unless we experience a major obstacle, I do not foresee how he could travel under his own power and beat us there."

"There's something strange about that man," said Omar, sharpening the blades of his naginata.

"You met him?" I asked.

Omar nodded, sitting up from slouching against the wall.

"He told us how crazy everything was inside the pod and encouraged us to be prepared to leave suddenly. As far as his trip, he said that it wouldn't take him long."

"Then he disappeared," Krista added.

I giggled.

"No, like he really disappeared," confirmed Omar. "One minute he was there, the next he wasn't."

"There must be a logical explanation," said Arjun. "People don't just disappear. I have some vague familiarity with the Tuareg. I came across them in the research. They're native to the area. Though I was under the impression there were none left, their heritage obviously continues."

"Did they have any special abilities? Like powers?" asked Krista.

Arjun smiled. "No. They were known for living in harmony with the desert. They were some of the few that could survive and thrive in the harshest corners of the Sahara. It would seem that in addition to his abilities, he still possesses some of his culture's mystique."

"I don't care how he helps us, just that he does," I said. "We are lucky to have made it this far, but now, we no longer have any help from transporters. For the first time, we're on our own, and Baghdad is a long way away."

"Huck has a map and knows how to drive," said Arjun. "I would suggest we set our focus always on the next pump house, ignoring the larger objective for the time being."

"Wise words, Arjun," said Omar. "Speaking of which, how far to the next fuel station?"

"Almost too far. The vehicle's tank size and pump houses are two aspects of the same system. To save resources, the First Builders spaced them between the pods at specific distances and sized the tanks accordingly. With half the primary storage, we'll have to completely drain the reserve tank again, possibly raid that of the buggy, and hope we can coast to the next stop."

"That's Arjun for you, encouraging you, then jerking the rug out from under your feet," said Omar.

"I don't see how ignorance helps in any fashion," said Arjun.

"Oh, it doesn't. But it makes people feel better," said Omar, slapping Arjun on the shoulder.

"Can you ask Huck to pull over?" asked Liesel. "I don't think Cesar is well."

"Sure," I said, rising to speak with him.

Minutes later, the truck straddled the crumbled edge of the asphalt and the pebbly shoulder as Cesar threw up in a tuft of grass.

"It's just motion sickness, I think," I said to Liesel.

"I thought that might be it. Not that he'd understand it," she said, rubbing circles on his back. "I'm having an issue with it, too. I appreciate the stop as much as he does."

"You never really answered how far the next pump house was, Arjun," said Krista.

"Another day of driving at least," said Huck, having returned from the bushes. "With no need to rush thanks to Arjun's invention, I'm trying to optimize fuel consumption. The inverts are leaving us completely alone. If we can make it to Baghdad and get reinforcements, maybe we can have an uninterrupted drive to the Hive."

"I strongly doubt that, Huck," said Arjun, pointing up. "We still have to deprive them of their senses. For all we know, there is a perimeter of Arthropods moving right along with us, just out of the signal's reach."

"Thanks for that uplifting image, Arjun," said Omar.

"I'm ready for a face-to-face fight with the little bastards," said Mathias. "I don't like all this emptiness. It's eerie. I might actually be relieved when I see one."

"You're a strange little man," said Omar, shaking his head.

"Bring it on, you shaved ape," said Mathias, puffing his chest.

"Guys!" said Huck. "Same side, remember? Look, we've already stopped. Why don't we break out lunch and chill? I think we've all been confined too long."

Mathias and Omar glared at each other before parting ways. Krista and I went off to see what edible things we could discover amid the sparse vegetation. I quickly found a patch of wild okra and harvested as much as I could carry. Krista, meanwhile, had found a porcupine and speared it with a perfectly aimed throw.

"Impressive," I said.

Krista flashed me a fleeting smile before resuming her trademark stone-face appearance. We returned with the porcupine, okra, and a handful of ripe red berries. Growing comfortable with fire-roasting our meat under the safety umbrella, we enjoyed freshly seared porcupine with berry sauce and charred okra. It was delicious. As I laid back enjoying the fullness in my stomach, I thought about how pleasant life on Earth had the potential of being. Having seen the diverse landscapes and knowing what else might be out there, I was overwhelmed with a sense of wanderlust. If I could stay alive, I'd have a lifetime to tour our planet's majesty. *Our planet.* That's exactly what it was.

•••••••••

After piling back into the carrier, we spent the rest of the day rolling over the increasingly monotonous terrain. I had given up on peeking outside. The only things that varied in the infinite landscape were the occasional rocky outcropping or another dilapidated town. By the time we stopped again, it was already dusk. Everyone proved just as exhausted from the boredom as by physical exertion, so in lieu of hunting, Huck caved and we pilfered our dry rations.

I woke as the light of dawn filtered through the ventilation slats of the cabin, covering the opposing wall in a pleasing pattern of soothing light. I made my way over the sleeping bodies littering the floor to Mei and checked her vital signs. Same. As much as I wanted to start a pot of coffee, I refrained, not wanting to wake the others. I grabbed my bow and silently snuck out the side door, avoiding the tailgate's noisy hydraulic lines. The faint glow had just begun to illuminate the campsite. Embers still burned in the fire, diffusing smoky essence into the air. Trusting the audible hissing of the speakers, I explored the perimeter of the area that had been too obscure the evening before.

We parked near the road, no longer under threat of pursuit. Huck had found a little clearing within an island of dense vegetation.

Staying within Arjun's proposed radius, I made my way into the woods, making sure to keep the carrier in sight. I heard a rustle in a bundle of low-lying shrubs and froze. Though the climate was too arid for blood midges, I'd seen enough unknown Arthropods to be ready for anything. I carefully pulled Ciro's bow from my back and nocked an arrow from my quiver. No sooner than I had the feather touching my cheek, I saw a fat black porcupine meander from the bush. I breathed out a sigh of relief. I hadn't taken a walk with the intention of hunting, but I decided to take advantage of the opportunity and stalked the slow creature.

A porcupine might not be quick, but it could fit places I couldn't. I found myself pushing through the dry spiky vegetation to pursue my prey. When I finally reacquired it, the animal was virtually motionless, munching on a cluster of deep blue berries. Again, I drew back my string. The creature turned its head towards me and for a brief moment, before I fired, I wondered if it knew its end was near. The animal released a muffled squeal as the arrow pierced its side, and it dropped to its stomach.

"Sorry, little guy," I said over its corpse. "Your death will help me live."

I carefully picked up the spikey animal the way Krista had demonstrated to avoid the quills and I marched back towards camp. In the intensity of my hunt, I had lost sight of the camp. *That was a stupid, Ariadne.* I kept walking in the direction I felt confident with. Thankfully, after a few nervous moments, I saw the carrier in the distance and felt the relief, silently resolving not to leave the camp alone again. The path was blocked by more vegetation, so I ducked through some brambles and hacked my way back towards the clearing with my dagger. The thorny branches began to tug my clothes and twigs lodged in my hair. Little gnats were starting to flood the air, biting me on the neck. I desperately wanted out of the woods. I ducked under a bizarrely growing tree and came face-to-face with Liesel, just as her eyes grew wide and she released a blood-curdling scream.

I spun to look behind me, raising my dagger in defense. Looming more than a meter over me was the carcass of a hook beetle, strung up on two wooden posts in an alarmingly familiar manner. I felt my blood run ice cold, shying away from my extremities as the porcupine slipped from my grasp into the dirt. Liesel's torturous screams were muffled by the racing adrenaline flooding my mind, cementing me to the ground as though I weighed thousands of tons. I heard something else. Someone calling my name.

"Ariadne! Ariadne!" yelled Hemant, his panicked voice entering my mind as though I had been submerged into a thick syrup.

I turned to face him, but my awareness had slowed to a crawl.

"Come on!" he yelled, grabbing my arm and jerking me back into reality.

We ran towards the carrier, Huck toting Liesel, and Hemant almost dragging me. Everyone in our party piled into the back.

"Hemant, I want you up front as a backup driver," Huck yelled, rushing everyone into place. "Mathias, in the turret. Omar, guard the gate. Arjun, take care of the others. Go!"

Everyone rushed around like bees as Arjun ushered Liesel, Cesar, and me into the carrier. By the time I entered, I had shrugged off my temporary adrenal-inspired fog. Within moments, the tracked vehicle was rolling.

"Someone please tell me what the hell is going on," yelled Mathias from the turret once we were a few kilometers down the road. "What is that thing?"

"A Demented sacrifice," answered Omar, resuming his battle-hardened persona. "Trust me, shoot anything that moves. They look like people, but they're animals."

My mind flooded with unanswerable questions. *Why hadn't Taha warned us? How far does their territory extend? Are we safe in the carrier? Why Demented? I could handle inverts, but why them?*

I took a shaky breath and watched the tremors in my hand, willing them to abate.

"Can this tug go any faster?" yelled Omar, as Cesar rocked in the corner.

"Not without risking our fuel. Arjun calculated—" Huck stopped mid-sentence.

"What's that in the road?" Hemant asked.

"Ambush!" screamed Huck at the top of his lungs.

"Ariadne?" asked Mei.

CHAPTER 45: HUCK

As soon as I saw the blockade, I slammed the brakes so forcefully that it locked up the tracks, causing us to skid to a halt. Barricading the road was a smattering of meter-tall concrete pillars blocking the path forward. The dilapidated barricades, which had lined the road for the last few kilometers, prevented us from simply driving around, funneling us right into the trap. The coast was clear, and for a brief moment, I hoped that maybe the trap had been abandoned. The thought crossed my mind to reverse out, but the shrubby vegetation made off-road travel unpredictable. Not to mention that we would already be gliding into the next pump house on fumes.

"Mathias, don't let anything approach! I don't care what it is," I yelled. "Hemant, Omar, I need those posts gone!"

Hemant scrambled out the door as I heard the bed's side door slam shut. Above me, Mathias chambered a round.

"Huck, Mei's awake!" yelled Ariadne.

"That's great, but piss-poor timing!"

"*¡Mierda!* Here they come!" Mathias yelled, as the carrier filled with the deep-throated *dum, dum, dum* of the fifty cal punctuating the air and raining its scorching shells into the cabin.

Out front, Hemant and Omar struggled to drag the first of the cumbersome pillars in an effort to clear a large enough path for the carrier. They had toppled the barrel-sized stone and we unsuccessfully attempted to roll it as the Demented's savage arrows arched overhead.

I could hear the harmless plink of the arrowheads as they careened with the vehicle's armored exterior. As long as that's all they had, we would be safe inside. Dodging the arrows shot from the distant tree line, Hemant sprinted back to the side door, throwing it open.

"We need Cesar!" he said, out of breath and struggling to speak over the gunfire.

"He can't!" yelled Liesel. "He's too frightened as it is!"

"We are all going to die if we can't get moving! We have to have his help!"

"Okay," Liesel cried. "Go with them, Cesar. Be careful."

I twisted my neck to watch him disembark. Cesar lumbered out through the door as Hemant guided him to the resting pillar. All around, the Demented ran suicidally into the clearing, only to be mowed down by the Mathias' powerful gun.

"Keep them safe, Mathias!" I yelled.

"Trying my best," he yelled. "The sick bastards are flooding in from everywhere! How many are there?!"

With Cesar's help, Hemant and Omar had managed to clear the first pillar and moved to the second.

"They're at the tailgate!" yelled Krista. "I can hear them outside!"

"I can't hit them from the turret!" said Mathias. "They're too low and close."

I heard him fire again.

"Well.. unless they climb the carrier," he said, spitting, "but then I get covered in overspray."

"Ariadne, we have to keep them back," I said. "Lower the gate. You and Arjun take out as many as you can!"

"They could get inside!" Ariadne said.

"If they get through Mathias, they will anyway!"

I heard the whine of hydraulics as the door descended.

"Arjun, grab one of the guns Hemant stole from Kano!" yelled Ariadne.

"I don't know how to use them!"

"You're the genius. Figure it out!"

After a fleeting moment, I heard the *tat, tat, tat* echoing from the cabin, painfully dulling my hearing.

"Got one!" yelled Arjun, continuing to fire.

Wham! I looked to my left. There was a male Demented crawling up the side of the vehicle. He stopped and stared at me through the scratched window before reaching for the handle. I mash my finger down on the lock mechanism as he beat his head against the armored window in frustration, leaving blood spatters from the intensity of the impacts. I reached down and opened the door's tiny vent and shoved my dagger through his lower abdomen. He fell back, grasping the wound before hobbling away.

In my distraction, I failed to keep an eye on the others. Hemant and Cesar continued to move the fourth pillar away as Omar spun to kill the attacking Demented fighters. Mathias was mowing them down, but they were slipping through his barrage. In minutes, we'd be overrun. I grabbed the external speaker, interrupting Arjun's signal.

"I can squeeze through!" I said. "Get back in the carrier!"

Hemant grabbed Cesar, whose shirt was stained with blood, and hustled him back to the vehicle as Omar held the attackers off long enough to get to the back.

"Don't shoot me!" he yelled as he came around.

"Everyone in?" I yelled, once Hemant was back in the cab.

"Go! Go! Go!" yelled Omar over Mathias' continued fire and the whine of the tailgate.

I restarted the engine and pulled forward.

"Cesar?!" yelled Liesel. "Oh my God, Cesar! Ariadne, help him!"

"What's going on?!" I yelled.

"Cesar's been hit!" yelled Ariadne. "It must've happened while he was outside!"

"You hear that?" asked Hemant.

I took my foot off of the gas long just enough to hear over our engine. It was hard to make out over the ringing in my eardrums, but sure enough, there was a distant revving. And it was getting closer. Hemant and I looked at each other, eyes wide with fright.

"They can drive?!" we asked in unison.

"You guys aren't going to believe this," said Mathias. "There's a crazy-ass looking buggy, and it's coming up on us—really fast."

I slammed on the accelerator, feeling the tracks sling sand as the carrier fishtailed so wildly that it almost jackknifed with the trailer before biting the ground and lurching forward. I pushed the pedal to the firewall. Within moments, I could hear the roar of the buggy behind us.

"My God!" said Mathias. "The thing is disgusting as they are! It's decorated with invert parts! The damn thing looks like it was painted by hand with hemolymph! Who the hell are these sickos?"

"Questions later!" yelled Omar. "Light them up!"

We heard the large weapon begin to spit its heavy slugs, then with the same cadence was a string of foul expletives erupting from Mathias.

"I'm out! Dammit! Of all times! We got any more ammo?"

I heard frantic rustling through supplies.

"Nothing but Yanus' crap! That self-serving buffoon didn't

store extra munitions! Get down here and seal off the turret. You can't do any more up there."

I struggled to keep the carrier on a straight path, constantly checking my side mirrors as I did. I could finally see it. Behind us was a sickening sight, matching Mathias' description. They must have stolen the buggy from the transporters. The buggy, while similar to ours, had been heavily modified. In the cab were several Demented warriors and even more clung to its sides. What I saw standing erect in their midst sent an icy saber through my heart. Barking commands from her position was a revolting human who would forever haunt my dreams.

Doop. Doop. Doop. Doop. Doop. I heard the fire of a small-caliber machine gun knocking on the tailgate, our armor rejecting every round.

"The bastards can't get us in here!" said Mathias, as their vehicle slammed into the trailer.

The impact sent a spine-jarring jolt through the chassis, which was directly tied to that of the buggy. Suddenly, there was an explosion that left my ears ringing, followed by screaming and yelling. I couldn't parse out what was happening. I brought my focus back up on the road just in time to steer away from the barricade I was veering dangerously towards.

"What's happening?" I yelled over the throbbing in my head.

"They hit us with something!" yelled Omar.

"Probably a small missile," added Arjun. It blew a hole in the roof. If they get another missile through that opening, the shockwave will kill us."

"If we survive this, Arjun, I'm having Omar give you a lesson in optimism," I said.

I began to swerve in a drunken zig-zag, hoping the movement would make it harder for our attackers to score a direct hit. I checked my mirrors. Arjun's theory had proven correct. Loading another round into her launcher, their leader took aim at our vehicle. Right before she could fire, I pumped the brakes, causing their driver to bump our trailer. The small collision caused her to drop the launcher from the buggy.

"Yes!" I yelled. "She dropped it."

"Whoo!" yelled Hemant. "Maybe they'll give up."

I glanced in the mirror and saw the woman, staring straight into my soul. Her hair was held back from her stitched face by what appeared to be the broken fangs of an eight. Her leathery vest revealed her scarred chest, her body as mutilated as her kin. She raised a wiry tattooed arm and pointed at me through the mirror, flashing her filed teeth.

"You okay, man?" asked Hemant. "You're as pale as a cave grub."

I swallowed.

"She's not going to give up, Hemant," I said. "Not now. Not ever. She's a huntress, and I think she just chose her prey."

I gave up on the swerving and drove like hell, ignoring the screams from the back. I desperately needed to get us to safety. We needed refuge, and we needed it fast. I frantically searched the landscape for anything promising. The terrain had become increasingly more mountainous and just over the rise was a large stone landform with a multitude of caverns recessed into its face. I raced along, desperately trying to stay out of reach of the pursuing buggy until I saw where there was a gap in the crumbling barricade.

"Hang on!" I screamed as I slung the vehicle hard left.

We busted through the weakened concrete, momentarily airborne as we left the roadbed before reaching the ground below. We landed with a hard crash, bottoming out the suspension. Again, were shouts of anger from behind, but I pushed everything out of my mind, thinking only of safety. Dodging the sporadic shrubbery and boulders, I pushed forward towards the looming mountain.

"They missed the turn!" yelled Hemant, slapping the dash in elation. "They're having to turn around!"

I nodded and pressed on. The caverns were much larger now that we were less than a kilometer away. After the abuse, the unforgiving terrain was ripping the heavy-duty vehicle apart. This was the type of thing it was designed for, but not at break-neck speeds. I nicked a large rock and the truck jolted up on one side so far I thought we were going to flip before it slammed back down, throwing everything asunder.

Catching up fast was the spry little buggy full of the twisted human descendants. The thing was so fast compared to our massive armored truck. We rocketed up an incline, making our final approach to the mountain.

"There!" I yelled to Hemant. "Everybody strap in. This is going to get rougher!"

I aimed toward a cave that was not much larger than our vehicle.

"What are we going to do when we get there?" he asked.

"No idea," I said, nervously smiling. "But they can't catch us, and we are almost out of fuel."

I plowed on, directly towards the opening. *This is going to be tight. I hope to the universe this works.* We hit the lip of the entrance and the carrier leaped up before slamming into the throat of the cave, and everything went dark.

CHAPTER 46: HEMANT

My head was pounding as I came to. Even surrounded by pitch-black darkness, a blinding white light rocketed through my vision. I could feel the warm wetness running down my face, tasting salty as I licked my lips. *What happened?* I struggled to remember as memories came in flashes. *Driving. Ambush. Pillars. The chase! Huck had driven us into a cavern.* I looked around futilely.

"Huck?" I said. "You okay?"

I heard a moan to my left. I ran my hands carefully along the seat until I felt his leg. I jostled it gently to avoid worsening any injuries.

"What?" he said, still groggy.

"Anything broken?"

"Um… maybe my brain. It feels like my body's been run over."

"Does everything move?"

There was no response for a moment.

"I think I'm good," said Huck. "Have you checked on the others?"

"Not yet," I said. "Anyone hurt back there?"

I heard groaning.

"I'm awake," answered Arjun.

Thank the universe.

"How's everyone else?"

"I don't know. Everyone buckled in, but they're all still coming to. That was quite the impact, Huck."

"Sorry about that," said Huck. "I panicked. Ditching seemed like the only viable option. We were going to run out of gas anyway."

"I hope we can find a way out," said Ariadne. "If we're trapped in here, we're not much better off than we would be out there."

"Caves rarely dead end," said Arjun. "It's likely there's another way out. It just may take time to explore the passages. There could be kilometers of them."

"Kilometers?" asked Omar.

"Maybe we could dig back out the way we came in," said Ariadne. "Maybe the Demented will be gone by the time we finish."

"I doubt it," said Huck. "The impact wedged that thing in pretty good. We'd risk a collapse even if we could get through the rubble."

"Do you think the bomb's okay?" I asked. "What if it's leaking radiation?"

"Oh, crap," said Huck. "I didn't think of that. I hope not!"

"If it makes you feel any better, exposure to radiation will worsen with time," said Arjun. "If it is damaged, the sooner we leave this wreckage, the better. It would mean our mission was a failure, though."

"Let's hope not," I said.

I could hear the deflation in his voice. If we failed, it would be devastating. I could hear low voices in the back as the last few woke. I felt along the utilitarian console above my head, scouring the metal for the switches to the cabin light. With any luck, the battery was still functional and would give us some illumination to work with. My fingers found the button and depressed it, bathing the cabin in a soft faint glow that seemed bright by comparison to the darkness.

"You look like hell," said Huck, through slitted eyes. "We need to get you bandaged."

"You don't look so hot yourself," I said. "That's a nasty bruise on your forehead. You're already turning purple."

I heard Arjun making his way to the pass-through.

"Everyone's up but Liesel, including Mei," said Arjun. "Huck, we lost Cesar."

"No," said Huck, distraught. "I was supposed to protect him. Liesel trusted me with his care."

"It is not your fault, Huck," said Arjun. "He took an arrow while they were moving the pillars. He died from blood loss before you drove into the cave. That's what Liesel was screaming about. You'll be pleased to know that before he died, he was pleased that he'd helped us."

"He was such a gentle, kind soul," said Huck. "I knew it was a risk bringing him."

"He wouldn't have lasted a day back in the pod without Miranda, Huck," I said. "He died honorably, and well, given the circumstances."

"I hate it for Liesel most," Huck said. "She was like a sister to him."

"That's why Ariadne was waiting until last to wake her," said Arjun. "Liesel's learning how quickly the surface can take those you care about."

Judging by the echoing sobs, she was no longer sleeping.

"We have to get out of here," I said. "Wherever here is. I don't hear any sign of our pursuers and this thing isn't going anywhere fast."

"You're right," said Huck. "Arjun, can you see if the tailgate or side door will open?"

"Sure thing," he said.

"What about me?" I asked. "I'm a little bulky to fit through the pass-through and I doubt we can open our doors. That's the wall right there."

"I was already thinking about that. The windshield. It was made to resist impacts from the outside, but not the inside. We can kick it out of the gasket."

"That could work, though it won't make my headache any better."

"Neither door will open," said Arjun, returning.

"We were about to try and bust out the windshield. If everyone could squeeze up into the cab, they could follow."

"There ample space above the carrier, too. It'll take a minute, but I think we can climb out through the gun turret single file."

"Let us get out first, so we don't hit you with the windshield, then follow," I said. "We'll clear the area."

I could see Arjun nod in the faint light.

"On three?"

Huck nodded.

On three, we kicked in unison. The windshield budged, but only slightly. We repeated the process until it finally fell forward, dangling from the rubber seal a few moments before crashing to the ground. Within a few moments, everyone was safely out, save for Cesar's body. After verifying that we were alone, I collapsed on the cave floor as Ariadne assessed each of our injuries.

"I can't believe he's gone," said Liesel, sniffling. "We spent most of our lives together."

"I'm sorry," said Huck, wrapping his arm around her. "He died saving us. I'll never forget him."

"I know. I kept telling him that as he was dying," she said, her lips quivering. "He was so happy. He smiled until he…"

Huck squeezed her a little tighter, kissing her on the head. Once Ariadne was satisfied with our condition, we were free to explore. All things considered, aside from Cesar's death, the group had fared well. The carrier's impact with the cave had brought down a rock slide behind it, protecting us from the threat, but also sealing us inside and crushing our buggy into oblivion. I had a nasty cut, Huck had ugly bruises, and others had comparable minor injuries. Mei still needed help to move, but that was due to her previous injury. It had taken four of us to get her out of the vehicle safely.

"We need to check on the bomb," said Arjun. "If it's safe, we'll need to prep it for transport."

"We need to dig it out," said Omar, pointing with his uninjured hand.

Indeed, the rock slide had washed against the side of the vehicle, burying the tank under a waist-high mound of debris.

"If you guys dig it out, Arjun and I can start hauling everything useful out of the carrier," said Ariadne.

"I can help," said Krista.

"No, you can't," said Ariadne. "You bruised some ribs. You're staying put. Doctor's orders."

"Fine," she said, crossing her arms.

"I can help you," said Liesel.

"I didn't want to volunteer you, not with Cesar still in there."

"It's okay. I think I can manage."

For the next few hours, we unloaded everything we could carry from the carrier and dug out the thankfully undamaged bomb. Arjun carried his transceiver, and I had the luxury of carrying a heavy-ass nuclear weapon—on my back. I wasn't sure if that was thrilling or terrifying. We bid goodbye to Cesar with Huck saying a brief eulogy, then guided by hand lights, moved deeper into the mountain. Trusting Arjun's expertise, we followed the cavern hoping to identify which one of the myriad interconnected tunnels might lead our way out.

"Seems like being underground has a tendency to save our lives, huh?" I said, shifting my heavy burden.

I heard a few chuckles from behind. As we explored, I caught a familiar sensation nagging in the back of my brain and pulled up next to Mathias.

"Do you still crave it?" I asked in a hushed tone.

"Every damn day," he said. "I knew a few guys who stopped using it back in the pod. They said eventually the depression wears off, but the taste for it never really goes away. Just lessens."

"Great. I wish I had never started on the stuff."

"Me too. But what's done is done. No use in griping about it now. I'll tell you what would help me out the most."

"What's that?"

"Some TLC from that one," he said, pointing to Mei.

"Dude, she just survived a hell of a wound. She can barely walk unassisted."

"I know, but she's something else."

I rolled my eyes. I liked the bearded wonder, but the more time I spent with him, the more he surprised me. I watched as he made his way forward, offering to help carry Mei's pack, which Ariadne was carrying in addition to her own. Left by myself, I meandered along towards the rear of the group, keeping an eye out for cave-dwelling inverts, but also enjoying the peaceful surroundings. There was something almost pleasant about being underground again. Humans might be meant to live on the surface, but it was clear that living my entire life underground had an effect on me. None of the others seemed uncomfortable in the claustrophobic subterranean network either.

I watched the twinkling on the walls as my flashlight reflected off sparkling minerals embedded in the rock wall. I stopped and grabbed a shiny crystal from the cave wall. It was obscenely sharp and about the size of a pea.

"Arjun, do you know anything about rocks?" I asked.

Arjun circled back, silhouetted by the light of the others. He studied the gem as I rotated it under my light.

"Not really, I'm afraid."

"Hold up," said Mathias, coming back to join our discussion. "I studied geology in Munich before I left, specifically dietary minerals, but there's a lot of overlap. I was never great at it, but I recall the basics."

Mathias took the stone. By now, the rest of the group had stopped to watch him intently. He examined it under the light and rubbed it with his fingers. He held up his mace and scratched a line into the metal's surface with a *Hmmm*.

"Mind if I break it," he asked.

I shook my head.

He laid the stone on a nearby rock and brought his mace down onto it with substantial force, shattering the stone.

"I believe it's a diamond," he finally said.

"A diamond?" I asked. "Aren't those worth a lot?"

"They certainly used to be," said Arjun. "Especially before the Arthropods arrived. Now, there's much less demand for them."

"That's funny," I said. "We're surrounded by the riches of old, and they're worthless. Ironic isn't it?"

"Not entirely worthless," said Mathias, pulling out a small pouch to collect them. "They have value to me."

We kept walking for another hour before stopping in an open area for lunch. I sat down on the cumbersome device, giving my shoulders a much-needed break. Without firewood, we were limited to dry rations. The wreck had physically affected all of us. We were dragging and beat. When Ariadne said Mei needed to rest, no one voiced a complaint. Mathias volunteered to take watch while we slept. No sooner than I'd laid my head down, I was out.

•••••••••

"Wake up!" Mathias said in an urgent whisper.

"What is it?" I asked.

"There's something in here with us," he said.

"Did you hear something?" asked Arjun, sitting up.

"It was like a clicking. It was coming from different directions. It almost sounded like…"

"Like what, Mathias?" asked Liesel.

"Like talking."

My breathing stopped as I scanned the dark cavities leading off from our location. How were we going to defend against an enemy in a labyrinth of darkness?

"Could it be another fatty?" asked Mei.

"I don't think so," said Arjun. "It is too dry for cave grubs here. And there hasn't been any mucus on the floor."

"I don't know what you're talking about, but it sounds disgusting," said Mathias. "In Munich, they only taught us about—"

We all froze as the clicking resumed. Mathias was right. The sounds came from multiple directions. *There's more than one.* The varying timbre and cadence made the chilling sounds feel like a conversation. I reached to wrap my hand around the comforting pommel of my war hammer.

"I counted three," said Huck.

"Same," I echoed.

"Any ideas, bug guy?" asked Mathias.

"This is new," said Arjun. "We should proceed with great caution."

"I want everyone's lights on full," said Huck. "It might attract them, but I don't want any surprises. Weapons at the ready. No rifles, too much risk. Arjun, your signal."

Arjun fumbled with his transceiver while the others readied their weapons.

"It won't turn on. The impact must have damaged it."

"Damn," I said. "It was cool while it lasted."

"I can fix it, just not at the moment."

"That's if we survive the moment."

"Weren't you saying earlier that I should practice optimism?" he asked, arching an eyebrow.

"Touché," I said.

"Shut up," said Huck.

I mimed zipping my lips. In our bickering, I failed to notice the clicking from the cave ahead was getting closer. Ahead, I swore I saw movement, though there was nothing visible. Huck must have seen the same thing. He motioned for Ariadne to nock an arrow. Liesel cowered in the midst of the group, completely untrained and inexperienced in combat, battling to keep her fear in check. Ahead in the glow, I *could* see movement. An eerie frigid sensation crept up the back of my neck as I realized the only signs of movement were the distortion of the sparkling gems in the wall. Oh, crap! An invisible invert. I was really starting to hate the bastards with a passion. Ariadne pulled the arrow's shaft back to her cheek and on Huck's signal, fired. The air raged with the shrieking of the wounded creature as the angry clicking of the other two sounded right behind my shoulders.

CHAPTER 47: ARIADNE

As soon as the creature started shrieking, I launched multiple arrows into the same vicinity. The grating shrills continued, but whether from the initial wound or additional impacts, I didn't know. I ran ahead towards the sounds, ignoring Huck's warnings. If I lost the creature, I might not have another chance. To my side, I could hear Mathias and Arjun, thundering forward with me.

Carelessly sprinting down the passage, I kept my eyes and light trained on the distortion ahead. I was oblivious to potential danger, singularly focused on keeping up with the wraith. Finally, we burst forth into a large chamber. I barely skidded to a stop at the jagged edge of a bottomless precipice, hearing the rocks I knocked off the edge plink down into oblivion.

"Dammit!" I said, hitting the ground at my side. "We lost it."

"I don't think so," said Arjun. "We're blocking the entrance and I don't see another exit, save for the abyss."

"Something tells me that would be fatal for it, too," whispered Mathias.

We stood rotating with our backs to each other, examining the room for any sign of movement. Aside from the pit, the egg-shaped room was scattered with stalactites and stalagmites. Across the dark maw were the remnants of a landslide. The landslide, long since over, still had sporadic pebbles rolling down. I pointed the phenomenon out to the others, who nodded. We avoided centering our lights on the spot, not wanting the creature to realize that we had identified its location. I readied my bow as Arjun drew one of Dieter's tiny sticky grenades from his pouch and armed it.

"On three," I whispered. "One, two—"

The count was interrupted by a hostile screech from the pebbly incline. Arjun flung the explosive toward the sound where it immediately clung to the creature's body. The wraith jumped the chasm toward us as we scattered. Before it could ensnare us, we were rewarded by a deafening pop and angry shrieking as we were misted with hemolymph. The creature collapsed to the ground in front of us, then was silent.

"You got it!" yelled Mathias. "I've got to get me some of those!"

"Don't advance until we know for sure," said Arjun, speaking more loudly than normal.

Arjun picked up a handful of the sandy, gravel mix that littered the floor and cast it onto the invert's invisible frame. The debris revealed the wraith's mangled thorax. Its body was reminiscent of a mantis. The camouflage dissipated, leaving behind a gray corpse with limbs slowly drawing inwards in death. Then the creature was still. Without warning, Mathias popped off two rounds for good measure, obliterating the creature's head and making Ariadne jump.

"Now we know," he said.

"Asshole," I replied. "You could've warned me."

Mathias shrugged.

"I have so much to share with the researchers at Baghdad," said Arjun.

"If we discover it, do we get to name it?" asked Mathias.

"That is the normal convention," said Arjun.

"Can I name it after me?"

"Um… That's considered poor etiquette, but there are no rules against it," said Arjun.

"How about… invisiblade?"

"No," I said. "That sounds ridiculous."

"Well let's see you come up with a better one, Miss Smarty Pants."

"Mantis wraith," I said.

"Alright, that's pretty good," conceded Mathias.

"Now can we get back to the others?" I asked.

We easily followed the passage back before eventually, we came to a split in the tunnel.

"Does anyone remember which way we came from?" I asked.

"We were running all out," said Mathias. "I wasn't exactly leaving breadcrumbs."

"I am afraid I don't remember either," said Arjun. "The column on the left feels familiar."

"That's as good a guess as any," I said. "Arjun's memory has served us well in the past."

"Then let's hop to it," said Mathias.

We headed down the tunnel on the left, hoping it would soon reunite us with our friends. Occasionally, we would hear human voices or phantom sounds echoing directionless through the cave's labyrinthine chambers. None of them were helpful at discerning the route back. After walking for far too long, Arjun voiced his concern.

"I think I chose poorly," he said.

"Should we head back or press on?" asked Mathias. "Didn't you say these things are all connected?"

"I did and they are, however, the connections may be vertical chambers, impassibly narrow shafts, or underwater rivers."

"Oh," said Mathias. "I vote head back."

They continued their discussion for a few moments, but I had lost interest. Ahead, there was something unusual scattered all over the ground. It resembled half-eaten Arthropod corpses. I crept closer and saw that they were aerial carcasses. Their exoskeletons littered the floor, disguised by brownish-yellow fungal protuberances.

"Arjun, come look at this," I said, waving him over. "What do you make of it?"

"It's strange. By the looks of things, it's an antenna bug lair, but I understood them to be surface dwellers," he said.

"Do the wraiths eat them?" I asked.

"No," said Mathias. "There isn't any evidence of teeth marks. The cracks in the exoskeleton look organic, almost as though they were made from the inside."

I looked at Mathias, surprised.

"What? I can't know stuff?" he asked.

I smiled.

"I think you're onto something," I said. "Arjun?"

"You're both correct," said Arjun. "It looks as though this parasitic organism, whatever type of fungus it is, invades the host and drives it underground. That explains why they're congregated here."

"How's that possible?" asked Mathias. "What do they do, hijack their brains?"

"I believe that's exactly what it does," said Arjun.

"Oh," said Mathias, his shoulders drooping.

"It drives the antenna bug to where the fungus thrives—deep underground."

"Wait!" I said. "We can use this! If we can infect the aerial network, they'd pass it to each other, right? We can take down the whole network!"

"That's brilliant!" said Arjun. "I believe the launchers could reach their hovering altitude, but we'd need to replace the neem to successfully disperse the spores. I need to harvest as much of the fungus as possible. Please, watch my back."

"How do we know the fungus won't hijack us?" said Mathias.

"We don't," I answered.

A look of concern darkened Mathias' face.

"I doubt it crosses over. Arthropod anatomy is dramatically different from our own. Fungus evolves quickly. I imagine since the Arthropods have similar anatomy to Earth's native insects, it was a simple evolutionary jump."

"I think I've collected plenty," said Arjun. "At least enough to fill our rockets."

"With any luck, it works on the others as well," I said. "Maybe this is the key to defeating the inverts!"

"That would certainly be convenient," said Arjun. "But seeing as the mantis wraiths live amongst the fungus, I would think they would've introduced it to the other species already. Bringing down the network would still be an incredible win for humanity."

"Agreed," I said. "Let's get back to the others. I really want to check on Mei and Liesel."

Arjun nodded. We took off in the direction we'd come from and easily found the split again. After ascending a mild incline we returned to the room in which we first encountered the wraiths. Thankfully Mei, Liesel, and Huck were there waiting next to another dust-covered carcass.

"Man, I'm glad to see you guys!" said Mei sitting up carefully from her reclined position against a stalagmite.

"Me too!" added Huck. "That was really stupid to run off like that, but I'm glad you're okay. Did you get it?"

"We did," I said. "I wasn't stupid. I wanted to kill it before it could kill us. And I was drawing it away from the defenseless."

"Who are you calling defenseless?" asked Mei.

"We still had to deal with this one," Huck said, ignoring Mei and gesturing towards the corpse. "I had to kill it myself. Honestly, it was a lucky shot. I didn't escape unscathed though."

Huck shined his light on the ground, illuminating the pile that was once his crossbow, then raised the lamp to shine on the side of his face he'd kept turned from us since we'd entered. Running from his ear to his chin was a long, deep gouge.

"Huck!" I yelled. "You should've started with that. Sit your butt down and let me have a look."

After Huck complied, I sat down to look at him.

"Oh, Huck, this is bad," I said.

"Liesel didn't seem to think it was too terrible."

"I love Liesel, but she has no medical training. No offense."

"None taken," said Liesel.

"You've got muscle and nerve damage. We'll need to get you on antibiotics after I stitch you up. You're lucky it didn't go through to your oral cavity."

"Then I really wouldn't be a good kisser."

I punched him in the arm. He winced, but it shut him up. I grabbed my medical kit and after giving him a local anesthetic, I began to stitch him up. When I finished, he eerily resembled one of the Demented, but I know once the stitches were out and the blood cleaned up, the wound would be much less offending.

"How do I look?" he asked.

"Not great, to be honest," I replied. "You're going to need to take good care of that."

"I'll get Liesel to help."

"Whatever you need to do," I said coldly as I stood.

"What happened to my brother and the others?" asked Arjun.

"They did the same thing you guys did," he said, pointing. "They went that way."

We reluctantly decided that staying put was the best option, knowing the other group would eventually try to find their way back to us. We lit an emergency fire log and raided another meal from our dry rations. After a few hours had passed, I was growing increasingly restless. Arjun and I left to pursue Hemant, Krista, and Omar. By the time we got to the tunnel entrance, we could hear their voices growing louder. Arjun took off down the tunnel. Within minutes, he returned with his brother and the others.

"We were just about to go search for you guys," I said.

"That's what Arjun just said," said Hemant, grinning.

"Did you guys kill yours?" asked Mathias.

"Sure as hell did," said Omar. "It was a team effort. When we cornered it. I stabbed it, Hemant crushed its abdomen, and then Krista chopped the damn thing's head off."

"Though next time Hemant drops his hammer, I'm pulling out my poncho first," said Krista, laughing. "That was gross!"

"How'd you guys fare?" asked Hemant.

"We're three for three," said Huck. "Though I lost my crossbow."

"Ugh, I suppose I have a remedy for that," said Omar, walking to his pack.

Omar dug out a long object, wrapped in a blanket.

"I grabbed this from the carrier before we left," he said. "I really wanted it for myself, but hey, you need it more than I do."

Omar unrolled the blanket and revealed a beautifully etched, wide red-hilted sword. I gasped.

"What on Earth?" I asked.

"I think it was Yanus' personal sword, not that he could ever be bothered to use it," said Omar. "It's unlike anything I've ever seen."

Omar flipped the sword through the chilly air a few times before handing it to Huck, hilt first.

"Use it well," he said.

Huck's eyes brightened.

"I trained with swords back in the pod," said Huck. "I've always been partial to the crossbow, but since the multipede attack, I've been questioning if it was the right weapon against the inverts. This, however, it feels… right."

"It's a *dao*," said Mathias. "The subtle curve of the minimally-tapered blade gives it away. It's of Wuhanian make like Omar's naginata, but far superior quality. The best blades are made in Pod Wuhan."

"A *dao*," Huck said under his breath.

"Now, if we're done gawking, can we get out of here?" asked Omar.

"Not yet," I said. "Arjun found something."

"A way out?" Omar asked.

"No, something better," I said.

Arjun explained what we found and its implications. Mathias and Arjun set to work saving the neem concentrate and replacing the rockets' payload with fungal samples. After refilling our canteens from an underground spring, Hemant strapped on the bomb. We set out along the way he, Krista, and Omar had gone after they mentioned that it led up. After a several-kilometer walk, a distant light appeared, first a pinprick, then growing bigger and bigger as we progressed. Within moments, we emerged from the tunnel out into the overwhelming daylight.

"Man, I'm happy to see the surface again, but how are we going to get out of here?" asked Hemant.

"I'm not sure, but perhaps we could try the rockets," said Arjun. "With the antenna bug network down, we'd have far less struggle traversing the open desert, which will be immensely challenging as it is. If we can make it to the famed Nile River, we could float most of the way to Baghdad."

"I don't have a better idea," said Huck, shrugging.

Arjun set to work readying the launcher before letting Mathias kneel for the shot.

"The projectile is fly-by-wire," said Arjun. "We can detonate it remotely when it appears at the same altitude as the antenna bugs."

Arjun unfurled a remote from the launcher, and we stood by anxiously. Mathias aimed towards an opening between the aerials, and as we collectively held our breath, he fired. The rocket rose, a corkscrew smoke trail behind as it reached the desired altitude. Arjun mashed the button. With a loud beep of acknowledgment, the rocket exploded with an underwhelming pop. We waited, but there was no noticeable effect.

"This is a waste of rockets," said Krista. "We should've saved the neem laced ones for the actual threats."

"I think this idea has more potential than anything we've tried," I said. "If they're deaf and blind, we actually stand a chance."

Mathias fired the remaining rockets. The task was perfectly executed each time but had no noticeable effect.

"Parasites take time to infect the host," said Arjun. "We have no way of knowing if it worked for a while."

"How long is a while?" Omar asked.

"Days, weeks, months maybe," answered Arjun. "Why do you ask?"

"Because," Omar said pointing to a closing dust cloud, "I think the Huntress just used those launches to hone in on our location."

CHAPTER 48: HUCK

"Into the caves!" I yelled, feeling a burning tug in my cheek.

The stitches would take some getting used to. With a groan from the over-burdened Hemant, we turned tail and rushed back into the oppressive darkness, temporarily blinded by the exposure to the sun's harsh rays. The lack of response to Arjun's spores was expected, but disappointing nonetheless. I guess I was hoping the spread would make the aerials drunkenly fall out of the sky. No such luck.

"What do you propose?" asked Krista as we ran deeper into the passage.

"Go back to the main chamber," I said, already breathing heavily from the downhill sprint. "Split up into the same groups and go the same directions. We already know the layout. Our best chance is guerrilla warfare. Pick them off one by one."

"What about Mei and Liesel," asked Ariadne. "They're not ready to fight."

"Right," I said. "Mei, I want you with Ariadne. Liesel, I want you with Omar and Krista. Hemant, I need you with me."

Everyone gave confirmation, but Mei was looking paler than

usual. I ran back and threw one of her arms over my shoulder as Mathias did the same with her other. I could feel her heart pounding to keep up. She was far too weak to do a fraction of the necessary exertion. A slight trail of blood drained down her neck from the fresh bandage. Before we got too deep, Hemant convinced me to let him stash the bomb in a shallow crevice he'd found, where it would be safe from discovery. We quickly stowed it and continued running. We finally arrived at the cavern, the distance having passed much more quickly than the first time.

"Arjun, take Mei," I said. "Hemant and I will try to hold them off at this bottleneck, then we'll follow you into the passages. Mathias, give me a rifle."

Arjun took over and each group vanished down the paths into obscurity.

"Hold them off?" asked Hemant, with a raised eyebrow.

"I'm making this up as I go, man."

"As if I couldn't tell."

"Shut up, I don't hear you— Wait. I hear them."

"Take the left side of the tunnel," I said. "When they come through, take as many as you can, then follow Omar. I'll follow Ariadne. With any luck, that'll split them up."

"Divide and conquer," said Hemant. "I like it!"

We waited anxiously, hearing their grizzly voices grow in volume as the minutes crept by. Finally, they were just around the bend. Their torchlight cast a horrendous maw-like shadow through the formations, threatening to swallow us whole. I nodded at Hemant, who returned the gesture, raising his war hammer. I cocked the *dao* back behind my head and waited. I had no idea how many of them there were, but I was going to take out as many as possible before vanishing.

The first of the men came through. I didn't hesitate. I brought my sword deep down into his torso between his neck and his shoulder, cleaving his chest nearly in half as his blood pooled at my feet. Out of the corner of my eye, I saw Hemant crush the skull of the one next to him, spattering the wall with gray matter. With whoops and guttural cries, the others backed up into the tunnel before firing arrows fruitlessly into the vast space.

I lowered the rifle from my shoulder and fired toward the torches. Nothing happened. The safety! I switched it to fire and squeezed the trigger. Never having used a weapon of the sort, the recoil caught me off guard, and I nearly dropped the thing. Some of my shots must have hit home as they were answered by gruesome howls.

"Now's our chance!" yelled Hemant.

We split off into the tunnels after the others. The entire time I ran, I chanted "It's me! It's me! It's me!" desperately hoping that Ariadne wouldn't put an arrow through my heart.

When I was away from the chamber, I switched on my light and ran until my lungs burned. The passage suddenly widened into a room as someone yelled "Stop!" I plowed my feet into the earth and slipped right off the edge of a precipice. Everything flashed through my mind. It was as though every thought I'd ever had wanted to spew forth simultaneously. I pushed through the memory onslaught, grasping for anything to keep me from falling to the bottom of the abyss. I felt my fingernails bend back under the force as I struggled to find purchase. *This is it.* I felt a sense of peace pass over me, knowing it was over. Just as I'd given up, I felt hands grip my wrists. Not one, but four. I kick the shaft's wall with my feet, desperate to find a foothold. Ariadne and Mathias pulled me up on my stomach. I rolled over on my back and stared up into their faces.

"Don't you ever scare me like that again," said Ariadne, tearing up.

I sat up slowly, inebriated by the flood of adrenaline.

"I'm sorry. If it makes you feel better, it kind of sucked for me too," I said.

"Glad you're okay," said Mathias, patting me on the back. "Now, how many of them are coming?"

"I don't know," I said, collecting my thoughts. "We killed two for sure. Possibly two more. A buggy holds about six, but they were hanging off the thing. I'd say we have eight to twelve total."

"Curse this injury," said Mei, no longer actively bleeding. "I wish I could fight. I owe them one."

"You just stay out of the way, sugar," said Mathias. "I'll take care of you."

"Sure, Mathias," said Mei. "But if you call me sugar again, I'll cut off your manhood and feed it to you."

"As long as you touch it first," he said, blowing her a kiss.

"Douchebag," said Ariadne as Mei flipped him off.

"Just wait until I'm better," muttered Mei.

"Shh, they are coming," said Arjun.

I listened intently and could hear the telltale throaty barking between the pursuers rapidly approaching. Judging by the voices, it only sounded like a couple. With any luck, the other half would be taken out by Hemant and the others. With our backs against the wall around the tunnel's opening, we waited. The two burst forth, the first moving so fast, he skidded right off into the pit, releasing a howl that would make your flesh crawl until it ended with a distant squish. I turned on my light, blinding the single remaining warrior as Arjun trapped him with his razor net, and Mathias delivered the fatal blow.

"That wasn't too bad," said Mathias.

"Don't say that yet," said Mei. "Neither one of them was the Huntress Huck mentioned."

At the mention of her, I shivered. Whatever fiend she was, she wasn't something I ever wanted to encounter again, but I knew without a shadow of a doubt that I wouldn't be leaving this cave until she made good on her implied threat.

"If the universe is smiling on us, maybe I shot her," I said. "Let's head back, but stay on guard. I'll take point. Mathias, help Ariadne with Mei."

We cautiously made our way back up the passage, making sure to follow the correct route. Before we arrived at the chamber, I could see the faint flickering indicative of a torch's presence. I waved to the others to halt while I proceeded forward. When I peered out from the tunnel into the space, I saw her. Flanked by two injured Demented and blocking the exit, she stood tall, her eyes boring right through me. I swallowed the lump in my throat and stepped out into the clearing.

"What are you doing?!" Mei whispered.

I waved for them to stay back. Ignoring me, they moved out to back me up. I could hear Ariadne and Mei gasp as they beheld the Huntress for the first time, undoubtedly reliving their previous experience with the twisted creatures. Her guards each had bullet wounds, blood draining down their legs. They must have been the ones I hit. I was amazed that they could stand. The Huntress didn't seem like one to tolerate failure. Again, she raised her arm, beckoning me forward in the flickering glow of the flames. I took a tentative step forward, hearing Mathias do the same. The guard closest to him flicked a knife into the wall centimeters from Mathias' head, warning him to go no further. *They're toying with us. She wants me alone.*

I stepped forward, readying my sword and stance. With unexpected fluidity, she strode forward, pulling two menacing crescent blades from behind her back. Each of the battle-scarred blades curved out from her fist and down in front of her fingers, neither more than thirty centimeters long. A smile passed across her face as she dropped into a low crouch with feline precision. Without warning, she pounced.

At first, panic raged through my system, but the training quickly took over. I dodged the attack, rolling out of the way. She growled when she hit the stone floor, but turned after me without a second's hesitation. Moving with surprising speed, she closed the distance between us. I couldn't outrun her, so I stood my ground. Flicking my sword up in defense, I parried her blow as she brought down both blades over my head. I slung her off, spinning out of her way, and bringing my sword in towards her side. With one hand, she blocked me as she deeply sliced my arm with the other, drawing blood. I flung her back, giving myself just enough time to glance at the wound. I'd live.

I flick my eyes back at her in time to see her licking my crimson deposit from the edge of her blade, purposefully slicing her tongue in the process and merging our blood. I shivered again, but this time from revulsion. With shocking speed, she barreled toward me like a cannonball. Our blades connected, time and again, and with such intensity, sparks showered the surrounding stones. She kicked my feet out from under me and pinned me down to the ground. Behind me, I could hear Ariadne yelling at her. When she was close, I could feel the steaming heat of her body, her primal stench nearly making me gag.

With surprising force, she pushed the flat side of the dao close to my chest with her blades, pricking me with their tips. She pushed hard and harder as I screamed with exertion, desperately trying to get her off. Effortlessly, she leaned down and licked my stitched cheek. I felt the bile rise in my throat as her tongue skipped over each knot in the thread. I began kneeing her between her legs to no avail. I dealt blow after blow, but all the Huntress did was emit a disturbing laugh.

At some point, Hemant and the others must have returned. I could hear Liesel screaming as Omar yelled threats at the guards. *Just in time to watch me die. Convenient.* Again, memories flooded my mind. I remembered Memo first suggesting the mission. I remembered the people like Mueller and Taha who'd helped us. I remembered the list of friends like Zeke and Kurt who'd fallen. All of it displaced the monstrosity hovering in my vision, bringing a meditative calm to my mind. Unlike the cliff, I resolved to survive. I knew what I needed to do, but it was going to hurt like hell. Before she could react, I drew the sword out from its protective position and felt the fire from the length of her blades as they pushed into my chest but were blocked by my ribcage. With a sharp flick of my wrist, a flash of surprise crossed the Huntress' face as I severed her head from her body and flung her spurting corpse to the side.

I could focus on nothing but the intense pain radiating from my chest. I felt tears streaming down my cheeks as I gritted my teeth, stifling a scream. With the Huntress gone, I knew the others were clearing the cavern of any remaining Demented. Even in the dim light of the cave, all I could see was bright white light—an effect of the pain. I saw Ariadne's face and heard my name, then nothing.

CHAPTER 49: HEMANT

I paced back and forth, waiting for an update on Huck's condition. Ariadne had the top of his jumpsuit peeled back as she and Liesel cleaned and sutured his chest. The two nearly parallel cuts had torn through some of his muscles, spilling blood over his chest. After giving him a local anesthetic, she and Liesel had gone to work, sealing up the lacerations. He owed his thanks to the curve of the blades and their proximity when he withdrew his sword. Once he was effectively bandaged, Ariadne revived him with smelling salts.

"Are they dead?" he asked, craning his head up.

"Yes," she said, pushing him back down. "Stay flat. You're in no condition to move. We need to get you on a stretcher."

"How bad is it?" Huck asked, wincing.

"Nothing major, thankfully. That was a huge risk you took back there. Your ribs stopped the blades, but they damaged several muscle groups. Your chest won't have its full strength for months."

"I'll manage," Huck said, rolling up.

"Huck, don't be an idiot!" I said.

"I'll be okay. She said my ribs blocked most of the blow."

"As your medic, I strongly advise against this," she said. "You need to convalesce."

"I'll take it easy. I promise. We can't stay down here. There's no telling how many more mantis wraiths there are in these tunnels."

"Fine," she muttered. "But we'll see how you feel when your meds wear off."

We gathered our things, preparing to move. As disgusting as it was, I patted down the corpses of the Demented for anything useful. The only trinkets they had were so revolting, that I abandoned the search. We reluctantly left the cool environment behind and took a painstakingly slow hike to the oppressively hot surface.

"Can you teach me to fight?" Liesel asked Ariadne. "I feel like a knot on a log when you're all battling and I'm cowering under the nearest rock."

"Of course," Ariadne said with a tight smile. "We'll start tonight after we eat. If the others aren't opposed, you can try their weapons and see what you're adept with."

"No one's touching my naginata," said Omar.

The conversation continued, but I tuned it out. We still had thousands of kilometers to reach Baghdad, and I had no idea how we were going to do it sans vehicle. Then the thought occurred to me.

"Um… I was thinking about how to get to Baghdad," I said. "I have an idea, but I don't think you're going to like it."

"No," said Ariadne. "Not just no, but hell no. I know what you're thinking. There's no way in hell I'm riding in that thing. I don't care if they're all dead or not. You'd have to drag me behind by a rope."

"That could be arranged," said Mathias.

"Shut up," she said.

"What if we cleaned it up? Made it look and smell halfway decent?"

"No. I want nothing to do with those creeps."

"Me either," said Mei.

"I'm not loving the idea myself," said Huck.

"Fine. But tell me, how are we going to walk to Baghdad? Like Ekon? The last time I checked, none of us were of Tuareg ancestry. We wouldn't last a minute out in the open desert. And that's not even considering what inverts might be out there!"

"He's right," said Krista. "It may be gross, but it's our only chance."

"Fine," said Huck. "We'll clean it up as best we can. How far do we have to go to the Nile, Arjun?"

"Farther than that buggy will carry us," he said. "According to the map, we're really close to a pump house, but the range of the buggy is only about half of the distance to the Nile."

"Can we walk the remainder?" asked Huck.

"Doubtful," I said. "Arjun's right. The desert and its inhabitants would likely kill us."

"What do you suggest?" asked Omar.

"We divert south to the green belt. It's not the way the transporters follow, so I don't know the conditions, but it would be less of a risk than the desert. To the south, there's food, water, and shelter. It'd be a longer trek and we'd still have to travel eastward on foot to the Nile, but it would be in far more favorable conditions."

"Then we go south," said Huck, as we stopped at the crevice to retrieve the bomb.

We quickly covered the remaining distance to the surface and emerged, once again blinded by the brightness. When my eyes finally adjusted, my sight fell on the repulsive carriage that would be our transportation for the next few days. It was even worse up close. As evening fell, we worked to strip the buggy of all evidence of Demented ownership. We slaved into darkness, flinging carcasses and tchotchkes from the chassis until it looked respectable. The smell was still horrifying, but it was a dramatic improvement.

"Can you wire your signal to the speakers, Arjun?" I asked.

"I don't know that the buggy has any, nor is the transceiver fixed," he said. "I'll have to work on it as we travel."

"What can we do about inverts?" asked Ariadne, still shaking from revulsion. "This thing has a gun, but I don't know how helpful that will be against a swarm. We've never traveled with this few of us."

"You still got the neem," said Mathias.

"He's right," said Arjun. "It would be quite potent, but we could soak the vehicle in the concentrate. Short of a spine back, I doubt the smaller bugs would touch us. The effect might last for weeks."

"Anything has to be better than this," said Mei, pinching her nose.

"It's settled," said Huck. "We'll slather the buggy with neem first thing in the morning. Everyone get a good night's sleep. I'll take first watch."

Like hell you will," I said. "See you in the morning."

•••••••••

I sat at the entrance of the cave, staring out over the alien landscape for any sign of threat under the cool moonlight. While I was doubtful anything would attack from the cave, I still had Mathias watching our backs. To my side, Arjun tinkered away late into the night on the transceiver. Putting aside my pleas for him to get some rest, he continued to work away. With the binoculars, I could see a pair of eights hunting far in the distance. We could easily fend off one or two, but dry climates were their habitat. I was almost certain that an attack would only draw more. I slunk towards the side of the cave and watched them warily. They had found something and were pouncing on it. I heard a squawk to my left and raised an eyebrow at Arjun.

"Sorry," he said. "I had to hear to make sure. I'm getting there, but without an Arthropod to test it on, I don't know if the signal works. The system's incorporated speaker probably isn't good enough to repel anything bigger than a pill bug."

"We can manage without it. You did a great job getting us this far without attack. We managed before without it. We can do it again."

"Yes, but we had a lot of help before."

"We'll be okay. I can feel it. Our mission… I don't know. It feels like destiny. I feel like nothing can stop us. We are going to carry Dieter's bomb to the Hive and shove it down their throats. Insects have throats, right?"

"They do, but it's called the stomatodeum—"

I stopped him with a wave of my hand, laughing.

"It was rhetorical, bud," I said. "I love you."

"I love you too, brother," he said.

The radio squelched a bit as Arjun turned down the volume. The night air was clean and fresh, unlike the hot, stagnant air of the day. Sprawling across the rocky landscape were little shrubs, indicative of moisture somewhere, not that we could find it. I'd be glad when we managed to get further south and into the safety of the familiar. I knew from my studies that the further south you went on the continent, the more verdant the environment became. I just wanted to be rid of the sand. Cool water would be amazing, provided it didn't have a local population of toadies. I felt my eyelids getting heavy. After insisting that Arjun get some rest, I let Krista and Ariadne take the watch and fell fast asleep.

•••••••••

In the morning when I woke, it was to the sounds of battle. I flung myself from my bivvy, my bulk getting tangled in the insulating fabric as I tried to hurriedly wrestle free. I lurched out of the cave with my hammer up raised to everyone laughing.

"You should see your face," said Ariadne, laughing. "I'm glad we weren't actually under attack."

I gave off a nervous laugh. Too tired to practice in the evening, Ariadne was apparently giving Liesel her first sword lesson with one of Krista's katanas. They had let me sleep in a little thanks to my late guard duty, but I had become the morning spectacle.

"Ha-ha," I said, mockingly. "You can make fun of me after I've had some coffee."

"Sorry, man," said Huck. "You slept too long. We need to get rolling. You can eat en route. If it makes you feel better, we didn't make coffee."

"Fine," I said. "At least the grumpier I am, the more the inverts have to fear. What's the plan?"

"We cover the buggy in Arjun's oil, head east for fuel, then south to the forest. The bad news is there aren't enough seats on the buggy, so we're going to have to ride fire-crew style on the sides. We'll rotate through everyone. It'll be slow progress, but our mathematician thinks we can make it."

I looked at Arjun who nodded. We loaded the gear, carefully stashing the nuclear bomb next to the gunner position, which also served as a cargo area. Arjun pulled out the vials of concentrated neem and began applying the compound to the buggy's exterior.

"Oh, God," said Krista, holding her hand over her mouth. "No wonder the inverts don't like it."

"It's pretty bad," echoed Omar. "My eyes are already burning."

"I kind of like it," said Mathias. "It reminds me of garlic naan. There used to be a great place in Kano that—"

"Enough, everyone," said Huck. "It stinks, but it'll save our lives. It sure as hell smells better than the buggy. Now, if everyone is done whining, let's load up."

I jumped onto the side of the buggy, still reeking of its hemolymphatic stench, which was only getting worse in the sun. It was going to be a long day. At least the thing had hand and foot rails for this purpose, not that I wanted to hang on them for hours. After one last survey of the site, we pulled out. I felt so small, being one of nine people, possibly for thousands upon thousands of kilometers in a vast sea of sand and enemies. We followed the road to the nearby pump house, which judging from its appearance, had been raided by the same Demented tribe we stole the buggy from. Ignoring the dried blood of its previous inhabitant, we filled up the buggy with the precious natural gas.

"Does that look strange to you?" asked Mathias, staring up at the sky.

I craned my neck to look at what had caught his attention. Overhead, the aerials were still present, but there was something different about their behavior. They normally held a static position in the sky, equidistant from each other like finely-tuned nodes. This morning, they had lost some of their precision. As far as the eye could see, the aerials hovered imperfectly, as if struggling to maintain their observant position over the planet's surface.

"It sure does," I said. "It looks like Arjun's idea did something."

"Look," Huck said, pointing.

I followed his gaze and saw where an aerial was slowly drifting down from the sky. Then another. Then another. Around us, the entire network was collapsing. One after another, each nodule fell from the sky.

"We did it! We did it!" said Ariadne, gently bouncing up and down with Mei.

"Yeah!" I screamed, hoisting Arjun onto my shoulders and spinning us around.

Krista and Omar were all grins, they gave each other a high-five before embracing.

Liesel carefully grabbed Huck, pulling him close and locking lips with him in a passionate kiss.

Mathias, swelling with pride, looked over at Mei.

"Wanna copy their example?" he asked, nodding to Huck and Liesel.

"That would be a resounding no," she said, rolling her eyes.

Mathias shrugged, still grinning with eyes upturned. I looked back at the falling network. We had done something. Truly done something that no one had done before. Even if we never made it to the Hive, we had dealt a significant blow in the war against the Arthropods that would go down in history. All because of Arjun and Ariadne's ingenuity. I couldn't have been more proud of my brother who I still held aloft.

Then I heard something. At first, just a whisper, but then becoming a roar. Piercing the very air was a collective screech, the likes of which had never been heard before. The roar sounded as though every Arthropod on Earth was simultaneously howling in fury at the loss of their communication network.

"I think we pissed them off," said Omar.

"You think?" Mathias said, pointing.

I followed his finger to the legions of Arthropods thundering towards us from every direction of the horizon.

"They may have lost our scent in Kano," said Arjun. "But they know who we are now."

CHAPTER 50: ARIADNE

As everyone darted around in the ensuing chaos, making preparations for the oncoming masses, I stood frozen in shock. It wasn't from the aerials falling from the sky. It wasn't from the infinite swarms converging on our location. It was Liesel's never-ending kiss. Right then I knew I'd made a mistake. I pushed him away before we'd even had a chance to try. Now I had to live with the regret, at least for a few minutes longer.

"Ariadne, what are you doing?!" yelled Hemant, grabbing me by the arm. "They're coming!"

Spurred out of my self-pity, I grabbed the compound bow and readied my arrows for the inevitable attack as we put our backs up against each other.

"I think we all know where this is headed," said Huck, raising his dao. "I love you guys. It's been an incredible journey. We've really accomplished something, and I can think of no one better than you to fight next to."

"Here, here," said Mathias, hefting his mace.

"If we're going to die, then I vote we take as many with us as possible," said Hemant, wrapping his arm around his brother.

"That bomb isn't going to waste on my watch. Arjun, I want you on the controls. The second they hit, blow them to hell!"

Everyone cheered, but with trepidation in their voices. We all knew it was going to be our final stand against the Arthropods. There was no way we were getting out of this one. I scanned the horizon. The multitude was innumerable.

"You'll always be my sister, Ariadne," said Krista, gently smiling at my side. "I love you."

"I love you too," I said.

"Are you sure you won't consider granting me a last wish?" Mathias asked Mei.

She rolled her eyes and kissed him passionately on the lips, surprising everyone. The air filled with juvenile jeers and whistles. Despite staring death in the face we had something to laugh about. Tears ran down my cheeks. *This is how it ends.* I looked out at the sea of inverts and wondered if I would feel the atomic blast, or if life would just… stop.

I glanced back at Arjun, who had unwrapped the bomb from its canvas bag. The innocuous white tube didn't seem all that threatening, but I knew it had the potential to level the desert for kilometers, turning the powdery sand into a thick glaze. Best of all, we'd wipe out untold inverts. Damn every one of the bastards and the space trash they rode in on.

I closed my eyes, taking in the moment. I could feel the scorching breeze stirring on my face. I could hear the sounds of those around me breathing, I felt the ground vibrating with the footfalls of the enemy. I also heard a strange hum. *The bomb? No, further away.*

"Do you guys hear that?" I asked, opening my eyes and looking for the sound's source.

The others could hear the faint hum too, and were trying to identify it.

"There!" yelled Hemant. "What the hell is that thing?"

"Where are the binoculars?" I yelled.

"Got 'em," said Hemant, rustling in his bag. "Here."

I looked at the object and I just about swallowed my tongue.

"It's a… It's a…"

"It's a what?!" yelled Huck.

"It's a plane," I said, dazed.

I could scarcely believe I was saying the words. Planes hadn't flown since the pods were built. Once the aerial network was in place, the other flying inverts would knock anything man-made from the air. Flying was impossible. Planes couldn't communicate, navigate, or use the complex circuitry humanity had become so reliant on.

"A plane? A plane?" Hemant yelled. "Arjun, don't blow us up yet. We may still get out of this!"

"The radio!" said Arjun. "With the antenna bugs down, I may be able to hail them!"

"How do we know they're on our side?" asked Krista.

"Right now anybody's on our side!" yelled Hemant.

Behind me, I could hear Arjun frantically cycling through the channels, trying to contact the plane. By now, I could easily see its fuselage with my naked eye. The fat, beige-colored aircraft blended in with the desert landscape. It looked… old. Now that it was closer, I could see small swarms of attacking inverts positioned around the craft. I could hear the rapid pop of the armaments it carried, fending off the nemeses like mosquitos.

"I have them!" yelled Arjun, jumping up and down. "They're here for us! They specifically asked for Ariadne!"

"But the only way they'd know that is—" began Huck.

"Ekon!" Mei and I yelled at the same time.

"H-How in the world?" asked Huck with a confused grin.

Everyone started screaming in elation. *Maybe we'd get out of this after all!*

"I hate to be a buzzkill," said Omar, "but we're not free yet."

The inverts had closed the distance so much that I could identify the oncoming species.

"Is there any way we can hurry this up?" I said.

"They've got something planned!" yelled Arjun. "They said take care of what gets through."

"Gets through what?" Huck asked. "Whatever they are going to do, they need to have done it an hour ago. What are they going to do, erect—"

Whoosh.

I spun towards the roar. At the front lines of the wave, the large plane began to lay down an epic curtain of fire. The heat from the inferno reached us almost instantaneously, evaporating my accumulated sweat and tussling my hair.

"Good God, what is that?" asked Krista.

"Napalm," said Mathias in awe. "It was outlawed long before the UTE was formed, because it inflicted excessive suffering on combatants."

"Let them burn," said Omar.

I watched as the plane bathed the inverts in flames as it flew around us in a massive circle, ringing us off safely from our foes with the inferno. A noxious scent rushed forth from the inverts broiling in their shells. The odor hit us almost as hard as the screams as the superheated fire combusted their internal organs, making their exoskeletons explode.

"Some are getting through," I yelled, pointing.

All around, various species were making their way through the flames, many of which fell shortly thereafter. With appendages still burning, bunches were headed our way. They arrived in seconds, and the battle began in earnest. Still unprepared, Liesel hung back underneath the buggy where she would be safe short of utter annihilation. Mathias let the machine gun on the back of the buggy rip, blowing the attacking hooks and eights apart. I fired arrow after arrow into the eyes of each invert the moment they were within range, dropping them like flies.

Brandishing his new weapon, Huck moved with grace, slicing smoldering appendages from the monsters as Hemant brought his war hammer down on their weakened carapaces. Refusing to hide with Liesel, Mei was throwing her knives bringing down the smaller beasts. When a gigantic multipede broke through our defensive line, Mathias jumped from the buggy's ammo-exhausted turret, bringing his mace down with all the inertia his squat body could muster, crushing the head of the pede. Before he could react, its spasming body whipped around and flung him far from the buggy and away from the protection of the group.

"No!" yelled Omar with unbridled rage.

Omar and Krista barreled after him, struggling to reach him before the eights could descend on his unconscious frame. I began to hear polie detonations from the raging wall of fire. Unable to pass through the fiery wall, the powder moths were dropping their explosive cargo on their own lines of troops.

"They're doing the work for us!" I yelled, loosing another arrow.

Everyone was so engaged that no one heard me. I glanced over to where Omar and Krista were battling a hook beetle and bone arachnid, desperately attempting to keep them away from where Mathias lay unconscious. Krista knocked off one leg after another with her dual katanas until the eight was maneuvering around solely on its four rear legs. It lost balance and rocked back, exposing its weak underbelly. She dashed forward, moving in for the kill. The creature's ploy had worked. The eight rolled forward again, swinging its remaining toothed legs around like a saw blade, chopping off Krista's left hand. Krista fell to her knees screaming. Omar drove his naginata deep into the hook's side, pulled it out, and in one fluid motion, turned and deposited the opposite end into the velvet patch of the eight's abdomen, slaying it. With a dying lurch, the hook sprung forward tearing a gouge of flesh down the length of Omar's back. Omar collapsed face-first into the sand as Krista, bleeding profusely, struggled to fend off attackers with her single remaining katana.

I fired my arrows at the inverts that swarmed the three, blinking away the tears that blurred my vision. The excitement of the plane was long gone, a hope that had arrived too late. I made my way to them, firing as I walked, doing my best to stave off the advances. With the circumference of fire roaring, the plane was coming in for landing inside the ring. In the sky, several dusters had cleared the blaze with their live explosive cargo. As the plane descended, its turrets still fired, killing the dusters and detonating most of the pill bugs in the air. The remaining polies detonated when they hit the ground, but one survived the landing and was bouncing directly towards where Hemant was fighting. Arjun, seeing the impending danger, sprinted to intercept the polie with his razor net. When the invert was several meters away from Hemant, Arjun ensnared it, inadvertently detonating it. The explosion blew him far back into the sand, his jumpsuit smoldering and his face badly burned.

"No!" cried Hemant, standing up from where the impact had knocked him to the ground. "Arjun!"

Hemant finished off the hook he was fighting and sprinted to his brother's side, tears flooding down his cheeks. Cradling his brother, his pleading voice carried across the battlefield over the plane's roaring engines as it grew closer and closer to the ground. I continued bringing down inverts, each arrow carrying more anger and hurt in it than the last. I hated the bastards. In a way, I wished the plane hadn't shown up. If we were all going to die, killing every one of the bloody things would've been a far better way to go than watching our *deus ex machina* rescue land seconds after we'd all perished.

The fire was burning hotter and higher than ever, keeping the would-be attackers away. I watched the bulbous plane teeter and totter all the way to the ground, where it bounced so high back up into the air that I thought they would leave again. After a few more bounces, the plane finally managed to stay in contact with the soft terrain.

I heard a loud grunt and turned back to Hemant. An eight stood looming over him, pulling out its abdominal stinger from his shoulder.

"No," I sobbed, collapsing to my knees.

I felt the will to fight drifting away from my body in the desert wind. Around me, my companions were dying. This must be like what Release Day felt like for so many. I felt my heart-rending into pieces. When another polie landed successfully and rolled towards me, I couldn't muster the gumption to rise. I already felt dead inside. I heard the sound of gunfire and the polie exploded, but not before blowing me back against the side of the buggy. I heard the crack of my bones as my head jarred back before I crumpled forward on the ground, my face to the side. Looking under the vehicle, I watched as Liesel, screaming, was helplessly pulled out from under it by a burning hook, unperturbed by the neem. I was going to have to powerlessly watch her be devoured. On the far side of the buggy, I saw where Huck and Mei each lay in the sand, covered in their own blood in addition to the black streaks of hemolymph.

I heard more gunshots, far quieter than the plane's turrets, and I heard footfalls and yelling of voices not our own. Someone was barking orders to get us onto the plane. I felt my body being carefully lifted and placed on a stretcher before being shuttled to the plane's hatch. I looked up at the bearded chin of my rescuer.

"Don't move," he said. "We've got you."

"Bomb," I said, choking on something warm. "You have to get the bomb."

"Don't talk. You're gravely injured," He said, looking towards someone else "Rico, look for a bomb. That must be the device he told us about!"

I heard a voice answer affirmatively. I felt my consciousness slipping away. As my vision narrowed, I looked over at the pair next to us that carried Mei on an identical stretcher. She was covered in blood, her arm hanging limply off the side and steadily dripping blood onto the sand. Mei's eyes were open, staring back at me—lifeless.

CHAPTER 51: SAMSON

"They're loaded up, Sam," yelled Hera, slamming the hatch. "Get this infernal behemoth in the air, now!"

"Working on it!" I yelled as I jumped into the ancient aircraft's cramped cockpit and buckled in.

"The fire's dying," yelled Ahmad from the turret below, dragging out the last word.

I'd left both the engines running while we were on the ground but pulled all the crew from their stations save for Remi. She remained in the plane, running back and forth between the port and starboard turrets, happily picking off the inverts that escaped the blaze. The woman liked dealing out wanton violence. Maybe even too much. *Whatever.* Right now, she was doing the thing I needed her to do most—cover our asses—and she was doing it well.

The rest of us had rushed out of the plane to collect the team of fallen citizens. We had been dispatched to perform an emergency evacuation for whoever they were. They must have been important to warrant our cross-territory flight. We'd apparently arrived just in the nick of time. They were damn close to being slaughtered. As it was, many looked like they might not make it. I was glad Hera was as exceptional of a sawbones as she was an engineer, having invented the napalm blaster parked next to the port machine gun. I dubbed it the squirt gun.

"Are they strapped down?" I yelled, pushing the throttle until the dinky metal levers wanted to bend against their housing.

"They're not going anywhere," she yelled back over the craft's intense vibrations. "Except maybe to the grave. It's bad, Sam. Real bad."

"If anyone can pull them back, it's you!" I yelled, already pulling back on the yoke, rushing the plane's climb. "And hopefully they'll survive my piloting skills."

"Don't even joke about that!" she yelled.

The lumbering whale of an aircraft was bouncing along the dunes, closer and closer to what was left of the wall of fire. I'd have to kiss Hera for that invention of hers—later. It had protected our landing and the lives of those on the ground. I pulled on the yoke as hard as I could, but the airspeed still wasn't enough to get us airborne, especially with the additional load of the new passengers and their gear. *Probably should've dumped everything that wasn't nailed down.* It was callous of me, but we probably should've left the dead girl's body, too. What a pity. They were all so bloody young.

I felt the front wheels begin to lift off of the ground as Rico continued to blast away at the inverts crowding our path.

"They're coming through in droves!" he yelled. "I can't take them all. We need to be in the air, like, now!"

"If someone else thinks they can fly this bathtub better than me, have at it!" I yelled, finally detecting the unnerving feeling of the separation from the ground. "We're airborne!"

I heard cheers from the crew as we passed over the smoldering carcasses at the edge of the fire line. I felt the intense heat radiating through the belly of the craft from its low altitude.

"Whoo! Cutting it close there, Sam!" yelled Rico, from his place at the port turret. "That toasted my ass."

"You know you liked it," yelled Remi back, laughing as she blew a few more hooks out of the starboard sky.

I turned the plane into a steep bank and pointed the nose back towards Baghdad, ignoring the nausea building in my stomach. I was finally getting a feel for flying now that I had three actual takeoffs under my belt counting our fuel stop. I couldn't believe I'd spent my life training and dreaming of heading a flight crew, only to find out on my maiden flight that I suffered from motion sickness. Nerves of steel and a stomach of mercury. Jesus.

I leveled the plane off at a few thousand meters and checked all the gauges. Everything looked good for the nearly five-hundred-year-old bomber. Then again, we had Hera taking care of the bird.

Long after the pods had been sealed, the Kano-Baghdad transport team stumbled on a squadron of old military planes in Pyramid City and brought them in pieces to Baghdad. They had been cobbled by the pod's top engineers into a single, functional aircraft and adapted to run on natural gas. Because of the plane's age, it had the unique ability to function despite the invert's omnipresent electromagnetic fields. Pod Baghdad's administration had been saving it for something of the utmost importance since if anything happened to it, the likelihood of coming across another was slimmer than the hairs on an eight.

After serving with the local transporters for my obligatory year, I returned to my birth pod as a citizen and trained as a pilot. I'd spent the last decade of my life practicing with the same people for hours every day. The aircraft just never left the staging area at the incline's base until, well… until today. We ran through scenario after scenario from the plane's historic flight manual, a book so old that only our chief trainer was allowed to handle it. We learned how to do preflight checks, fly using only our instruments (save for the compass), and practice for emergencies. All from the comfort of the pod. From the second the wheels left the ground and I started barfing, I knew all the theory in the world couldn't have prepared me for the real thing—much like Release Day.

Shortly after our unusual deputy prime minister returned from his stint at Pod Kano, Prime Minister Lafet announced that we would be deployed on our first mission. Deputy Prime Minister Okoro, who insisted everyone call him Ekon (including himself), had discovered a promising mission to destroy the Hive. We weren't privy to all of the details, but we knew that it was a smaller group than had ever been attempted before, and they carried with them some promising device. Admittedly, I was nervous about the mission, having never actually flown before. Flying an ancient craft as a first-time pilot into hostile territory to pick up strangers would give anyone the shakes. But we'd done it!

I panned the skies, still amazed at the lack of aerial network. I'd become so accustomed to them during my time on the surface that the skies felt empty without them. It was the strangest thing. *This is what the skies looked like to my ancestors.* Once we were about halfway to Kano, the antenna bugs had begun to fall from the skies in waves radiating from our destination. At first, we thought it might be in response to something we had done, but then we realized it had been a result of the citizens that were now lying unconscious in the cargo bay. Initially, we'd been worried about whether we could find them, but as if in answer to our question, the legions of Arthropods pointed the way. I'd kept the radio on for old-time's sake, enjoying the low static, tying me back to the pilots of antiquity when Arjun's signal had broken through. I'd just about flipped my lid, nearly dropping the mic in between my rudder pedals. I felt my stomach gurgling again and reached for another sick bag.

"Hey, Samson," said Hera, plopping into her vacant copilot seat next to me. "Stomach again?"

"It's getting better, I think," I lied, tucking the bag away and swallowing the bile. "Who's tending to the injured? Ekon will have me mucking stalls if something happens to them."

"Relax, *mon nounours*. Remi is keeping an eye on them," she said, putting her soft hand on my arm. "She's making Rico operate both turrets and getting a kick out of his whining."

I chuckled. "Your squirt gun made a hell of a show. Probably saved their lives."

"Thanks. I sure tested it enough. They're still picking glass out of the arena sand. The barrage used up all our napalm. It'll take months to source the chemicals to fabricate more."

"It was worth it. Speaking of used up, we're almost out of gas," I said loudly over the engines and gunfire. "We'll have to land in Pyramid City again to tank up or we'll never make it back."

"Just make it quick. They're in rough shape."

"How bad?"

"Lacerations, amputations, contusions, fractures, blood loss, concussions, burns, envenomed… The only one who's conscious is so plagued with the Shock, I'll be surprised if she's every right in the head again. She's sedated now."

"Holy hell. Were you able to stabilize them?"

"Temporarily. One of the girls must be a medic herself. She was better supplied than we are. If not for the antivenin she carried, the husky guy would be dead already. I medicated everyone, halted the bleeding with bandages and styptic, and stitched what I could. Though it was difficult when the pilot can't hold the plane still," she said with a sly smile.

"Hey—"

"I'm kidding about the pilot but not about the motion. We've got to get them to a proper medical facility as soon as possible or half of them won't make it."

"How long do they have?" I asked. "We still have a good ten hours of flight time, plus refuel."

"Don't take your time," she said, dropping her eyes.

ACKNOWLEDGEMENTS & AUTHOR'S NOTE

I can't believe I've turned a dream into two books. It's the most amazing thing to see my creative work not only in physical form, but being bought and distributed throughout the world. Writing continues to be such a rewarding and fantastic experience.

That being said, I couldn't write without my wonderful support system. As always, I want to thank my wife, Jessica, and daughters first, who sacrifice so much of their time with me so that I can focus on the writing, design, and promotion of the series. I also want to thank my test audience: Jessica Matthews, Deshea Surratt, Ariel Wells, Emily Wan, Missy Wood, and Ross Kyzar. Their editing and feedback were invaluable.

At this point, I've been fortunate to hold a number of book-related events and obtain placement in several independent book retailers. Through this, I'm learning that there is nothing more important than an author's relationships with fans, local libraries, and shop owners. Thank you so much to all of the people who've bought and reviewed my work and believed in me from the beginning. It is the coolest and most humbling thing to have supportive fans who want to see me succeed.

Lastly, it was important to me to tell this story with authentically diverse voices from an inclusive perspective as they experience the harsh realities of a corrupt, dystopian world. The characters represent varying ethnicities, genders, sexualities, religions, body types, and abilities. This is something I did my best to handle with care and I hope it is reflected.

—Ryan

RYAN MATTHEWS

The Release Day Saga is the debut series of Ryan Matthews, an English as a Second Language (ESL) teacher and graphic designer. In addition to writing and teaching, he enjoys spending time with his family, taking insect and mushroom pictures on hikes, and plowing through his extensive reading list. He also dabbles in foreign languages, open-world video games, and the French horn. Ryan holds a Bachelor's Degree in Art and a Master's Degree in Education. He lives in Tennessee with his wife, daughters, and the family pets, Luna and Coda.

@ryanmatthews501
ryanmatthewsauthor.com

NEWSLETTER

For the latest updates, events, and behind-the-scenes information, visit Ryan's website and subscribe to his newsletter.

RATE & REVIEW

If you wish to support authors like Ryan, please leave reviews on sites like Amazon and Goodreads for all of your favorite books.